Bisbee '17

BISBEE '17

A Novel

by Robert Houston

The University of Arizona Press

Tucson

First University of Arizona Press paperbound edition 1999

♾ This book is printed on acid-free, archival-quality paper.
Manufactured in the United States of America
04 03 02 01 00 99 6 5 4 3 2 1

Library of Congress Cataloging-in-Publication Data
Houston, Robert, 1940–
Bisbee '17 : a novel / by Robert Houston. — 1st University of Arizona Press paperbound ed.
p. cm.
ISBN 0-8165-1939-0 (paper)
1. Copper miners' strike, Bisbee, Ariz., 1917—Fiction.
I. Title
PS3558.0873B57 1999
813'.54—dc21 98-42406

British Library Cataloguing-in-Publication Data
A catalogue record for this book is available from the British Library.

For the patience of Pat

Acknowledgments

The number of people involved in giving substance to this book is far too great to be fully acknowledged here. I would, however, like to thank a specific few, and hope the others will understand that my gratitude extends equally to them. First, for their aid in documentation: Leland Sonnichsen, Tracy Row, and the staff of the Arizona Historical Society; Barbara Hooper and the staff of the Bisbee Mining and Historical Museum; the University of Arizona Special Collections Library; J. Bankston of Bisbee; Alex Dresshler of *The Arizona Daily Star;* and James Byrkit, whose dissertation on the book's subject is unequaled.

For granting interviews: Carl Nelson, Art Kent, John Pintek, Kate Pintek, Eugene Stevens, John Lanigan, and (especially) Fred Watson, all of Bisbee; Florence Borazon and Rachael Riggins of Tucson.

For financial assistance: *Mother Jones* magazine, in which I first published the article this book is based on.

For advice, encouragement, and information: Vance Bourjaily, James T. Farrell, and Wallace Stegner.

For their faith and hard-nosed editing: Tom Engelhardt and Wendy Wolf of Pantheon Books, and Joan Holden.

For his patient ear: Charles Neighbors.

For his example: the late Dan R. Houston, labor leader, honest politician, and humanitarian.

And most of all, for endless coffee, conversation, and remembering: Ray Ewing of Bisbee, IWW, retired miner, bindlestiff, timberbeast, riverboater, railroader, and gentleman—without whom this book could not have been written.

Foreword

The major events in this book actually happened, although a number of details have been altered. Many of the characters are based on real people (none now living). Here, too, the author has taken great liberties that may upset scrupulous biographers. But the book pretends to be neither history nor biography. It is a novel, a fiction. The truth it seeks is of another kind from that of the scholar. If it is history at all, it is as Homer chose to write it—a storyteller's history.

Why do they mount their gatling gun
A thousand miles from ocean,
Where hostile fleet could never run—
Ain't that a funny notion?
If you don't know the reason why
Just strike for better wages,
And then, my friends—if you don't die—
You'll sing this song for ages.

—JOE HILL

Part One

Prologue
June, 1917

We've never known a summer like it. On paper, we've been at war with the Bosch three months now. Halfway around the world, at a place called Chemin des Dames, French and German soldiers duck artillery in mud so deep that it sucks the wounded under and smothers them. Our Boys aren't there yet, but they're coming. The first regiments are on ships somewhere in the Atlantic dodging U-boats, on their way to the mud.

In England, Hun air machines dip out of rain clouds to do what no one since William the Conquerer has done. Twenty of them slip past all shore batteries and antiaircraft guns to toss bombs down onto London itself. Smart insurance agents in America are offering War Policies before it's too late. Protection from bombardments and aerial attacks of any kind, anywhere in the Forty-eight.

Still, the Germans are desperate, the papers say. A dispatch from Berlin reports that even lunatics are being made into soldiers. "We are honored," the director of Imperial Asylums has written to the Kaiser, "that our inmates are allowed to serve the Fatherland. But they have become an unbearable burden to the army. They refuse to obey orders, desert their companies, and become vagrants. They are of little military value, and many have been sent back to their asylums. In the meantime, the death rate at our asylums is increasing rapidly, due to underfeeding." The Kaiser is disappointed. It was a pet project.

Things have metamorphosed. Hamburger steak has become Salisbury steak. Sauerkraut has become Liberty Cabbage. Schmidts have become Smiths. The devil has become a German.

Teddy Roosevelt tells a patriotic rally that German-language newspapers are "a fit subject for the censor." "The English language," he says, "does pretty well without German or any other tongue." The St. Louis schools are dropping German from their curriculum. English, the schoolboard says, teaches Americanism.

It should be the best of times to turn a buck. Mining is the business—profits highest in history. But things threaten us, everywhere. In Petrograd, Russian workers and soldiers are rioting, demanding something called a "people's Soviet." And in Montana, an outfit named the Industrial Workers of the World, the Wobblies, has got the whole state shut down in a strike. They claim they're socialists, too, like the mobs in Russia. The *Saturday Evening Post* is fighting back. It sends boys buttons with pictures of yellow dogs on them. The boys form Yellow Dog clubs and pin the buttons on neighbors they catch making disloyal remarks.

A wave of dachshund poisonings is sweeping the country.

We are surrounded. It's been less than a year since Pancho Villa raided New Mexico. Now all along our southern border he issues a call to arms to his old troops. Black Jack Pershing isn't here to chase him off anymore. Border towns stock arms, drill guards, swap dark rumors.

There is safety nowhere. Huns from the north, bandit armies from the south. We are confused. We are afraid, some of us. The government orders the round-up of all slackers who fail to register for the draft. Loyal Americans are asked to turn in their neighbors. It is a duty, our salvation.

Something is growing, swelling, stretching, ready to explode. We can almost touch it, almost feel it enclosing and suffocating us. We are churning with a sense that something we can't name is terribly, intolerably wrong. Is waiting to swallow us.

Big Bill Haywood: New York City, June 28, 1917, 4:00 P.M.

No one has recognized you yet as Big Bill Haywood, but somebody will. The crowd attracted by the young anarchist speaker beside the subway entrance will be sure to know the leader of the Wobblies, the roughest, toughest, most hell-raising union in history. Your Stetson, boots, scowl, single eye, and black western-cut suit are as much trademarks as Bill Cody's beard. But you deliberately stand on the Fourteenth Street side of Union Square, just beyond the edge of the crowd. The situation is too explosive. You've already spotted the phalanx of blue-coated bulls hidden around the corner, reinforcements for the dozen mounted ones who ring the crowd. Any one of them would love to hang an inciting-to-riot charge on you. You can't have that. Not now, of all times.

The ragtag crowd is composed of immigrants, mainly, in run-down shoes and frayed coats who huddle against the misty rain. It seems you've seen a hundred thousand like them today, pushing things, unloading things, cleaning things all over Manhattan. You've been walking since dawn. You've had no sleep since Jim Thompson blew into town yesterday from the copper mines of Montana and Arizona. You left your flat in the Village at daybreak, before the rain began. Your sometime secretary, Giovannitti, was sprawled on the couch asleep. Thompson nodded in an armchair, still wearing the black frock coat that makes him look like a skinny raven. You listened to the two of them argue through the night. There may be a telegram for you today from Arizona, Thompson said. You've been hoping for it for months, and you've been afraid it would come for months. Now it has caught you by surprise. You might have to leave for Arizona in a few days. If you do, you're convinced that you may change the course of civilization forever. You believe fervently that it can be done, and know that it is a thing to be afraid of.

The June rain has soaked through your coat, and your

shirt sticks to your skin. Your feet are numb. Back at the flat, they'll raise hell with you again about your health. You hadn't meant to stop when you came across the rally, but the speaker grabbed your attention. He's good. He handles his voice well, drops it almost to a whisper to get the crowd straining toward him, then bursts out with one of the old, good lines about the master class or wage slavery that always gets a cheer. And he knows how to project from the gut so that even the bystanders across the street catch the right phrases.

The speaker is good, but you know you're better. And that disturbs you, too. You should be up there with the kid, should at least know who he is. You're almost fifty now, and spend a lot of time in salons these days, over in the Village. You're a Public Figure. Mornings pass long and dull, with reports and policy statements and committee meetings that squeeze your ulcer like a fruit juicer. Afternoons on end you sit huge and hunched in one armchair or another, surrounded like a Buddha by younger radicals, telling stories about busting broncos and scabs on the frontier. When there still was a frontier. You drink black coffee and dream about the shots of rye whiskey the pill pusher says will put you underground in a year if you go back to them. You try to understand the damnable war and to read all the new revolutionary-theory books from Europe. You don't have much luck with either. Sometimes you feel you're drowning in a bastardly mudslide of statistics and nit-picking political theories and bohemian college kids and coffee cups. Your fists, big as double-jack sledgehammers, stay clenched in your coat pockets nowadays, or in your lap, useless as tits on a boar hog. While the world blows up.

The mounted cops ride closer to the edge of the crowd, like sheepdogs. They signal to one another. They're tight, ready for something. Why in God's name doesn't the speaker's outfit have spotters out? Greenhorns! They should have been able to smell the cops' setup. You would have had your own boys outflanking the bulls the minute they showed up. You have no patience for this anymore.

You know your patience for most things is shot. You started out to reforge the world twenty-odd years ago in Silver City, and now things are worse than ever. You weren't even able to head off the most terrible war in history, this capitalists' shooting war you swore you wouldn't let interfere with the class war. And then you let yourself get talked into coming east to play this Eminent Man business. It's no damn good. You're impatient for the smell of Home Run cigarettes in a miners' hall in the mountains of Nevada. For the way the boys whoop when you step up onto the bed of a wagon to speak in a muddy mining camp in the Mesabi range. For the solitude of a hard-rock miner's cabin where you can read your Marx and Shakespeare without telephones and the klaxons of taxicabs. Where something clean and clear *happens.* They tell you you're a Spokesman and that you belong here in the center of things. For a while you believed them.

One of the mounted bulls bumps a woman who steps too far out into Fourteenth Street traffic. The woman staggers, then yells at the bull that he's a cossack son of a bitch. The speaker sees the commotion and roars at the bull, too. The crowd takes it up, a ragged smattering of hoots and oaths. You tell yourself that now is the time to move on. But you know what it will be like when the bulls get the young speaker to the Tombs. You remember the way your ribs ache after the splat of a rubber hose.

The pencil-mustached sergeant in charge of the mounted cops reins his horse back. That means he isn't ready yet, but you know the setup is still on. You can sense it the way an Appaloosa can sense a snake.

Something catches your eye. Down by the subway entrance, toughs with their caps cocked over their eyes slip out in groups of three and four. Nonchalantly they take up positions around the speaker and work into the crowd. You're taller than most anybody else in the audience, and even at this distance your one good eye picks them out.

You look for the mounted sergeant. He sees the toughs, too. One of them makes a small sign to him, a little flip of his cap. The sergeant nods. It's an old con: start a free-for-all, break some bones, arrest the leaders. Why in damnation aren't these people ready for it?

You take a deep breath and pull your stomach in. In spite of the impatience, you feel a sense of excitement you haven't felt in God knows how long. Maybe not since the days in Utah and Colorado with the old Western Federation of Miners. Back when you knew who you were. You move closer to the crowd.

But calm now, calm. You think of the telegram, the decision you have to make if it comes. Speakers on soapboxes, swallowed up by Manhattan, aren't enough anymore —if they ever were. The country's going crazy. Half the radical leaders you know are either in jail or on their way there. Who next? Soon the first American troops will land in France to get slaughtered in J.P. Morgan's damnable war. Soon the whole world will blow sky high, or be gassed to death. Soon the scissorbill scabs and the bosses will get together and have a witch-hunt. It has started already. The newspapers have gone stark mad. There is so little time left.

A big redhead, probably a Mick, has been keeping the audience more or less out of the street and leading the cheers when they don't come quickly enough. You've watched him move up and down the fringes of the crowd and figured him for part of the speaker's outfit. He's less than three or four yards away now. Slowly, so as not to attract attention, you edge up beside him.

"You," you say. "Turn around easy."

The Mick turns casually, as if he were asking for a match. His face is round and flushed and hard, like a polished apple. But when he takes in your features, his eyes open marble-sized, and he takes a step back.

"Jesus! It's Big Bill Haywood. Ain't you?"

You feel a thrill, the same private thrill you always feel when a workingstiff or a reporter recognizes you. But you keep your face composed, scowling. "Hold yourself natural," you say, "and take a look at the front of this crowd."

The Mick stands on tiptoe. You watch him read the situation in a single long glance, as coolly as if he were checking out a passing shopgirl. "Aye," he says. "So it's that game they're wanting, is it?" He eases himself down and looks up at you again.

"Do you know the man on the soapbox?"

The Mick winks. "Like me brother. Dago or not."

"Can you get to him?"

"Has a cat got an ass?"

"Then go. Get him into the subway. After they smell the thing you won't have long. Drag him if you have to."

A thin man from beside the Mick steps in between the two of you. "It's Big Bill Haywood, ain't it?" he asks the Mick, with a trace of a Yiddish accent. The Mick nods, winks at him, and slips away through the crowd toward the speaker. "I seen you at the Lawrence strike, Bill. God, you was fine," the thin man says.

You clap the man on the shoulder, then carefully check to see if the the bulls are on to you yet. The sergeant is busy spreading his men to block any possible retreat across Fourteenth Street. There's not much time left. The thin man with the Yiddish accent has recognized you already. Soon others will—and then the bulls. You've done what you can. Leave now.

But at the head of the crowd, you see the toughs slipping closer to the speaker. The one who signaled the sergeant before tries to catch his eye again. For a moment, when he climbs a few steps up to the square, you get a clear view of him. He holds his arm abnormally straight. There is a billy club in his coat sleeve; you know the trick, have used it yourself. Women are scattered in the front rows of the crowd, girls from the sweatshops on the East Side. They'll be the first to get it. The Mick's red head works too slowly through the crowd.

The sergeant's horse, glistening in the drizzle, throws its head back as the sergeant reins it around for a last check of the foot patrolmen hidden behind the building. There is an insufferable arrogance in man and horse that telegraphs itself to you like a slap. The sergeant signals to the tough again. He moves toward the speaker.

The thin man beside you tugs at your coat. You pull away from him and spin on your heel. You can't bear to meet his eyes. He wants to collect a debt that you can't pay now. Behind you, the crowd breaks into a song. It's from the IWW songbook.

They don't get to finish it. You hear a woman scream, and you dodge the rearing horse of a mounted bull. You keep your steady pace and throw a quick look back for the speaker. He's vanished into the circle of toughs. You're in the middle of Fourteenth Street. Drays swerve and automobiles *oogah.* The foot patrolmen charge from behind their building. A dozen or so workingstiffs rush past you. The foot patrolmen part before them. The disorganized crowd is easier pickings. You hear a pistol shot, then the screaming and shouts behind you become general.

You keep walking steadily down Fourteenth Street until the confused noise fades behind you. The excitement drains away, leaving your ulcer clenched. You were almost you again, but you walked away. You think of the telegram from Arizona. It's so late, too late for all the little fights. There may be time for only one fight, the big one, before civilization blows itself up.

You remember the pistol shot you heard behind you. Where is the kid who was speaking? The poor naïve son of a bitch. You look for a saloon. Just one drink, no more. One drink to blot out the cop's arrogance, the dull crack of that pistol shot, the tug on your coat sleeve, the gray city rain, the telegram.

By the time you get home, the wet streets are glistening under dim street lamps. The drink—the two drinks—haven't helped. Your flat is teeming, as usual. All the windows are thrown open against the heat of the rainy evening, but even that can't erase the sense of too many damp bodies soaking up the air. Giovannitti raises his hands in an Italian gesture of exasperation when he sees you. Some of the people around Giovannitti you recognize: a clubwoman from uptown who wants you to speak, an artist who wants you to pose for him—wants to make a cube out of you or something—a coed from the antidraft league at Barnard who wants to sleep with you, a French syndicalist who needs money, and Jim Thompson. Besides those a half dozen others, workers, mainly, who will want to hear you offer them coffee "sweet as love, black as night, hot as the fervor of revolution." They want to go home and repeat that to their families tonight. They want some of Big Bill Haywood to rub off on them. You wish you could let them rub you away, down to the bone, past the nerves.

"Where the hell, Bill? Where the hell?" Giovannitti waves his sheaf of papers at you accusingly. More reports, letters, more Public Man. He's excited. He's a poet, a theorist, a strategist, and prone to that sort of thing. But he's a good organizer and has guts.

"Not now, Arturo," you tell him. "Please."

"No sleep again?"

"No sleep." The people in the room are all on their feet now, expectant. They'll cling to you soon, like ticks. You throw your shoulders back, fix your one eye on your bedroom door and make for it. You wave at Jim Thompson and Giovannitti to follow you.

Your bedroom is dim, only the lamp on the bed table burning. The air is less close here. You take a deep breath. Giovannitti bounces in behind you; Thompson sidles in and perches solemnly on the edge of the bed. You fall into your armchair by the window. You wonder if they've found the bottle of rye in the kitchen and dumped it yet. Giovannitti tries to get you to take off your wet clothes but you motion him away. You haven't the patience for it.

Thompson holds a crumpled telegram in his thin hands. He's been with you since '05, when you and the others founded the IWW. The Greatest Thing on Earth, the first posters said. You look for your voice. It has to be steady now, and clear. Big Bill Haywood can't get tired. "That the telegram?" you ask Thompson, too abruptly.

He holds it out to you. "That's the one."

You don't take it from him. "I'll not read it now. What does it say?"

"Bisbee's voted to go out. They've contacted Butte. They're calling for the general strike, Bill."

Your eye remains on the telegram. So that's the way it comes. A dozen words in a telegram, and the thing you've preached for so many years pounces on you. The ultimate weapon, promised in the IWW constitution that you helped write. You'd imagined years more organizing first. Every detail in place, every worker ready. But the war's snatched that away, too. And now there's the telegram, demanding a yes or no you're no more able to give than you were able to look that thin workingstiff in the eye this afternoon. Are you in control at all anymore—of anything? You need so desperately to think now, to drive out the muddy weariness and impatience. Giovannitti slaps the iron bedstead. "*They're* calling for it. What the hell kind of way is that to run a union? You know what this means, don't you?"

"Tell me what it means, Arturo." He doesn't notice the sarcasm you're too tired to keep out of your voice.

"Oh, Christ, Bill! You're going to count on a few thousand copper miners to hold out so hard and long that you shut down a whole industry—in the middle of a war. No—more. You're talking about tying the whole country up, about breaking up the biggest war machine in history. Because if you leave it intact, it'll turn on us and rip our guts out. Bisbee may not realize that, but you do, don't you?"

While Giovannitti is pacing and making his speech, you're watching Thompson. Now he catches your eye, and a slight smile flickers across his hollow face. "Reckon Bill knows that, Arturo," he says.

"Then . . ."

"Just hold still a minute, Arturo. You talk to the boys on the central committee when you were through Chicago, Jim?"

"I didn't see all of them. Most, but not all."

"What do they say?"

"They've advised against it, you know that. But they won't try to stop it . . . as long as you don't."

"Of course they advised against it." Giovannitti paces between you and Thompson. "Bisbee! You might as well try to call a general strike from Mars." He plops onto the bed beside Thompson.

"Any answer from Butte yet?" you ask Thompson.

"No."

Giovannitti bounces back up off the bed. "What would they say? They lost a hundred and thirty men in that Speculator shaft fire. They're madder than hell and they've got the whole state shut down already. Even the AF of L won't buck 'em. What do they have to lose?"

Your eye moves up to the map of the United States pinned above your bed lamp. You have only to turn slightly to shift Giovannitti away to your blind side. Bisbee, Arizona. The Queen of the Copper Camps. It's such a speck on the map, but it may be the last place on earth the plutocrats would expect you to launch a war from. It's a world you understand, and Giovannitti doesn't. Giovannitti is an eastern boy, and you know his arguments already. Arizona, he'll say, is just barely a state. He's not even sure whether the wild Indians have been removed yet. There are more people in Trenton than in the whole of Arizona. Bisbee is somewhere in the mountains on the Mexican border, in the middle of nowhere. They still wear guns and shoot each other over card games out there. Giovannitti's certain that Phelps-Dodge Copper is run by mad Englishmen and Tamburlaines, and you'll concede him that.

But as your eye moves up the map to Butte, you see what Giovannitti doesn't. Butte and Bisbee, two prongs of a pair of pliers to squeeze and squeeze until something cracks, collapses. Between the two of them, they control almost all the copper there is, and you've already got Butte. There's a quarter of the world's known copper in Arizona. And with no copper, there's no munitions industry, no shell casings, no wire for trucks and tanks and air machines, no alloys . . .

And yet you still can't clear your mind to say, Yes, this is the place to set the charge that will bring the whole tottering capitalist machine down before it destroys the earth. What are you afraid of? You've never been afraid of losing. No power anywhere can shake your faith that the working people don't want this war any more than you do. Why are you afraid of winning, then?

Giovannitti comes between you and the map. "We don't have the strength, Bill. The war's changing things. People are changing. The companies are organized now like never before."

You push yourself out of the mohair armchair and go to the window for air. The whiskey is retreating, draining you even more.

"What will it take?" you ask Thompson. Your mind tries to shuffle things, to calculate, to find the key to end this damnable uncertainty.

Thompson shrugs. "People. Like always."

"People!" Giovannitti snorts. "You know what you're taking on? Phelps-Dodge, not just Nowhere, Arizona. You know how big Phelps-Dodge is?"

"I know just how big it is, Arturo. To the dollar." You turn from the window. "Who was in Bisbee when you left?" you ask Thompson.

"Not many that you know. Embree's the local secretary and a good man. Frank Little just left but is laid up in

Phoenix with a busted leg. Bo Whitley's coming down from Butte. He's one of the best of the new boys."

"I don't know him," you say. And add to yourself, I should.

"Used to be Gurley Flynn's old man. Wrote a couple of songs for us."

"Oh. That one."

"He's good, but he ain't enough."

Giovannitti breaks in. "What's enough, Jim? Big Bill Haywood himself?"

Thompson looks up at you from under his thin eyebrows. "Maybe."

"Dio!"

"How did it feel to you, Jim?"

"It's tight, Bill. Bisbee's the hardest-ass company town I've ever been in. The boys ain't got a good clear-cut issue like the Speculator fire up in Butte. The companies are screaming their heads off about the war and patriotic duty and such. If you're asking me, I'd say that we got to get something in there that's bigger news than the war. And that ain't easy."

"What's the law like there?" You've read the endless reports Giovannitti passes you. But you need something more. Something real.

"The sheriff? You know Harry Wheeler, don't you?"

"I've read about him in the papers."

"Well, he's hard to figure. No telling which way he'll jump. The boys elected him big last time, but so did the companies. Best I could tell he ain't on nobody's payroll. But he's a tough little SOB, they say. Real fast-draw six-gunner. Old school."

"Christ!" Giovannitti says. "Cowboys and Indians now."

Your interest quickens. There's something in what Thompson's saying that you can touch. Something about a kind of war you can understand, whose rules you know. You take a deep breath. "Can we win it, Jim?"

Thompson doesn't speak for a long while. "We can win it, I think. Reckon we'll have to if we support it."

"Bill . . ." Giovannitti's voice is pleading. "Nothing's the same now."

Your patience, stretched tight as a rubber band, pulls

you around on your heel to face him. "Then what, Arturo? What in hell do you want us to do?"

"Let this war thing cool a little. Just that. Wait."

The rubber band snaps. "Wait! God almighty damn. For what? In six months the world may be in smithereens, boy. And who's going to be around to pick up the pieces if we wait? Let me tell you something. Back in the free speech fights in Seattle in nineteen-nine, when they were stuffing the jails with Wobblies like chickens in a breeder—except the food was worse—they asked the men questions. 'What's your religion?' the bulls asked them. 'The IWW,' the boys answered, down the line. 'Who's your best friend?' the cops wanted to know. 'Big Bill Haywood,' the boys said, to a man. And when the Pinkertons kidnapped me and Moyer and Pettibone to Idaho and tried to stretch us for murdering their governor, who got us off? Darrow and his three-dollar words? No. It was the nickels and dimes the workingstiffs kicked in for the defense fund that got us off. Wait? God in heaven, I owe more than waiting, Arturo!"

Your eye leaps from Giovannitti back to the map. You listen to the sound of things falling together in your mind, as sure to you as the clank of switches on railroad sidings. The connections take final, solid shapes: Butte, Bisbee, the whole copper industry. Then, out of the chaos of a country exhausted by a stupid war, a new thing, a workers' commonwealth, something the world has never seen before, the Greatest Thing on Earth. You'll never have to walk away from another fight. It can be done, Thompson said. Then, so help you, it will be done.

You take the telegram from Thompson and stare at it as if it were a kind of totem. Then your eye moves from the telegram to the too big stomach under your vest. It's a middle-aged man's stomach. Nothing you've done here in the East has lasted. Nothing. And Giovannitti says wait!

"You say it'll have to be big, Jim."

"Big as you can make it."

"Arturo?" You let him slip back into your sight. "You told me Mother Jones was in town, I recollect."

"Bill," he says, "for God's sake don't even think about it. Nobody's ever shut down Bisbee."

The bedsprings squeak as Thompson gets to his feet. "I

called her up today. She's here working with the antidraft people. She's madder than hell—at everything."

"Anybody heard from Gurley Flynn yet?"

Giovannitti slaps his papers against the bedstead and sighs. "I spoke with her mother today up in the Bronx. Says she and Tresca are going to stop over in Chicago for a few days. She's exhausted from her trial in Duluth, Bill. She won't want to know you right now."

You turn to the window again and shut it against the sound of the traffic outside. Yourself, Mother Jones, Gurley Flynn. There's not a miner in Bisbee who wouldn't know any one of you on sight. Gurley Flynn's only twenty-six or so, and the papers tell you she's almost as famous as Theda Bara now. Nobody, man or woman, can take over a speaker's platform or work a picket line as surely as she can. Even though she's living with that Italian anarchist who's even more excitable than Giovannitti, there's nobody solider anywhere. She's been quirky lately, you'll grant . . . but she couldn't refuse to go. Not if the cable came from you.

And Mother Jones. She must be eighty-seven now, but still the best cop baiter in the country. She sat on the platform with you when you founded the IWW, was working the underground railway before the Civil War. She's always said you were the only man in the country who could sweet-talk her.

Thompson said it would have to be big. Bill Haywood, Mother Jones, Elizabeth Gurley Flynn. What's bigger? The excitement you felt for a moment this afternoon returns, grows; your hand tightens around the telegram. Oh, by Jesus, it would be fine.

"Arturo? Anybody at your flat tonight?"

"No. Not even me."

"Mind if I stay over? I'd like to sleep tonight, and think."

He fumbles for his key. "Think, then. Think that if you take on the copper trust at Bisbee, you take on the war, damn near every newspaper in the country, and maybe even the government."

You drop the key into your pocket. "Jim? You disposed to head back West?"

"Montana, Bill. Got a wife there now, remember?"

You take his hand. "We'll stay in touch."

"Reckon."

Someone in the parlor bangs out a series of chords on your borrowed upright. An uneven chorus of voices follows: "There's a pow'r, there's a pow'r, that must rule in every land—One Big Industrial Union Grand. . . ."

For a moment, the fear you felt today falls back over you. But you shake it off like the afternoon's rain from your Stetson as you take it from the hat rack. Big Bill Haywood can't be afraid.

Orson McCrea: Cochise County, Arizona, July 1, 3:00 A.M.

The monsoon, the *chubasco,* has come at last. Fat cumulus clouds grow in the distant Gulf of Mexico, lumber across the wastes of Chihuahua, clip the tops of the high sierra of Sonora, bust open over the emptiness of southern Arizona like overloaded Papago water skins. Walls of water rip churning and brown through dry washes. They freight rocks, rattlers, dead branches, gophers, skeletons, down to the arroyos and cactus flats of the desert. An hour after the rains stop, the water is gone. Soaked up by the desert like memories of the Apaches, deported at last only a generation before. The monsoons will come every afternoon now, all through July and August, like grudging payoffs to the things that wait, dormant or dying, through the other ten dry months. It is the time for plagues of things—blister beetles, mosquitoes, thumb-sized toads, Wobblies.

The rains were done by the time they called Orson McCrea up out of the Czar shaft in the middle of the night shift. Said Mr. Dowell himself wanted him. Now.

Just me? McCrea asked the guard who came for him. Yep—said to put one of his jigger bosses in charge of the shift and report to Mr. Dowell in the warehouse of the company store within twenty minutes. Why? What the hell was up? Bad cave-in somewhere? The guard didn't know, except that there hadn't been any cave-in signals sent from any of the whistles so far as he knew.

McCrea doesn't wait for the cage to hoist him up to the surface. Not when the manager of the Copper Queen Mining Division himself wants him. He jumps onto a skip full of ore and dangles by the cable to the top of the shaft. They'll burn him for doing it if they find out. But he'll never make it in twenty minutes if he follows regulations. Besides, his belly feels like it had a piece of dry ice in it already—why not get the devil scared out of himself and bust a few safety regs to boot? Only reason they'd call him out like this is if he's got his tail in a sling anyway. God-bless, he'll hate to lose his job now. One step away from foreman, and a new house to pay for up on Quality Hill, and sure as hell they've found something to can him for.

He has to crank the old Overland for what seems like five minutes before it starts—and the crank flings back on him once so that he's sure he's sprained his wrist. Must be the fault of the blessed rain that afternoon. He's planned on a new Studebaker with an electric starter next year, but now . . .

And when he gets to the warehouse, what is Miles Merrill doing there at the loading door? Near midnight, and the chief of security hanging around a dark warehouse? The dry ice in his belly stays there, but his gut loosens. What was fear before turns into a kind of excitement. Something big is up, and they've called *him,* Orson McCrea, just a shift boss, because of it. He gets out of the Overland quickly, but with dignity. Merrill is watching—one important man watching another important man approach.

McCrea steps into the fuzzy circle of yellow light by the door where Merrill is waiting for him. Merrill gives him his huge hand and nods his walrus mustaches and bald head at him. He's in uniform—tight leggings, campaign hat, and gunbelt. "Orson," he rumbles.

"What's up?" McCrea asks. He tries to sound casual, tries to soften his West Texas whine, tries to stand a little taller than his thin five six.

"Nothing important," Merrill says. "Just need a little help here, and all my boys are tied up. You mind?"

McCrea deflates, but catches himself before Merrill notices. He hopes. "They told me Mr. Dowell was here."

"He is," Merrill said. Closemouthed as a lockjawed snapping turtle, McCrea thinks. Comes with the job, he expects. "You go on in. I'll be along." His eyes leave McCrea's and, by way of dismissing him, swing around the square and up Brewery Gulch. Checking, always checking. McCrea lets his own look follow Merrill's for a minute before he slides the warehouse door open. Quieter than usual tonight. The sound of the clock on the Pythian Castle striking three echoes off the cobblestones and buildings of Brewery Gulch undisturbed by the singing and shouting that usually drift down from the cardrooms and saloons. Most of the lights on the Gulch are out. Lights in places like Cockeyed Jimmy's cardroom, or the blackjack room old man Johnson runs over the assay office. Lights that never go out. Only a dozen or so miners hang out in little groups in front of the door to the Turkish bath across the square, or under the tile awning of the Orpheum Theater. They watch him and Merrill, pretending not to. When he turns so that they can see his face, one of them breaks away from the group and saunters off up toward O.K. Street. The IWW hall is on O.K. Street, in the Pythian Castle. McCrea is uneasy. He has read about the monstrous things the Wobblies do to their enemies.

A drunk cowboy, asleep and teetering in his saddle, clops over the cobblestones from one streetlight to the other. The miners spit and watch him pass without a word. Too quiet, McCrea thinks. Any other time one of them would have stampeded the horse and taken bets on how far the cowboy would get before he fell off and busted his head.

"They waiting for you," Merrill says. "Better get on it."

McCrea nods and slips in the door. Holy Jesus, he thinks as his eyes adjust to the light. Not only Dowell but Captain Greenway! Managers of *both* mining companies, Copper Queen and Calumet & Arizona, too. The two biggest men in town here in the middle of the night. He looks around for Lem Shattuck. Add him and you'd have all three of the mining outfits here at once. But Lem is an independent, not in the same league with the Copper Queen and C & A. Not one of these Yale men like Greenway and Dowell.

There are only a dozen others besides himself in the warehouse. McCrea recognizes Tom Matthews, Phelps-Dodge's purchasing agent, and Greenway's security chief, Wilson. The rest are men he knows from the mines, foremen and shift bosses like himself. Men on their way up in the company—or already up. He tries to keep his face grave, composed, as they nod at him. Dowell, balding and clean-shaven, offers his hand; it is smooth but firm. Returning the gesture, McCrea wonders what his own feels like: He has been soaking his hands in glycerine and rosewater ever since he's been made shift boss. Get the miner's calluses off them.

"You're the last of us, I believe, Orson," Dowell says in his tight, precise voice.

"I was underground when they called me, sir." McCrea hopes it doesn't sound like an excuse.

Dowell lets go of his hand and makes a little gesture of forgiveness. "No harm," he says. McCrea steps back, respectfully but with dignity. Dowell raises his arms and motions for the other men to come closer. Greenway, casually slapping his riding boots with his crop, leans back against a vegetable crate, just a little apart from the others. McCrea has always thought Captain Greenway should be in picture shows like Douglas Fairbanks, or maybe in Richard Harding Davis novels. He never has been able to figure Greenway. Better to his men than the others, but even when he's having a drink with them down across the border in Naco, he always keeps a kind of fence around him. Never married either, even though McCrea has heard that every rich woman on the West Coast is after him. McCrea has been trying to get on his good side ever since Greenway shook his hand at a picnic three years ago. Always takes his hat off to him in the street, always wonders if Greenway has noticed him. An important man, and McCrea sometimes feels that importance is something that can rub off on you if you stay close enough to it.

"Men," Dowell says. His voice gets lost in the stacked crates and boxes of the dim, crowded brick warehouse.

"A little louder, I think," Greenway says.

Dowell nods without turning. His face flushes. "Men, I apologize for getting you down here at this hour. But we need a little help, and boys we can trust. There's some equipment—important equipment—we need to move out of here tonight. Equipment of a . . . delicate nature." He clears his throat and looks embarrassed and awkward, as if the words he has at hand don't please him. "There are elements here in Bisbee—in the country, I might add—that would misinterpret our purposes if they knew we had this equipment. So we need men whose . . . discretion we can depend on. Am I clear?"

He waits. One of the men behind McCrea says yessir, and he goes on: "There's an element of loyalty involved here, of patriotism perhaps—even of Americanism, I think. None of you will say anything to anyone about this, I hope. Not even to your families."

McCrea still doesn't understand, but he takes the chance to say yessir before anyone else. Greenway casually lets his eyes wander to him. The hunk of dry ice in McCrea's belly melts a little.

"Good," Dowell says. "This shouldn't take long. We're just going to ask you to help us load some crates from a boxcar on the siding behind the store here—load them on handcarts and push them over to the dispensary. The equipment is, as I say, too . . . delicate to leave here in the warehouse. So we're going to leave it in the dispensary basement for the time being. I might add that the government is in agreement with us."

Be dogged, McCrea thinks. War stuff, then. Some secret kind of gas maybe.

Greenway flicks his crop at Dowell and laughs. "Medicinal equipment, Grant," he says. "Tell them that. Good medicine."

Dowell tries a tight smile and ignores Greenway as if Greenway were a kid who had made a bad joke. Tom Matthews, the purchasing agent, who has kept quiet and stands just behind everyone in the shadows, takes a step into the light and makes a notation in a leather note pad. Dowell watches him nervously. Almost defiantly, Greenway holds on to his broad grin as Matthews writes.

McCrea can't figure it: What is somebody as important as Grant Dowell doing worrying about what his purchasing agent writes down in a book? It is something that a man on the way up like himself ought to know, and he promises himself he'll find out.

"Any questions?" Dowell asks. McCrea shakes his head with the others. "Fine, just . . . fine." Dowell says. He is clearly glad there aren't any. "I believe Miles is waiting at the siding for you."

Outside, McCrea notices that the miners who were in front of the Orpheum and the Turkish bath are gone. Two men—a sheriff's deputy and a town policeman—have taken their place. They pace slowly across the mouth of Brewery Gulch and O.K. Street. Whenever someone approaches, they signal to three or four company guards who lounge a hundred yards away, against Dowell's Packard twin-six touring car, parked next to Greenway's white mare by the dispensary. They all wear side arms. The sheriff's deputy holds a sawed-off shotgun. At the Orpheum, the marquee advertises *The Spoilers.*

Merrill climbs into the boxcar first and asks one of the foremen to come with him. Dowell waves across the square to the dispensary, and a company guard lifts a bundle of what looks in the streetlight like sheets from the back of Dowell's Packard machine. His boots echo from the dark brick buildings around the square as he struggles toward the boxcar with the sheets.

Too blessed quiet, McCrea tells himself again. He looks at the lights that climb straight up the mountains around him. Streetlights and house lights and lanterns in miners' tents fade out above him into the stars so that he can't tell, at the very top of the mountains, which are stars and which electric lamps. Too many lights. Quiet downtown and yet so many lights in the miners' cabins. Who is up so late, and why? In the distance, a steam whistle hoots a warning to a hoistman. Somewhere far up Brewery Gulch, where the Mexes live, a burro answers it. Dogs speak to one another from hilltop to hilltop. He hasn't seen downtown Bisbee this quiet since . . . since never, he supposes.

The man from the dispensary heaves the sheets up into the boxcar. McCrea hears Merrill and the other man talking tersely to one another. They sound as if they're straining with something heavy. After a time, Merrill comes to the door of the boxcar and motions half a dozen more men to come up. McCrea is not one of them.

Dowell and Greenway and Matthews wait by the warehouse. When Merrill orders the men into the boxcar, Dowell calls to McCrea and the rest. He slides the warehouse door wide and points to a row of shoulder-high, two-wheeled handcarts against the wall.

"Two men on each cart," he says. McCrea steps ahead of the others and takes the first handcart. A man he recognizes as one of Greenway's C & A foremen takes half the handle and they maneuver the rattling cart outside to the boxcar.

When they get there, Merrill and another man have what looks like a long crate or coffin covered with a sheet ready to slide off onto the cart. McCrea helps them, and the C & A foreman holds the cart steady while they slide three more of the heavy crates, all covered, onto the cart.

"Four's plenty," Merrill says. "Don't want to spill 'em."

McCrea and his partner ease the handcart over the uneven cobblestones of the lot behind the warehouse. Greenway cuts ahead of them across the square. The company guards jump to attention as he approaches, and one of them unlocks the heavy steel trapdoor over the stairs to the basement of the dispensary. The rattle of the cart sounds up the dark streets and alleys as McCrea and the other man grunt and shove their way across the square with it. McCrea is nervous—for all the noise they were making, they might as well be setting off dynamite.

Greenway doesn't appear to mind, though. Easy self-confidence flows from him. He stands at the open trapdoor to the basement erect but loose—like an officer waiting at ease. He motions for McCrea and a guard to get down onto the stairs. "Two men on each end," he orders. "One of those crates slips and you'll personally come see me in the morning," he tells his foreman.

"Yessir," the foreman says. He and a third guard wrestle a crate into position and slide it slowly toward McCrea and his partner. McCrea braces and takes the weight of the thing on his shoulder. It is heavier than he thought, and for a moment he staggers. Greenway swears at him, and he steadies.

The basement has been cleared as much as possible. Traction frames, medicine cabinets, operating tables, have all been shoved to one side to leave a whole wall clear. Greenway slips past McCrea and the others on the stairs to direct the stacking of the crates. Straining, McCrea notices as Greenway brushes by them that he has a faint scent of lilac water. Lilac water. McCrea makes a note of it—he thinks his wife has some. He'll try it tomorrow.

"Tight against the wall," Greenway tells them. "Stoop to your knees and ease it off your shoulders. Be gentle with it."

McCrea is the smallest of the men, but he is sure he is straining hardest. For a second, the crate slips precariously and thuds against the wall. It is the company guard's fault, but McCrea takes the weight of it. He thinks his gut will split with the strain, but he holds and eases the crate back into a horizontal position. Greenway steps over and takes part of the weight. "Good man," he tells McCrea. McCrea manages a smile.

When the crate is down and shoved flush against the wall, in the corner, Greenway steps back and mentally measures distances. "You boys start on the next one," he tells McCrea's partner and the two other men. "You," he says to McCrea. "What was your name again?"

"Orson McCrea, sir." He tries to straighten his cramped back, to match Greenway's military stance. Even with that, he still has to look up six inches to Greenway's eyes.

"McCrea, then. Look here, those crates will have to go lengthwise, don't you think? You look like a man with a good eye for distances."

"Lengthwise, sir?"

"Lengthwise, yes, damn it. Lengthwise. If you had to get to a thing like that in a hurry and it was flush against the wall with five others like it stacked above it, could you do it? If it was butt-ended against the wall, not flush, don't you think you could get around it with two men on a side easier? Use your imagination, man."

McCrea is confused. What in God's name is a man like Captain John Greenway asking his advice for? "I . . . I'd think so, sir. Wouldn't risk a-pulling the whole stack over on you that way."

"Good," Greenway says. "Always rethink, consider possibilities, McCrea. Most men don't do that."

"Yessir," McCrea says. Rethink. Possibilities. He makes a note of that, too. He'll write it down when he gets home.

"So then," Greenway says, clearly pleased. "Take ahold of that end and help me shove this thing out from the wall before you go up for the next one."

"Yessir." He braces his foot and pulls the crate away from the wall until he can get a double handhold on it. Greenway watches, then steps around and puts a riding boot against it. Between them they slide the crate around so it sticks lengthways into the room.

"You see?" Greenway says. He gives the crate a last shove with his boot and steps back. As he does, his spur catches the sheet and jerks it away from the crate. "Damnation!" he curses under his breath. The whole crate is exposed. He throws a quick look behind him to make sure no one else is in the room. McCrea, still on his knees, grabs the end of the sheet and pulls it back up. His eyes meet Greenway's.

"What was written on that crate, McCrea?" Greenway asks sharply.

"I didn't see it, sir," McCrea says.

"Don't lie to me! I know good and damn well you did."

McCrea drops his eyes. "Captain Greenway, sir, I know how to keep my mouth shut. I don't want to know nothing that's none of my business. It's just that . . . well, sir, if there's anything that needs doing, most anybody can tell you I'm your man. If I seen anything on that crate, it just makes me feel that, well, that I might be needed even a little more now."

"Pull that sheet back off," Greenway orders.

McCrea is confused again, but the feeling of something important happening to him, around him, is stronger than ever. Carefully he pulls the sheet off the crate.

"Read it again," Greenway says. "Take your time."

McCrea has trouble concentrating. Captain John Greenway, the man who has founded five towns so far, who was Teddy Roosevelt's right hand at San Juan Hill, who was just about the biggest football star Yale ever had, is taking Orson McCrea into his confidence. It is a wonder, a marvel.

He reads the stamped letters on the wooden crate, this time slowly:

> Marlin Arms Corporation
> New Haven, Connecticut
> Two (2) ea. Air-cooled Machine Guns, 7.5 mm
> Spec. USA 21–3

His eyes meet Greenway's again.

"Are you a Christian, McCrea?" Greenway asks.

"Mormon, sir."

Greenway considers. "That'll do. Have you ever read Saint Augustine?"

"No, sir."

"The City of God, McCrea, is at stake. The sons of bitches want to build the City of Man where we've built the City of God. They want to tear down, destroy. I'll roast in hell before I see that. Do you understand? A Mormon should understand the City of God, surely."

McCrea looks away. "I never went to college, Captain Greenway. I've never even been to Salt Lake."

Greenway's face relaxes into a soft smile that doesn't seem proper for it at all. "Stay with me after this is done. I'll arrange it with Mr. Dowell. There will be other things that need doing."

McCrea answers Greenway's smile, cautiously, humbly. The most important thing that has ever happened to him is beginning. "Yessir," he says. Humbly.

Jim Brew: July 1, 7:00 A.M.

Too old, Jim Brew tells himself as he drags himself up the haulage tunnel of the Copper Queen Southwest. Wore out and too blessed old for the graveyard shift. Timbering all night in a hot-spot drift where the heat is so high the water in the air turns into underground rain. Then coming out here where the air gets sucked in through the cracks in the mountain so hard the wind blows forever, and it's always 40 degrees. If the miner's consumption don't get him, the god-amighty winds in this shaft will.

Bo Whitley once said that Jim Brew looks like a sly bear. Hunkered over when he walks, with arms that swing down nearly to his knees. Eyes just a little Oriental, inherited from a Cherokee grandmamma on his daddy's side. His hair is cut too short on the sides and too long on top. His ears are as flat as if they had been pasted back to his head. For the most part he's reconciled himself to being too old and broke-nosed and stumble-footed ever to have a wife. But every now and again, alone at night in his room at Mrs. Stodgill's boardinghouse down in Jiggerville, he thinks maybe not. Someday, when he gets a little ahead, he'll marry him a cantina girl from Naco. He's already sending money to two of them. One of them even gave him a present, a good cavalry sword she snitched from a Mex officer.

But the thing Jim Brew would appreciate more than anything else is a change room, a bathhouse. He comes up all sweaty and stinking like this and has to walk home through the early morning mountain chill in the same dirty long johns he's worked in all night. If he had a wife to keep a hot bath for him at home, it wouldn't be so bad. At the union meeting the other night Bo Whitley said that if Saint Peter was a company man he'd send you through the pearly gates in your sweaty long johns, same as here. Jim Brew thought that was pretty rich. He told it to all the boys on the graveyard shift. Bo Whitley is smart. Got a schoolhouse in his head. Everybody else thinks so, too, which pleases Jim Brew. He practically raised Bo Whitley after Bo ran off from his family. He's his cousin, too. And now that Bo has come back a big man with the Wobblies, he still stays with Jim. Jim knows most of the other stiffs at the boardinghouse always thought he was a little queer, probably from the time a Chink hit him in the head with a rock in a fight up in Tombstone. But they respect him now.

If the union has gone through with the strike like Bo says they're going to, they might get a change room. Jim should know if they're on strike as soon as he comes out of the tunnel. Bo said the strike had already been decided on, and the final meeting last night was more or less a formality. Bo says the IWWs are syndicalists. Jim doesn't know what that is, but it sounds all right. Bo says that means the union will take the mines away from the bosses. Jim guesses he'd rather have the union pay his wages than the company.

He can see the end of the tunnel, and he opens his carbide lantern to get ready to shake the burned carbide out of it at the mouth of the mine. He knows the number of bare light bulbs above by heart. There are three more before the collar of the tunnel. If they can get a change room out of it, Jim guesses he'll go on strike all right. Nobody should ever be able to say that Jim Brew was a damn scissorbill scab. And if they get six dollars a day like the Wobblies want, he can get a little ahead and marry a cantina girl from Naco. They make good wives if you treat them right. Everybody says so.

He'd like to stay in Bisbee, maybe get a pension if they win the strike. Hell, he's looking sixty in the face now. He's too old to be a tramp miner, a "ten-day boomer," anymore. Too old to hop freights and sleep in mulligan camps by the side of the railroad track. Leave that to the younger stiffs. They like it.

Jim Brew has seen a little bit of all of it. He remembers he was seven years old when the Yankees came and his daddy and mamma had to leave Alabama. He remembers San Angelo, Texas, and how his mamma cried when her good rocking chair got burned up in the range war. He remembers Bisbee when Heath and his men shot up Mr. Goldwater's store and the boys got mad and busted through Mule Pass to Tombstone and lynched Heath. He's seen a man get killed with a hammer in Tombstone Canyon, with an ax in Brewery Gulch, with a gun in Naco. He's worked everywhere from the Orphan Girl Mine in Nevada to the Sunshine in Idaho. He's double- and single-jack drilled, mucked, trammed, and skinned in every kind of hard-rock mine on God's green earth. He's seen Geronimo, and fought his braves. He's dealt faro in Sonora, California, and black-jack in Goldfield, Nevada, during the gold boom. Once he got so well thought of that they made him faro banker in Butte, which was the best job he ever had. He's placer mined in Oregon and prospected from the Dragoons to the Superstitions.

What he's really wanted to do most was be a peddler. But there's always been a woman that needed money or a panguinque and conquian-grande game that needed sitting in on. Oh, he'd love it, though. Get something that people wanted to buy and set up a stall somewhere. Souvenir rocks, maybe, for the people who come through on the Drummer's Special from the East. When they win the strike he'll do that maybe.

He knows the strike is on as soon as he steps out into the yard. Over the quiet pulse of the steam hoist he can hear the singing and hollering. And the mounted company bulls are all around the collar of the shaft to search him and the other boys. Looking for swiped dynamite, they say.

Then Miles Merrill, the chief company bull, makes a little speech about the Wobblies being German agitators and how he's sure every patriotic miner will ignore them down at the gate and will show up at work tomorrow. He doesn't get finished before one of the stiffs with a Swedish accent tells him to go fuck himself. Merrill gets huffy and asks him why he doesn't go back where he came from. The guy says he can't because he's an Indian, and most of the other miners laugh. One of the company scissorbills makes a remark about German spies and the Swede hits him. The company bulls break it up.

The world has cracks in it, like the mountain above the mine. All month Jim Brew has felt it. You don't know who's a union man and who's a company fink. The Mexes all might be Villistas, to hear the company union men tell it. You don't know who to speak to on the street anymore. The distrust is like a fog, creeping up Tombstone Canyon and Moon Canyon and all the canyons of Bisbee. Who the hell do you turn to? Who's a German spy? Who's a company spy? For his money, Jim Brew will stick by Bo Whitley. If there's anything Jim Brew has learned it's that you got to go by the people in an outfit to know whether the outfit is any good.

At the gate, the company bulls make sure everybody keeps moving. Just outside, on the railroad right-of-way, a half dozen deputies with carbines are keeping the way clear. Jim looks around for Sheriff Harry Wheeler, but doesn't see him. The deputies are being bossed by Wheeler's deputy, Shotgun Johnson, strutting with his sawed-off 12-gauge.

Some of the day-shift people are trying to get in through the picket lines. Lord, there are a lot of the boys on the line! Like a company picnic. The day-shift scabs aren't having too good a time of it. Neither are Shotgun Johnson and the deputies. Jim Brew would sure as hell hate to try to run that picket line. When the Wobs call a strike, they call a good one.

He gets to the gate and the boys on the picket line are hollering for him to join them. Most of the other men going out the gate join, but who knows how many do it for fear of getting their ass busted if they don't? Just up ahead three or four of the boys on the line have got hold of a scab who Jim heard yell "traitor" at one of the Wobs before. Now he's down on the ground and the boys are kicking hell out of him with their miner's boots. Shotgun Johnson breaks it up and shoots off one barrel of his 12-gauge in the air.

That calms the boys down a little. But the scabs still have to dodge rocks to get through. They're looking worried. Jim guesses it's because they know they got to get back through that line after they make their shift. And there's more than one thing can happen to a stiff underground, too. Jim would hate like hell to get in a cage to go underground thinking that the hoistman with his hand on the brake might be a Wob.

Jim feels a tap on his arm. Bo Whitley is motioning him on to the line. Bo is grinning that grin he has sometimes that makes him look like a kid with the devil in mind. Jim remembers it well from when Bo was a boy. If they weren't men out on a picket line, he'd like to hug him.

Instead he takes a kick at a deputy. Bo slaps him on the back for that. Jim's been in strikes before. He even carried a Wobbly card once, back in '07 at Goldfield. Everybody carried one then, from the mayor to the newsboys. Big Bill Haywood got so carried away in that one that he even tried to organize a Bronco Busters' local over in Salt Lake.

But Jim is a little worried, too. He ought to be studying about a pension. What the hell kind of life is it for a man without a pension? Soup kitchens and missions and a poorhouse.

But he can't let Bo down. So when the deputy whirls around, Jim brings his lunch pail down on him. The deputy ducks and Bo pulls Jim out of the way, back into the crowd.

All the scabs who are going in are past now. A good half of them gave up and went home. A dozen or so even got on the picket line. Bo jumps up on a fifty-gallon oil drum that Nigger John Brown is holding for him. He tries to say something, but most of the boys are still worked up and yelling cuss words at the deputies and company bulls. So Bo and a fat fellow who seems to be Bo's assistant start a song to get everybody's attention. Jim remembers it from Goldfield and joins.

Hallelujah, I'm a bum!
Hallelujah, bum again!
Hallelujah, give us a handout
To revive us again!

It's a good one to get the boys in a better mood, and by the time they get to the last chorus, everybody is singing it at the top of his lungs. Even the Bohunks and Dagos who don't know what it means.

Lordy, Jim feels good now. He'd forgotten how fine a strike could be. Like a tent meeting, except the preaching makes more sense.

The deputies stand back now that they see there's not going to be any more trouble. Shotgun Johnson tries to make sure that the pickets stay off company property, but can't so he gives up. Then the speechmaking begins. Jim can't understand a lot of it because it's in Finn and Bohunk and Mex. But he and the other stiffs holler and clap just like the Finns and Bohunks and Mexes do. That's the Wobs for you, Jim thinks. The AFL won't look at you unless you're a citizen. The Wobs take anybody, even niggers.

Then Bo Whitley speaks. Jim is proud. Bo's good, uses his hands a lot, and makes his voice sing like a revival preacher's. The crowd gets quiet now. Bo tells about the girls in the shops, and the dark mills, and the children with their legs cut off so that capitalists can sail on big boats to Europe. He says that capitalists are fat and live off the blood of the workingstiff. He tells about the widows and orphans from the unsafe mines. Some of the boys are crying before he gets done.

Then he tells what the Wobs want. Six dollars and eight hours a day, collar to collar. Water hoses on the pneumatic drills to keep down the dust that gives you the miner's consumption and can kill you in less than a year. No blasting during work shifts, so the mines don't cave in and the dust choke you. Two men on all machines underground, so if one gets hurt he's got somebody to go for help before he lays there and dies. The boys cheer him after every demand.

"How many of you boys ever had a physical examination?" Bo asks. Some of the men laugh, but most of them make faces and groan. "Now ain't that funny?" he says. "I had me one when I went to rustle me a job last week. Fellow asks me if I want to join the company's union before I go in to see the doctor. 'No thanks,' I tell him, and pull out my red IWW card. 'I got me a *real* union,' I says." The boys whistle and clap. "Then he sends me in to see old Doc Bledsoe." Somebody hoots, and a couple of boys make raspberry noises. "Old Doc Bledsoe, he pulls on my earlobe and looks at my tongue and tells me to wait outside. Few minutes later the fellow that asked me about the union comes out. 'Sorry,' he tells me. 'Doctor's report says you got two flat feet, polio, one arm, apoplexy, consumption, and three balls'!"

The crowd breaks up laughing. Jim looks around him and sees that even the deputies are smiling. Bo goes on. "'*So,*' I says to him. 'Does that mean I ain't healthy enough to work for Captain Greenway?' ''Fraid so,' the fellow tells me. 'But one thing I want you to know for sure. The fact you're a union man ain't got a thing to do with it'!"

One of the boys has brought up a washtub from somewhere and beats out a tattoo on it with a pair of sticks. The rest of the men slap one another on the back and clap and whistle. Jim is so proud of Bo he thinks he'll split open. Bo holds up his hands for quiet.

"You boys as sick of that horseshit as I am?" he shouts. The men roar back at him *yes, hell yes!* "You ready for a fighting union that ain't afraid to take on Captain Greenway and Grant Dowell and even old Walter Douglas himself up in his company president's chair in New York?" *Yes, hell yes.* "You ready for One Big Union?" *Yes, hell yes.* "You ready to give the mines and mills and factories to the people they belong to—to the great working people of this country?" *Yes, hell yes!*

Bo jumps down off the oil drum and the fellows crowd around him to shake his hand. Then the fat man who seemed to be Bo's helper struggles up on the drum and announces that his name is fellow-worker Hamer and that there will be a big rally this evening up in City Park on the Gulch, and that there will be some surprise speakers. He says he has some IWW membership cards for the men who don't have one yet and that he can sign them up on the spot. Dues are two dollars to join and thirty-five cents a month for everybody.

Bo sort of fades into the background, and Jim sees him keeping his eye on the train station, off to the left. A crowd's gathering on the station platform. Jim makes out Captain Greenway in his riding boots and campaign hat. He thinks he sees Sheriff Wheeler standing on the other side of Greenway, but can't be sure since Wheeler is such a runt and Greenway so tall. He's sure he sees Grant Dowell, though, and Tom Matthews. A few of the boys from the Copper Queen band are forming up behind them. For the first time, he realizes maybe he should be afraid. Wheeler and Greenway and Dowell and that bunch—they don't forget things.

Jim takes his Ingersoll out of the watch pocket in his Levi's and checks it. Getting on toward 7:30, time for the Drummer's Special from El Paso. With that collection of big wigs, must be somebody important coming in.

A Wob taps Jim on the shoulder and says to him, "You signed up yet, fellow worker?" Jim is indignant that the stiff doesn't know he's a friend of Bo Whitley's and of course is signed up. Then the fat man who said his name was Hamer works through the crowd selling cards with songs on them for a nickel apiece. Jim looks through them for one of Bo's songs and doesn't find one. But he buys three anyway.

Then Bo jumps back on the oil drum and asks the boys if they'd like to serenade some friends of theirs. He points to the station platform where Captain Greenway and Sheriff Wheeler and the others are. The boys clap and hoot some more. Bo tells them to make it loud, and asks the stiffs who have song cards to share them. Jim shares his with a

Jew jitney driver he knows named Bronstein. Bo plays the tune first on a harmonica, then tells everybody to turn toward the station platform and sing with him. He makes a mock bow to the ladies on the platform with their parasols, who all turn away except for one slight girl.

Then he leads the singing, and Jim imagines the music echoing off the canyons for miles and miles, even as far as Mexico:

> We have fed you all for a thousand years
> And you hail us still unfed,
> Though there's never a dollar of all your wealth
> But marks the workers' dead,
> We have yielded our best to give you rest
> And you lie on crimson wool.
> Then if blood be the price of all your wealth,
> Good God! We have paid it in full!

Harry Wheeler: July 1, 7:20 A.M.

You are Harry C. Wheeler, the last of the real sheriffs. You came across the Great Nowhere to find the Wild West, and almost missed it. You were a scout with the Apaches in captivity back in Fort Sill, Oklahoma, when you were barely twenty, and one of the best, by God. Then at thirty you were commander of the Arizona Rangers and able to hit 197 out of any 200 bull's-eyes. Five four or not, you were so tough that all you had to do was tell a man to turn himself in, and he did. You could draw with the best of them. And even in '09, when the pussies disbanded the Arizona Rangers to get ready for "civilization" and statehood, you kept going. Took a Cochise County deputy's job just to keep your hand in. Suffered that for three years, tracking men on horseback through the snows of some of the most god-awful mountains in creation. Talking to eastern reporters and storywriters to pass the weeks. Getting more famous. Preparing to be sheriff of the roughest county in the West before the pussies took that away, too.

And you made it. Just in time, because the SOBs are after your county.

Right now you are standing on the El Paso and Southwestern railway station platform in Bisbee waiting for the arrival of the 7:30 A.M. Drummer's Special from El Paso. You are standing beside the last of the real men, Captain John C. Greenway. He is general manager of the Calumet & Arizona Mining Company and one of the half dozen most powerful men in the state of Arizona. You are flattered. Captain Greenway is over six feet tall, imperially slim, blond, and a hero of the Spanish War. You are a little chubby, and were discharged after the Philippine campaign, an enlisted man, when a horse stepped on your foot and broke it. You are flattered, but a little ashamed, too. But as always, you keep your voice level and quiet, a voice of authority. You respect Authority passionately. Almost as much as you respect Right. Almost.

You are not a happy man. You came home from OCS in California less than two weeks ago, washed out. They told you simply that you were "not officer material," and no more. Out of all the impressive things you have done, you wanted nothing so much as to be an officer in the United States Army, like your father, and your uncle, General Fighting Joe Wheeler.

You left your house on Toughnut Street in Tombstone before dawn to get here on time. Alice, your wife, and little Sunshine, your daughter, were still asleep when you loaded your bedroll and rifle into your cutdown racing Locomobile and set out across the desert. The afternoon's heavy clouds had cleared off during the night, and the moon made the mountainsides a pale blue. You thought that the sparse shrubs on them made them look like the dotted Swiss bedspread over Alice's body in your neat white bedroom. Then your mind wandered to the lounging Greek women painted on the cloth ceiling in Remedios's room. Remedios is the Mexican whore who is "your woman" above the Line on Brewery Gulch. It was an unmanly thought and you dismissed it. Now is not a time for whores. These next few days could be the most important ones of your life. According to the telegrams the mining companies have intercepted, a foreign revolution against the United States government might be beginning. Here, in Cochise County.

There have been strangers from foreign parts pouring into town for days. Tough guys, troublemakers. As you drove by the courthouse on your way out of Tombstone this morning, you stopped for a moment in front of the O.K. Corral on Allen Street and got out to clear your head. The stablekeeper knows you and said nothing when you walked to the spot where the Earp-Clanton shoot-out happened, a generation ago. It was empty in the moonlight and smelled of horseshit. But you didn't notice. You stood for maybe ten minutes on the spot where the old-timers said Wyatt Earp had stood.

As you drove slowly down the deserted Allen Street, the only real street left in Tombstone, the ruins of the Birdcage Theater, of Earp's Oriental Saloon, of the Crystal Palace Dance Hall, were sharply silhouetted in the moonlight. It seemed to you that you had never really seen them before, and they appeared almost whole, restored, in the blue moonlight.

Now you hear the whistle and see the tail of steam as the Drummer's Special rounds Sacramento Hill. The crowd of miners off by the post office to your right hoots back at the train. They've been listening to radical speakers since six—Bohunks and Mexes and Dagos who can't even speak English without an accent. And singing. Songs that make you want to flat puke sometimes, songs making fun of God and policemen and bosses. Just now they've been listening to a young blond type with a crooked nose who Captain Greenway tells you is Bo Whitley. You knew his daddy—a good man, rode pony express in the old days—and are ashamed for the boy. He comes from good people and shouldn't be mixed up with such a bunch. Captain Greenway seems to know a good bit about him; he says that Grant Dowell has a file on him. The Copper Queen has files on every man in the district, Greenway says. That should come in handy.

There must be five hundred men on the picket line. You'll have to see that they cut that number down: too many for public order. A good half of them break off from the main bunch at Whitley's signal when the train comes into sight, and begin to spread out up and down the track by the station. Most of them keep their distance from the platform. They know you, know you're not a man to be messed with.

"They'll be checking the train for strikebreakers, I imagine," Captain Greenway says. You nod. "I don't suppose there's any point in my asking if you're prepared, is there?" he says confidentially. Beside him, Grant Dowell looks worried and takes a nervous swipe at his balding head. Standing a little apart, as usual, Tom Matthews takes everything in and keeps his face a mask. His son is arriving from Princeton today, which is why you're all there. A welcoming party. Art Matthews is the first Bisbee boy to win his commission and get orders for France, with the Princeton Rifles. That makes you a little uneasy, too. He's barely twenty-two, and you'll be forty-three next year. It's not fair, but you have to be careful not to show any resentment. They all know about your washing out of OCS and they'll be watching you.

You check the Wobblies spreading out along the track. They're thorough—seem to have group captains that post them at even intervals. The Whitley boy's directing them. You admire that kind of operation. Discipline—nothing's ever done right without discipline and authority.

You don't have enough deputies yet, and that worries you. Shotgun Johnson, your chief deputy, is watching you for orders, his sawed-off shotgun resting loosely in the crook of his arm. He's a thin stooped man with a mean streak to him you don't like, but need. You know he'd love to use his shotgun. And start a riot. But you'll have no riots, by God, from anybody. Not while you're sheriff of Cochise County—elected to that job by the largest margin since Texas John Slaughter.

There are no strikebreakers on the train, you've been told. That puzzles you. But it's not your place to ask why not. Still, you're glad there aren't any. You hate a damn Wobbly like a snake, but you're in favor of the workingman. He has a hard lot and you've always felt a little bad about breaking a strike, even when you were commander of the Arizona Rangers. It's just these I Won't Work IWWs that piss you off. They got no sense of decency, of Americanism.

Whitley starts the pickets to singing and leaves a fat man to direct them. Grant Dowell knows the fat man, too, and says his name is somebody Hamer. You make a note of that, then walk casually over to Shotgun Johnson.

"Keep 'em off the right-of-way, Shotgun," you tell him quietly. "Leave the company guards to keep 'em clear of company property, but be ready in case anything starts. Make sure people get off the train without being molested." Johnson grins and touches his hat brim to you. "No trouble," you tell him, and mean it. Railway platforms always make you nervous. You have four bullet-hole scars on your chest and arms from a railway platform, left from the day you got your first blood in a shoot-out up in Benson. The wife of a man named Tracy was trying to get away, and he came to the train with a pistol to stop her. You were a ranger then and she ran to you for help. Tracy got four slugs in you before you could draw, but you got him on your way down with one shot. Nobody's ever got the drop on you since. You pull your black coat back to expose your pistol butt and check it to make sure it's sitting easy in it's holster.

The train chuffs into the station. Grant Dowell, with another swipe at his bald head, waves his hands like a hen's wings to the Copper Queen band. There are less than half of them here; the others went out with the IWWs. They step forward and strike up "When Johnny Comes Marching Home." The tuba player is trying to hold the company standard and play the tuba at the same time. He fails miserably. There's only one drummer, and he's nervous because the damned Imperial Wilhelm's Warriors are trying to drown him out with their singing.

Captain Greenway takes Tom Matthew's arm and leads him to the front of the small crowd that has gathered to welcome Art Matthews home. The crowd begins to clap and cheer politely. A handful of Wobblies makes obscene noises and gestures at the ladies, damn their eyes.

Bo Whitley is keeping his boys back pretty well and seems to be checking the train windows for somebody in particular. The Wobblies have dressed a man in a clown suit and he's doing cartwheels along the right-of-way. Somebody else leads a mule in a frock coat up and down beside the station platform. It has sandwich boards hung over it with arrows pointing toward the mule's ass. The words Scabs' Entrance are scrawled above the arrows. One of the Wobblies runs up and slaps a gummed sticker on the big Brooks twelve-wheeler locomotive as it passes him. As the locomotive eases up to you, you see that the sticker has a picture on it of a black cat hunched above the word Sabotage. You reach out and rip it off before the glue dries.

One bunch of the Wobblies breaks loose from the others and rushes the baggage car, right by the platform. Captain Greenway steps toward them and slaps at one with his riding crop. The man cowers. Another of them flings a piece of dung from the mule in the frock coat. The dung hits Captain Greenway's boot. Greenway doesn't flinch. The Wobblies back off from him. By God, Jack Greenway is a man.

The band gets louder to compete with the Wobblies. The locomotive is making an awful hissing, and the mule, upset, begins to bray and kick up its heels. The Wobblies along the track make catcalls at the salesmen who are trying to get off the train, and whistle at the ladies. The racket and confusion are awful, and you're afraid things are about to get out of order, but Jack Greenway is still cool. Grant Dowell has slipped back into the safety of the ladies with their parasols. Tom Matthews searches the detraining passengers for his son. A slight girl in a voile shirtwaist steps up beside him—Art Matthews's fiancée, no doubt, though you've never been introduced. You're not a member of the Bisbee Country Club. Or of the Bisbee Yale-Harvard-Princeton Club. You were too busy learning to be an Indian scout to go to college. West Point would have been different, but you were too short to get in. Your father never forgave you for that.

Most of the passengers are off by now, and still no Art Matthews. For the first time you see a touch of concern on Tom Matthews's face. He takes the girl's hand and pats it. Mrs. Matthews, a largish woman in a black dress and veiled flowered hat, steps up beside them and looks questioningly at Tom. He drops the girl's hand and whispers something to his wife. She looks comforted.

At the very end of the platform, near the last car of the train, the Wobblies seem to be congregating. They're shoving one another to get close to the train. You're too short to see what it's all about, but Captain Greenway knits his eyebrows and says, "The sons of bitches are going after Matthews's boy, Harry. They're going after the uniform." The slight girl breaks away from Tom Matthews and runs toward the commotion. Matthews jerks his derby off and goes after her.

Quickly (but coolly) you push past Greenway and the band to catch up with them. Beneath the noise, you can feel the faint jingle of your spurs. They comfort you. The girl has nearly reached the end of the platform by the time you catch her. A big ugly Jew Wobbly reaches out and swats her behind as she goes past. Then he sees you and ducks back into the crowd.

It's hard to see past the crowd, still, but you catch sight of the red lining of an officer's cape on the top step of a Pullman coach. The girl is trying to shove through the crowd to the steps. A colored porter reaches out for her but the crowd shoves him back. You touch her arm and lead her away. Tom Matthews takes her from you and nods his thanks.

By the time you turn back to the crowd, Bo Whitley is ahead of you. He's telling the Wobblies to stand back. They seem to obey him naturally, as they do you. You step in beside him and the two of you make a path through the men. He could be a good man, you think, if he'd leave these damned outside agitators alone.

Now you make out Art Matthews clearly. Envy stabs you for a moment when you see his spit-shined riding boots and the way his cape with red lining flows over his slim six foot four. You pull a miner in overalls out of the way and he turns, fist cocked, but drops his hands when he sees who you are. Let the kid in the uniform get *that* kind of respect, you think, and stand as tall as your five four will let you.

Art Matthews is smiling, which surprises you. Then you see the other two people, standing on the bottom step in front of the Matthews boy. The few miners remaining between you and the train are reaching out to take their hands, and the two, a man and a woman, are smiling also and shaking as many hands as they can. Now you're even more surprised. The crowd is ignoring the Matthews boy, and he seems as interested in the two on the steps in front of him as anyone.

"Let 'em through, let 'em through," Bo Whitley shouts beside you, and the crowd begins to form ragged lines on either side of an imaginary aisle. The man and woman turn and each takes one of Art Matthews's hands. He leans down to say something to the woman that makes her smile even more. She's a damn fine-looking woman of average height, somewhere in her mid twenties, with a good figure underneath her old-fashioned white shirtwaist and lace collar. The man with her is a tall Dago with a flowing red scarf and rimless glasses. You peg him as a pussy.

They're radicals, no doubt about it, and well known to the strikers. But why would Art Matthews be friendly with them? You turn to Tom Matthews, who has moved up beside you, for a gesture that will tell you how you should react. He looks displeased, nothing more. His boy spots him and waves. The girl beside Tom Matthews waves her handkerchief, and the Matthews boy smiles at her and shrugs to tell her he can't get through the crowd yet. She's crying.

Whitley has got some sort of order restored now and the man and woman walk together down the imaginary aisle. The Wobblies break into cheers. The woman walks with her head slightly cocked, as if it were a habit, and as she passes close by you, you're struck by her sharp blue eyes. The band straggles down the platform behind you and the tall Dago waves to them. They break into "Marching through Georgia."

Then the woman stops. Her smile fades and her eyes lock onto something in the crowd beside you. The tall Dago follows her look and his mouth turns into a prissy frown.

They're both looking at Bo Whitley, whose eyes are fixed on the woman. There is something happening between the two of them, but you can't make out what it is. The woman starts to speak, but Whitley turns sharply on his heel and walks away from her, up the platform toward the main body of strikers.

You hear someone call Whitley's name. It's Art Matthews, who, looking disappointed, is waving at Whitley's retreating back. The Dago puts his arm around the woman's shoulder and leads her away. One of the Wobblies shouts, " 'The Rebel Girl,' boys!" and begins to sing.

And the grafters in terror are trembling
When her spite and defiance she'll hurl;
For the only and thoroughbred lady
Is The Rebel Girl.

You feel a hand on your shoulder. Jack Greenway is standing at your back. "You a Joe Hill fan, Harry?" he says. His eyes don't meet yours; they are following Bo Whitley.

"Not particularly."

"The Tennyson of the working class, Harry. He wrote that song for the famous little lady you just almost met. We've got a celebrity with us now."

You look up at him to see if he's serious. There's a slight mocking smile on his lips that you're not sure how to respond to.

"Oh, they've called out their heavy artillery on us now. That's Elizabeth Gurley Flynn, and if I'm not mistaken, the Italian-looking gentleman with her should be named Carlo Tresca. Do you read the *New York Times,* Harry?"

"No, sir, I don't."

"It's not necessary. Well!" He takes his hand from your shoulder. "I wouldn't be surprised now if Big Bill Haywood himself showed up. Think you could handle that, Harry?"

You're affronted. "I'd welcome it, Captain Greenway."

"Good, good. Bully." Greenway pats your shoulder a last time. "We'll have to talk, Harry. Drop out for a drink this evening, eh?"

"Thank you," you say without committing yourself. "We'll see how this business here goes, I think."

"Of course. I *would* like to talk with you, you understand."

"Yessir." You do understand. You've just received an order.

You follow the progress of the Dago and the Flynn woman up toward O.K. Street and the Pythian Castle, where the Wobblies have set up their headquarters. Elizabeth Gurley Flynn. Be damned. You saw her name in the *Bisbee Review* just last week. But you didn't expect her to look like that—somehow she should have looked like that fat sheeny, Emma Goldman. You wonder momentarily if you should deputize some women if the damned Wobblies are going to play it this way, but decide against it. You've handled plenty of women up on the Gulch before with no problems. What's the difference?

Wobblies all up and down the train are drifting back toward the main body of pickets in front of the post office. They're slapping one another on the back and whooping and hollering. The passengers—drummers in skimmers and derbies, mainly—who are waiting for their baggage, watch them nervously. One or two seem to be seeing to it that their bags are put back onto the train. You don't blame them for not wanting to stay. The man with the braying mule leads it up and down the length of the train, cussing.

You notice another bunch, now. Women and children, for the most part, gathered in little knots at the edges of the platform, with beat-up suitcases and cloth bundles. Not many tramp miners have families. These must be the families of the older ones, property owners, who know what to expect. They're leaving town It's a bad sign, like animals you've seen running before a forest fire.

You pull yourself together and excuse yourself from Captain Greenway, who is waiting his turn to greet Art Matthews. Tom Matthews and his wife and the slight girl are all embracing Art in a cluster. The girl is still crying. The remnants of the Copper Queen band, silver braid catching the morning sun, straggle on with "Marching through Georgia." There's a hell of a lot to do yet. Pickets to thin, deputies to round up (Grant Dowell tried to get you to deputize the company guards that morning, but you refused. What the hell kind of fairness would that show the miners?), headquarters in the dispensary to set up, patrols to send out, damn Wobbly leaders to meet with.

You haven't gone twenty paces before Grant Dowell catches up with you. "Ho, Harry," he says. "I . . . ah, wanted to congratulate you on your statement in the *Review* this morning. Good strong stuff. I like your phrasing: ' . . . a direct blow to the government of the United States,' was it? Your own phrase, I assume?"

"Yessir," you say. Grant Dowell is not a Real Man. He's efficient, you'll give him that, and has power. But there's something about him, a kind of calculation and slipperiness that you can't deal with. He won't meet a thing directly, head on, the way a man ought to.

"Doesn't hurt to be prepared, does it? Lots of German sympathizers in these Wobblies, you know."

"I've heard that, yessir."

"God's truth, it is, Harry. I expect to be able to prove it before long."

"I'll be interested," you say.

"No doubt, no doubt. Have you made any definite plans so far?"

"To keep the peace, Mr. Dowell."

"Fine. Well . . . fine. The company is—so far as I can speak for them, of course—behind you one hundred percent. Whatever you need, let me know."

You pick up your pace again. Dowell falls behind, puffing. "See you at Jack's tonight," he shouts after you. You wave without turning around. At Jack's, he said. They've never encouraged you to call Captain Greenway that before. You've never even been in his home.

In front of the post office, the fat man—Hamer, was it? —still leads the pickets in songs, though they've thinned out considerably since the train has gone and the shift change is over. A Mexican is setting up a tamale stand nearby, and men circulate among them with lemonade and hot ears of corn. That'll pass soon, you know, when the money runs out. Shotgun Johnson seems to have it well in hand. Three of Bisbee's six-man police force stand near the huge American flag hung over the post office, looking worried. A hell of a lot of good they'll be.

You pause a moment in the square between the company store and your offices in the dispensary. Up Brewery Gulch, the stores are open and clusters of miners hang around in front of them, chewing and spitting and whispering. You can't see far up the Gulch, just to the Palace Meat Market and Cockeyed Jimmy's cardroom, before it winds behind Muheim's Brewery. They tell you the Gulch shut down last night, for the first time in memory. You wonder if Remedios knows you're in town. She must. Word travels fast when you come down from Tombstone.

You wonder if she'll try to get in touch with you. The girls are forbidden to come down off the Gulch, but they have ways. Your cock uncoils below your gunbelt. You'll have to call Alice and little Sunshine first thing. They'll be worried.

You take one last look around. Bo Whitley is standing alone right under the flag by the post office, watching you. Your eyes meet. He nods. You nod. Hell of a strange kid. Dangerous, maybe. You'll have to remember to ask to see his file. And to find out what's between him and that Flynn woman. You have a feeling you'll need to know that before this whole thing is over.

He'll have to learn who you are, too. Because you're Harry Wheeler, last of the real sheriffs.

Art Matthews: July 1, 8:00 A.M.

Art Matthews's welcoming party has taken a roundabout way from the station to avoid what Jack Greenway calls, with a laugh, the wrath of the masses. They slip off the platform on the east end, toward Mexico and away from the strikers in front of the post office. The ragtag Copper Queen band follows, but in front of city hall Grant Dowell dismisses the group. The band goes inside city hall to change. None of them wants to be caught alone by the strikers in his Copper Queen uniform. Most of them will be on strike by evening anyway.

The slight girl hangs on Art Matthews's arm as they walk. She is Rachael French, the daughter of the head of Phelps-Dodge's smelting operations down the road in Douglas, but everyone knows her as Bunny. She has blond hair so fine the light shines through it and makes it seem to glow. Her mother thought she looked like a little bunny rabbit when she was a baby. She has always been told she is lucky because she has a tiny mole on her chin that people say passes for a natural beauty mark. She has always been proud of her teeth, too, and has sweet breath from chewing mint leaves. She is Art Matthews's fiancée, and has been thought of that way since she was thirteen and he fifteen. They've seen very little of each other since he was sent away to prep school and then Princeton while she stayed home to go to finishing school.

Art Matthews has slipped his gloves underneath his epaulets in a jaunty way popular with the other chaps in the Princeton Rifles. His red-lined cape is thrown back so that Bunny can take his arm more easily. His father walks ahead as a kind of honor guard, and his mother walks beside him so that she can judge the extent to which the army has been misfeeding him. Everyone is telling him how well he looks and how proud they are of him. He is a little worried that the long train trip has wrinkled his jodhpurs. Grant Dowell catches up with him in front of city hall and apologizes for the terrible state of affairs. He hopes it won't spoil Art's leave. Art will see enough of this sort of confusion in France, he bets.

Art smiles at them all and endures their chattering, even though he's a bit embarrassed by it. But, aside from appraising Bunny's thin figure as she sways against him, his mind is elsewhere. It has been one bloody strange morning.

He's excited about having had breakfast with Elizabeth Gurley Flynn and Carlo Tresca. He knows some chaps at school who are awfully keen on them, and they'll be envious when he writes them about it. Himself, he doesn't go much for politics, but Gurley Flynn is pretty famous back East. Tresca was not very friendly and complained about the food. He insisted on talking Italian to all the Mexicans on the train, which they didn't think much of. But Gurley Flynn chattered to Art as if he were an old confidant of hers. She asked him all about Bisbee, and wondered if he knew a fellow named Bo Whitley. She seemed pleased and wanted to know more when he told her Bo had taught him to play baseball and had been a childhood hero of his, though of course they didn't see much of each other socially. Tresca scowled a great deal while they were talking about Whitley, and Gurley Flynn changed the subject before Art could ask her how she knew Bo Whitley.

Art knew that Gurley Flynn and Tresca were living together in a state of Free Love, and that excited him, too. It seemed to him that he could smell recent lovemaking on her above the odor of the breakfast bacon. He's heard a lot about Free Love among the radicals and thinks it's not such a bad idea. But he's a little ashamed of the thought with Bunny on his arm. Gurley Flynn's clothes were crisp and clean, while Bunny's are fluffy and flowing and somewhat dusty.

Gurley Flynn asked him what he thought of the strike, and he admitted that he hadn't seen a paper since he left Princeton. But when he told her his father had wired him about it, she seemed very interested in who his father was. She asked him all sorts of questions, some of them darned intimate, about his father's habits and position. Art was pleased, though, to find out they were both Catholic. But she was pretty down on Catholicism, and he owned that he wasn't too keen on going to church either.

Over after-breakfast coffee he had asked her about the IWW and socialism, and she tried to explain them to him. But there wasn't much time, and he was right well confused about the difference between socialism and syndicalism and anarchism. The differences mattered a great deal to her, but all three systems seemed bloody impractical to him. The only time they almost had words was when she told him he was going to get butchered in a capitalist war, and he tried to explain to her that he had to go and fight Prussian militarism and monarchy. She told him she thought that was pitiful.

They walk past Brewery Gulch now, then start up School Hill, where his family's big brick house is. They pass between the magnolias of the company offices and the Copper Queen Hotel, which Colonel Roosevelt called the only real hotel between Saint Louis and San Francisco. There are knots of men—salesmen and businessmen—standing on the hotel's two porches smoking cigars and watching the activities of the strikers.

Then they start the long climb past the dark brick Presbyterian church and the YWCA onto Opera Drive. Everything in downtown Bisbee has always seemed to Art to be made out of the same batch of dark brick, as if the builders wanted to make the streets look like the dark canyons they occupy. It's dashed depressing.

He had forgotten how many hills Bisbee has. When he was a schoolboy, he always thought Rome must look like

Bisbee. His father apologizes for not having had the auto waiting but says it seemed better to walk, what with all the turmoil. Art tells him he doesn't mind. All the other company officials moved to the new suburb of Warren a few years ago and sold lots to one another except his father, who said he didn't really mind the smoke and smells of Bisbee and who, besides, wanted to "keep an eye on things." Art has never questioned the explanation.

The striker with a mule dressed in a frock coat followed them as far as the Copper Queen Hotel but didn't dare go any farther. Art noticed that some of the striking miners even doffed their hats to Captain Greenway and Mr. Dowell, and looked guilty. He has always heard that the Bisbee miners were "good boys" and is, in truth, surprised by the strike. Strikes have always seemed to him to smack slightly of ingratitude.

They take it easy going up the winding streets and long flights of steps past the miners' wooden houses. The ladies musn't tire themselves. Art notices that the miners' families, and the solitary miners in the jumbled boardinghouses, watch them through windows and screen doors. None of them seems to want to come out onto his porch. At one time, when he was a boy home for summer vacations, they would all greet him by name when he passed by. He even knew some of their names, too. He searches out Bo Whitley's family's cabin. Strangers' faces watch him from the window now. He's still hurt that Bo didn't recognize him this morning, and is surprised to see him back in Bisbee. He was glad at first to see him, helping Sheriff Wheeler, but now he is puzzled about Bo and the Flynn woman and all this strike business.

Ralph, the colored chauffeur, spots the family first and takes the long flights of stairs to the house two at a time to alert the other servants. By the time Tom Matthews leads everyone up the last flight of stone stairs the whole household staff is waiting on the wide front porch. Guadalupe, the maid, is shy and beaming as usual, and Concha, the ageless cook, maintains her dignity, but Art thinks he can see a tear or two. Mexican women aren't supposed to cry a lot. Only the Chinese houseboy, Johnny Fourth of July, is missing. Apologetically, Ralph tells Mr. Art that he got drunk and went on strike with the Wobblies. He's sure Johnny'll come back when he sobers up. Mrs. Matthews shakes her head indulgently. These people! So like children.

Ralph is sent to the station for Art's luggage. Jack Greenway and Grant Dowell apologize for not being able to sit awhile, but business does call. Greenway mentions to Mr. Dowell that he's borrowing a man named McCrea for a few days, and winks. He's sure Dowell doesn't mind. Dowell looks serious and warns Greenway to go very slowly, very cautiously—about what, Art isn't sure. Greenway laughs his good rich laugh and tells Dowell not to be an old woman. Art has always wanted to be like Jack Greenway, even more than like his father.

His father comes in from sending Ralph for the luggage just in time to hear Dowell warn Greenway. He looks serious, as he always does, and rests his hand on Greenway's shoulder. "Listen to Grant, Jack," he says. "We've got to stick together in this, you know."

"Of course we have, Tom. Of course," Greenway says. His mood is still light.

"We haven't heard from Walter yet," Tom Matthews says. Art assumes he means Walter Douglas, president of Phelps-Dodge's mining division. Walter Douglas lives in New York and Canada, and comes down in his private railway car, the Cloudcroft, every now and again. His father founded Bisbee, and he has the biggest house in town, next door to Jack Greenway's.

Greenway looks soberer and merely nods. Art wonders how the mention of Walter Douglas's name can mean so much to a man like Jack Greenway, especially when they don't even work for the same company.

While the other men are talking and Bunny has gone with his mother to "freshen up," Art looks around the living room to see if things have changed. Everything is still as proper as always. The silver dish with calling cards, their corners all correctly turned up, still sits full by the door. The white curtains, starched, still hang as bloody straight as ever. The doilies his grandmother made still cover all the chair arms, and the family Bible still lies on the largest doily of all, on the parlor Bible table, beside a neat stack of folders and company papers. His father's hunting prints and his mother's landscapes still hang with military regularity along the wall.

Art feels at home and, at the same time, just a tiny bit smothered, as always. He's sure the strict English regimen of Bisbee's proper people hasn't changed either: high tea in the afternoon, dressing for dinner, tails and top hats at the country club. The chaps at Princeton always get a laugh when he tells them about the mining engineers struggling up the burro trails of Bisbee in morning coats and spats for tea. They tell him he's a colonial.

And then he sees the one thing that has changed. Over the door. A 12-gauge riot gun and a thirty-aught-six rifle. His father has never allowed guns in the house before. His mother comes in and sees him staring at the guns. She takes his hand and tells him not to worry. It's just a "precaution." "You know about those IWW people, I suppose," she says. "Or don't they teach that at Princeton? I know Harvard is such a radical place, but I assumed that Princeton . . ."

Art begins to tell her about Gurley Flynn and Tresca, but his father's conversation with the other men catches his ear. Dowell and Greenway are reading statements they're going to give to the *Bisbee Review* for the next morning's edition. There is no rush. Phelps-Dodge owns the *Bisbee Review,* too.

" 'Regardless of any question of merit in the demands,' " Grant Dowell reads, " 'this company will never negotiate with an organization founded on principles inimical to good government in times of peace, and treasonable in times of war.' "

"Bully," Jack Greenway says.

Dowell goes on. " 'Any demands by this organization will be refused, even though such refusal may result in the company's shutting down its mines for an indefinite period.' "

"Does that check with Walter Douglas?" Greenway asks.

Dowell looks to Tom Matthews. Art wonders why he doesn't answer for himself. "Standing orders to use that wording," Tom Matthews says.

"Ah!" Greenway says. "My turn?" Dowell and Tom Matthews nod. Greenway unfolds a handwritten note he has taken from his shirt pocket. " 'To all loyal and patriotic employees of the Calumet and Arizona Mining Company and friends among the public,' " he begins. Then he looks up for approval. "That should cover the bases, I reckon." Dowell smiles. "The rest," Greenway continues, "is more or less in the same vein as yours, you know. I mention the nationwide conspiracy to cripple the government in the war—a conspiracy in whose existence I wholeheartedly believe, needless to say—and end with . . . let me see . . . oh yes . . . never negotiate, etcetera, then: 'Bisbee is the highest-paid camp in the world, and the conduct of its mines is proverbially clean and high grade. C and A plans to continue operations unchanged.' Does that jibe with what Lem Shattuck's outfit will say?"

"More or less," Grant Dowell says. "Lem's a bit more cautious, of course. German wife and all that puts him in a rough position."

"Damned old reprobate," Greenway says. "You boys see Harry Wheeler's statement in the paper this morning? I reckon you might have had a hand in that wording, Tom?"

"Not a bit," Tom Matthews says. "He phoned it in from Tombstone last night all by himself."

"Why, that little bastard! I didn't know he had it in him!" Art's mother looks offended and retreats toward the kitchen. "Sorry, Lavinia!" Greenway shouts after her.

"Well, that should do it, I suppose," Dowell says and picks up his hat.

"No other choice," Greenway says. "Can't negotiate with rattlesnakes. Stop 'em here, or hand 'em the whole shooting match on a silver platter. Did I mention I got a letter from Teddy on this whole Wobbly business?"

"From *who*?" Dowell says.

"Colonel Roosevelt," Tom Matthews reminds him quietly.

"Teddy compares that I Won't Work outfit with Danton, Robespierre, Marat—that French lot. Says they're criminals. Says if the government won't stop them, then there should be enough decent people to do the job. Eh?"

Art has studied the French Revolution at Princeton, but finds it hard to compare Gurley Flynn with Charlotte Corday or that kind. His eyes are drawn back to the riot gun and the thirty-aught-six.

"We expect to hear from Walter soon," Dowell says to

Greenway. "That right, Tom?" Tom Matthews nods. "Things should keep till then, Jack. Harry Wheeler will meet with the strike people, I expect. He'll stay on top of it."

"Harry Wheeler couldn't stay on top of a turtle with polio unless somebody told him how to," Greenway says. "Don't forget that McCrea lad, Grant. I'll give him back to you when I'm done."

Dowell sighs, and takes his hat to leave. Art's father walks them to the foot of the steps. Art hears Greenway say as they clack across the front porch, "Bring your boy along tonight, Tom! My house, seven sharp. Time he learned some things about the real world."

Art is still puzzled. Why does everyone seem to defer to his father? Dowell outranks him, clearly. While he is alone in the room, he removes his cape and sits to wait for someone to bring him tea, as he knows someone will sooner or later. From the Bible table, he picks up a folder marked Phelps-Dodge Corporation, Copper Queen Mining Division, Confidential. He has never bothered about his father's business before, but his curiosity is up. Besides, he is an officer in the United States Army now.

At the top of the papers in the folder is a formal business letter from the Thiel Detective Agency. It is signed by Agent 34, and no one else. Art leafs through the pages, which contain an alphabetized list of names. From its length, he surmises it must list every adult male in the district. He is astounded and, as he reads a few of the entries following the names, shocked.

Bauer, Louis, Bisbee 6, 89 O.K. Street. Butcher. Born in Arizona. Republican. Now working at Tovrea's shop in Lowell. Was raised in Douglas; rather shiftless and does not have a job long; is married to a Mexican woman and has several children; inclined to be a radical and was a strong supporter of radical ex-Gov. Hunt. Has spoken in favor of IWW and is not to be trusted. Worked at P.D. store and was fired on account of his work not being satisfactory. A very ignorant, unreliable proposition. NO GOOD. 5-18-17.

The rest of the names all have similar entries. Church, politics, family, attitude toward IWW, attitude toward corporations, money in the bank, lodge, newspapers read—and at the end, GOOD or NO GOOD. The last page in the folder is another letter from Agent 34, which says he has managed to infiltrate the IWW leadership and will maintain contact with Tom Matthews as arranged.

What the hell is going on? Art wonders. Contact with his father, and not Grant Dowell? Agent 34 and all that kind of cloak-and-dagger stuff. He comes home to get in a little bird shooting and walks into a bloody damn war. And why was this Flynn woman so interested in his father? And dash it all to hell, why does he keep finding himself thinking about the Flynn woman and not Bunny, who is his fiancée? It's a rum setup already, and he's not been home an hour.

He hears his father's footsteps on the porch and quickly puts the folder back on the Bible table. Bunny sways in with a tea tray just as his father comes through the front door. His father mumbles something about leaving the young people alone and goes to look for that damn darky, Ralph, who should be back with the bags by now.

Bunny pours his tea for him. Her face is small and she smells heavily of face powder. She keeps her eyes downcast. Art wonders if she feels as awkward as he does.

"I'm glad you're home," she says at last. "There's not been much to do while you were gone. I was afraid you'd go away to war without seeing me again." Her voice is small, too, and a little pouty.

Art takes her hand as she gives him his English china teacup. Her hand is as small as her face, and feels cold. "Never," he says without much conviction.

Bunny raises her eyes to him at last. She lets him retain her hand, but it lies limp in his. Her face is as pouty as her voice now. "I was afraid you had taken up with that radical person on the train. Oh, but that's a terrible thing for me to say. You've just gotten home."

"That Flynn woman? She's not our kind of people at all."

"I know that. But I thought maybe that was just why you did like her. I've been reading about that . . . well, Free Love." She drops her eyes again, then blurts out, "Well, whoever knows what kinds of bohemian people you've met at college!"

"Where in the world have you been reading that sort of

thing?" Art says. He feels rather worldly as he sees himself through Bunny's eyes. Dashing, even.

Bunny is contrite. "Magazines," she says softly.

"Do I *look* like a bohemian?'

"No, but . . . well, it's one thing to go up to the girls on the Gulch, but to seriously have anything to do with somebody as notorious as that Elizabeth-whatever person . . ."

"The porter seated us together at breakfast. That's all. Besides, she has her lover with her."

Bunny withdraws her hand from Art's. He's afraid he's been too dashing. He shouldn't have used the word "lover" so casually.

"I just wanted to know," Bunny says. Her voice is less pouty now. "I just get a little jealous here all by myself. I suppose I have a right to. You . . . mean a good deal to me, Art."

Art leans over and kisses her cheek. It tastes like talcum powder. Her dress is low cut, and she wears a tiny gold chain with a cross in her cleavage. Art sneaks a look, but doesn't see much cleavage.

"I understand," he says, wanting to sound sympathetic.

"Your mother has arranged a little thing at the country club for you. Did she tell you?"

"Good God. A party? With all that's going on?"

"Well, it *is* for the Fourth, too. And we . . . *she* thought you and I might . . . have something to announce, you know."

She waits for a comment. Then, in the face of Art's silence, continues. "Your father says we should all try to go on as usual through these horrible times. He's being very brave."

"Yes," Art says absently. He tries to imagine Bunny with no clothes on. He can't. There is an awkward pause.

"More tea?" Bunny asks at last.

It's not at all the way Art has pictured it. Alone in his room in Princeton he's had fantasies of Bunny in black garters. And now that he's home, all he can think of is some woman he met on a train. Bunny all but gave him permission to go visit the girls on the Gulch, but is worried about a woman he knows he couldn't get close to with a ten-foot pole. Then Jack Greenway wants to teach him something about the "real world." And his father is connected with a mysterious Agent 34. And Bo Whitley is connected with that Flynn woman, besides being involved some way with the IWW or Harry Wheeler, or both.

He wonders if he could see the reflection of Bunny's underclothes in his spit-shined riding boots. In two weeks he'll be on a boat for France, maybe never to come home again. Somehow everything that's puzzling him matters more because of that. There are things he has never understood that he has a right to understand now, decisions about people he has a right to make that he never did before. Perhaps he *will* go see a girl up on the Gulch. And he *will* find out more about the Flynn woman. And he *will* go see Bo Whitley if he wants to. If the world is upside down, he can bloody well afford to take a look at its underside before he goes and gets his head blown off in a bloody trench.

He stands. "No, Bunny," he says. "I think I'll not have more tea. I think I'll see if I can find me a drink of whiskey."

Bunny looks shocked.

Bo Whitley: July 1, 11:30 A.M.

Bo Whitley sits with a man named Hamer on top of Sacramento Hill watching a Mexican air machine do lazy tricks over Naco, across the border. They sit cross-legged on the ground with a bunch of miners' kids, who are smoking snitched tobacco. The kids tell them the Mexican air machine appears every day and drops a bomb on the railroad siding. Even though Whitley's muscles are cramping underneath him, he does not move. He wants the cramping; it gives him something to focus the stour of his anger on. He watches, but doesn't see, the air machine. It doesn't concern him now.

There was artillery during the night, the kids say, that lit up the sky. Hamer is excited by the idea; it's all new to him. But Bo Whitley remembers the far flashes and thuds that followed seconds later, like thunder after lightning, as far back as '11, when he left Bisbee for good.

Back in '11, the El Paso and Southwestern Railroad sent out special revolution-watchers' excursions. The bosses and mining engineers and their families went down to Naco with skimmers and parasols and lawn dresses to watch the fighting. Until the blood got too close and survivors began to fall back across the border without arms or noses, or to take pot shots at gringos. Then they went back to baseball, in which the players didn't shoot at the spectators.

Now the top of Sacramento Hill is about as close as anybody comes to the fighting, except for the miners and cowboys who risk the Villista rifles for the cheap whores and cheaper booze in the Naco casinos. Everybody else leaves the border to Sheriff Harry Wheeler and his border riders. When the fighting gets heavy, Sheriff Harry drives his cutdown Locomobile across to bring back the wounded. Once he got so mad that he took a leave of absence and went to hunt Pancho Villa down alone. At last, having failed, he wrote Villa and got a gentleman's promise from him that he had no specific designs on Cochise County, Arizona. Wheeler is known as a determined man. People were reassured.

The air machine does a roll, then cuts down through the late morning mare's-tail clouds to buzz Naco. The man named Hamer says that he bets the plane's pilot is one of those Americans who answered that recruiting poster he's seen everywhere, the poster that reads: Atención, Gringos! Come South and Fight with General Villa for Gold and Glory! Whitley only grunts an answer. He is trying to make a decision, while his mind is rummaging around in old memories that he has stored away like yellowing unpaid bills.

In three days, eleven tons of dynamite placed in forty-seven separate holes will blow the peak of Sacramento Hill to kingdom come. It will be the biggest Fourth of July spectacular in Arizona history and will signal the beginning of what Phelps-Dodge engineers envision as the largest open-pit copper mine in the world. The pit will take sixty years to complete. When it is worked out at last, it will have eaten up the entire mountain, including at least three towns, and will have left a gigantic hole that is a mirror image of what the mountain once was. But now that does not concern Whitley either.

The air machine buzzes low enough to bring a few puffs of rifle smoke from both sides of the border. Then it climbs out of range and drops down sharply again to toss out a single bomb over the railroad siding by the customhouse. The bomb looks as small as a pebble from the top of Sacramento Hill. One of the miners' kids says the Mexes make their bombs out of dynamite and scrap iron wrapped in cowhide. Hamer laughs at the backward Mexes.

The bomb falls wide of the freight cars on the siding and throws up some ground behind an adobe shack at the town's edge. When the pilot starts to climb again, something goes wrong—a rifle bullet in the engine, maybe. The machine levels off, dips, tries for altitude again, then goes into a slow, silent spin. Halfway to the ground it explodes. When it hits the ground on the American side of the border, it explodes again. The smoke and dust billow much higher than the tiny bombs did. Hamer says it looks to him like it hit something, possibly a house or a small store.

A couple of the kids cheer and clap and one of them yells, "One less Mex!" The rest giggle. Whitley tells them to shut up. But he does not pity the pilot. He figures he expected what happened, sooner or later—maybe was even relieved. The kids move away down the hill. Bo follows them down with his eyes. He has been watching on and off a man below them at the ragged edge of the skirt of miners' clapboard cabins that climbs the side of Sacramento Hill. The man is dressed in the cheap seven-dollar suit an order-taker from the company store would wear. But it is too late for order-takers to be at work: Already the burro trains and wagons are starting out with their morning deliveries.

"Jesus H. Christ," the man named Hamer says. "Don't take much, does it? *Poof,* and the damn thing's down." Hamer is chubby—fat, really—with only a few almost invisible strands of blond hair left on his crown. He is just under thirty, the same age as Bo Whitley.

"Why didn't any of you boys tell me, Oscar?" Whitley asks him. The man he's watching has disappeared behind a goat pen.

"What the hell, Bo? Tell you what the hell?"

"You know damn well. That she was coming in."

"Oh. Well, Jesus, Bo. The buggering telegram didn't come till late last night. And you was so busy setting up pickets . . ."

"You was afraid to tell me, right? All of you. You figured it was easier to let me just find out when she got off the train and make a damn fool of myself."

"Hell, pilgrim. Afraid of what?"

"That I'd roll up my bundle and leave you stiffs to run this damn strike by yourselves."

"Oh, hell . . ."

"Well, that's fine. Now you don't need me anyway. You got her and her boyfriend to do it for you."

"Bo, now don't get your ulcers in a uproar. She's a woman and he don't even speak English unless he has to."

"I been a Wob for eight years now, Oscar, and never once have a bunch of stiffs pulled a stunt like this on me."

Hamer looks away and studies the dispersing cloud of dust from the air machine. "Haywood's coming in, too," he says quietly.

"Be goddamned," Whitley says. He tries to control his anger. "If that don't beat all. When?"

"Morning train, I reckon. Mother Jones'll be with him."

"That does it, all right. I'll be on the next ore train out." He turns toward Bisbee and massages his cramped legs. So much smoke and steam hang over the canyons that the town looks as if it were built in the crater of a volcano. The smell of the city gasworks floats up to him from Jiggerville. The very pit of hell, he tells himself. The valley of the shadow. Through the haze he makes out the snaky outline of Brewery Gulch running north from Tombstone Canyon up into the mountains where the Mex mule skinners live. The Broadway of the West, they call it. Forty saloons, and nobody has ever counted the whorehouses up on the Line, the invisible boundary the whores are forbidden to pass. Everything in its place, Whitley thinks. The top on top and the bottom on bottom. It's a god-awful town, a detestable place. He could never hate a human being the way he hates Bisbee.

He looks for the man in the order-taker's suit again.

The man still hasn't come out from behind the goat pen.

"Suit yourself," Hamer says. He doesn't get up. "Way you run out of that strike committee meeting this morning when you heard she was invited, I reckon the boys won't be surprised. Lots of them didn't even know she was your wife."

"She's not."

"You know what I mean." Hamer still hasn't taken his eyes off the tiny crashed plane in the distance. A rooster tail of dust from a automobile cuts across the mesquite flats toward it. "Must have been one hell of a bust-up."

Whitley shrugs. He is thin, but has nothing of the slump of a skinny man. He is too short to be really striking on first glance, but his habit of standing with his shoulders thrown back, accenting the muscles underneath his shirt, does not give him the attitude of a man ashamed of his body. His hair is as blond as Hamer's, but full. It curls loosely from underneath his cloth cap, which he wears pushed back on his head with the bill slightly to the side. His suspenders keep his pants high so that the cuffs just touch the tops of his brogans. A pair of brass knuckles weights one pocket down. His face has clean lines, except for his nose. Looked at straight on, his nose is a little crooked, off center, really, like his cap bill. It gives him the odd appearance of always looking just beyond and to the side of the person he's talking to. Gurley Flynn used to tell him it was a needed flaw.

"No worse than most bust-ups, I suppose," he says. He stamps his feet to get the circulation going again. He's known Hamer a month. They met in Butte, organizing. Hamer's a money man, a bookkeeper and a strike fund-raiser.

"I wouldn't know," Hamer says. "Never tried it. Any children?"

"A boy. Seven now."

"Ever see him?"

"No."

"You and her couldn't have been but kids yourself."

"I was twenty-one. She was eighteen. That's old enough."

"Rather not talk about it?"

"I don't care."

Hamer pulls a plug of chewing tobacco from his shirt pocket and offers it to Whitley. Whitley shakes his head and spits. "What happened?"

Whitley scans the cabins below him for the man in the order-taker's suit. He sees nobody but a jigger boss's wife hanging out clothes. "She come out on a speaking tour to the Mesabi range. She fell in love with the West and the miners and I was the first one she met, I reckon. After a couple of years of her traveling and being in jail—and me doing the same—I took it in my head I wanted to settle. She was in New York with her people, then, and I 'boed across to get her. She didn't come."

"Any reason?"

"Her daddy asked her that, with me setting on the couch between 'em. 'I just don't love him anymore,' she told him. 'And besides, he bores me.' " Whitley picks up a rock and flings it toward a streetcar far down in Tombstone Canyon below him. "Come on. Let's get off this goddamn mountain. I got an ore train to catch."

Hamer heaves to his feet and brushes the seat of his overalls off. "We need you, pilgrim."

"Like hell."

"You ain't going to let a ball and chain get in the way of the union, are you?"

"There's other strikes."

"Not like this one. Haywood don't come down to no chicken-wire makers' strike."

"One organizer more or less don't make no difference."

"I ain't no good on a picket line, Bo. I got more ways than Noah had bugs to get ahold of strike money, but ain't nobody can work a line like you."

"Haywood can," Whitley says. He starts the long scramble down the mountain, toward Bisbee. Hamer puts his hand on his shoulder, and Whitley pulls away.

"Sorry," Hamer says.

There are two things above all others that Whitley can't abide. One is bosses, and the other is to be touched by another man. He's always guessed that both had to do with the green house he grew up in at the end of the hunared and six steps from Brewery Gulch. He was ten when he left the house in the middle of a Saturday night and went to live with his mamma's cousin, Jim Brew. He never told Jim what happened between him and his old man that night. Never told anybody, and nobody asked. People don't try to get too close to Bo. It's always seemed to him that it's their choice, not his.

His old man is dead of the miner's consumption now, and his mamma of cholera. His sister is somewhere in California, married to a Bohunk stevedore. But as he strains through the haze, he thinks he can still make out the hundred and six steps. The last time he climbed them was in '11. He ran home after Gurley Flynn sent him packing, and made it in time to watch his mamma die. Nobody in Bisbee cared then that he was home. Bisbee has never given a damn about him. Not yet anyway.

When his mamma was gone, he swore he'd never come back here. And now he's back. Two weeks ago, when the news got to Butte that Bisbee was thinking of coming out on strike, he walked and thought all night, then packed his blanket roll the next morning. In one way, it's like he's come back to his old man, too. In another, it's like a strike in Bisbee is his own property. Either way, Bisbee owes him something. He'll be thirty on the Fourth of July. He's got things to sort out, to settle. To put in their right places. But he didn't count on Gurley Flynn being one of those. And that burns him.

"Where's she staying?" he asks Hamer.

"They put her up with a hoistman's family up on . . . what do you call it? Chihuahua Hill?"

"Tresca, too?"

"Naw. Wouldn't look right, the committee thought. They got him in a rooming house up on O.K. Street. Nobody else'd have him, I reckon."

Bo kicks hard at a hunk of dead mesquite on the path. He's always wondered if the son of a bitch bothers to take off his little rimless glasses and red scarf when he's making love to Elizabeth. Now he wonders if she'll slip into his room at night, like she slipped into Bo's in Duluth before they were married.

The path turns into a woodcutter's burro trail, then cuts across the tag end of the steps that run between the houses of Jiggerville. The steps descend past the goat pen that Bo saw the man in the suit disappear behind. Bo checks. The man is gone. Hamer is puffing to keep up. "Whew, pilgrim," he wheezes. "Only straight-up-and-down town I ever seen. One good rain and seems these damn houses ought to come sliding flat down on top of one another. And guns—I ain't never seen so many guns in one place in my life. What do they do—teeth babies on 'em?"

"Something like that," Whitley says. He slows for Hamer to catch up.

"Hell of a town to win a strike in."

"We won't."

"What?"

"We won't win it."

"That's a hell of a attitude, fellow worker."

"I was born here."

"Big Bill Haywood ain't nobody's fool. He's coming down for it."

"Bill Haywood's damn near fifty years old and never been to Bisbee." The steps swing around between two houses and dead end at a tent pitched in what once was a chicken yard. From inside the tent come voices in a language Bo can't make out—Serb, Finn, Yiddish, they're all here in Bisbee. A half-grown boy squats over a latrine trench dug behind the tent. He looks at Whitley and Hamer with sleepy eyes and doesn't move. The buzzing of flies rises from the trench.

Out of the corner of his eye, Bo sees a movement. He turns in time to see the order-taker stepping behind a red house just past the tent. He looks back at the shoeless kid, and things slam together, like a string of freight cars coupling. A kid shitting in the open air like a dog, Tresca, Elizabeth, Bisbee, bosses, his old man . . . they all focus for now on the order-taker's suit vanishing behind the red house. His body tenses. He feels relief, like the Mex pilot must have felt.

"Got company," he says to Hamer.

Hamer looks alert. "Where?"

"Man in a suit. Yonder on the other side of the house."

"Want me to flush him?"

Bo grins. "Send him to me. Special delivery."

Hamer does a mock salute and casually walks toward

the red house. Bo's body is light; he can hardly feel it. He reaches into his pocket and pulls his knucks out. As he slips them on and seats them, they weigh nothing at all. The kid on the trench stands and buttons his pants. With sleepy eyes he watches Hamer round the corner of the red house. Bo motions for him to stand out of the way. The kid sees Bo's brass knucks and his eyes open wider. He says something in the language Bo heard coming from the tent. Bo shakes his head and motions him toward the tent again.

The sound of a scuffle comes from behind the red house. Bo steps to the other side of the tent, closer to the corner of the house.

When the order-taker backs into sight, his hands held out to protect himself from Hamer, Bo rushes him. He grabs the collar of the man's cheap suit and spins him around. "Uh-uh, buddy, uh-uh . . ." the man says and covers his face. Bo jerks the man's hands away and swings his fist that weighs nothing at all. The man staggers back against the house, swinging feebly at Bo. Bo grabs the fist that hits him on the shoulder and shoves the man toward the latrine trench. The man goes down onto one knee.

Bo is on top of him, flings the man's body flat. The man's suit rips in his hand. It feels good, and he pulls until the lapel comes off. The man tries to kick Bo, and Bo straddles him. He pins the man's arms down with his knees.

Then with deliberation and ease, he brings the knucks down on the man's skinny freckled face. The man grunts. The thud of the knucks vibrates up Bo's weightless arm.

He doesn't know how many times he's brought them down before Hamer and the kid from the trench pull him off the man. It can't be too many times, though. The man's face is still recognizable.

"You gonna kill the son of a bitch, Bo!" Hamer yells. The people from the tent, dark people in black clothes, are outside, yammering. The woman in the red house screams at him from her back porch. Bo feels Hamer's and the kid's hands on him, under his arms.

"Don't goddamn touch me," he snaps, and swings at Hamer. The kid jumps out of the way, but Hamer holds on and pulls Bo backward off his balance. Bo scrambles around in the dirt to get a footing, and Hamer lets go. Bo finds his footing, stands, and backs off from Hamer, fist cocked. He notices his body now, notices he's panting. The man in the order-taker suit rolls over on his side and covers his face.

"Find out who the bastard is," Bo orders. Hamer, cautious, stays out of range of Bo's fist and goes to the man. He kneels beside him and rolls him over on his back. One of the man's eyes is cut and closed; the other tries wildly to find Bo. Hamer helps him to a sitting position.

"You're dead, you son of a bitch, you're dead dog meat in the sun," the man babbles. "God'll punish you in hell, you son of a bitch."

Bo waits for him to calm. A man from the tent runs to the boy and pulls him away, toward the tent. The woman on the back porch yells that she's going for her broom.

"Who the hell are you?" Hamer asks the man.

"You, too, you son of a bitch. Deader'n hell," the man says. Hamer slaps him.

"Who the hell are you, pilgrim?"

"All I done was come with a message. All in God's world I done." The man's babbling is turning into a whine. Bo steps up into his line of vision. He's afraid the scissorbill SOB is going to cry.

"Who you got a message for?" Bo asks him. "You Western Union?"

"Got a message for you, you dead son of a bitch." Bo makes a mock threatening motion, and the man's hands fly to his face again.

"Cap'n Greenway says he'll talk to you whenever you want. Just to you. Says leave a message for him at the C and A hospital. Says give him a time and place and he'll be there."

Bo looks closer at the man's face. Even with the shut eye and torn cheek, he's sure he recognizes him. "You a local boy, ain't you? You one of the McCrea bunch from up Tombstone Canyon." The man doesn't answer.

"You want to carry something back to John Greenway for me? Huh? Want to be a good little goddamn scab?" Bo says. He steps past Hamer, who is still kneeling, and jerks McCrea to his feet. "I got something for Cap'n Greenway all right." McCrea is limp. Bo lifts him off his feet for a moment, then shoves. McCrea stumbles backward.

He hits the edge of the latrine trench, tries for his footing, and swings his arms like windmills to keep his balance. It doesn't work. He goes down in it, catches himself on its edges, and comes to rest sitting up. Hamer whoops, then laughs. A gurgling sound comes from the latrine trench. McCrea makes *uh, uh, uh* noises. The woman from the red house charges off her porch with a broom and makes for Bo. He ducks her first swing and dances away from her.

"Take that to Cap'n John-ass-Greenway!" he yells at McCrea. "Tell him it come from the Wobbly mailbag! Tell him there's lots more of it."

Hamer is running from the broom now. He hollers for Bo to come on. Bo throws a last look at McCrea, hoots, and takes off at a trot after Hamer. Captain Greenway himself wants to see him. Son of a bitch. Not Gurley Flynn nor even Big Bill Haywood. Just Bo Whitley. There's one ore train, he tells himself, that's going to leave Bisbee without him today. He's got an invitation to consider.

Elizabeth Gurley Flynn: July 1, 3:00 P.M.

Elizabeth Gurley Flynn is troubled. She told herself that she came to these desert mountains to crack the copper trust, and her mind is full of an ex-husband. She knew Bo Whitley was from Bisbee. When Bill Haywood cabled her to come to Arizona, she didn't consciously think of Whitley. But when she stepped off the train and saw him, she knew she had expected to find him. That made her angry: She couldn't explain herself to herself. She is still angry, and there's so much else to do. Damn it.

She has stolen some time for herself, away from the others. All morning she has been in the disorganized strike headquarters, planning, advising, arranging details. With each year, she finds it harder and harder to face the chaos of another IWW strike. She stands now at the foot of the Pythian Castle, her thoughts jumbled and uncertain. The clock on the gold and white Georgian cupola of the building has just struck three. Tresca is still in the green wainscoted meeting room above. He hated the idea of coming to Bisbee—said she should have outgrown her "noble savage" stage. They've fought about it all the way from Chicago. He gave her a questioning look, a warning, when she left the meeting room. He's Italian and will raise holy hell when he knows she's been to see Whitley. But she has to go. There's too much at stake in this strike. She has to put herself in order for it first.

Around her on the narrow street that snakes off into the mountains—O.K. Street, was it?—miners in overalls sit on walls, or stand and wait. They'll go upstairs by turns and ask for relief, for bags of beans or flour or for money to buy them. The committee will take their names and give them what it has, and promises of more. They'll hope, as she does, that the money will come from somewhere to keep those promises. And she knows the worst of the strike hasn't even begun.

The miners and their women are afraid, like children themselves, playing hooky. They turn their faces away when strangers walk by as if they expected to be reported to this Greenway or Dowell or Shattuck she's learning about. She's weary already at the knowledge of a job that has to be done again and again. The huge job of teaching them that what they're doing is all right, is good. Is, in a way, holy. But she can't let herself be weary yet; that will come tonight and all the following nights and afternoons of speeches, skits, schools, picnics, dances, songs. All the things she must arrange to let them know they're not alone.

That's why she has to find Whitley, to sort out the past. When she saw him in the crowd at the depot, it was as if a hand had jerked her away from Tresca, out of Bisbee, and dropped her back in the muddy cold of the Minnesota iron ranges again. Eight years ago, when she was eighteen. Bo Whitley was no longer the abject tramp miner on her father's couch in South Bronx, as she has tried so hard to remember him. There she could send him away with a flip remark about how boring he was. Here he belongs, like the sharp stones and sparse trees of the mountains around her. In New York, or in the mill towns of Paterson and Lawrence, she can love the soft sound of Tresca's Italian *cariños* at night, his ability to wind with her through the tight mazes of political theory. But the West is harder, with another voice. Like Bo Whitley, who won't get out of her life.

It has been six years since she has seen him. He was the first man who ever touched her naked body. She has a son by him. And she remembers cold nights with the faint sweaty male scent of Whitley beside her on borrowed beds from Duluth to Leadville. Is that what's left to deal with? Or is it something else? What? Damn it all to hell.

She plunges through the crowd of miners. Directly across from the stairwell in the Pythian Castle is a flight of metal steps that leads to the floor of the Gulch. Without caring where she's going, she takes them. She can feel the heat, the stillness in the overcast afternoon. She has to hold her long black skirt high to get down the steep steps, past some newsboys dragging a smaller boy down them on his butt. At the foot of the stairs she finds herself in a winding alley beside a doorway with a sign above it that says Lyric Theater, Stage Entrance. The dark brick buildings follow the twists of the alley, so she can't see the ends of any of them. Everything winds or curves in Bisbee, she thinks, even the buildings. Nothing is level, nothing is flat or straight. Nothing is wholly visible. It reminds her of pictures she has seen of towns in the Middle Ages. She has always imagined people who lived in those towns smothering to death. She shudders.

She's got to find air, to breathe. She takes an uphill direction from the Stage Entrance, which has a bill beside it advertising Vera the Medium. Past a newspaper office and a storefront, in whose window a fat sign painter scratches his naked belly with painty hands, the alley merges into a street. She can see the company store at the downhill end of the street and has her bearings now. She is on Brewery Gulch. They have always told her it is the most notorious street in the West. Fine. She is pretty notorious herself. She smiles at a Serbian woman who hurries by under a black shawl.

Brewery Gulch could be a good street. Lots of boardinghouses along it and above it. They're probably full now, men sleeping in shifts, because of the war. Tramp miners without families. Good men usually, not company scissorbills. A sign in the window of a restaurant called the French

Kitchen, Meals and Rooms, 50¢, says No Scabs' Lunches Fixed. A man handing out IWW news bills rides by on a burro. Up and down the street men stand in front of saloons and cardrooms in little knots and talk in low voices. There are pool halls and smoke shops and barbershops and pawn shops crowded onto every inch of curb space. Horses and mules worry at one another beside a few automobiles. This is not company territory. It is the miners' world, and so the IWW's.

She strikes out uphill along the cobbled street. The only other women she sees hurry by with their heads down. The saloons and boardinghouses and cardrooms seem endless. She'll talk to the committee about the saloons. They're no good for a strike. Liquored-up pickets can't be depended on. They'll police the saloons themselves if that little snit of a sheriff can't be counted on to do it—and she'll bet a dollar to a dime he can't be. In front of one saloon, called the Saint Elmo, a miner asks her if she'd like to make two bucks. She stops, gives him a head-to-toe, and tells him yes. The man looks startled and leers at a couple of his buddies. He has a gold tooth. She takes a red IWW membership card from her skirt pocket.

"Two bucks for a piece of the Greatest Thing on Earth," she tells him. Before she leaves, she's signed up all three of them and given them each a pad of propaganda stickers to post. She's feeling better. She's at home.

Past a concrete bandshell and fenced-off open space above street level—which must be the City Park she'll speak from tonight—the Gulch narrows and tames. It's mostly grocery stores and houses and lumberyards now, and the pavement fades away. In the distance, past the smokestack of what looks like a steam laundry, the houses that climb the hills seem all to be made of stone and adobe, like villages she's seen in pictures from the Mexican revolution. She decides to walk to the laundry and find out if the women who work there are organized or not, then turn back. She can breathe now. There is a strike to run and a world to make. If the way she feels about Bo Whitley is uncertain, this, at least, is not. Ever since her father took her to socialist Sunday School instead of church, she has had that one certainty. Had he taken her to church, Tresca tells her, she would have been a nun.

Brewery Gulch is an amphitheater, she realizes as her eyes travel along the cabins and boardinghouses that rise up steep as New York tenements on the mountainsides. Impossible stairways and burro trails and narrow streets take off from the Gulch with seemingly no sense to them. Red and blue and yellow houses teeter at the edges of high unmortared rock walls, one above the other to the very tops of the mountains. She can see children hanging from makeshift bridges between the houses. Noises echo and magnify from hillside to hillside: a child practicing scales on a piano, a husband yelling for his wife, an unhappy goat, a dog war. Every balcony and porch is a box seat. They'll all watch us and remember us, she thinks. Win or lose. Something will change. At least that.

Just before the laundry, she rounds a sharp curve in the floor of the Gulch, and is stopped short. Ahead of her rise half a dozen huge wooden houses, out of place in the narrow canyon. Next to and behind the big houses, scrambling up the hillside, are what seem to be dozens of smaller, one-story row houses, all green. Each smaller house has three or four doors in it, and a little private porch for every door. Women lounge in cane-bottom rockers on the porches. Some houses have only white women in front of them, others all Mexican or even Chinese and colored. Women in unbuttoned shirtwaists, or just chemises, hang from a score of the windows in the big white houses. One of the houses has an arched false front with Monte Carlo Club painted in red across it. Others simply show numbers— Thirty-one, Nine, Forty-three— in Gothic letters. A ground-glass door faces her with The Mint etched into the glass. "Nellie Gray" on a player piano seeps like smoke from under the door.

The women mostly ignore her or stare sullenly. She returns their stares. The women will hate the Wobs before this is over; the money that goes for strike relief doesn't get spent for whores. If she could just get through to them that they are the most exploited of all. . . . Her eyes catch those of a redhead leaning on a second-story window sill in one of the numbered houses. For a moment she sees herself in one of the windows, her black hair loosened from its tight bun and her shirtwaist unbuttoned. Briefly she thinks she sees returned understanding in the woman's eyes.

Then the woman sticks out her tongue, squeezes her

breast, and makes a noise like a fart. Elizabeth turns on her heel. You don't grow up a tough kid in South Bronx and not know what that means. Elizabeth Flynn, she tells herself, you can be such a *god*damn fool sometimes. No wonder Bo thought he could treat you like a bourgeois housewife.

Bourgeois housewife! Let a bourgeois housewife face a line of mounted bulls the way she does. Her resolution strengthens. She's acting like a schoolgirl at a cotillion, damn it, worrying about seeing a man. Is that what she came a thousand miles for?

She throws one last look behind her at the whorehouses before she rounds the curve. Whatever those women may be, they wouldn't waste two seconds worrying about handling Bo Whitley. She has been told he lives in a section called Jiggerville. He must know she'll come looking for him. Somewhere in her abdomen, a tiny thrill of excitement rises. She draws her anger back up around her to squelch it. How many times will she make a fool of herself before she learns?

Jiggerville is not Wobbly territory. There are boardinghouses, but fewer here than around the Gulch. Most of the board-and-batten cabins are for families—on land leased, the jitney driver told her, at a dollar a month from the company. With a one-month lease. So it's scissorbill territory. People with precious little to lose, but with at least something. It will be harder going here, committees to talk to the wives, pounding and pounding until *scab* is a dirtier word to them than *hunger.* Most of the houses fly American flags. That will be the hardest defense of all: Give them a word like *patriotism* to hide behind and they close up like oysters. And turn mean.

The bosses are already at work on it. On the way to Jiggerville, she scans a copy of the *Bisbee Review* the jitney driver leaves on the seat beside her. The phrases leap out at her obvious as warning flares. "High treason stalks in our midst in the guise of the Bisbee branch of the IWW. . . . It is nothing short of treason, incipient and terrible. . . . Men with no interest here, with no wives and homes and no means of support, seeking to use the miners of this camp for their sinister purpose. . . . A deep-laid plot to cripple the

United States in its war." Build the hysteria, she thinks. Make animals out of them. The job before her is huge. Her weariness creeps back on her as she climbs the long flight of stairs to Stodgill's boardinghouse, where they tell her Bo lives with a man named Brew.

The clapboard house is long and white, with a wide shady porch. A woman comes out to show her where Jim Brew lives, and tells her she cannot be in the room after dark. Brew's room is on the side of the house, with a little porch and screen door of its own. Fig trees grow around the porch. Down in a dry wash under a Chinese elm tree, an old man in a round Albanian cap fixes shoes that other men throw down to him from a bridge. There must be a gasworks nearby; the odor of it hangs in the still air, as if the trees themselves gave it off. Harmonica music comes from the room. Elizabeth smooths her long black skirt nervously and touches the bun of her hair to make certain it is in place. Some women are wearing things called flapper skirts now, which come above their knees. She won't. Short skirts are a capitalist trick to save cloth.

When she knocks, a tall heap of a man comes to the door. He wears only a pair of overalls and an undershirt. He looks at her from eyes that seem to be habitually fixed in a surprised expression, and waits for her to speak first. She asks for Bo. The man shuffles back a step and mumbles something into the room. She hears bedsprings squeak. Then the man shuffles farther back out of the doorway and vanishes into the darkness of the room. Bo takes his place at the screen. He has no shirt on and is barefoot. His suspenders cover the nipples of his breasts, but his tight stomach and chest muscles are cleanly outlined. He stands in that cocky way he has always had, one leg thrust in front of him, his chin poked out as if he were daring you to take a swing at it. " 'Lo, Elizabeth," he says through the screen. "Slumming?"

"How are you, Bo?" she says.

"Fine. Just dandy."

She stiffens as he lets his eyes travel up and down her body. "Can I come in?" she asks.

"We can talk here."

"Bo, I've come from a long, bad trial. It's been a hard

morning. No games." She remembers there was another trial once. Her first big one, during the IWW free-speech fights in Spokane. The bulls would arrest a Wob for speaking on a street corner, and by the week's end so many Wobblies would have ridden the rails into town that the jails were full and the bulls had to let them all go. If they survived a week in the bullpen. But not her; she was a leader and had to be tried. She was nineteen and pregnant then, and Bo had demanded she not go to Spokane to begin with. So during the trial she wrote him to stay in Missoula and attend to his job there. She didn't mean it, but Bo did. Not once did he come. She needed him, and he had decided to punish her for not leaving the IWW and staying home to have their baby. She never lived with him after that. Or forgave him.

Thunder rumbles close-by. Bo doesn't answer her. She spins and starts down the stairs. "Wait," he says. He opens the door for her and makes a huge sweeping bow. She hesitates, then goes in. The room smells of motor grease and carbide and sweat. The tall heap of a man stands in the shadows in a corner of the room. Like a stuffed moose. She can't see his face.

"Lizzie Flynn, Jim Brew," Bo says. "I reckon you've both heard me mention each other. Jim's my cousin, Elizabeth. You remember." He's being too polite, too controlled.

"Mr. Brew," she says and offers her hand.

The man moves out of the shadows and takes her hand. His own feels like tree bark. His eyes dart around as if he's looking for a place to hide as he mumbles something unintelligible.

There is an awkward silence in the room. The thunder peals just above now. It rolls and echoes, trapped in the steep canyons. With only one window, the room is dim and cool. She can make out an iron bedstead, a high-back rocker, an oak dresser with a washbasin and pitcher on it, a chiffonier, and a bedroll in the corner. No more.

Jim Brew makes uncertain movements, and winds up pointing to the chair. "Set you down, ah . . . ma'am," he says. He seems to need to swallow two or three times before he can speak at all. "I got to . . . ah, go . . . get some shoes fixed." He stoops and picks up a pair of brogans that seem perfectly fine to Elizabeth, then backs out the screen. The spring thwangs, it closes behind him. Elizabeth steps aside for him, then takes the rocker Bo motions her toward. From there she can see now a sword—of all things—and a pistol hanging over the door. Is there anyone, she wonders, who doesn't have an arsenal in this town? Even the family she's staying with has a rifle and pistol by its door.

Bo stays on his feet and plays a verse of "The Rebel Girl" on his harmonica. She breaks in on him. "I brought a picture of Buster. I thought you might like . . ."

He holds out his hand for the picture of their son. She slips it from her purse and gives it to him. It is her favorite. Buster is wearing his sailor suit and sitting on a pony. Her father told her she was acting like a silly bourgeoise when she had it made. Bo takes it and sits on the unmade bed. For a long time he studies it in the dim light. "He looks like me," he says at last.

"He looks like my father." That's a lie, and she knows it.

"Then Lord pity him."

"Amen." They both laugh nervously. She recognizes his smile, a tough-kid's sassy grin. She wasn't nervous before. But now they're alone, and Buster's picture establishes a kind of intimacy between them. Again she's hit with the sense of being jerked backward in time.

"I was wondering when you'd get here," he says.

"We need to talk, Bo."

"I tried that six years ago. I came two thousand miles to talk."

"Not talk about that, Bo. I was . . . what, twenty then? I didn't want to hurt you."

"Like hell," he says, and hands the picture back to her. "Does he know who his father is?" His smile is gone now.

"Of course he does."

"Is Tresca good to him?"

"He adores him." She says it defiantly. It's an exaggeration. She wants to tell him that it's none of his business.

"He damn well better."

"You've never written him."

"I don't write so good. Besides, I never have a return address."

"You write songs well. I've seen them."

"That's different. People write 'em out for me."

She drops her eyes as she puts the picture away. For a moment she compares the face in the picture to the one in front of her. It's the same. She takes a deep breath and rocks back in the chair. "I . . . I came to ask you a favor, Bo."

"Ask me a favor? Mercy goodness."

"Don't fight me, Bo. It's not easy."

"No. You were never good at asking favors. But try me."

"You know Bill Haywood's coming in."

"So they say."

"He's really thinking in terms of a general strike, Bo."

"I told the strike committee they were crazy to send that damn telegram to him."

"You don't believe in the general strike?"

"Oh, hell, I don't know. I'll leave that to you and the other big shots. But I'm sure of one thing. We don't need Big Bill Haywood to shut Bisbee down."

"What *do* you need?"

"What we got."

"Be that as it might, he's on his way."

"And you're here, too."

She comes back at him more quickly than she should. What does she have to be defensive about? "And I'm here, too."

"Uh-huh. You're as sure as Haywood that you can win this general strike thing?"

"Bill thinks it's now or never."

"Bill thinks that. And you?"

She hesitates. "I want to talk to Bill. I need to know the strategy . . ."

"Shut her down and keep her down. That's all the strategy we've ever needed."

"And that's still enough now?"

"If it ain't, why did you come, Lizzie?" He grins again.

"That's not important."

"No?"

"No . . . oh, damn, I don't know if it is or not. Bill asked me to come. That's all."

"Just that—you sure?"

"I was tired, Bo. I *am* tired. The whole stinking world's

tired. Maybe I'm trying to remember what it was like not to be tired. All right?"

"I'm not tired. Sure there's no other reason you came?"

"I know what you're trying to get me to say, Bo Whitley, and I won't. No matter what reason anybody has for being here, the strike is on and nothing can stop it. And it's got to be won. Period. We can't let us get in the way—we don't matter that much. Period again. You can take that as a request or a threat—as you like."

"Don't preach to me, Lizzie."

"I'm not preaching."

Bo leans back on the bed and rests on his elbows. It makes her even more conscious that he has no shirt on. "You know, I didn't think we could win this thing a few hours ago. Now . . . I ain't certain. I was set to leave town this morning."

"I was afraid of that."

"I still don't think *you* can win it—nor Bill Haywood either."

"I'm not sure what you mean."

"I ain't either. I got to do some more studying on it. Things are happening."

Things are happening. Things have always been happening with Bo. She remembers so vividly now the sense of raw, almost violent energy that drew her to him. With Bo there was never any need to think, to play with the kinds of subtleties Tresca's mind and world demand. Only to share his energy. It was so easy to relax into that, to let it carry her along. She doesn't remember ever feeling this weariness then . . .

"But you'll not fight me."

"You love this Tresca stiff?"

"Yes, I suppose so."

"You suppose so?"

"Yes, then. I do."

"Why don't you marry him?"

"You've never understood that, have you, Bo? You've never understood that I won't be somebody's property."

"Any man's dog, eh?"

"You bastard. And you want to know why I left you."

She gives the rocker a last violent rock and gets to

her feet. He springs off the bed and blocks the door. His speed surprises her. The energy again. "You didn't come here just to ask me not to fight you, Lizzie. You could have sent Tresca for that and we'd have settled it right up, man to man."

"I'm leaving, Bo." The thunder rattles the windowpanes and the wind rakes the fig tree against the house.

"Do you know what a damn fool I felt like in your old man's flat? Do you?" he says, his face tight with anger. His voice is uneven and clipped. "Every time I see your picture in the paper with that . . . that damn gigolo . . ."

Behind him through the screen she can see trees lashing in the wind. The old man who was repairing shoes in the wash is trying to get his things gathered as the waves of rain come closer together. A man in his working diggers, a scab she supposes, hurries to the middle of the bridge and throws a pair of shoes down to the old man. The old man stops gathering his tools, picks up the shoes, spits on them, and throws them back to the scab on the bridge. It's an action Bo would understand, an action she may have come too close to forgetting.

"Bo," she says. "I'm sorry. I truly am. It couldn't be helped." The words sound limp, like wet cloth. She puts out her hand and touches his chest. He takes the hand and moves it in slow circles on his skin. His chest feels warm, firm. It is a map of a landscape she knows. She doesn't pull away.

The Model T at the foot of the stairs has already parked and *oogah*ed its horn before she notices it. Bo tries to lead her farther into the room, away from the persistent *oogah*ing. But she's certain that Tresca has come looking for her. She strains to look past Bo, through the screen. She can't see inside the car; the isinglass curtains are closed. Tresca's hired a car, she's sure! Damn him! She wrests herself away from Bo and runs to the screen.

But as she throws the screen open, the *oogah*ing stops and she sees the uniform climbing out of the Ford. It's that bourgeois snit of a lieutenant from the train. She's relieved —and inexplicably angry again. He has his head down against the rain and doesn't see her yet. But there's no place for her to go to get away from him. She steps back into the room. Bo is beside her now. "That son of a bitch," he says when he sees Art Matthews start up the steps, cape whipping in the wind.

Bo takes her hand again. What in God's name was she about to do? She came to sort things out—and now they're more muddled than ever. The sense she had this morning of being jerked back in time hasn't gone away. It has grown stronger. Is she a blockhead eighteen-year-old again? She fights to calm her breathing, to find her control.

"He's dehorn drunk," Bo says. "Where the hell did he learn that? He was a pretty decent kid." Bo hates drunks. She remembers his stories about his old man. He slapped her once for drinking a glass of beer.

"I met him on the train. His father . . ."

"I know what his father is. He'll beat hell out of the kid. Five to one the kid don't know a damn thing about his old man's business."

"No. I couldn't get anything out of him."

"Figured you'd try."

Art Matthews spots them and makes a ragged path around the front of the house toward Jim Brew's little side porch. "Ho!" he shouts through the rain. "The gang's all here. Don't start without me!"

She lets her fingers slip from Bo's hand. He catches them up and squeezes them. "I'll get rid of him."

"No. Carlo's waiting for me."

"Let him wait."

"Bo. It's been six years. I don't *want* to stay. Let it go. It's over."

"Like hell," he says.

Art Matthews hits the wet steps to Jim's porch, slips, and catches himself on the railing. He looks up at Bo. He has a sloppy grin on his face. His eyes are bright and harmless, like a spaniel's. "Bo," he says. "By God, Bo—we've come home, Bo. Welcome home!"

"Yeah, Art," Bo says. He lets go of Elizabeth's hand. It falls to her side, limp. "Welcome home."

Art Matthews: July 1, 4:30 P.M.

Will wonders never cease? Art Matthews has never had so many things happen to him in one day. The train ride with the Flynn woman, the excitement of real Wobblies striking around him, the strange joy of standing up to Bunny and his father, then—best of all—his afternoon on the Line. A bunch of all-right fellows hang out up there, and he never spent four dollars so well in his life: He got not one, but *two* women. When they found out who he was, they said they gave him "special treatment," like his father got. Old dad! He never would have guessed. Well, he can't blame him. After all those years wondering what it would be like to lie with a woman, it turned out to be everything it was cracked up to be. Oh, how fine it must be to be in love with the one you're with, too. Some striking, sophisticated woman who knows things.

Like the Flynn woman. And to think, Bo tells him they were married once. So she's a divorcée, too! He can't think of anything better than to have found her and Bo together. He dropped by just to see Bo. He wanted to talk about old times and tell him about the afternoon. He imagined Bo would be proud of him, when he told him he made both the rowing *and* polo teams at Princeton. Bo's always been so keen on sports. But Bo and the Flynn woman just looked at each other when he told them, and Bo rolled his eyes strangely. That disappointed Art.

But he's sure it was just the awkwardness of things. It must be awfully touchy to see a woman you were married to once. Neither one of them much wanted to talk. Bloody uncomfortable. And him wet and all, too. He was positively afraid for a moment when he pulled out his flask of Scotch and offered Bo a shot. Thought Bo was going to pitch him out the door. The Flynn woman did take a sip, though, and he could swear it was just to make Bo mad. She seemed to think it was pretty funny, but Bo didn't. Even a radical like that Flynn woman is a woman at heart, he supposes.

And now, as icing on the cake, the Flynn woman has accepted his offer of a ride back into town. How lucky that it's raining. He would have liked to stay and chat with Bo some more, but after all! Besides, Bo didn't seem glad to see him. Awkward situation or not, he could have been more civil, at least. Art supposes it's that Wobbly outfit that's got to him. He was surprised to find out Bo had become so notorious, but he doesn't think that's the kind of thing two gentlemen should let come into their personal lives. Politics is one thing, and life is another. But he still thinks the world of Bo. When this strike business is settled, he's sure they'll get on again. He hopes he isn't jealous of that Flynn woman. Art had rather have that Dago of hers after him than Bo.

The Flynn woman seemed anxious for him to just drop her off at first, and he was hard put to come up with some excuse to keep her with him. He really didn't want to spend too much time downtown with her, since there's that strike element clogging up the street. And to tell the truth, he's more than a little worried that his mother and Bunny will see him. Bunny is a quiet sort, but when she takes a notion into her head, she can crack a mean whip. His mother told him that, and women know those sorts of things about one another.

He thought he might get the Flynn woman to take in a picture show with him. There's a double bill that looks pretty good at the Eagle: *Fall of a Nation* paired with a new Chaplin film, *Mirth of a Nation.* But she told him she had to speak at some meeting or another at the park this evening. She's not too interested in mediums, either, so she didn't go for his invitation to see the one they call Vera. He supposes it's just as well. He's got his own meeting to go to, out at Jack Greenway's house. He'll have to sober up for that one. He bets Jack would understand about going to the Line, though. Jack's a man's man.

He's just about run out of suggestions for things to do by the time he gets the Flynn woman to the bottom of Chihuahua Hill, where she says she's staying. But then he has an inspiration. He figures she's pretty knowledgeable about strikes and that kind of thing. So, even though he knows his father would kill him, he mentions the list of names on the

Bible table at home. He shouldn't have done it, he knows, and he feels guilty. But, hell *in vino veritas,* they say. He'll regret it later, but *carpe diem,* they say, too.

She perked up at that, all right. She didn't press him on it, which he thought was pretty decent of her. But she didn't seem as anxious to send him away, either. She told him that there might be hope for him yet, even though he was a bourgeois "swell." But she was good natured about it, so he didn't mind. He hasn't told her about old Agent 34 yet, though. That might be going too far. But she has asked him if he would like to meet some people. She has to go up to the house of the family she's staying with first, then go to something called a strike kitchen down in the Finn Hall in Lowell camp. Somehow today it seems perfectly ordinary to him to agree to go along. Oh, but they'll pitch a proper cat fit about that at home.

Mostly Mexicans live on Chihuahua Hill. He's surprised to find that she's staying with some white people there. They have to park the Ford at the bottom of the hill by city hall and climb up to where she's staying. He rushes around to open her door for her, but she beats him to it and opens it for herself. She's a hell of a strange woman, all right. He hesitates before offering his arm for the long climb up the hill, but when he does she takes it. She seems bloody tired. He's none too sure on his feet right now and hopes he doesn't trip her up.

The rain has settled into a steady, soaking downpour. As they climb higher on the steep steps, he can see down to the Gulch and Main Street. The Gulch is running pretty well. He tells her how every year children and dogs get caught in it, and how one year he swam out to rescue a miner's kid's dog. He tells her, too, about the year that the Gulch ran so deep in a storm that it flooded a boardinghouse and Camel James came floating down to the Copper Queen Hotel naked in a bathtub. She doesn't believe him, but he swears it's the truth and she laughs. It's the first time he's seen her laugh. The water laps down the steps as they climb, and he's upset that nobody told her she should bring her rubbers for rainy season here. She'll ruin her boots. He wonders if famous union women like herself get paid well enough to throw away boots. He's shocked when she tells him she gets eighteen dollars a week, like everybody else.

She's staying with some people named Ewing. Mr. Ewing is a hoistman at the Irish Mag shaft, and wears overalls. His wife has on a print dress and sunbonnet. They're embarrassed when he comes in and keep apologizing for the house, which is a yellow board-and-batten cabin with green trim. Through a window he can see a small garden on a flat patch of ground and a wooden outhouse. It all makes him nostalgic. They have an undeterminable number of children who wander in and out with the chickens and stare at his uniform. That pleases him. The girls' dresses are made out of the same print flour-sack material as the boys' shirts.

The Flynn woman leaves him in the parlor, where she sleeps, and goes to change her wet clothing. So far as Art can tell, there is only one bedroom in the house. He wonders where the deuce the children sleep. On a side table he sees a birth-control pamphlet by a woman named Sanger. So the Wobblies are involved with that outfit, too!

It's all very uncomfortable while the Flynn woman is gone. He begins to wish he were back up on the Line. He sits while the Ewings stand. They don't seem to be very good at polite conversation. The parlor is decorated with paper doilies and calendars from Hubbard's Mortuary. It is furnished with two cane-bottom chairs, a hand-hewn table, a pressed-wood clock with a gong made from a spring, a mohair couch in none-too-good repair, and a Warm Morning stove. An old Smith and Wesson six-shot revolver hangs over the door. That makes him even more uneasy and he offers Mr. Ewing a drink of Scotch.

Mr. Ewing takes him into the kitchen. Evidently these people do their drinking in the kitchen while the women and children stay out of sight in the parlor. There's no ice, unless he wants to ask Mr. Ewing to chip it off the block in the icebox. They drink standing up. There is only one chair in the room. The floor is of tamped earth, and there's no gas, of course. Art feels nostalgic again when he sees the leather water bags in the corner that he knows come up by burro everyday. He offers a toast to Mr. Ewing's health. Ewing thanks him, drinks, and asks him what kind of whiskey they're drinking. Art thinks it's a joke at first, then realizes the man is serious. He feels like an ass. To cover his discomfort, he takes a chaser from a gourd dipper in a water bucket by the cabinet. There are a bloody awful number of flies and strings of dried chili peppers everywhere. That Flynn woman has guts to stay here, he'll give her that all right.

He's awfully glad when the Flynn woman comes back. He tells the Ewings he's sorry they're on strike and they give him an odd stare. The Flynn woman looks absolutely tip-top. She has a lace collar on over her fresh white shirtwaist. Black and white are good on her. He doesn't believe he's ever known a woman with black hair and such blue eyes before. On the way to the Ford he tells her she looks tip-top. He's a little disappointed when she says her mother makes all her clothes for her.

He worries that they'll run into her Dago at the Finn Hall. He mentions it casually and she tells him that the man won't see her again until the meeting that night. He feels better. And daring.

The Finn Hall is a barn of a wooden building with a false front on a muddy piece of treeless ground. He has to admit to himself that he's more than a little afraid when they go inside. The building is mainly one big open room with chairs stacked around the sides and a makeshift podium at the end opposite the door. An IWW emblem hangs on a banner above the podium, with some words in Finnish that have exclamation points after them. There seem to be a couple of other rooms behind the podium. Hefty women with black shawls come in and out of them with kettles of food, which they put on long tables.

The place is right gray and dismal, but it's the men who disturb him. There must be two hundred of them lounging about. And they're a rough-looking crowd if he ever saw one. A good many of them are staring at him. The Flynn woman asks him if he'd like to inspect the kitchen with her. He doesn't think so. He wants to stay near the door. Besides, the smell of whatever stuff they're cooking isn't doing his stomach good. He hasn't eaten since morning.

Some of the men are spread out on blankets sleeping; others sit in small groups arguing. Most of them wave or clap when they catch sight of the Flynn woman. They are dressed in ragtag items of clothing—suit coats, overalls, shoes with run-down heels, old dress shirts without collars. Oddly enough, they all seem to be close to his own age, or a little older. Fellows who should be able to find work fairly easily.

He tries to catch parts of their conversation. Much of it is in foreign languages he can't understand. But even the English he can't make much of. Everybody seems to be a stiff of some sort: harvest stiff, straw stiff, and Lord knows what else. They refer to one another as bindlestiffs. As best he can tell, that has something to do with their bedrolls, which they call bindles. They look as if they could all stand a good military delousing. He imagines most of them will come around before the war's over and register for the draft. The group nearest him is engaged in a conversation about religion. They don't sound as if they're keen on it. He has to listen to them refer to a Jerusalem Slim several times before he can make out that they mean Jesus. One of them says that Jerusalem Slim was probably a Wob. Art thinks that's grand. He'll have to repeat it to someone.

The chap who called Jesus a Wobbly breaks off from his group and approaches him. Art needs a drink bad. He tries to pretend he wasn't really listening to them. The man, who can't be much over twenty, asks Art if he can "glom a snipe."

Art begs the man's pardon, and someone yells that the man wants to bum a smoke. Art apologizes that he doesn't smoke.

"Well, do you take a drop, then?" the man asks him. His manner is insolent, but polite enough. He's thin, with a day or two's growth of beard, and thick Mediterranean features. Art is more nervous than ever.

"I do, yes," he says.

"Then come have a set. You can snitch a sip if you do it quiet. No drinking on a strike, you know. Are you partial to mule?"

Art begs his pardon again. The man leans closer. "I mean, you ain't too much of a swell to take a sip of corn liquor with a workingstiff, are you, colonel?"

Art knows he's being made fun of, but he's at a loss to know what to do about it. He takes the straight-backed chair the man offers him. Another of the Wobblies, a chubby man with some teeth missing, slips a bottle from the bindle leaning against his chair. He offers it to Art.

It's poisonous stuff, Art thinks. But he drinks a decent swallow and tries to smile. He coughs instead. The men laugh. Art slips out his silver flask and offers it around. When it comes back, it's empty.

"We was wondering about you, colonel," the Mediterranean-looking man says. Art decides his name should be Guido. "A friend of the Flynn's are you?"

"An acquaintance," Art says. His tongue seems thicker now. Can't afford to get polluted, he thinks. Got to get out to Jack Greenway's house.

"Ah!" the man says to the other Wobblies. "He's an acquaintance, fellow workers."

"You a bellhop, 'bo?" the man with the whiskey asks, and hands the bottle around again.

Art begs his pardon and takes another swallow of mule. It goes down easier this time.

"Ain't that a bellhop's uniform you got on?" the man says.

Art stiffens. But suddenly what the man said seems wildly funny. "Oh, that's good!" Art says. He knows he's giggling, but can't do a thing about it. He should have had lunch.

The Guido-looking sort elbows a fat man beside him. "Ask him if he's a friend of J.P. Morgan's, Hamer."

The fat man smiles faintly. He seems more serious than the others. "Why's that?" he says.

"Why, he's fighting his fucking war for him, ain't he?"

That seems funny to Art, too. He can't stop laughing.

"Watch that language," a man behind Art says. "Big Bill don't take to cussing."

"Big Bill ain't here yet," Guido says.

"He's a-coming. Never fear."

"A drink to Big Bill," Guido says. The bottle goes around again. "Borrow me your hat a minute, colonel," Guido asks Art. Art hands it to him, and he puts it on backward. Then he does a kind of belly dance and sings a verse from "Yankee Doodle." Everybody except the fat man named Hamer laughs. Art is relaxing now.

One of the women in black shawls comes down to see what the commotion is, and the Wobblies hide the bottle. Until she leaves, the conversation dies. When it starts again, it's quieter. Guido makes a couple more jibes at Art, but the whiskey seems to have mellowed everyone and he doesn't get much response. Art is glad. Things are slipping away from him. That mule is a pretty strong proposition, he thinks. The voices around him don't seem to come from anyone in particular. Some of the fellows talk about how things are in the lumber camps up in Oregon, and call the loggers timberbeasts. They say the bunkhouses are full of lice and the employment "sharks" send men out on jobs that don't exist. Art thinks that's pretty rum. Somebody ought to do something about it.

Others swap stories about life in the hobo jungles. The conversation roams over mine cave-ins and bad food and missions and jails like one of those Jack London novels. Art leans back and lets himself imagine what it would be like to go hoboing. It sounds pretty god-awful, but dashed romantic, too.

The conversation stops when one of the men says he's an IWW and a KKK, too.

"How the hell can you do that?" the fat man, Hamer, says.

"I figure this way," the man says. He hasn't talked much and sounds southern. "The IWW is out to take care of the workingman. The KKK is out to take care of the white man. Well? I'm a white workingman, ain't I?"

Art doesn't think much of that. "That's des— des—despicable," he says. He realizes he shouldn't try to say much now. A couple of the fellows slap him on the back. He feels pretty much one of the boys now, and takes off his cape. He's forgotten about the Flynn woman.

Hamer says he just got down from Butte with Bo Whitley. Art wants to tell him about Bo, but Guido breaks in to ask if Hamer was in the Speculator shaft fire. Art has read about it.

"It was awful, pilgrim," Hamer says. "A hundred and twenty-eight burnt alive. Oh, I seen some of them with my own eyes. Company had put in concrete bulkheads—without no manholes in 'em, of course, like the law said. The boys that was trapped in there tried to claw their way out. Clawed their fingers down to nubs, some of them. I seen it on the ones that wasn't burnt to cinders."

They fall silent. Then the man with the whiskey says, "I was up at Everett, Washington, when we come up the river on the *Verona.*"

"Bad as they say?" the klansman Wobbly asks.

"Sheriff said we couldn't dock. Said they didn't need no more labor agitators in town. Had him God knows how many of his dehorn scissorbill buddies behind him. When the shooting was over, some of our boys had done floated off down the river. Ain't found some of them yet, they say. Guess you know who they tried. The Wobs."

"My brother was at Ludlow," Guido says. "Them Rockerfeller gunmen was the worst ever seen. Raked them tent cities with machine guns and burned the tents with the women and children still in 'em. Found eleven of 'em burned up in one tent alone. Little kids."

Art has the impression that they're talking for his benefit. That they're saying things they've all heard before. They keep watching him out of the corners of their eyes for reactions. He tries to look sympathetic. And by damn, he *is.* Bloody shame, all of it.

"Could get worse here," the man with the whiskey says. He checks to see no one is watching and offers the bottle around again. "I hear that that Sheriff Wheeler is a pisser. Damn mean town, from the looks of it. Tightest company town I ever been in."

Hamer takes a slug of mule. "You don't wear the copper collar in Arizona, pilgrim, you don't eat."

There is another silence as everyone considers. Guido breaks it with a soft chuckle. "I ever tell you boys about the time they had me up on a free speech rap in Fresno?"

"I don't believe a word of it already," Hamer says.

" 'What's your nationality?' the DA asks me. 'IWW,' I tell him. 'Then you're not a patriot?' he says. 'Wouldn't you fight for the country?' 'Not me, boss,' I answer. 'I live in the city!' He was a little perturbed by then. 'No,' he says. 'Fight for your native land, I mean.' 'I don't own no land,' I tell him. 'The landlords own all the land, and the bosses own all the machines. If you own any land, I'll fight you for it!' "

A rift of wheezy laughs and hoots goes around the group. Art joins in. That last drink of mule was positively good. He thinks this is sort of like shooting the breeze with some of the fellows down at the club in Princeton. Sort of.

A man with long hair picks out a tune on an old piano up on the podium. Some of the men near him start to sing. After a while others join in. All the while the black-shawled women scuttle back and forth with kettles of food and dishes. The long tables are so full they're bending in the middle now. Art recognizes the song: it's the one about pie in the sky that some of the bohemians sing at parties back East. Guido leans over to tell him it's by Joe Hill. Hamer asks if he'd like to buy a songbook. Art gives him a dollar for it. Hamer tries to give him change but he won't take it. It's the least he can do.

He opens the book and tries to focus on the songs. A lot of them seem to be by that Joe Hill and people with odd names, like T-Bone Slim. Art likes that one. He wishes someone had ever given him a nickname. But his mother said nicknames were undignified. The songbook is red, and the motto on it says: To Fan the Flames of Discontent. Art has always been taught that you should count your blessings and be content. It's all very strange to him. A lot of the songs seem to be set to the music of hymns, but the words! Father Mandin would pitch an absolute fit.

He's just about to join in the singing when he spots the Flynn woman up by the piano player. She whispers something to him and he breaks off the song. One of the women clangs on a triangle gong. Men begin wandering up toward the food, and the buzz of conversation gets louder. He's hungry enough to eat his boots, but it doesn't seem right to go and just eat without paying something. The smell is still pretty putrid, but he's always up for trying new dishes. After all, he's had just about everything on Lüchow's menu.

The Flynn woman saves him the trouble. She weaves through the crowd with a dish for him, and a cup of coffee. The dish is full of something that's all in a heap. He tries to get up for her, but has trouble doing it. She motions for him to keep his seat.

"Smells good," he says when she hands him the plate.

"Ever had it before?" she asks. "It's coll."

"I don't . . . ah . . . know." The words keep slipping away. The Flynn woman still seems fresh, even though she's been in the hot kitchen. Only her eyes look tired.

"No, I don't imagine you spend much time in hobo jungles." She watches him to see if he eats it. He's sure he sees a smile on her face. He takes a few bites. There seem to be hunks of onion and liverwurst squished around in mashed potatoes. He's never had real Wobbly food before. It's actually edible if you don't think about it so much. He might not make such a poor hobo after all.

"You're really not so bad," she says. "Not just any bourgeois would have told me about that list."

Art's mouth is full and he has trouble swallowing. It's pretty lumpy stuff after all. "Strictly confidential, of course." He winks at her. By now most of the other Wobblies who were sitting with him before have wandered back. They wolf their food, Art notices.

"You plutes eat your chuck like the world was full of it," Guido says.

Art begs his pardon. "Plutocrats," the Flynn woman whispers to him.

"Ahhhh!" Art says between mouthfuls. He tries to eat faster. Plute. That might be a good nickname. They're a good bunch, these Wobblies. Lots of imagination.

"Would you do me one more favor?" the Flynn woman asks. She pulls up a chair and sits beside him. He remembers the odor of sex he thought he smelled on her in the dining car this morning. Damn straightforward woman. Not coy like most of them he knows.

He nods.

"Could you get me a look at that list?"

Just like that, he thinks. Bam! Right out in the open. Why doesn't he learn to keep his mouth shut? He's in a hell of a spot now. His father would kill him. Absolutely. It's unthinkable. But he's surrounded by hundreds of dynamite-throwing Wobblies, too. Now you've done it, Matthews, he tells himself. You're damned if you do and damned if you don't. He decides his only hope is to make a joke out of it. Maybe tell her something else to get her mind off the list. Surely she can't be serious, anyway. The other Wobblies in the bunch around him seem to be busy talking again.

Maybe they won't hear the whole thing. He hopes to God they don't.

"Oh," he says, and tries a laugh that comes out wrong. "Old Agent Thirty-four wouldn't like that at all, would he?"

She's watching his face the whole time. She doesn't change her expression. The men who seemed to be so busy talking fall silent and put their forks down. One of them, Hamer, draws his chair closer.

"Pinkerton?" the Flynn woman says flatly. "Burns?"

Art tries to swallow. He can't. "Thiel, I think I recall."

"Your father's the contact?"

"Miss Flynn, I really shouldn't . . ."

The man with the whiskey slips the remains of the bottle from his bindle. He hands it to Art. The Flynn woman doesn't object. "Wet your throat, shorthorn," he says. "Ain't nobody going to hurt you."

"Does he say where he is?" Hamer says. Art feels he should trust the man. He's Bo's friend. "What his job is? Anything like that?"

"No, no, he . . . I really think I've . . . I shouldn't . . ." He can feel the sweat trickling down inside his uniform. He unbuttons his tunic. He doesn't feel well at all.

"Does he say what he's got in mind?" the Flynn woman says.

"No, nothing. Just that he . . . exists. And that he's one of . . . you."

"Oh, fine, pilgrim," Hamer says. "Just fine."

"You expected it, didn't you?" the Flynn woman tells him. Her voice is sharper than Art has heard it before. Who in the Lord's name has he got himself mixed up with?

Hamer sighs. "I reckon."

"God, I shouldn't be here," Art says. He looks around for his hat and cape. They lie in a heap on the floor. He wants to run out, to get away from the nauseating smell of the stuff he's eating and stand in the cool rain. The hall is out of focus and the last drink of mule is stuck somewhere in his throat, trying to come back up.

The Flynn woman covers his hand with hers. Her hand is cool, like he imagines the rain would be. "It's all right," she says. "Your father will never know."

"Oh, please, no . . ." Art says.

"Who's his old man?" Guido says.

"Matthews," Hamer says. "Company purchasing agent."

"How do you know?" the Flynn woman says, and turns on Hamer.

Hamer toughens. "He's a friend of Bo's, ain't he? So am I."

Their eyes hold each other for a moment. Then the Flynn woman nods and turns back to Art. "Will you get the list?" she says.

Art looks down at his boots. Army boots. He's a soldier, an officer. His country is at war. Soon other men like himself will be dying to defend it—perhaps even he will. "You're not . . . not really German-supported, are you?"

The Flynn woman's hand rests lightly on his. "It doesn't make one jot of difference to us who wins this war. I swear that to you."

The world *is* upside down, he thinks. And this is what the bottom side of it looks like. "The list," he says. "I don't know. I'll try. I'm just . . . not doing so well right now. Please."

The Flynn woman pats his hand. "It's all right," she says. He must seem such a bloody fool to her.

The man at the piano begins to play again. Art turns up the bottle of mule and finishes it. It stays down, but he's not sure how. He'll have to come up with *some*thing now—maybe just slip the list out for a couple of hours. That shouldn't be so bad. And after all, it doesn't seem sporting that Dad's side in the thing has such a stacked deck. He knows other chaps at school from families just as good as his who have gone out and actually worked in the streets with these people. Why, there's that John Reed fellow from Harvard—actually in jail with Haywood once. Reed's living in a state of Free Love with some woman, too, the papers say.

Damn plutes. Free Love, that's an all-right proposition. And the bohemian sorts he's known aren't really all that bad, after all. With some sort of private income, it could be a swell enough life. The more he thinks about it, the less keen he is on going to France.

The Flynn woman leaves him to check on the weather

outside. She comes back in and says that it looks as if it should clear up enough for their meeting. Art jerks himself straight in his chair. Joseph and Mary! He's got his own meeting to go to. And oh, is he snockered. His father will kill him. Positively kill him.

The fellow who has been plinking around on the piano launches into "The Star-Spangled Banner." Art is surprised. There's patriotism in these—what's the word?—stiffs, after all! Then the Flynn woman opens his songbook for him to page 23, and sings out the chorus with the rest of the Wobblies.

> And the Banner of Labor will surely soon wave
> O'er the land that is free from the master and slave . . .

Ho, he thinks, that's rich, that's grand. He'd love to see maybe old Harry Wheeler's face at this one! Wonderful. Just wonderful. Bloody Star-Spangled Banner, even.

Orson McCrea: July 1, 7:00 P.M.

Orson McCrea sits in a shaft of rainy evening light and listens to the voices from Captain Jack Greenway's parlor. His head throbs, and he is a little drowsy from the shot Dr. Bledsoe gave him at the C & A hospital in midafternoon. The leather armchair is comfortable, and he wishes he could go to sleep. But he can't. Captain Greenway has given him things to study. He has been trying, but he can't make heads or tails of them. Captain Greenway's houseboy came and brought him some sandwiches on a copper tray a while ago, but he hasn't been able to eat more than a few bites. His jaw is swollen and painful, and the bandage on it keeps him from opening his mouth very wide. Captain Greenway has also sent a message home for him, and he hopes his wife isn't worried. She lies awake and prays all night when she's worried.

After Captain Greenway took him to Dr. Bledsoe this morning, and bought him new clothes, he had McCrea stay with him through the afternoon. Captain Greenway is the strangest man McCrea has ever known. He rode his white mare, Caesar's Consort, home and had his chauffeur drive McCrea behind him. All the streetcar conductors clanged their trolley bells when they saw Captain Greenway. McCrea guesses that's because Captain Greenway is president of the streetcar company, like he's vice-president of the light and gas and telephone companies. Walter Douglas is president of those, and McCrea supposes Mr. Douglas doesn't mind Captain Greenway's being president of one company anyway.

Captain Greenway lives in the second biggest house in Bisbee. Walter Douglas lives next door and has the largest house, but he's never there to use it. They both live in Warren, really, which Captain Greenway explained is a suburb, a new thing that automobiles and trolley cars are making possible. Captain Greenway is vice-president of the Warren Land Company, too, and Walter Douglas is president. Their houses sit on a hilltop right at the end of a long green mall. All the other houses line the green mall, and are smaller. The mall dead-ends into the baseball park. It looks like pictures McCrea has seen of the grounds of castles and things in Europe, except for the baseball park.

McCrea guesses Captain Greenway likes kids a lot. He spent an hour during the afternoon at the swimming pool his company built for kids in Warren. He would throw dimes into the pool and watch the boys dive for them. He told the girls not to, though. Then they went to the company offices in Warren and all the big shots waited at the window while Captain Greenway played another game with the boys. This time he put dimes on spots on the sidewalk and had the boys rollerskate by and try to pick them up. He said "Bully" and "Capital" a lot when the boys got the dimes, and tousled their hair. Then the rain drove them inside.

McCrea liked it all except for Captain Greenway's nigger chauffeur, who kept talking while McCrea was trying to watch Captain Greenway. The chauffeur didn't seem to even know he was a nigger.

Now McCrea is trying to figure out what's going on in the parlor. He can make out most of the voices so far. He first recognized Grant Dowell's, then Tom Matthews's. People are coming in faster now, and he has trouble keeping the voices straight. He can hear Miles Merrill every now and again, and Captain Greenway's security chief, Wilson, and he thinks he can even make out Lem Shattuck. Then there is a hush, and he can hear Harry Wheeler's quiet controlled voice greeting everyone. Captain Greenway's hearty laugh weaves in and out among the voices, and McCrea can hear him giving orders for drinks and sandwiches.

McCrea again picks up the diagrams that Captain Greenway gave him. There is a picture of a railway car—a gondola—on the top sheet, and an incline. Attached to it are other sheets with pictures of wheels and axles. There are dimensions and formulas and computations that McCrea can't follow at all. He tries to rest his head on the cool leather of the chair back, but the pain won't let it stay there. He wishes he were home. With every throb of pain he sees the face of Bo Whitley. He doesn't think that he's ever really hated anyone before. But he knows what hate is now. Hate is Whitley. There is nothing, nothing he wouldn't do to pay back the filthy thing done to him.

He stands and paces the study to keep awake. Captain Greenway has more books than the Copper Queen Library, he bets. Most of them seem to be Greek or Latin or from England, bound in leather. His wife has a Latin textbook at home, and he resolves to put it on a shelf in the parlor. Two books are open on Captain Greenway's huge mahogany desk. McCrea flips through them without losing the captain's place. The first one is by an Englishman McCrea is sure he's heard of. The man's name is Carlyle, and the book is about heroes. Captain Greenway has been reading a section of the book about natural leaders and the rights of men who are destined to rule. It looks interesting and McCrea resolves to read it one day. The other book is by a German. That surprises McCrea. The German's name is Nietzsche and the book looks far too heavy for pleasant reading. McCrea decides he might as well go back to the things he is supposed to be studying. Before he sits, he opens the door a crack so that he can see into the parlor. He will need the light. The thunderstorm outside is letting up, but the clouds still hide the last of the sun.

Along with the diagrams is a list of names, with a little biography of each man attached. All of them have GOOD written at the end of the biographies. Captain Greenway asked him to go through and circle the ones he knew to be the best leaders in town. Captain Greenway uses the word *leader* a lot. There are at least two dozen names. McCrea has circled his own name and nine others. Satisfied, he looks at his work, then picks up the diagrams again. He is dismayed. There is no help for it. He will have to ask Captain Greenway to explain them to him. That's Whitley's fault, too.

Through the door, open a few inches, he can see the men in the other room settling. The Mexican houseboy, who has been taking everyone's rain slickers, is hanging them in the vestibule to dry. Captain Greenway and his security chief are setting up an easel and leaning a stack of diagrams against it. McCrea stands again and walks to the door for a better look. Maybe he can at least make sense out of those diagrams.

Captain Greenway lives in a copper house. The walls are wooden, of course, but all the light fixtures are copper, even the huge chandelier, which is made of a dozen copper lilies hanging upside down with light bulbs in them. The door handles are copper. When he went to the bathroom earlier, McCrea noticed that the faucets and tubs were copper. The desert painting around the top of the parlor walls is done in copper tones.

Captain Greenway is leaning against the marble fireplace waiting for the men in the room to quiet down. The room is decorated with hunting trophies and pictures, as is the study. McCrea noticed a picture of the captain with President Roosevelt on the study wall earlier. They were dressed in hunting clothes and holding up an antelope between them. Elsewhere, the captain's Yale diploma in mining engineering and pictures of himself in various uniforms—football, military, lodge—hang in clusters. One of the largest pictures is of two men in Confederate officers' uniforms with a child between them. Someone has written "Daddy, Granddaddy, and Jack" on it. Most of the other pictures are of Captain Greenway with important-looking men and groups of men. They all seem to have large stomachs and top hats, except Captain Greenway. He is slim and wears a campaign hat.

There is no trace of a woman's hand in the house. And only two of the pictures are of women. One has "Mother" written under it. The other is of a younger woman in clothes that were in fashion a dozen years ago. There is no name under it, but it hangs so that Captain Greenway looks into the woman's eyes whenever he is sitting at his writing desk. She is a little skinny for McCrea's taste, but he can't deny she looks as if she should be on the cover of one of his wife's *American Woman* magazines. Or maybe in a painting in a church. Beside the desk is a gun cabinet with five rifles and two pistols in it.

McCrea can't see many of the faces in the parlor well, only Captain Greenway's and Harry Wheeler's. The rest of the men are hidden in the captain's big wing-back chairs, or sitting on the leather couches with their backs to him. The captain is dressed in a silk smoking jacket with Japanese pictures on it. Harry Wheeler's black suit is clearly store-bought, like the one Bo Whitley tore off McCrea this morning. He looks uncomfortable. McCrea feels better. He knows how it is for Harry.

"Gentlemen?" the captain says. "Everyone sufficiently provided for?" Everybody nods or murmurs. They all seemed to be served whiskey except Harry Wheeler. He has coffee.

"Sorry to see Art couldn't make it," Captain Greenway says to Tom Matthews. "Tied up with Bunny, I reckon?"

"No. Drunk," Matthews says.

Captain Greenway laughs his hearty laugh and everyone seems to relax except Harry Wheeler and Lem Shattuck.

Captain Greenway starts to say something, but Lem Shattuck stands up. "Before we get too comfortable, boys, I got something to say. Everybody in this room knows I got as much to lose as the next feller, maybe more." Lem is the only independent owner left in town. His belly hangs over his belt, his hair looks like it's slicked back with bearing grease, and his mustache droops over his mouth like ragged pine straw. He doesn't belong to the country club, Orson has heard, and isn't even an Episcopalian. He has a German wife who goes around barefoot, and he sends his kids to school in patched clothes. His oldest boy has just run away to Mexico to avoid the draft. The boy's mother didn't want him to go kill Germans, she said. Lem owned a saloon once. He got his start in mining by standing miners to drinks and then letting them work the bill out on his claim. Most of them like him for that. He flat outsharped them. McCrea reflects that he is a Mormon and can never make his fortune that way.

"You boys can stand a long strike better than I can," Shattuck goes on. "Copper's thirty-five cent a pound, higher'n it's ever been. And I damn well need the money. But I've always got on with the union—used to be a miner myself, as you know. I got to keep getting on with them. They strike me too often and I ain't got other businesses to keep me going. So I'll tell you this: I ain't got no more use than the rest of you for this IWW bunch, and I don't think most of my men do. I won't negotiate with 'em for now. But I won't step out front and low-rate the unions in general either. You need money to help out, I got it for you. You need some good loyal boys to do a job or two, I got 'em for you. But otherwise, I'm laying low, so to speak. And if you boys don't come up with a way to get the men back to work soon enough, I'm settling with any union on any terms I can get. Thirty-five cent a pound for copper won't come back soon, and this war ain't going to last forever. I'm getting what I can while I can. I just want you to know that."

He looks around fiercely at the other men. Although McCrea can't see their faces, he imagines they avoid his eyes as Harry Wheeler and John Greenway do.

"That's a damnable attitude!" Grant Dowell blurts out. "I have my stockholders to think about just the same as you do, Lem. But there's more than just a dollar-a-day raise involved here. We're at war, damn it. Or I suppose you'd rather not talk about that, had you?"

Shattuck fixes his eyes on Dowell. McCrea has heard that he personally went after men with double-jack sledgehammers in the old days in his saloon. "You care to explain that remark, Grant?" Shattuck says slowly. McCrea sees Harry Wheeler sit up straighter in his chair and put his coffee down.

"There's more than either war or raises involved," Captain Greenway says. "So much so, boys, that we damn well can't afford to squabble amongst ourselves."

"Well!" Dowell says. He is relieved. "I should say so."

Shattuck looks around at Greenway from under his heavy eyelids. "If there's something more important involved than my mine, I damn well don't know it."

Greenway smiles at him, the soft smile that McCrea saw in the dispensary. It still bothers him. "What's involved, Lem, is Christian civilization," Greenway says. He waits a moment for his statement to sink in. "Would you like to sit a spell, Lem?" Shattuck looks bewildered and sinks into an armchair. Greenway rests his arm on the marble mantelpiece and props his foot on the hearth as if it were a bar rail. McCrea thinks he looks like pictures he's seen of English hunters in India.

"Christian civilization, gentlemen," Greenway says. "Wobblies are the advance guard of the Antichrist. Do you boys believe in the Antichrist?"

"Jack . . ." Grant Dowell begins.

"No, now let me finish, Grant. It's all there for you in the Bible. The Antichrist, the Good Book tells us, will come to establish the Kingdom of Man and destroy the Kingdom of God. Now you've seen the IWW posters, I reckon, just like I have. No God, No Master, says one of them. Now what's that if not a proclamation? Make an earthly paradise, they say. Not godly, but earthly.

"They're the signs of this damnable century. No God, no master! Horseshit. People have always had a God and a master. Without them, there can't be any civilization. As we know it, in any case. Oh, it's not just Wobblies in it—they're tied up with other outfits all over the world. Mainly Jewish-inspired, I might add."

He looks around at Harry Wheeler. Wheeler has picked up his coffee cup again and listens intently.

"The men who *can,* who *know,* who are *able* to rule, are the ones who, in nature, must. Without them, there is chaos. Without them there would be no arts, no progress, no 'peaceful discourse,' as the saying goes. They are the men who are entitled to their reward for providing work for those who can't provide it for themselves. They are above the normal restrictions of men, but bound by even higher laws. They are us, boys. Like it or not, it's our duty.

"Now this IWW outfit. Who the hell are they? Drifters who don't vote. Slackers who refuse to fight for their Christian, enlightened government. People who have no families, no backgrounds, no talents, and no respect for those who do. People who recognize no authority, no goal beyond this jackleg idea of an earthly paradise. They hook up with immigrants who have none of our traditions, our language. And whose interest do they serve? Ours, or a nation's we're at war with? Their aim is to shrink the soul of man, and to replace it with one mass soul with no face.

"They're enemies, gentlemen, enemies. Plagues, blots, things to be exterminated—a cancer to be cut out before it consumes the body. It isn't too much to say that we are engaged, whether we like it or not, in a kind of holy war. Am I not right?"

His smile is still intact. Harry Wheeler sits with his coffee cup in midair. He is waiting for more. McCrea hears uncomfortable scraping and foot-shuffling noises from the men whose faces he can't see.

Lem Shattuck heaves to his feet again. "Well, Jack. Like I said, if there's anything more important involved here than my mine, I still don't know it. They're a no-good bunch of low-class sons of bitches and they want my mine. To save it, I'll make a pact with the devil himself if I have to. You fight your holy war. I'll give you a check. But for the rest . . . I don't want to know." He nods to Greenway, then to the other men in the room one by one. The silence is heavy as he walks to the vestibule and waits for the houseboy to dig out his top hat, cane, and raincape.

At the door he pauses, then turns toward Dowell. "Give my best to Walter Douglas when you tell him about Jack's holy war, Grant. Walter's a big 'un for holy wars, I reckon."

McCrea's breathing is heavy. He has never heard anyone stand up to Captain Greenway that way before. Greenway bows slightly as Lem Shattuck closes the door behind himself. His smile grows and turns into his hearty laugh. "Capital!" he says. "Lem Shattuck is the salt of the earth."

"Whatever he is, Jack," Grant Dowell says, "we need him. If he breaks, this goddamn strike could have us by the short hairs. And, well . . . the truth is that 'extermination' is a pretty puffy word, don't you think? I mean, what would Walter think?" He stands and paces to the picture window beside the marble fireplace. At the window he turns and faces Tom Matthews. "Good question, eh, Tom?" he says, and swipes at his balding head. "And the stockholders. They're as patriotic a bunch as you or me—most of them British, in fact, and damned bothered by this war business. But 'exterminating' and 'holy wars' . . ."

"I don't propose that we include the terms in our quarterly reports, Grant," Greenway says.

"Still . . ." Dowell says.

"Walter will be in touch soon," Tom Matthews says. "No sense in getting upset just yet, Grant."

"Oh . . . well, I suppose you're right." He wanders back to his chair.

"Details, then," Greenway says. He takes his foot off the fireplace, picks up his charts and diagrams, and positions them on the easel. They are covered by a black piece of paper. "My men are close to seventy percent out, including Mexicans. Of the thirty percent still working, we have to count machinists and such. They're AF of L, of course, like yours are, Grant, and we can count on them to cooperate. That means then that the strike is right near eighty to ninety percent effective. I assume that jibes with your situation?"

"Same story, essentially," Dowell says.

"That gives us a figure of about five thousand men out. At least half that many would go back if they weren't afraid. Right?"

"Sounds reasonable. Don't forget to add Lem's men. He's shut down totally."

"They're added. Twenty-five hundred active strikers, then. Plus sympathizers in the mines. Saboteurs, perhaps. And how many outside agitators? They can do a hell of a lot of damage." He pulls the black piece of paper from the first of his diagrams. "Roughly, these are the mine shafts we know of. Some of the early ones, and some of the leasers' workings, we don't have charted anywhere. Miles of shafts here, gentlemen, miles. Some of them under the city itself—almost all of them under some inhabited place. Think of the opportunities for holocaust: dynamite here, for example . . ." He touches a point on the map. It is too far away for McCrea to make sense of. "And the post office and library sink into the earth. The air blast would of course make peashooters out of these shafts here and here. Men and machines would spew out of them all over the camp."

"We've thought of that," Tom Matthews says quietly.

"And Grant still maintains that we don't exist in a state of war? Holy or not, Tom, it's war, by damn."

"We're prepared for it, Jack. You know that as well as I do."

"No, we're not. No matter what we've got in the dispensary. That's just my point."

"Convince me then," Matthews says. McCrea can see Harry Wheeler straining forward in his chair to see the diagrams.

"This next chart," Greenway says, "is one I've made up myself over the past few weeks. It shows the points needed for a military force to control the city. The Tombstone Pass, the Naco Road, C and A offices, Copper Queen offices, post office, telegraph, telephone, etcetera. How many armed men would you need to do it? Harry, you're a military man. You tell me."

Wheeler looks embarrassed. He narrows his eyes to study the chart, then clears his throat a couple of times. "Oh . . . quite a few less than they've got, Captain Greenway." That sounds a little lame to McCrea, but he isn't sure. He's not a military man.

"Precisely," Greenway says and smiles at Wheeler. Wheeler relaxes. "In a word, we are at their mercy. Harry, I understand you met with their 'leaders' today. Could you tell us what happened?"

"Well," Wheeler clears his throat again. "They agreed to keep off company property, and to keep the number of pickets down so as not to obstruct traffic."

"No more?"

"They asked me to deputize some of their men. Said they'd keep their own peace."

"Did you?"

"I did not."

"Did they mention the aeroplane?"

"Sir?"

"The aeroplane that was shot down over Naco this morning. It was a Villista machine, is my understanding."

"As best I know, it was."

"You know the IWW sent a brigade to fight with the Villista forces, I reckon."

"Yessir, I recall that." McCrea tries to read Harry Wheeler. He is still nervous, but in control. Perfectly respectful, but in control. McCrea is glad he voted for him.

"Aerial attacks, sheriff. Villa raided Columbus last year. He's weaker now. But with support within the United States, with spotters here to guide him and immobilize us . . . That's not wild talk, Harry. I have my sources."

"I didn't question that," Wheeler says.

"Have you considered calling in the army?" Greenway asks.

"I have," Wheeler says.

"I wouldn't . . . not at this point."

"Oh, now, Jack . . ." Dowell breaks in.

"Walter Douglas will back me to the hilt on this, Grant." Greenway's eyes never leave Wheeler. "Where are the nearest soldiers? That's a rhetorical question, of course. Fort Huachuca. And what kind of soldiers are they? Buffalo soldiers. Can you conceive the terrible blowup we would have on our hands if the government decided to send in buffalo soldiers to run Bisbee, Harry? Niggers, Harry. Will you turn the town over to the darkies to save it from the Wobblies? What will the people say to that?"

"Troops could come from other places, captain," Wheeler says.

"Not likely. The guard has already left for France."

Wheeler studies his boots and considers. "I'll think on it. Ought to have an observer, at least, I'd imagine."

"Fine. An army observer. We just don't want it to appear you've decided you can't handle the situation, do we?"

"I haven't decided that."

"How many deputies do you have now, Harry?"

"Roughly two hundred since yesterday."

Greenway leaves his chart and paces back and forth in front of the mantel. He has the air of a man deliberating.

"Two hundred. Against how bloody many? Twenty-five hundred . . . maybe more? I've got reports of at least four hundred of them from outside bedded down at the Finn Hall. Not good military odds, eh, Harry?"

"There's been no violence yet, Captain Greenway."

Greenway stops his pacing. He turns on his heel sharply. "None? Let me show you something, Harry." He leaves the fireplace and comes toward the study. McCrea is terrified. He backs to the chair by his diagrams and drops into it. He picks up a diagram and tries to look at it. He can feel his heart, in spite of the dulling medicine Dr. Bledsoe gave him. He has always been terrified of dying from a heart attack.

The door to the study opens. "Orson?" Captain Greenway says. His shadow makes a tunnel of darkness toward McCrea. "May I ask you to step in here a moment? Don't be afraid." His voice is gentle, as if McCrea were a skittish horse. "And whatever you do, don't be surprised at anything I say. Just agree with me. You understand?"

"Yessir," McCrea says. He fumbles his way to his feet in the dim light. When he follows Greenway through the study door he tries to walk as steadily and precisely as possible.

Under the glare of the chandelier, he feels as if he were a body on an operating table. He tries to keep his face stern, like Harry Wheeler's. But humble. It isn't easy to do with so many blessed bandages. Everyone is staring at him. The shot Dr. Bledsoe gave him makes him unsteady. He's absolutely sure he'll fall and bleed all over Captain Greenway's Oriental rug.

"Most of you know Orson McCrea. You do, certainly, Grant."

"Lord God," Dowell says. "What happened to you, son?"

"I . . ." McCrea begins.

"Wobblies happened to this boy, Grant. One Bo Whitley, in fact, not six hours ago. And without provocation. What will happen now? You'll arrest Whitley, perhaps, Harry? How many men can the jail here hold?"

"At the most twenty-five."

"Arrest one and you've got to be prepared to arrest them all. You can't do that. But this boy here, who has a family . . ." He notices McCrea has trouble standing. "Would you like to have a seat, Orson?" he asks gently.

McCrea shakes his head and stands taller.

"This boy here may have given us the solution. I asked Grant if I might borrow him today, Harry, because he came to me last night with an idea that he wanted to discuss with me. 'Captain Greenway,' he says to me. 'There's many of us who like to think of ourselves as soldiers in the trenches, like our boys in France. We hate the Wobblies for the snakes they are. But we have no organization, no structure. The merchants have their Citizens' Protective Association, but we boys in the mines have nothing,' he says. 'I'm coming to you because you're a military man, and might help us.' I was touched.

" 'There's a many of us would like to be on our way to France, Orson,' I told him, 'but for one reason or another, can't be.' "

McCrea tries hard to keep his eyes straight ahead. He remembers what Captain Greenway told him in the study. He has a role to play, even if he doesn't know just what it is.

Greenway has paused, and out of the corner of his eye McCrea sees Harry Wheeler put his coffee cup down. He is staring hard at Captain Greenway.

"So," Greenway goes on. "I say to him, 'I'll be glad to offer what advice I can, Orson—*after* it's cleared with Sheriff Wheeler. How many of your boys are there?' 'More than a few,' he tells me. 'We won't know until we get organized.' 'You'll never organize,' I say, 'until you get you some leaders. Good, loyal boys you can trust. Citizens, I'd suggest. Family men. Preferably men with a military background. Can you come up with some names?' 'Yessir,' he says, 'I think so.' It was while he was coming up with those names that he was jumped, gentlemen. Two of them did it, one of them with brass knuckles."

"Let the boy sit," Tom Matthews says. McCrea thinks he should protest, but Captain Greenway takes his arm and leads him to a chair.

"He's got those names with him tonight. He asked me if I would take charge of the organization. 'No,' I told him. 'There's only one man should in any way officially take charge of an outfit like you have in mind. That man is Harry Wheeler.' "

Wheeler's eyes stay locked on Greenway's. McCrea is

relieved, until Wheeler shifts in his chair and lets his eyes wander to McCrea's bandaged face. "What kind of outfit are you thinking of, McCrea?" he says.

"Don't make the lad talk, Harry," Greenway says. "It hurts him to."

"All right, then. What kind of outfit is he thinking in terms of, Captain Greenway?"

"I'd say—and of course this is just offhand—a defensive force. Men from every part of the mines, from all over the district. Men who understand discipline. A show of force, so to speak, no more."

There is something at work in Harry Wheeler's face now. Excitement maybe, or agitation? McCrea can't tell. "I see," he says.

"What would you do, Harry—for example—if Curley Bill Brocius's gang was to come in here riding their horses into saloons and shooting up things like they did when we were kids? Like when Texas John Slaughter was sheriff."

"You know what I'd do, Captain."

"Well, then. What's the difference? These aren't our people, Harry. They're outsiders. Foreigners. Already this Flynn woman—if you can call her that—is here. And that Dago of hers. Scores more on every freight train. And tomorrow . . . surely you know who's due in tomorrow?"

McCrea sees Wheeler's face still working. "No, sir, I don't."

"Big Bill Haywood. Didn't Grant tell you?"

"I haven't seen Harry today," Dowell says. "Not since Art came in."

Wheeler's face hardens. His eyes narrow. "I've been right busy today, Captain. Do you mind if I ask how you know that?"

"We have our sources, Harry. You understand."

"I understand I should have been told that, Captain." Wheeler's voice is still calm, but sharpened now by an edge of anger. "I understand that if I'm supposed to enforce the law I can't have fewer 'sources' than you do." He stands. McCrea looks toward Greenway. His smile still plays around the edge of his lips, but he's not happy. Didn't mean to make old Harry mad, did you, Captain? McCrea thinks.

"Doesn't alter the fact, Harry. It's you and Haywood now. And this boy here has come up with the best idea yet for keeping the peace."

"You can form whatever organization you want to, Captain Greenway. I can't stop you."

"And yourself?"

"I see no cause to get involved in it."

"What will it take, Harry?"

"I reckon I'll have to decide that when the time comes . . . sir. And if you'll kindly call your boy to get my things . . ."

Wheeler takes a step toward the door and no more. A stumbling and bumping, like a scuffle, starts suddenly on the front porch. Wheeler crouches, and Greenway's security chief, Wilson, leaps up. Miles Merrill flings himself out of his chair and kneels by the window, pistol drawn. Greenway stands, a statue, listening. Then something is pounding at the door, something like a mob, McCrea thinks. He knows he ought to throw himself in front of Greenway and Grant Dowell and protect them. But the medicine's got him.

The pounding stops, then begins again. Harry Wheeler cautiously throws back his suit coat from his pistol. He holds up his hand for everyone to freeze, and motions the houseboy to stand back. He walks carefully to the door. "Who is it?" he calls. His voice is steady. Authoritative, McCrea thinks.

The pounding stops again. "Who wants to know?" a muffled voice says through the door.

"Sheriff Harry Wheeler."

"By God," the voice says. "Old Harry. How the hell are you, old Harry?"

Tom Matthews pushes to his feet. "That's Art!" he says. His tone is more questioning than angry.

"Let him in, Harry," Greenway says.

Wheeler slips his Colt .45 double-action back into its holster and turns the bolt on the door, which flings open so quickly that he barely has time to jump back out of its way. Art Matthews lurches into the vestibule. McCrea knows it isn't proper for him to gawk, but he can't help himself. Art's tunic is undone down to his waist and his cape is on backward. His boots are muddy, and there are swatches of mud on the hem of his cape. He's drunk. Gloriously drunk. He sweeps his cape in an arc at the men in the room.

"Lo, the bloody plutocrats!" he says. He has trouble with "plutocrats." His eyes are slits and he's hatless. "An injury to one is an injury to all, gemmun. Remember that. Remember the bloody *Maine,* too!"

"Where the hell have you been, boy?" Tom Matthews growls.

"Consorting with the proletariat, pappa. Wanna hear some— somethin'?" He tries to throw his arm around Harry Wheeler's shoulder, but Wheeler shies away. He settles for the houseboy, who smiles and looks as if he wants to run. Art throws back his head and sings:

> Onward Christian soldiers! Duty's way is plain;
> Slay your Christian neighbors, or by them be slain.
> Pulpiteers are spouting effervescent swill,
> God above is calling you to rob and rape and kill,
> All your acts are sanctified by the Lamb on high;
> If you love the Holy Ghost, go murder, pray, and die.

He hugs the Mexican houseboy. "Like that, fellow worker? Wanna hear some more? 'Onward Christian soldiers! Rip and tear and smite! Let the Gentle Jesus bless your dynamite.' . . ."

Tom Matthews has moved faster than McCrea thought a man his age could. He shoves the houseboy out of the way, and grabs Art's shoulders. Art tries to pull back but Tom slams him against the wall.

"Not in this goddamn house, not in this goddamn house, you insolent son of a bitch!" he yells. "In that goddamn uniform!"

Art doesn't struggle. He stands, his arms pinned, and looks his father in the eye. "Wanna go up on the Gulch with me, pops? I'll get you a half-price lay—one buck, American. Or had you rather talk about old Agent Thirty-four? Huh, pops?"

Tom Matthews grunts and slaps Art. Art's head lolls. He grins. Tom slaps him again, then smashes his fist into his face. Harry Wheeler steps up and grabs his arm. Tom swirls on Wheeler, then remembers himself and drops his fist. Even the Matthewses don't mess with Harry Wheeler, McCrea thinks, not even an old pisser like Tom Matthews.

By now, Captain Greenway is beside Tom Matthews. "Take the boy home," he tells him. "He's been under a strain."

"He'll not sleep under his mother's roof tonight. No, by God," Tom says.

"Put him up in the Copper Queen," Grant Dowell says from across the room. "On my bill."

Tom Matthews stands, shaking. He tries to speak but can't. Harry Wheeler takes his arm. "I'll help you with the boy, Mr. Matthews." McCrea can only see Wheeler's face in profile, but he's sure he looks satisfied. That don't seem right, either.

"Thank you, Harry," Matthews manages to say.

Art Matthews has recovered. "For every dollar a man gets that he didn't earn, another man earned a dollar he didn't get! Fight, tiger, fight!"

Greenway turns to McCrea. McCrea drops his eyes. He's in bad with the big people for sure, now. Watching what's none of his business. "Thank you, Orson," Greenway says. "Would you wait in the study?"

McCrea looks deferential and keeps his eyes lowered as he makes his unsteady way to the study. It's totally dark there now, and he fumbles for a light switch. He finds a lamp and sinks into the leather chair by his diagrams. Someone closes the door to the study completely so that he can hear only a mumble of voices from the parlor.

When the study door opens, McCrea realizes he's dozed off. There are no other voices from the parlor now. Captain Greenway is alone. "Bad show, that," he says. "I apologize, Orson." McCrea tries to focus the sleep out of his eyes and stand. Greenway tells him to keep his seat.

"That was Whitley's work, too," Greenway goes on. He walks to a bar in the corner and pours himself a drink of Scotch whisky. McCrea knows his wife would never let him keep it in the house. He should, though. "Whitley will come to me, you know. He will," Greenway says. "He's too good for that crowd. I've watched him. I could make something out of him."

He pulls a ladder-back chair up, turns it backward, throws his legs over it, and sits facing McCrea. "I've never had a son, McCrea. Do you?"

"Yessir. Two."

"You Mormons have lots of children, don't you?"

"Yessir."

"I'd like a son. It's good for a house to have young men in it." He points to the picture of the woman above his desk. "I could have had sons by her, Orson. But she wouldn't take me. She's got her a Scottish laird dying of consumption in a castle now. They tell me she's known as the most fascinating woman in Europe. And she's nursing a dead man. I've never done anything in my life but what I've kept her image in front of me."

If he could only shake that medicine, McCrea knows he'd be all right. He'd hurt, but he could stay awake. Captain Greenway's voice is soft, and he wants to listen, but the words just aren't holding together.

"The world is shrinking, Orson. This is the last place a man can breathe. Now they want to suffocate me here, too. I've been waiting for them."

McCrea tries to answer, but can't. His head is more weight than he can bear, and he lets it sink.

But the pain jerks him up. He looks around, afraid. Captain Greenway has his soft smile now, and he's drawing back his hand to slap McCrea again. McCrea watches the hand. It's aimed at his swollen jaw. He flinches, and the hand stops.

"Have you made sense out of those drawings, Orson?" Greenway says. "You'll have to stay awake now, won't you? Shall I ring for a cup of coffee? No—Mormons don't drink that either, do they? Then control yourself. Control, damn it, man. Look here."

McCrea lets the pain help him focus his eyes. Greenway is pointing things out on the diagram. He's explaining patiently about the number of times a wheel will have to turn to make a cord of a certain length attached to its axle grow taut. He's explaining that you can measure exactly how many revolutions of a railroad car's wheels there are in each hundred feet the car travels. He's explaining how many hundred feet there are between the Bisbee depot and the Copper Queen company hospital, down the incline at the base of Sacramento Hill. He's explaining how a cord could be attached to a dynamite plunger to make the plunger fall when the cord grows taut. McCrea is controlling himself now. He's fully awake.

Part Two

Big Bill Haywood: July 2, 4:15 P.M.

The Golden State Limited brakes, jerks, hisses. You throw out a hand to steady yourself against the window frame. To calm your impatient anger, you've even tried to count the numberless gallows frames that mark the hoists of Bisbee's mine shafts. But your anger won't let you. It has had you up and pacing from window to window in the black and gold observation car since they brought the *Bisbee Review* aboard in Douglas, twenty-five miles back. FIRST CONTINGENT OF AMERICAN ARMY REACHES FRANCE, the headlines told you, above a photograph of that hypocrite Pershing. And then scattered all down the page, in a single column, those other headlines and subheadlines: 200 NEGROES KILLED IN EAST ST. LOUIS RACE RIOT. *City on Fire.* Terrified Blacks Run from Buildings to Face Bullets or Rocks. Mobs Roaming City, Killing at Will.

It all makes a fearful, twisted kind of sense to you. Mother Jones is reading you something aloud, but your mind won't stick on it. Backyards flick by the window. You imagine bombs from flying machines ripping the yards open, and children and young men and women falling into them as if into open mineshafts. Like a quick flash on a motion picture screen, you remember the swollen face of the Negro you saw hung in Salt Lake, when you were a boy. Where is sanity, one shock of sanity in all this terrible harvest? Nowhere, you're certain, but in you and those workingstiffs who line the tracks outside your window. You know now that you should have come even earlier.

The train brakes past a white gabled building with a sign, Copper Queen Hospital, hung over its porch. You lean forward against the window frame, as if your urgency could push the car faster. In an armchair next to you, thin in her black dress and hightops, Mother Jones slaps the newspaper flat and snorts. "And would you listen to this lovely swill," she says. You force your mind to settle on her voice.

" 'Wobblies!' " she reads through her steel-rimmed spectacles. " 'Arizona's plague! What is our sin, O Lord, that this sword should be set upon us? We have given our boys and men to thy army; we have bought of the Liberty Bonds and given freely to the Red Cross. We have tunneled our mountains and set trees in our deserts and builded towns and cities in our canyons and toiled without ceasing and looked always to the skies for inspiration.' "

She looks up, rolls her eyes heavenward, and crosses herself. When she goes back to the paper, her Irish-accented voice is a Sunday School singsong. " 'Arizona's plague! Ah, but there is a virus for every poison and a toxin for every afflicted spot. We can and will cleanse the chambers of our mountain valleys of these foes of the health, hope and happiness of our people and our government. After the Cross and the crown of thorns comes the resurrection. . . ."

She crumples the paper and flings it onto the carpet. She raises her eyes past you and takes in the whole length of the observation car. "Swill!" she says. "Damned swill!"

A hotshot drummer tips his coffee cup to her. "You tell 'em, ma'am."

She looks back up at you. "That's what we've got a-waiting for us, Bill Haywood. They'll have us praying to the flag now."

"If they could, I reckon they would," you answer abstractedly.

"I'll tell you another thing, too. I haven't missed a flat-out labor war since the days of the Molly MacGuires, but I've not seen such hysterical horse hockey as this yet." She fires the drummer a hard look. "The sons of bitches."

Through the window you see that you're on an incline coming up into a narrow canyon. Bisbee is no longer a speck on a map. The houses and tents are thick and real now, and the mines seem to sit right on top of the tracks. From somewhere comes the stink of a gasworks. You remember the first time you read Dante, in a Colorado silver camp. You wondered how he could have conceived hell so well without ever having been in a mining camp. Under the heavy thunderheads, the mountains are scarred blue and green and gray from oxidized copper. Huge pipes, gallows frames, flumes, dirty and rambling tin buildings, obliterate a whole mountainside. Steam hangs flatly over it all. This is not the wildcat, dozen-man mining country you knew. This is something else, a new thing that's eating up your West. There are no bosses here; they're all hidden away behind prospectuses now, in another state, another country. You slip your hand into your coat pocket and close it around your Iver-Johnson .38 revolver.

"Not an easy place to get into, Mother, if it was blocked off right."

She looks past you through the window at the sheer mountains. "Nor to get out of. Don't forget that."

"It don't look to me like those boys out there are studying leaving." You sweep your hand toward the men who trot alongside the train checking for strikebreakers. You've looked for goon squads yourself ever since you left El Paso. There aren't any. That bothers you. The companies should have at least tried to bring them in by now.

The train jolts again. You crane and see Bisbee's brick depot ahead. Outside, the crowd of men on strikebreaker watch is thicker now. Deputies stand in knots just beyond them—nearly as many as there are strikers. They all have sidearms. Most wear bandoliers and carry rifles, too. But the boys' spirits are high. They slap the train and wave at the passengers. The scene looks almost like a holiday. Little crowds of bystanders—kids and Indians, for the most part—hang at the edges of the crowd. Hot-dog and tamale vendors wait for the train to pass so they can get back to business. You try to read all the faces. There has to be something in them, some clue, some secret that will tell you if what you've come for is really here—or anywhere.

And then they spot you. Over the hiss of steam and *poof* of airbrakes and screech of steel wheels, you hear them call your name. All along the line, the word spreads. Big Bill's here! That's Big Bill Haywood, by damn!

You help Mother Jones to her feet so they can see her, too. Then, with a last jerk, the train stops. The observation car is still far from the depot platform and is blocked on one side by an empty ore train. But the boys who have spotted you are already yelling and waving to the crowd of strikers at the depot. The few drummers and other passengers move past you to collect their things from the Pullman coaches. You wait for them to leave. Your boys will want to see you, uncluttered.

But where is the thrill? As you watch the crowd grow, you feel less the excitement you've looked forward to than a kind of dread. It's as if that damnable vague fear you've felt since New York has built a wall between you and all your other feelings except anger and impatience. You hand Mother Jones her crutch and take her arm as she hobbles toward the observation platform ahead of you. She's eager; you can feel the tension in her thin arm.

The boys are on the platform before you reach it. They shove to get closer, to touch you. You hear your name a dozen times crackling through the growing crowd. A handful of women shoves with the rest. One of them is crying. A miner grabs Mother Jones, kisses her on the lips, and she raises her hands in a prizefighter's salute. A cheer rises to cover even the thunder that rolls in across the mountains.

At your feet a boy of nine or so reaches to touch your pant leg. The crowd is crushing him against the platform. You stoop and pick him up. He looks surprised. As you lift him, he kicks to free himself from the crowd. His face is a marvel: big Bohunk eyes that grow even bigger as you shift him astride your shoulders. Flash powder goes off and you feel him jerk in fear. You hold him tight around his waist and shout to him that it's all right. He laughs. You can see his scuffed brogans and too short overalls hanging down over your black suit coat.

He accidentally knocks your Stetson off. One of the miners grabs it and whoops as he waves it over his head. The others nearby clap, as if he'd caught a pop foul. Down the length of the train, you make out Gurley Flynn and Tresca on the station platform, waiting and clapping. You hold up your hand for quiet. "Fellow workers!" you shout. They keep shoving and whistling and cheering. You try again. "Fellow workers!" Some of the stiffs nearest you wave for quiet, too. Slowly the jostling and shouting and whistling fade.

You introduce Mother Jones and a hullabaloo breaks out. Her black hat sits cockeyed and her glasses have slipped down on her nose.

"I don't know about you boys," she yells when her voice

can be heard, "but I'm here to give somebody hell! Who's with me?"

The cheering begins again. It keeps going as latecomers swell the crowd and the boys lift Mother Jones down among them. You let it go on for what seems to you a full five minutes before you call for quiet again. "Fellow workers!" you shout. "Mother Jones isn't done yet. She'll have more to say later, I promise you. A good deal more—and she'll keep saying what she has to say until the bosses are where they belong: down in the mines with a shovel in their hands like everybody else!" As the cheering returns, you see the deputies behind the crowd laughing at something their skinny, shotgun-carrying leader says. You ignore them.

Then something wholly unexpected happens. You ask for quiet and begin to speak, but you don't tell the crowd what you'd planned to—the particulars, the tasks. As your words begin to come, the anger, the fear, the impatience, all rise and burn away like impurities in a blast furnace. The words take you over, give shape to a vision, carry you higher and higher on a great hot wave of conviction. You tell the boys about the wonderful dining rooms in the mines and smelters of the new world they'll make with you. They'll eat the best food that can be bought, and they'll dine to sweet music from unexcelled orchestras. They'll have a gymnasium and a great swimming pool and private bathrooms of marble. They'll take their work breaks in museums with masterpieces of art. A first-class library will grace every mill, every smelter. All roofs will have gardens, and all chairs will be Morris chairs, so that when they become weary on the job they can relax in comfort. You give them the future, the paradise they can live to see here on earth, not in some sky-pilot's harp-plucking afterlife.

When you finish you notice Mother Jones watching you oddly. She looks almost amused. Have you made a damn fool out of yourself? But then you look to the faces of the miners. There is no amusement on them, no skepticism. They're quiet, eager, waiting for more. They understand, they know, they are you. You stand motionless in awe of the silence.

Until it is split apart by the deputy's sharp shout. "Runaway!" he yells. "Goddamn runaway!"

By the time you pick him out at the rear of the crowd, he's already breaking for the railroad tracks. You spin to see what he's running toward. Not fifty yards away, on the parallel track, the last car of the empty ore train is moving alone down the incline. It's picking up speed, and the deputy runs at a long angle to try to head it off.

The men nearest the car break for it, too. You swing the boy from your shoulders and push toward the far edge of the platform. The other men part to let you by. But before you even reach the platform steps, the boy is already down them and racing for the runaway car. You run after him and yell for him to come back. He ignores you. He's being a hero for you.

Your breath comes short in the mile-high air. You know you'll never make the car. Only the deputy and the boy have a chance for it. You grab one of the miners who's running past you and tell him to go—quick—to the depot and telegraph the next station to set the derail for the car. You shout for the boy again. Your voice is lost in the yells from the crowd.

The deputy reaches the car first and swings himself up onto the ladder. The boy, arms flailing, catches the coupling and somehow throws himself onto it. A handful of other men lunge for the car and miss. It has its speed now. No one else will make it.

The deputy throws his rifle away and goes hand over hand for the top of the car. You keep your pace, but the car is far outdistancing you, growing smaller. You make out the deputy reaching the wheel for the handbrake, see him struggling with it. It's not moving. The boy still dangles from the coupling. You try to wave him off, but the car rocks around a bend in the tracks and disappears behind a tin building.

You throw all your strength into speed. Your side stabs you. No less than fifty men have outdistanced you by now. But you're still tall enough to see over them, if you can just make the bend. You trip over a tie, flail, get your balance back, then throw yourself forward until you stumble to a stop, your heart ripping from your chest.

The car is still rolling. The deputy, failed at the frozen handbrake, huddles in the cinders a few hundred yards ahead of you. You strain to focus on the coupling, but it's only a dark knob on the end of the car. And then it's gone.

Coupling, car, everything, in a silent flash, rolling smoke. Pieces of things spin away through the overcast air. Everyone stops, frozen, like figures in a news photo.

Then the sound and shock wave hit. Some of the boys ahead of you, smaller men, are knocked to the ground. Behind you, a woman screams. The car is devastated. You can't even make out the wheel trucks as the smoke billows up into the wind. Slowly, one by one, the men around you find their voices and break for the hospital building. The car exploded short of it, but you can see at least half of its windows gaping black, like missing teeth. You can't bear to think of the pieces of things spinning away from the explosion, and of the boy. So you shut your mind off with action. You race for the deputy who tried to stop the car. He is painfully picking himself up from the cinders, and as he does, hunched beneath him is another form. It is the boy.

He blinks up at you with frightened eyes. You drop to one knee. A half dozen other men stop and press in. Beside you, the deputy bends over and brushes the ashes and dirt from the boy's hair.

The air you gasp for comes harsh into your throat. "You hurt anywhere, son?"

"No, sir. Don't reckon."

"Can you stand up?" the deputy asks.

The boy nods and lets the two of you help him unsteadily to his feet. The last of the crowd races past the little circle of men that surrounds and hides you. You notice the deputy's hair is matted with blood.

"I'd look to that," you tell him.

"Directly I see the boy home," he says. "I know his daddy."

Your eye catches his a moment. "I'd be obliged."

He drops his eyes, embarrassed. "He ain't yours to be obliged for." Then, in a tone wavering between embarrassment and anger, he says, "Why in hell don't all of you let us be? What's this here boy got to do with Morris chairs in mills?"

He scoops the boy away from you and pushes through the circle of onlookers. You get to your feet, still breathless and weak from your run. Damn the man! The boy is safe: That's all that does, or ought to, matter now. Because of that, you and the deputy almost touched, almost reached one another. But then he stepped behind that damnable wall of ignorance, that blankness you know so well. The wall you've got to smash somehow, once and for all. What does the boy have to do with Morris chairs in mills? Everything, you want to shout after the deputy. Everything! He's got to see that. Now, here, you've got to make them see, to share your sure knowledge of all the awesome and rigorous connections you know exist among things.

Ahead you see a nurse weeping on the hospital porch, her long white skirt whipping in the wind. Around her, men and women in bedgowns wander aimlessly through the wreckage. Thunder tumbles down the canyon. Deputies shove people back from the grotesquely twisted rails around the crater. You're still a little above the scene on the incline, and you can make out the forms of Tresca and Gurley Flynn and a young blond man. They are arguing with the shotgun-wielding deputy you saw cracking jokes while you made your speech.

Dust clogs your dry throat. You'd give a hundred dollars for a drink of whiskey. You know this was no mere company propaganda stunt. It was a message to you. There will be no second chances here.

Suddenly you're conscious of a presence beside you. A man who barely comes to your shoulders stands with his hands on his hips and calmly watches the chaos around the crater. He wears a dark suit with the coat thrown back over a pistol and holster. There is a badge on his lapel.

"The wonder is," he says without looking at you, "that the walls held. I'd have expected the whole blamed building to collapse. Wouldn't you, Haywood?"

You follow his gaze back to the wreckage. "Wonders never cease, Sheriff."

"They tell me there was a boy almost killed in that."

"There was."

"Don't reckon that was in the plans, was it?"

"Is that a question you'd expect I'd know the answer to?"

"Well." He looks up at you. "I can't figure why the company would want to blow up its own ore car and hospital."

"That would take a deal of explaining to you, Sheriff." You fix your eye on him.

"Might at that." He glances at the lump in your coat pocket. "That what I think it is, Haywood?"

"Most likely."

"You mind giving it to me? I'll see you don't need it."

"Is that a request?"

"No."

You hesitate, then take the revolver from your pocket. What good is one pistol, or a hundred pistols, now. The wrecked hospital tells you that. You've got to have something stronger, bigger than guns.

"I'll see you get it back when you leave town. You ever used it?"

"Hadn't you better see to your men, Sheriff?"

His eyes meet your single one again. They're hard, steady. The dailies in New York think he's good copy. Don Quickshot, one called him. But he's a little man with a gun, and with the power of guns behind him. Merely that.

"You've been in town less than half an hour, Haywood. There's an ore car—war materials—blown up, a hospital wrecked, and a child nearly dead. That's a bad start."

"Somebody intended it to be, I'd imagine." The wind blows the smell of rain to you through the lingering sharp odor of smoke from the explosion. You hear a crunch on the cinders of the railbed behind you. Mother Jones, with a pair of women supporting her, stops beside you.

"The boy?" she says.

"He's all right."

Wheeler takes a step toward the explosion site, then turns. His hand rests on his gun butt. "There's a night train to El Paso. Why don't you go, Haywood, before it's too late?"

"I reckon it already is."

Wheeler measures you with a look. "No," he says. "Not yet." He touches his hat brim to Mother Jones, then with an about-face in the crunching cinders, walks steadily away toward the wreckage.

"Harry Wheeler?" Mother Jones says.

"Harry Wheeler."

"He's a stubby little midget, ain't he?"

A smatter of rain pelts your back. You clutch your warm vision to you. Secretly, you exult. Harry Wheeler is hard, real, solid. He is something you can see and fight. Yes, this is the place you should be. God forgive you, you're almost grateful for it.

Harry Wheeler: July 2, 8:00 P.M.

That Haywood is *not* a pussy. So much you know. Whether he is a Real Man or not remains to be seen. You bet he has used that pistol, and would have used it again. You wonder why he gave in to you so easily this afternoon. But you don't let your mind dwell on it. It's enough to know that a man will give in easily, if you have to count on him. You don't expect you'll have to count on Big Bill Haywood for much but trouble.

There is authority in the man, if he'd only use it. But he won't: None of that damned bunch has any respect for Authority. You've been reading up on them from some things that Captain Greenway gave you. Every man a leader, they claim. Horseshit. No bosses. Horseshit. Greenway's smart, no doubt about it. But if he thought that he could give you a big head and make you overstep your authority last night, he was wrong. You're nobody's fool.

Naturally, the damned army observer, only a lieutenant colonel from Columbus, New Mexico, was on the same train as Haywood. And just your luck that he was one of the first off the train and already safe in the Copper Queen Hotel dining room before the explosion hit. If he'd actually seen it, he'd have changed his tune. But he has no imagination. Nobody knows who set the explosion, he says. There's nothing troops could do now that the local populace can't. You spent nearly an hour with him, but you can see that Greenway, Dowell, and Matthews have him on a leash. Why they're so dead set against troops is beyond you. But they claim that even Walter Douglas says no to troops, and they're not about to cross Walter Douglas. That leaves you in this fix. What is your authority now? You've always thought of yourself as a soldier. Always known that to give orders you've got to know how to take them. Now you've asked for orders. And there's nobody to give them.

But you won't let yourself be stampeded. Not by damned Wobblies, not by Jack Greenway's holy war. You tried to get that across to Haywood today. You'll not desert the sure wisdom of the sign you keep tacked in your office: "To do the right is not difficult. But to know the right and wrong of a thing, that's the task." When you know the right and wrong of this thing, you'll do the right. And nobody will get in your way.

You're alone now, sitting on the cot in the tiny room behind your temporary headquarters in the dispensary. You just got a call through to little Sunshine before she went night-night. While you were in the phone office you made sure that Kellogg, the manager of the phone company, knew that he was on standby to monitor calls. Or shut down if need be. You hope to hell it doesn't come to that. But a boy was almost splattered all over the railroad tracks today. Where will it stop? Is even little Sunshine not safe?

There's no sleep for you yet. This thing has drawn you tight as a new boot. You push up off your cot and walk to the small library desk in the corner of the windowless room. Your drafts of telegrams to Governor Campbell and President Wilson asking for troops lie ready to be sent. To hell with the army observer. Beside them are files on Bo Whitley and half a dozen other IWW leaders in town. They read like police blotters. You've also got an intercepted telegram that went out last week from IWW headquarters. It calls for a general strike, whatever that is. As best you can tell, they want all the mines and smelters in the country to go on strike until every single company settles with the Wobblies. If that's not treason yet, it's within spitting distance.

So you're trying, Lord knows you're trying, to get help. You buckle on your gunbelt and slip into your coat. You've got to get out of this tight room and do something, even if it's wrong. You made a decision after the explosion today. Not to act, necessarily, but to be prepared to act—if your hand's forced. That shift boss Greenway put you on to yesterday lives up on Quality Hill, you recollect. He didn't seem especially bright to you, and is a Mormon to boot, but when you compare the decent way he acted with the horse's ass the Matthews boy made out of himself, he's first rate.

In the outer office a deputy sits lazily reading a western novel. He rises when you pass through. You double-check the city directory for McCrea's address, then give the deputy a few orders and tell him where you can be reached. He tells you not to worry, that he's got everything under control. You doubt it.

Your racing Locomobile and horse stand side by side outside. You poke your head back into the office and tell the deputy to see that your horse is taken care of. You won't need him tonight.

The Locomobile turns over on the second cranking. You listen a moment to the even monotone of the engine. To test it, you stand a half dollar on edge on the hood. It stays there. You've done all the work on it yourself. That's part of the American Genius, the *Review* says.

Satisfied, you ease the Locomobile away from the dispensary onto Main Street and up the snake of Tombstone Canyon. Wobblies hang out on every corner. You suppose the rally up in City Park is over by now. You checked it out earlier; there didn't seem to be as many of them there as you had expected, what with so many big-deal Wobblies in town. You couldn't stay through the whole thing; your stomach was turning. One of their damned speakers, who had some sort of Dago or Frog accent, got worked up and held high a red IWW card during his speech. "Don't a-register for the draft!" he told the mob. "Don't a-buy Liberty Bonds! Let this-a be your Liberty Bond!" And he waved the damn thing around like it was a crucifix.

When the hollering and whooping died down, you heard—very quietly—the voices of some children playing on the balcony of one of the houses on School Hill, over the Gulch. One of them began to sing "America," and the others joined. Voices pure as mountain air. Not many of the mob heard it. You were sure the ones who did looked ashamed.

The Wobblies, gathered in little groups, yell at you as you pass them. Your deputies don't dare stop them. All you need is one of those scummy free-speech fights on your hands, too. You wonder where they get their money from, if not from the Bosch. Doesn't make sense that they could make enough from the sweaty hats they pass around at these rallies and speeches. You make a mental note to try to get hold of their account books. You wish to hell one of the private dicks you're always reading about was on the company payroll. You'd think they could afford that, at least.

You gear down for the turn up to Quality Hill. It's peaceful here up the canyon—where the Wobblies are missing. Not many boardinghouses, and the few that do exist are high-class ones for foremen and machinists. The road to McCrea's house is barely wide enough for your Locomobile. It zig-zags up the steep hillside. McCrea lives in a neat white bungalow on the top knob of the hill. You can see all of Bisbee lighting the canyons below you, like civilization itself filling the desert mountains. You feel a rush of what you've always secretly called your responsibility reflex. They depend on you; you can't desert them. This rotten century hasn't changed that, at least.

Mrs. McCrea, a plain woman with a worried, scrubbed face, is flustered when she sees that it's Sheriff Wheeler himself at the door. You're pleased by that. McCrea looks positively terrified when he comes in from the sleeping porch, where he was apparently about to get into bed. Tonight, his bandages don't keep him from talking, but he stammers like a kid caught poking around in a little girl's panties behind the barn. He seems obsessed with this afternoon's explosion. You assure him that you'll find out which of the Wobblies is responsible. That visibly calms him.

When he seems fully in control of himself, you accept the glass of apple juice his wife offers you and sit him down. His wife leaves you. You feel comfortable here. The house is like your own, clean, simple, in order. You're careful of your words with him. "McCrea," you say, "I want you to be straight with me. I've got no use for a man who won't deal that way. I think you're a man who will."

He nods, but looks a little helpless and apprehensive.

"Last night Jack Greenway was doing all the talking. I want to know one thing: Was he talking for you truthfully or not?"

McCrea hems and haws, and finally winds up with a

yes. "I have that list of names right here with me," he says, and painfully reaches to take a sheet of paper out of the drawer of a commode.

You wave it away. "I don't want to see it, don't want to know who's involved. I only want to know one thing: What strength can you muster?"

"Captain Greenway was right, Sheriff." You really don't like the whining tone of his voice. "Myself, I got no way of knowing until we get the boys together."

You ponder. McCrea seems to get more nervous. "There'll need to be a good many," you say. "You couldn't afford to show weakness. Do more harm than good."

He nods. You wish the hell he'd take the initiative on something.

"There'd have to be a deal of closed-lip about certain parts of this, of course. Are you a close man?"

"I can be," he says.

"I suppose Jack Greenway can size a man up," you say. "I'll have to accept that. Any military training?"

"No, sir."

You reckoned not, from his bearing. Another strike against him. You'll have to make do, though. "I wouldn't have any part of a thing that was more than show of strength, you understand. Something like a patriotic organization, a Loyalty League or some such thing. A morale booster and . . . protective association. Not deputized, not official. Just something that'll make the IWWs think twice. No more monstrosities like this afternoon."

He gets nervous again. You offer him a plug of tobacco. He refuses. Mormons!

"Would you consider . . . ?" he starts timidly. "I mean, do you think a rally of some kind might be a good idea? Captain Greenway says that the Fourth of July is something we might think about helping us out. He thinks nobody but a skunk could refuse to be loyal on the Fourth. He says . . ."

"McCrea, I frankly am a damn sight more interested in what you have to say."

He swallows hard. "We . . . I . . . thought maybe tomorrow night might be a good idea for a rally. With the parade coming up the next day, you know, if we had enough fellows we might even march in it. Strike the fear of the Lord in the IWWs. Captain Greenway sa— "

"Go on," you say.

"I thought maybe the baseball field down in Warren? Since the team went out on strike . . ."

"Not much secrecy possible there. Reckon the IWW will want to bust things up, if they get the chance."

"Oh," he says, wilting. "Yes."

You stand and pace to the window. The man is forcing you to get more involved right now than you want to. You can't afford to look bad if it doesn't come off. But if it does work . . . A Loyalty League. Good name—calls the shot cleanly. Your mind races ahead. A way to test, finally, who's right-thinking and who's not. A weapon even the government doesn't have against this Wobbly Menace. Just how big could it be? you wonder. Patriots' groups all over the country, like during the American Revolution maybe. A virus for every poison, the *Review* said today. You can almost feel the poison seeping through the air.

Your eyes wander down Quality Hill. The steeple of Saint Patrick's Church rises above the trees and houses, outlined against the streetlights of Tombstone Canyon.

"The church," you say, more to the windowpane than to McCrea.

"Sir?"

"You'll have your rally in the church." A church! Not even the IWW would risk busting up a meeting in a church.

"The Mormon Church? I'm not . . ."

"No, McCrea, damn it. My church. Saint Patrick's."

"Could you?"

"You don't know Father Mandin. I do. You can have your rally in Saint Patrick's. I promise you that."

"Oh. I've . . . never been in Saint Patrick's." Can't he come up with a better comment than that? you wonder. Is the man a nitwit?

You try to picture the church packed—sanctuary, steps, loft, aisles, courtyard. How many men could you get in it? Fifteen hundred? More? "It'll do," you say. "You'll need to get under way tonight. Do you have captains in mind for Douglas and Tombstone, too?" Captains. You like the word; it has a good military sound.

"Yessir."

You continue to stare out over Bisbee. "Do you know what happened to Tombstone, McCrea?"

"I'm not sure I know what you . . ."

"Back when they closed the mines, man."

"Oh. It . . . just died, I reckon."

"No, McCrea. It was murdered. Ask them that were there then. When the pumps were pulled, the mines flooded. Forever, McCrea. Labor agitators pulled those pumps. Labor agitators." You picture the canyons of Bisbee dark, with roadrunners and rattlers nestling in the ruins of the Copper Queen Hotel. A ghost town, like the dozens of others you've patrolled in Cochise County. The biggest ghost town of them all. You turn from the window abruptly. "My name's not to be involved in this yet. You understand?"

"Yessir."

"I'll be standing by tomorrow night. I'll decide whether to talk to the boys then."

"Do you want me to ask Captain Greenway and Mr. Dowell to be there? And Mr. Shattuck?"

"Forget Shattuck. The other two, yes." If the thing flops, better Greenway is in the audience than you. "I don't think they'd take it poorly if you contacted them right away."

McCrea gets to his feet again. "I'll go right now."

You take your hat from the table by the door. The table has a silver plate for visitors' cards on it. The plate is empty. You notice a faint scent of lilac water in the air. McCrea hurries to see you to the door. As you leave, you turn to him one last time. He's only three or four inches taller than you. "Don't disappoint me, McCrea," you tell him. He nods. Harry Wheeler is not a man people let down.

Outside, the number of stars seems almost obscene to you. You stand a moment by the running board of the Locomobile and let your eyes follow the sky to the point where it vanishes behind the ridge of the divide to Tombstone. In the opposite direction, the endless desert darkness of Mexico waits beyond the lights of Naco. In either direction, emptiness.

You feel a terrible sense of isolation. It's as if you're alone in the whole world, as if Bisbee were a boat on the ocean. You think that the first settlers must have felt this way fifty years ago. They had to find laws, customs, defenses, that fit this awful isolation. Now it's happening all over again. And there's only one man they can look to. Dowell, Greenway—they have the money, but you have the Law. From under the seat of the Locomobile, you bring out a pewter whiskey flask. It's full, and you take a long swig. The burning in your throat holds back the cold isolation of the stars and desert. That's good, the first good thing you've found since you got the phone call that the damned Wobblies had voted to strike.

At the dispensary, you slip your flask into your hip pocket before you go into your office. The deputy, under a bare light bulb, jumps to his feet when you come through the door. You grunt to him and keep walking toward your cubicle.

"Sheriff Wheeler." You pause. "I thought you'd want to . . ."

"I don't want to hear nothing unless it's good news," you tell him without turning.

" 'Tis. We lost one of them."

"One of them what?"

"Them Wobblies. One of the big shot ones."

You turn to him now. He's hangdog but pleased. "Haywood?"

"No—I wish it was. It's that Dago, Carlos or whatever."

"Tresca?"

"Yessir. Left town. Johnny Medicovich that runs the motor stage to Douglas come to tell you. The Dago's taken the last stage out. Johnny heard him and that woman of his having an awful row. Dago said he was going to catch the next train east from Douglas."

"He say why?"

"Johnny seemed to think it had more to do with the woman than the strike."

It could be a trick of some kind. They're slippery bastards. Gone off to get more German money, maybe. Maybe. But where there's a woman involved, who the hell ever knows? The thought of the Flynn woman, alone now, causes a little thrill to run through your groin. You squelch it. It wasn't a manly feeling. You'd near about as well have a whore on the Gulch as somebody like that.

You grunt at the deputy again and go into your cubicle. The antiseptic walls depress you. You slip the flask out and take another slug. You're not a drinking man. But there are times. You reach to unbuckle your gunbelt, then stop. You think of Remedios, "your woman." Remedios is warm, listens but doesn't talk much. You need something warm to drive away the coldness of the stars and the dark desert. Something to bury yourself in for a little while. In the morning, the Wobblies will still be waiting.

You check yourself in the small mirror you've tacked onto the wall. You need a shave. But Remedios won't care. You'd vowed not to do this, but the whiskey makes a man need things. Even if he doesn't want to need them.

The deputy is surprised when you come back through the office. You wave him down into his chair. "Going for a walk," you say.

To avoid being seen, you climb up Opera Drive to City Park, then swing down onto the Gulch beyond the cardrooms and saloons. It's quieter here, people asleep. They've learned long ago not to notice who goes by on the way to the Line. Nonetheless, you stick close to the edge of the road, in the shadows.

Remedios has a room in one of the green cribs on the hillside behind the Mint. A good private place. You stop in the shadow of a chinaberry tree to take another shot. The flask is half empty now.

Nobody has seen you so far. You begin the climb up the steps, then the wet path to Remedios's crib. Out of habit, you scan the mountainside ahead of you. Nobody on any of the paths or steps.

And then—you can't even be sure you're seeing them at first in the dark—you spot two people outlined against the pale sky. They're on High Road, the old wagon trail that leads to Dixie Canyon and the High, Lonesome Road across the desert. You strain to focus. The whiskey doesn't help. But it's two people all right, a man and a woman. Just standing there, watching. They're looking in your direction, and you cuss the streetlight you've just passed under. Who in hell would be up on a deserted wagon road at ten o'clock at night, what with Wobblies on a rampage?

You hesitate, consider going back. But the coiling in

your cock won't go away. To hell with whoever's on High Road. What you do is your own damn business. And what are the chances that they've recognized you anyway? You climb on. One last time you look up toward High Road before you step onto Remedios's porch. The woman is out of sight. The man still stands, watching.

There's no surprise in Remedios when she answers your knock. She simply smiles her slow, Indian-Mex smile and takes your hand to lead you inside. Her face is wide and olive, but her eyes have that Oriental slant to them that has always driven you wild. Ever since your first time with an Apache squaw back at Fort Sill.

"I have wait you," she says. She's dressed in a cheap satin dress, and smells of heavy Mex perfume. You know little about her. She's from Sonora somewhere, and has a kid or two—they all do—that she's farmed out to some woman in Naco to raise. She's in her late twenties, you guess, with a grown woman's full round curves. What you do know about her is the way she uses her mouth, the little bites up and down your body, the noises she makes when she wraps her legs around you. That's what brings you back to her. She never charges you, though you've left money hidden here and there on occasion. You pay her with something that is worth more to her than money: protection.

She's made a shade for her bare light bulb out of some red paper. It makes the room glow. The walls are rough planks, with the biggest decoration a niggerish plaster shrine to the Virgin of Guadalupe that has an always lighted candle in front of it. Otherwise, scattered pictures from magazines hang here and there among half a dozen hooks with dresses on them. A Chinese screen in one corner gives her privacy: You've always wondered what those swooshing and squirting noises are that she makes behind there when you finish with her. The bed is high, brass, with a blue satin bedspread. The clay charcoal brazier that gives her heat in the winter sits underneath the only window in the room.

But the ceiling is the best part; it's a genuine balloon ceiling, a painted cloth she claims she got from one of the girls' rooms of the Birdcage Theater in Tombstone. Nymphs and satyrs chase one another around the border.

The center is a huge painting of a glen in the woods with lords and half-naked ladies lounging among deer and rabbits. It's real art, you know that. And it hung in the Birdcage, where Luke Short and Doc Holliday used to spend their nights. You've lain with Remedios after lovemaking, wondering what their women were like, if they were better than yours.

"Sit," Remedios says. "Your boots." She points to the ragged armchair in a corner of the room. You unbuckle your gunbelt—after a quick check behind the screen—and collapse into the chair. You're tired, God how tired! You hadn't realized. Remedios squats to pull your boots off. You slide out your flask and take another long pull. Not much left now. Got to slow down.

Your boot comes off with a jerk, and Remedios lands on her butt on the floor. She giggles and holds out her hand for the whiskey. You shake your head. You don't like to see women drink. She shrugs and gathers herself for an assault on the other boot. You're relaxing now; the red glow in the room reminds you of a good fire on a winter evening. You feel safe.

Your other boot plops off, and Remedios reaches for your tie. You push her gently away. You want to prolong this peaceful moment. She looks at you, puzzled. "In a minute," you say. Her eyes watch you like that squaw's in Oklahoma. You're not really listening to yourself as you begin to talk. You're remembering. Remedios sits on the bed and listens quietly without understanding. You're sleepy, and the words are a song you're singing to yourself.

". . . Fort Sill," you're saying. "The Apaches adopted me —first white man they ever did that to. I wasn't but twenty or so, and I helped 'em out. They couldn't leave the reservation, but I was a scout and could. There was a scummy bunch of hill people in those days, used to come down and take the Apache's cattle, and know the Apaches couldn't come after them. I took it on myself to bust the thing up, and did. Me and a handful of horse soldiers. That's when they adopted me.

"But then the Spanish War came along, and I had to leave for the Philippines—a deal of us did, and the colonel arranged for a going away ceremony. Parade, band, all of it.

And the Apaches showed up; I had a woman among 'em, too. Must have been five thousand of them, with the old chief himself in front. The colonel saw them. He was a hard old boy, a friend of my father's. Won his commission fighting Indians. He sent me to find out what the Apaches wanted. They said they'd come to say good-bye to me. Had themselves all painted to dance for me."

The memory has hold of you now and won't let you go. Remedios doesn't move. You finish the whiskey and close your eyes. Apaches are all around you, spread across the low hills of Oklahoma.

"I was right touched. Any man would have been. When I rode back to the colonel to tell him what they wanted, I thought he'd be pleased. But he told me to get rid of them —said so many Indians made him nervous. I didn't say a word. I was a soldier, and I had an order. I rode back straight to the chief and ordered him to leave. He just looked at me. For a full minute, it seemed. Then he turned to the others and told them in Apache what I'd said. I didn't explain, couldn't explain. I had an order.

"The old chief pulled his blanket over his head and turned his back on me. Then they all did, all five thousand of them, like dominoes. Not a one of them looked back when they left."

You don't know if you're actually talking or not now. You know the words are low, that Remedios isn't hearing anyway. "I went back after the war. Rode to the reservation. They didn't any of them speak to me. All along the line, they put their blankets over their heads and turned their backs. My squaw had a baby by then. Indian baby, by a brave."

The room is quiet. You can hear Remedios's breathing. You ask her to come to you, in Apache. You haven't spoken it for years. She doesn't understand and sits waiting on the bed.

Your head is spinning now. You focus on Remedios's Oriental eyes. You fight to your feet. The whiskey flask hangs dead in your hand, like an empty pistol. You fling it hard across the room. It smashes the clay charcoal brazier.

"I had orders, goddamn it!" you hear yourself shout to her. "I'll never regret it to the day I die. Do you understand, damn it! I had orders!"

Remedios comes wordlessly to you. She eases you down onto the bed, and loosens your tie. You have no strength left. She slips your coat off, then unbuttons your shirt and piles the studs neatly on the armchair. By the time she has your shirt off, you feel your cock straining against your pants. She massages it, gently. You tell her in Apache that it feels good. She unbuttons your pants and lowers her head.

Above you, the nymphs and satyrs chase one another around the border of the ceiling Doc Holliday lay under. Tomorrow the Wobblies will still be there. And so will Harry Wheeler. You reach for Remedios's full breast.

Elizabeth Gurley Flynn: July 2, 10:00 P.M.

Whitley hasn't spoken since they left the last street behind. Elizabeth doesn't know why she's here with him at all, on an old wagon road high above the town in the cool damp of the night. She only knows that she had to get out of the smoky meeting hall of the Pythian Castle before she screamed, and Whitley was there to take her away. For the past hour they've plunged up and down the nonsense streets of Bisbee while Whitley mumbled explanations of things they passed as if he were a tour guide. She hasn't the slightest idea why he's doing it, but that doesn't matter. It was what she needed.

It's the first chance she's had to think since the explosion and Tresca's leaving. She was sure she'd never get through the rally. And then the stuffy strike committee meeting! How long had Tresca been planning to leave? He wouldn't tell her—wouldn't explain anything to her. Just showed up at the Ewings' with his valise before the rally and let her make a fool of herself at the motor stage office. She thinks she may be in a kind of shock, and needed someone to lead her around like a mule while she tried to come out of it.

Tresca's leaving was hard, even though she knows he's right. This is not his world, his kind of strike. Carlo is at home in Paterson, New York, Chicago—among tenements and basement printing presses, not Arizona gunslingers. So why should he waste union money here? But there was a brutal unfairness in his leaving, too. He wasn't afraid to stay, she knows that. It was more as if he were playing with her. Stay here with Whitley, he was saying. Find out where you belong. He was throwing her away to prove she'd come back to him. She doesn't need that now: Christ, she needs a man with her, not against her. But none of that really explains the thing that she's felt most strongly of all since he left—a sense almost of relief.

Nor does it explain why she is here with Whitley, alone on a bare mountainside with only the light of the stars and a bright moon.

Whitley stands at the edge of the wagon ruts, shading his eyes against the moon. He seems to be watching something on the Gulch below. She steps up beside him and strains to see down through the darkness. All she can make out are the outlines of the whorehouses she saw yesterday afternoon.

"It's Harry Wheeler," he says. His voice is contemptuous.

"Where?"

"There, by the streetlight above the Mint."

"I don't see him."

"He's out of the light now."

She watches the steps far below them a moment more, then turns back to the cool light of the stars. Damn Harry Wheeler. There was nearly a child dead, no older than her Buster. Wheeler could have stopped it, she's certain. He's in collusion with the fatcats who planned it. And now he's celebrating with a whore, down there in that tangled town. Add that bitterness to her other jumbled emotions: frustration with Carlo and a terrible sense she's being unfair to Bo. Why in the name of all the saints is she here? She could have stayed in Chicago to get her strength back. Nobody would have faulted her after that terrible trial in Duluth. She asks herself for the dozenth time: Would she have come to Bisbee if she hadn't known Bo might be here?

Bo turns away from his watching. "He's gone into a crib," he says.

"A what?"

"A cathouse." Bo says the word harshly. It's as if something about Wheeler were her fault.

She doesn't answer. She can feel one of Bo's moods working itself up. She recoils from the thought of having to deal with it. Now, of all times. She can't make him out clearly in the dim light, but she can feel him near her. She's never been able to sense a man, physically, that way before.

He walks a few paces ahead of her up the dark road. "You were good with Haywood at the rally," he says.

"Anybody looks good on a stage with Bill." Haywood was at his best tonight, more elated than she's seen him in years. There's no one better. He can hold a crowd that doesn't speak six words of English. Takes his huge hand and spreads the fingers apart and lets it hang limp and weak, like working people without organization. Then he wraps it up into a fist, the biggest fist she's ever seen, roars "IWW," and smashes it down onto the lectern. It always works. You have to have a fist like Bill's to pull it off. He can make her believe things she's almost forgotten she could.

"I didn't see him at the strike committee meeting afterward."

"No."

"Nor Mother Jones either."

Elizabeth sighs. "She's . . . with Haywood." She hadn't wanted to go into this. On top of everything else, this. "He's been on the wagon for months, Bo. But he . . . fell off after the rally tonight. Mother Jones is sitting with him."

Bo stares off ahead of him, up the dark road. His back is to her. "What does that mean?"

"Take your pick," she says. "He's worst when he's on top of the world. Or worried."

"Is Tresca a dehorn, too?"

Damn! He's stalking her again, throwing her off balance. She should have known. He keeps his back to her and takes another step up the old road. Then he stops, as if he's listening to see if she follows.

"Don't want to talk about him?"

"I'm going back down, Bo. Show me the path."

"No, not yet. I thought you might want to get it off your chest."

"No, thank you," she says curtly. Of all people to offer her a shoulder now! She wishes Mother Jones were free tonight. Since she lost her husband and all her family in a yellow fever epidemic, she's never had a real home, and has spent more time in and out of jails than any woman in the country—yet the woman's spirit! Where does it come from? If only she could break off a little piece of it, like a starter culture for bread. . . .

"Rather talk to Art Matthews?" Bo says. His voice is noncommittal.

"I asked you to show me the path, Bo."

"Or haven't you been invited to Art's little party tomorrow night? Engagement party, ain't it? I didn't see your name in the guest list in the *Review* today. Mistake, I guess."

She moves away from him down the road. He can play his games alone up here till doomsday. She got up the hill; she'll find a way down.

"Think I'll go to the party," he calls after her.

She stops, turns to him again. "You'll what?"

"Go to Art's engagement party."

"What on earth are you talking about?"

He faces her now across the half dozen yards between them. "They got to have a band and waiters, ain't they? And if they're working, they sure ain't striking." He moves closer. She can see his grin. "Figure I'll do me a little organizing."

She's stupefied. "At the Bisbee Country Club?"

"Yep. Me and a couple of other stiffs might."

"Why, for God's sake?"

"Why not?"

She shakes her head, speechless.

"Give me one good reason why not," he persists.

"You want a hundred?"

"The bombing today—you're worried about how they're going to use that on us? Or tell me about how they're going to use the Fourth to work up the scissorbills against us. Oh, hell, I know all that, Lizzie."

"Bo, Jesus, there'll be more guns around that place than . . ."

"More than one way to get somewhere if you know the land well enough."

"Have you talked to Haywood?"

"Should I? I wasn't planning on inviting him."

"*Jesus,* Bo. Christ Jesus."

"You want to come?"

"Ohhhh . . . I'm in no shape for this." She sinks down onto a boulder beside the road.

"Bet Tresca never took you to a country club. Of course, I ain't got my tails with me. . . ."

"Bo, just . . . shut up a minute, will you?"

He throws his leg out in front of himself again, in that cocky pose. The bastard. In the middle of what could be the most important strike in their lives, after she's just said good-bye to the man she's lived with for four years, he brings her up here to talk to her about something nitwitty like this. They're in one of the most damn isolated spots on earth surrounded by who knows how many gun-crazy cowboys on the Fourth of July with a war on and he wants to bust up the bosses' biggest social blowout of the season. It's childish, politically pointless, wasteful.

Then suddenly she sees the look on the face of that little snot Art Matthews is engaged to when they walk in to her party. Art's old man going red above his stiff collar. All the girdled richbitches flapping their handkerchiefs and squawking—the stuffed officers from Fort Huachuca sputtering and yelling orders at one another like Keystone Cops. Why not? Bo said. Of course. It's so clear. Why not? How long has it been since she's said that?

Suddenly she's laughing, without meaning to. The idiot, the grand idiot. She tries to catch her breath to stop the laughing and can't. But, no—she doesn't want to stop it. Tresca would have catfits if he knew, and that seems even funnier. She sees Bo's grin widen, hears his own laughter. She holds out her hands to him. In her laughter there's a relief as clean and natural as this stupid spangled desert sky. She lets herself relax into it. Bo steps to her, takes her hands and lifts her. Her eyes are blurred from laughing. He pulls her after him along the wet rocky road. They trip against each other and she's sure they'll fall off the edge of the mountain on top of Harry Wheeler in his whorehouse.

That gives her another giggling fit. Oh, God, she's needed a Bo Whitley, the bastard.

She makes out the dim shape of walls ahead of them. As they come close, she sees that they form a stone house that looks long empty and untended. Bo leans against it and throws his head back gasping. He pulls her to him and she lets herself fall against his chest. She drops her head onto his shoulder to smother another rush of giggles. "You son of a bitch," she says and pummles his ribs.

He lifts her head and wipes her tear-streaked face with his handkerchief. She smells the damp stone walls, the bittersweet of desert trees after a rain—nothing that reeks of the mines or machinery below. The sense of relief has wound through her whole body now and left her limp.

Bo hesitates. "Would you be here if Tresca wasn't gone?" he asks.

"Shut up with Tresca." She puts her arm around his neck.

"No, I mean it. Do you love him?"

She hesitates. "Not now." She braces herself against the stone wall with one hand and with the other brings his face down to hers.

"Not tired anymore?" Bo says, close to her lips.

"Not now." She holds his head tight, kisses him, presses herself against him. To hell with Tresca. She's not any man's dog; she's no man's dog. Bo's hands slip down to the small of her back and pull her hips against him. His motions are firm, quick, and she moves with them.

He pushes away from the wall, finds a doorway, empty, and draws her into it. "Careful," he says, and helps her over a low stone stoop. The house has no roof, and framed by the ragged stone walls the stars above appear even thicker. There is no floor, only packed leaves from an acorn tree that grows in one corner of the room. Bo takes his coat off and spreads it on the leaves.

"You planned this," she says.

"Uh-huh," he says and slips his arms around her waist again.

"Maybe I did, too," she says, and draws him down onto the coat and the cool, wet leaves.

The mountain night wind slips cold into the empty doorway. She's been someplace between waking and sleeping, floating, letting go of things. Heavy things, bags and boxes full of them. She lifts her head. Bo stands in the doorway, shirtless. Beyond him, only a few lights from the Mexican huts of Zacatecas dot the far mountainside.

"Bo?" she says, full of ease and sleep. She has the odd sense that they're back in Montana, that she's eighteen and incredibly in love and calling him to bed. That nothing at all has happened since then, or will.

"I'm here," he says.

"Where are we?"

"High Road, it's called."

"This house, I mean."

"Used to be a watchman's house in Geronimo's time, they say."

She stretches and curls tighter on his coat. "Aren't you cold?"

"I suppose. I wasn't thinking about it."

"What were you thinking about?"

"When I was a kid. My mamma used to say Geronimo just sat up here on his horse like he was trying to figure out why in hell anybody would want to put a town down there. She used to say she understood that."

"Was it different here when you were a boy?"

He turns so sharply it startles her. "It was never different, and never will be. No matter what Bill Haywood thinks he can do."

She doesn't want to think about Bill Haywood now, nor strikes, nor . . .

"We need to talk." Bo's voice is harsh.

"About what?"

"About us."

"No we don't," she says quickly.

"I need to know things, Lizzie. About the way you feel."

"Don't you already? Come here." She stretches her arms out for him.

He kneels, but doesn't move closer. She wants him to come to her again, to keep the warm half-sleep on her. In Montana they would lie until nearly dawn some nights, not thinking.

"No . . . it'll eat me up until you tell me. Why did you come here? For me? You knew I'd be here."

She sits up and pulls his coat around her shoulders. She hands him his shirt. "Put this on before you freeze."

"Answer me, Lizzie."

"Yes, Bo . . . I imagine I thought you'd be here."

"And you came here for that, didn't you?"

She looks past him at the lights from Zacatecas. Did she come for him? Why does he want to force her to think at all now? She needs something else from him. During their lovemaking, she had it, had his energy, his toughness. She wants that to be enough. It seems that she's been doing nothing but thinking for longer than she can remember. She needs desperately to learn how to feel things again, the way Bill Haywood made her feel today that the world was full of possibilities. Or the way Bo once made her feel that love, too, was full of possibilities. Not to think things to death, just to feel and do. It strikes her suddenly that the secret she wished she had from Mother Jones must be precisely that. To believe, to act. To live this strike, this life, and to let the rest go to hell.

She lets her eyes focus on Bo again in the dim light. "Yes. I came here for that."

"And Tresca?"

She pulls Bo's coat tighter around her. "Tresca's . . . gone."

Bo's hand reaches out and slips under the coat. He lets it rest on her breast. It is cool as the leaves beneath her. "I never quit loving you, Lizzie."

A rush of tenderness, almost desperate tenderness, swirls over her. She trails her fingers along his bare arm and presses his hand harder onto her breast. Give yourself some stars, Flynn, and some mountains and a man and see what happens to you. Like a farmer's daughter on a hayride. She knows she ought to keep him at a distance, to put her energy into the general strike, where it belongs. But she pulls him closer and slips her arms around him. The coat falls open. Bo feels warm against her bare breasts.

"Tell me about the country club, Bo," she says.

"We'll set 'em back on their cans," he says. "Like we used to."

She doesn't know whether she loves this man or not—

has never known. But now, for this time, this place, she can —she will. Tomorrow, next week . . . is tomorrow, next week. No more. Love and fairness and next week, next year: what do they have to do with one another?

As she pulls Bo back down onto the leaves with her, she has a last glimpse of the lights of Bisbee through the broken doorway. They seem to outnumber the stars. Wheeler must be down there somewhere in his whorehouse, she thinks. Wheeler, too. Wheeler is tomorrow, too.

Jim Brew: July 3, 9:30 P.M.

Striking is one thing; busting into the country club is another. If he wasn't so afraid that Bo would think he was letting him down, there's no way in hell he would have got roped into it. To begin with, he's too blessed old. Taking the streetcar out to the car barn in Warren, then sneaking through the desert behind the country club in the dark! Lord! There's no point in it that he can see. He doesn't mind roughing up some scabs. But country boys and country clubs don't go together at all.

They're lucky to have gotten as far as they have, Jim thinks. There's only four of them: Bo, Miss Flynn, the man named Hamer, and himself. Bo says he doesn't think they'll really get anybody to join the strike, but he and Miss Flynn are doing a right smart of giggling about something. Hamer doesn't seem to think much of the idea either, so he and Jim bring up the rear.

They've snuck through the golf course, which has more rattlesnake holes and railroad tracks in it than places to hit the ball, so far as Jim can tell. He's never been this close to the country club before. It sits right in the desert foothills of the Mule Mountains, overlooking Naco. You can see it a long way off. Bo showed them how to get to it down an old burro trail that nobody but Bisbee kids knew about.

There are floodlights all around the club, and more fancy cars than Jim can remember seeing in one place before. Jim and the others pause for a minute at the edge of the lights while Bo figures out the best way to get in. It won't be easy. Seems to Jim that he can see a deputy with a rifle leaning on every third car. That's why there weren't many of them at the rally in the park tonight. Probably for the best, too, that they didn't hear the things the Wobs have planned for the Fourth. Some of the stuff would piss off a pope. Jim sort of regrets that. He's always looked forward to the drilling contest and burro races and parades.

A motor van from the company store is parked just back of the clubhouse unloading something. Bo thinks their best bet is to make a run for it and sneak in through the kitchen. Hamer doesn't like the idea of running. Bo and Miss Flynn laugh at him. Then he laughs, too, and everybody feels like they're having lots of fun. Even Jim feels better.

Bo dashes out into the lights first. Miss Flynn is right behind him. Hamer and Jim have kind of a footrace, and Jim wins. When they get close to the clubhouse, Jim sees it's all made out of redwood with big gables and a wide porch around three sides. American flags fly from all the gables and bunting hangs from the eaves. Band music, a waltz, comes from inside. They all catch their breath a minute and listen to the music. Miss Flynn says the people are dancing on the edge of a cliff, and Hamer says amen, let it crumble.

Suddenly a couple of men in butcher's aprons come out of a door. Bo and Hamer and Miss Flynn go up to them and say something that Jim can't catch. The men look upset, but take off their aprons. Bo and Hamer put them on and go inside with a load of meat from the back of the truck. The two men get into the van and drive away too fast. Bo and Hamer come back out to say that the door leads into the kitchen and they can get into the ballroom from there.

Jim's nerves act up, and even Miss Flynn asks Bo if he still thinks it's a good idea. Jim doesn't believe he felt as nervous as this when he fought Geronimo's braves. But Bo tells them to come on, and they do.

The people in the kitchen look surprised when they see Miss Flynn. They're mostly Mex cooks, but there's a white woman supervising them. Jim talks a little Mex and Bo asks him to tell the cooks that there's a strike on and they have to go home. The woman supervisor makes for the door. Miss Flynn picks up a skillet and the woman stops.

"Hay una huelga," Jim says. *"Por qué están aquí? Vámonos!"* He thinks that's what Bo wanted. Anyway, it's as close as he can get. The Mexes seem to understand and jabber among themselves a minute.

Then one of them says that they have families and have to feed them. Jim translates. Bo says that the Mexes should take whatever food they need for their families and go home. Jim translates and the Mexes jabber some more. Then the one who seems to be the spokesman throws up his hands and cusses and starts gathering up bread and pots full of food. It all smells pretty good to Jim. He'd be just as glad to go with the Mexes, but he's feeling good about translating.

The woman supervisor, a chubby woman with gray hair and a Cornish Cousin Jack accent, wails that they're stealing. Miss Flynn tells her she thinks that's a miserable attitude for a working woman who's feeding the biggest thieves of all. Hamer laughs.

One of the Mexes tries to pick up a case of whiskey instead of food, and Bo whacks his hand. The women have made baskets out of their aprons and the men take double armloads of everything from raw meat to lettuce. They're scuttling out the door as fast as they can. Some of them are laughing. A waiter busts through the swinging doors and yells at them when he sees what's happening. Hamer grabs the waiter by his white jacket. The man shuts up. Hamer tells him he's a goddamn scab and that he better go home. The man follows the Mexes out the back door. Hamer doesn't seem to care if the man tells the deputies outside or not.

Bo and Hamer take off their butcher's aprons. Bo has his tough kid's grin now. He whacks Miss Flynn on the bottom and she throws a loaf of bread at him. She's a cute little shit, Jim thinks. Bo peeks through the swinging doors out into the ballroom. They've planned it all pretty well. Bo and Miss Flynn will stop the band. Jim and Hamer will position themselves in front of the bandstand and keep whoever they can away until Miss Flynn has a chance to make a little speech. They don't figure they'll have long. Bo's counting on surprise to get them through. Then they'll have to run like hell. Miss Flynn won't be able to run so well, but she thinks the deputies won't rough her up much anyway.

Bo turns to them. "Ready to let the plutes know the One Big Union's in town?" The Cousin Jack supervisor finds a cane-bottom chair and plops in it. She looks horrified.

Jim can't stand it. He can tell Bo's worried sick. He never could abide seeing him worried. When Bo was a kid, Jim would sit up with him half the night sometimes and show him card tricks to keep him from worrying about his mamma. So what the hell. No reason Bo should have to go first. Jim Brew's good for something besides eating beans and farting. Before he has time to study on it, he flings the swinging doors open.

He's less than a yard into the ballroom before he freezes. No matter how much he wants them to, his feet won't move. It's as bad as the time Reverend Jackwood caught him crapping in the church basement. The room is long as a change room in a mine, with big beams across the peaked roof. To his left is the bandstand, and just in front of him two sets of French doors to the porch. A huge electric chandelier hangs from the center of the roof and sends sparkles of light down on the people. To his right against the wall is a long table set up for a bar with half a dozen stiffs in white jackets and bow ties pouring drinks and punch. The floor is hardwood, waxed to shine like somebody had put a sheet of glass over it. Deer heads and paintings and crystal light fixtures and flags and bunting hang on the paneled walls. A light breeze blows the green curtains out into the room like willow limbs, and his nose picks up a faint mixture of cigar smoke and perfume. He's never seen anything like it, even at the White House casino and whorehouse down in Naco.

But most of all it's the people who stop him. Maybe a couple of hundred of them. Half of them dancing, swirling around to a waltz in the middle of the floor. Officers in dress uniforms and capes, bosses in tails and patent-leather shoes, women in gowns that have a dozen yards of material in them. All swirling around in the sparkles of light from the chandelier. It's like a picture on a calendar. He feels like a son of a bitch.

But then Bo has his coat sleeve and pulls him along toward the bandstand. Nobody has really noticed them yet; they're all too busy. So the bandleader is surprised as hell when Bo jumps up and grabs for his baton. Bo wins it by shoving the man off the bandstand. The band straggles to a stop. The dancers trail off like dolls on music boxes winding down. And for a moment there's the loudest silence Jim has ever heard. Everybody just stops stock-still and looks toward the band. Mr. Dowell and Captain Greenway and Dr. Bledsoe and Mr. Matthews and Art; nearly every big shot he's ever seen in his life is here. It's awful. He wants to die.

One of the army officers, a major, is the first to move. He throws his shoulders back and steps toward the bandstand. He's a tall graying man who holds himself as straight as an ironing board. Jim throws himself in front of him. The major looks up at Jim and stops.

"There's a strike on in this town!" Bo yells and looks toward the band, then the waiters behind the bar. "Anybody working here tonight is a scab and a traitor to his fellow workers. We know you're here and now we know who you are. Look to yourselves, then go home and look to your families. There's not a real man among you that would leave his family alone and scab at a time like this. Go home!"

The crowd starts to mumble now. A big woman standing next to Mr. Matthews looks as if she's about to have an apoplexy. She's poking at him and he's turning red as a whore's bloomers. But nobody else has moved. Jim keeps scanning the people to head anything off. His eyes stop when they get to Captain Greenway. He's dressed like an advertisement, relaxing and watching Bo. Jim could swear the man is smiling.

Miss Flynn starts to speak just as the French doors slam open and a covey of deputies tumbles into the room. Captain Greenway, who is right by the door, flings out his arm to stop them. "You'll not get rid of us!" Miss Flynn shouts in that funny Bronx accent she has. "You'll not go on gorging yourselves and dancing while your wage slaves starve in your bloodstained mines and mills. You're drinking our sweat tonight, not champagne. You're paying your killers and gunmen with our blood. But we're here to tell you that we can stop every wheel in creation, and we mean to do it. Your putrid war . . ."

"Treason!" somebody shouts from the dance floor.

"Murderers!" Miss Flynn shouts back.

Jim knows now is the time to get the hell out. Run while they've got a chance. The bosses are getting ahold of themselves. One of the deputies trains his rifle on Miss Flynn. Half a dozen other men and women take up yelling "Treason!"

And then the thing Jim expected least of all happens. A girl, the slight girl he remembers waiting for Art Matthews at the train station, breaks away from Art's side and marches toward the bandstand. Mrs. Matthews runs out of the crowd and tries to pull her back, but the girl shakes her off and keeps coming. Looks neither left nor right, but marches straight for Miss Flynn.

She's all alone on the waxed dance floor. A pale girl in a cold blue gown. For a moment Jim can't get it out of his head that the dance floor is ice, and the girl is sliding across it. And he can't stop her. He can't knock her back like he could have the army officer. He's never pushed a woman around in his life except squaws and whores. Hamer isn't moving either. He's in the same fix. Jim looks to Bo. Bo seems as helpless as Hamer. Only Miss Flynn looks ready; she shifts her position ever so slightly, like she's bracing herself.

The girl cuts sharply around to the end of the bandstand and up the steps without slowing her pace. On the stand, the musicians shove to get out of her way. She stops like a soldier coming to attention just two feet away from Miss Flynn.

"You hussy," she says so everybody can hear. "How *dare* you do this at my engagement party? Don't you have any sense of decency?"

Bo hoots first. Miss Flynn struggles to keep her face straight but doesn't have any luck at it. She bursts out laughing. Right in the pale girl's face. The pale girl doesn't flinch.

Instead her hand flies up quick as a mule's hind leg.

Catches Miss Flynn square on the eye. Miss Flynn can't stop laughing. So the slight girl makes a fist out of her hand and slugs Miss Flynn on the nose. With the other hand, she reaches for her hair.

"Bunny, don't!" Art Matthews is to the bandstand before Jim can head him off, but Hamer catches his cape and jerks him backward just as he leaps for the stand. Matthews splats down on his back. Then Miss Flynn stops laughing.

The girl has ahold of her hair, pulling hard. Miss Flynn clasps her hands together to make a double fist and brings it down on the pale girl's neck. The girl screams and lets go. Miss Flynn swings again, and the girl totters off the bandstand. Art Matthews tries to get to his feet and catch her, but it's too late. She sprawls beside him.

Bo grabs Miss Flynn and pulls her toward the kitchen door. Hamer bolts behind them. The deputies shove through the crowd and a dozen of the younger men join them.

"No shooting, no shooting!" Mr. Dowell shouts. Jim moves as fast toward the door behind Bo and the others as his stiff bones let him. The Cousin Jack supervisor woman gets to the swinging doors just as Bo and Miss Flynn do. They run her down.

Jim gets through the swinging doors just in time to fling them back hard into the deputies. It slows them a second but not enough. Bo and the others are at the back door and Hamer is yelling at Bo to take one of the cars outside. Jim leaps down the back steps right behind them, and stumbles. He pitches forward into the hard caliche dirt. Bo, seeing him go down, doubles back to help.

And then it's too late. Before Jim can get to his feet, a herd of deputies from the parking lot charges around the building. He looks up at the leader of the deputies. It's Shotgun Johnson. Oh, shit.

Jim lunges for the nearest deputy, who sidesteps and catches him on the side of the head with his rifle butt. Jim sprawls but doesn't feel any pain yet. A young fellow in tails dives on him like a football player, and Jim flings him off into the crowd.

But it's Bo they're after. A couple of the deputies push Hamer against the spare tire of a roadster and shove a rifle into his belly. Bo swings in half a dozen directions at once, without connecting much with anybody. Shotgun Johnson dances just out of Bo's reach and hollers at the other deputies not to shoot. Miss Flynn throws herself into the ring of deputies beside Bo and kicks at anybody who gets too close.

It's turned into a kind of party now. The deputies whoop and jump out of reach of Bo and Miss Flynn like they were fighting cocks. Some of the young men in tails laugh; Jim hears one of them offering odds. He tries to get to his feet again, but something heavy hits him between the shoulders and he goes down on his face.

He has a harder time getting up than before. When he gets to his hands and knees, Bo is alone. He can't see so well now that the deputies have closed in tighter, but he catches sight of Miss Flynn pinned against the building by three or four men and the Cousin Jack supervisor woman from the kitchen. The laughing and hooting from the crowd has tapered off into a more serious growling noise. Like a pack of coyotes makes when it's chucking a rabbit back and forth among itself. Jim catches a glimpse of Art Matthews like a beanpole at the edge of the pack, trying to pull men away from Bo, but getting flung back himself.

Bo has to be tired. Jim can see the deputies throwing up their rifles to ward off his fists. Bo goes down. They kick at him now, Shotgun Johnson closer in than the others. They're going to kill him, kill him slow. Jim can't see anything except Shotgun Johnson's boots and Bo's face through Johnson's legs. He doesn't give a good goddamn where he is or why; he's got to stop those damn boots. He lunges to his feet.

He slams into the circle of men around Bo with his arms outspread like an ore scoop. He hits their backs, catches them off balance, and the whole circle stumbles before him. He roars things at them that don't make any sense even to himself. Three or four of them trip over Bo and he sees Bo flail at one of them with his brass knucks.

Jim has no idea at all what he's doing. He's grabbing at whatever he can reach, slamming whatever heads he can slam together, flinging whatever's flingable. Before the heavy things start hitting him on the back of the head and neck, he sees Bo on his feet again, and it's all right. Bo's up and swinging again. It's fine, it's okay. Bo's okay.

"You all right, pilgrim?" Jim's on his back and Hamer is kneeling over him. The floodlights hit his eyes like rock chips from a dry drill.

Jim tries to nod his head but can't. He feels as if there's a sack of potatoes on it. The best he can do is inch it over on its side so he can look for Bo. Things don't focus so well, but he can make out Captain Greenway a few feet away. Greenway stands with his hands on his hips, looking down. Every now and again he flings out one of his arms to order a deputy to do something. He seems angry.

Jim struggles to raise himself up on an elbow. He wants to throw up. He's not sure whether he really remembers what happened or not, but between Greenway's legs he sees Bo sitting on the ground holding his head in his hands. Art Matthews is kneeling beside him. Miss Flynn comes out of the kitchen with a bucket of water and a wet dishtowel and kneels, too. She wipes Bo's face. Captain Greenway orders the Cousin Jack supervisor to bring a wet towel for Jim, too, and Hamer wipes his forehead with it.

Jim's vision is better now and he sees the others: Shotgun Johnson leaning against the clubhouse with half a dozen men squatting around him; the slight girl sobbing in Mrs. Matthews's arms; Tom Matthews trying to pull Art away, and Art shoving him back. Jim feels like a bear in a circus. As things begin to make sense to him again, he remembers his anger. Whatever else he's done all his life, he's held his goddamn head up. Never laid on the ground with people gawking at him. He's been beat up before, but not like this.

And Bo. The sons of bitches would have kicked him to death like a snapping turtle if it hadn't of been for him and, he guesses, Captain Greenway. The sons of bitches. There's not a real white man among 'em. He tries to get up again to go for Shotgun Johnson, but Hamer holds him down.

Bo gets to his feet and Miss Flynn helps him over to Jim. Art tries to take Bo's arm, but Bo shoves him away. He stands wavering over Jim. "You okay, cowboy?" he says.

"I'll do. You?"

"I'm alive." Bo tries to grin, but winces.

"We arrested?"

"Damn if I know." Bo looks to Captain Greenway.

"I'll press no charges on behalf of the club," Greenway says.

Tom Matthews is beside him now. "By God, I will. I'll press every charge in the books."

"Checked that with Walter?" Greenway asks him.

"Have I . . . what the hell does that mean?"

"Just what it says. Better make sure Walter wants this thing to turn ugly before you jail these people. It will, you know."

Matthews steps back from Captain Greenway and looks him straight in the eye. "You're serious, aren't you, Jack?"

"Do I make sense, Tom?"

Matthews sighs. "I suppose so. You'll handle Wheeler?"

"I'll handle Harry Wheeler."

Art Matthews, not touching Bo but still beside him, speaks across him to Miss Flynn. "I'll give you a ride back into town."

Tom Matthews steps in front of Greenway and spins Art around. "You'll rot in hell if you do, boy."

Art's back is to Jim. He can't see the expression on Art's face, but he knows it must be a dilly. His old man backs off from him and his face reddens again. The slight girl, still boo-hooing, rushes up to fling herself into Art's arms. He pushes her away. "I'll come back after I get these people home," he says.

"You'll not come back," his old man says. "Not to this family."

Art doesn't answer his old man right away. Instead, he turns to Bo. "Then I'll bloody well not come back," he says. Jim thinks the look on his face is kind of like the ones they put on statues of Civil War soldiers in town squares.

"Then you'll be hunted down like a dog along with the rest of them," old man Matthews says and spins on his heel.

"Art, oh, Lord . . ." the slight girl says. Tom Matthews takes her arm and tugs her gently toward her family.

Art doesn't turn back to her. "I'm sorry, Bunny," he says. "Ready, Bo? Miss Flynn?"

Miss Flynn shrugs. Hamer helps Jim to his feet. Jim

can't count the places that ache. But most of all, the humiliation hurts. Nobody, Mex or white man, Indian or mine boss, has ever done to him and Bo Whitley what this bunch did tonight. And now he's letting them lead him off like a sick mule. He feels as if he's got a hunk of something sharp lodged in his throat. Something that he's got to get out, one way or the other, before he chokes. One way or the other. Soon.

Art Matthews: July 3, 10:15 P.M.

Art wishes Bo and the Flynn woman were in the front seat with him instead of this big lump of a Brew chap. He's dying to talk. He feels unspeakably . . . elated. He's just done the most moving thing in his life. He's free! For the first time he was able to tell the old man to go diddle himself! And he might as well be sharing it with a dead horse as with Brew. Too, Bo's monopolizing the conversation. He seemed all right when they put him into the car. But then he started rambling and ranting like a Chinese opium eater. The Flynn woman is doing her best to shush him, but with no luck. He seems absolutely compelled to let the words out.

He's said some perfectly shocking things. First he went into some long story about his father and a hundred and six steps. He told how his father used to come home so snockered to the gills at night that he'd have to get up the hundred and six steps to Bo's house on his hands and knees. Then he went into how he used to have to sleep with his father, and that was the shocking part. When his father was drunkest, he'd think he was in bed with Bo's mother. He'd start to whisper to Bo and touch him and . . . do things to him. It was pretty lurid. Now Bo's telling about his father dying of the miner's consumption. He begged Bo to hold him as he was dying. Bo says he couldn't bring himself to touch his father. He ran out of the house and never came back. And the oddest part is that somehow he muddles it all up with Bisbee, as if it were Bisbee's fault.

Art thinks he'll have a conniption fit if he can't get the subject back to tonight. "Never is easy to break the old paternal tie," he says over his shoulder. "Take tonight, for example. Poor old Dad must be destroyed by . . ."

Bo interrupts. "This goddamn town! I shined shoes and I ran errands for any two-bit racket store owner that would let me. And the bastards kept telling me someday I'd make something out of myself. I had one pair of khaki britches and two work shirts. I didn't finish sixth grade. I quit and went to work scooping mule shit in the mines so I could make a buck to send Mamma after the sons of bitches killed the old man. And they kept telling me I could make something out of myself!"

"Dad's a plute, all right," Art glances behind him. "Always has been and always . . ."

"For God's sake, hush!" the Flynn woman says. "Can you find a doctor? Even the company hospital if you have to. Bo's bleeding."

Art checks Bo in the rearview mirror. He is bleeding pretty bad. Art thinks he remembers a doctor of sorts in Lowell. He steps on the gas.

"The same sons of bitches that was there tonight," Bo goes on. "Who the hell's made something out of himself now? Hey? Whose goddamn town is it going to be?"

They bounce onto the pavement that runs through Lowell. Art has the windshield open. The night air is exhilarating. Everything is exhilarating. "Ours!" he says. "Every stiff one of us!" Brew looks at him a moment, then lets his head sink back onto his arm. By God, even Brew was magnificent tonight. Everyone was. Art rips his black tie off and flings it into the wind. No more of that, ever.

"They'll remember us, Lizzie," Bo says. "It was just what we wanted."

Art glances over his shoulder as they pass a street lamp. The Flynn woman is trying to keep Bo's sweaty hair from blowing against a great bloody scrape on his forehead. She hesitates a good while before she answers. "Yes, it was just what we wanted."

"Bunny is really a nouveau riche," Art says. "They know what they want."

Bo's voice has been slurring steadily and he's tilting in

the seat. The Flynn woman cradles his head on her shoulder. Art looks back at the road just in time to see they're about to miss the turn to the doctor's house. Damn! He swerves. The car rocks, bounces, then skids. Art jerks the wheel back. Brew slides into him like a sack of potatoes. Miss Flynn yells. The wheel rips out of Art's hands. He yells too. And then it's all a blur.

They come to rest just under a brass plaque that says "Phelps-Dodge Mercantile Company" on it. One front wheel spins noisily. Art leaps out to see to his passengers. But they aren't any more hurt than they were already. Bo's more or less laughing. Brew hardly seems to have noticed. "Just get going," the Flynn woman says. "Find the doctor."

But the car won't move. The other front wheel is hooked over a concrete threshold. Art spins the back tires until they burn.

"Hell, we'll walk," Bo says. He jerks the back door open and pushes Art and the Flynn woman away so he can walk alone. Art calls for Brew to help them with him. But he's gone! Stalking alone up the street toward downtown Bisbee. Hadn't said a word since they left the country club, and now this. Bo shouts for him to stop. But he turns into a dark alleyway and vanishes. *Poof!*

Bo keeps sort of ranting as they make their way to the doctor's house in Upper Lowell, and the Flynn woman keeps agreeing with him and shushing him. She doesn't seem very enthusiastic. Dr. Bankston isn't pleased that they wake him up, and makes Art and the Flynn woman wait in his parlor while he attends to Bo. The parlor is dim, and everything has fringes on it, so that Art is reminded of a funeral parlor.

The Flynn woman is very quiet. There is no sound but the ticking of the doctor's old mantel clock and someone snoring in the bedroom. Art gets nervous and begins to scratch himself in inappropriate places. He's relieved that the Flynn woman doesn't notice. He feels he should do something dramatic, something to keep the night from being over. He imagines what the fellows in Princeton would think if they could see him now. He wants to tell the Flynn woman about it, but he can't bring himself to breech the brown study she seems to be in. The look on her face is almost one of distress. He remembers seeing the same look on his mother's face once. She got all dressed up and took him to a party, but when they got to the house it turned out they were a week late. His mother simply couldn't accept that.

Finally he can stand it no longer. "Well, I guess we're all in the soup together now."

"What?" the Flynn woman says, as if she'd forgotten he was there.

"I mean, here we all are prols together now. I suppose you'll want me to move in with some family of stiffs."

"No." She's still distracted. "I wouldn't think that would be necessary.

"Oh." Art is disappointed. The clock takes over the room again. Art tries to imagine the map of the rest of his life. Everyone should have a cause to live for, something that matters. The problem is to know how to go about that. He feels as if he'll burst unless he can get somebody to talk to him about it. The Flynn woman sighs heavily. Her eyes have little worry lines around them, and traces of dark circles beneath. Even at that she looks a peach with her hair mussed.

"Is it always this . . . invigorating?" he asks.

"No, thank God."

"I'd think you would be on top of the world tonight. You were a grand success. We all were, don't you think? It's impolite to fish for compliments, but . . ."

"Were we? And now what do we do?"

"Why, more of the same."

"Until?"

"Until . . . until . . . I suppose I really don't know. Until you win!"

"And then?"

"Well, isn't that all? Then you do it again someplace else." This is one hell of a note, Art thinks. She's asking *him* questions. "Isn't that what this Wobbly thing is all about?"

She has that almost distressed look once more. "Out of the mouths of babes," she says. But when she catches Art watching her, her face relaxes. She actually smiles at him.

Art's embarrassed.

"Oh, it was funny tonight," she says. "I've just got to

learn to . . ." A sharp shout of pain comes from the doctor's office. "Oh, Bo," she says, her smile vanishing as if she were remembering why they were there. "Poor Bo."

Art slides across the couch closer to her. Wonderful things are waiting for him. There is courage in him he never knew he had. He thinks of Chopin and George Sand and people like that. He reaches out and covers her hand with his. "Be strong," he says.

She looks down at his hand, surprised. Then she turns her head away and makes a sound that, under other circumstances, Art might think was smothered laughter. "Mother of God," she says. "How could we not win!"

Jim Brew: July 3, 10:30 P.M.

They would have wanted to take Jim to the doctor, but he's never been to one of the sons of bitches in his life, even after he spent a week in the Mormon stope cave-in up in Utah. They took Bo, and that's all right. He's pretty bad. But Jim had to figure a way to get that sharp something out of his throat before it chokes him. He's never felt quite this way before. Nothing he can think of will work. Getting drunk is what Shotgun Johnson and Mr. Matthews and the others would like to see him do—make him look as low-down and no-good as they treated him. Naco and one of the whores is out. He goes there when he feels good to begin with.

He's made it as far as Main Street now, where it hits Brewery Gulch and runs on off up Tombstone Canyon. What's left of the graveyard shift is going to work: a little trickle of men with lunch pails, whose wives walk along beside them with rifles. Wobs hoot at them from corners and do a deal of cussing. A few bump into them on purpose, and the men keep walking with their heads down. At the mine gate, deputies have to open up a way for them.

It's no blessed good ever since the strike started. Nobody looks you in the face anymore. People lock their doors at night and keep their guns oiled. Nobody knows who anybody is. Jim can feel the fear crawling up the canyons like the stink of smelter smoke. The first day or so was fun, with Bo and all the famous people and the singing that was as good as a camp meeting. But it's turning mean. The strike's for the best, all right, no doubt about it. But Lord! What in the world is it all about, in the end? People got to keep living.

Jim wanders up Main Street a way, past Woolworth's and the Fair Store and the English Kitchen, where the scabs eat. There's a sign in the window that says: We Serve AMERICAN Dishes Cooked by AMERICAN Cooks. Everything's closed but the restaurant and the pool hall and the *Review* office. Any other night before the Fourth, it would be like a carnival. It's no blessed good.

People look at him funny as he passes. His shirt is half tore off, dirt and blood all over his face. And it hurts him to walk. So in front of the Palace Livery he takes the trolley. He rides all the way to the turn around at the end of Tombstone Canyon, where the divide rises up black against the sky. The fresh wind helps some as the trolley clacks and sways along, so he's paying a little more attention to things on the way back down. Which is why he notices for the first time the funny things going on around the fish-eaters' church.

One hell of a lot of horses and autos, even down onto the canyon, and deputies hanging out under the trees. Lots of them. He swings off the open trolley as it slows for the curve at Castle Rock. He's got to get his mind on something besides that sharp thing in his throat. Maybe they got some good speakers up at the church. No matter what they're saying, he loves a good speaker.

To avoid the deputies, he scrambles up to the churchyard a back way, through a leaf-choaked gully. He breaks into the light beside a man munching an apple. The man looks a little surprised to see him—he's a striker named Engelhardt from down in Moon Canyon, married to a girl from El Paso. Brew starts to ask him what's up, but the man winks at him and shakes his head. Jim understands; this is some kind of meeting against the strike. By damn! He's never seen so many people in one place since the time he heard Billy Sunday up in Leadville. As he works closer to the church, he recognizes the voice of Father Mandin. He's right heated up about something—God or the Wobblies, Jim can't make out which. He finishes as Jim gets to the window, though, and the first thing Jim sees is him motioning for somebody to come stand beside him on the podium.

It's Harry Wheeler, all decked out in a suit and tie! He holds out his hand for somebody else to come onto the stage, too, and that shitty shift boss, McCrea, joins him. The crowd claps a lot. Jim peers in the window to get a better view. And be goddamned if the whole bunch from the country club aren't standing up at the front of the church! Mr. Dowell, Captain Greenway, Mr. Matthews, all surrounded by their security boys wearing sidearms. Son of a bitch! They've even still got their tailcoats on. And they clap for Harry Wheeler, too.

The whole hot-damn crew of them, up there with the Catholic preacher, and Jim Brew standing outside with his shirt tore up and his face bleeding. A stiff tries to shove in beside him at the window and Jim slams the man out of the way. The rotten bunch of sanctimonious bastards!

Wheeler says something about this being the finest display of Americanism he's ever seen. Of course he's not officially connected with it, he says, but he can't resist the call of patriotism. Then he wishes them all well and lets McCrea take over. McCrea announces that there's a new place in the parade tomorrow between the Boy Scouts and the Serbian float. It's for something he calls a Loyalty League. They'll all form at the church, he says, and the company store is lending them five hundred American flags, which can be bought afterward at a 10 percent discount. First come, first serve. He seems nervous and stammers a lot. He has a bandage around his head.

Jim thinks of Bo, and what his face looked like when he saw him last. The scummy shits! He's about to start hitting something and get himself shot, he knows. He's got to get the hell out of here.

He stumbles back through the crowd. No gully this time; he's in too big a hurry to get the smell of the scissorbills and bosses out of his nose. He imagines himself forty feet tall like that giant who said fee-fie-fo-whatever. He'd scatter the scissorbills like pigeons, sweep their cabins off the mountains, and squash their mine shafts like pack-rat tunnels.

Unclog. Something to unclog with. To stop this awful damn feeling that the whole camp is choking to death.

The streetcar ride back downtown doesn't help now. All the cabins are full of people about to go hungry, or taking money from them that watched him lie like a runover dog in the dirt tonight. He has to rest half a dozen times climbing the stairs to Mrs. Stodgill's. Old and tore up. Broke-nosed and big-footed. Made a fool of.

He doesn't bother to take his clothes off when he falls across the bed.

The sun is just spilling over Chihuahua Hill when he wakes up. He's stiff in even more places now than last night. But the idea has come. Sleep cleared something, and the idea has unclogged the rest. He rolls off the bed and, bracing himself on the wall, slides to the commode and pours a basin of cold water. He scrubs carefully. It gives him time to think, to make sure.

When he's dried himself he holds his sore back and stoops to untie Bo's bindle roll. He knows what's in it; Bo showed him the first day. He hurries a little; he reckons Bo is staying somewhere with the Matthews kid and Miss Flynn and will come home to change.

Bo called the stuff hell-fire. Said it was made out of phosphorus and something. Jim shoves a book by a man named Bellamy out of the way and gently lifts the newspaper-wrapped package. His thick fingers, worse from swelling, have trouble with the knot in the string around it. He has to bite it in two.

The stuff is in sticks, like dynamite. But homemade, not as neat. He lays it on the bed like a baby, then changes his shirt. He puts on overalls now, so the stuff won't show when he ties it to his chest. His Ingersoll shows 4:50, time enough.

At the trolley stop on Naco Road, the sideburned conductor who picks him up is sleepy and doesn't want to pass the time. Jim is glad. He massages his stiff legs and wonders that he's not nervous at all. He's not thinking either, really. His mind sways like the trolley.

The conductor is surprised when Jim gives him another nickel at the carbarn in Warren. He doesn't expect anybody to ride all the way to the end of the line by the country club at this time of morning. Nobody else is in the car; it's too early even for the strikers and Mex maids.

No need to slip up through the golf course now; the deputies are gone and the parking lot empty. And the club looks different in the morning light. It's nothing but a wooden building in the desert now, with vacant flagstaffs. Jim hurts when he slips over the gate. But he doesn't hurry. He's picking things out: the place he lay in the dirt, the corner of the building where they surrounded Bo.

Up the graveled drive, his limp gets worse. He rests halfway and picks him out a good spot. Bo said you had to throw the stuff hard and make sure it hit something solid, then flatten yourself quick. Jim imagines he should avoid the porch. Too many chances of its skittering there. Broadside will be best, toward the front so that the crystal chandelier will most likely go. The beams will be important. He mentally places his shot as carefully as a charge in the mine.

He checks his Ingersoll again. Five twenty-eight. The article in the *Review* said the charges on Sacramento Hill would go off at 5:30. Eleven tons of dynamite, charge after charge for at least ten minutes. In town, the noise will cover his piddling little explosion like it was a ladyfinger firecracker. He waits at ease. He'll be back home in bed before anybody even realizes what happened.

The first charge from Sacramento Hill reaches him like a roll of thunder out of the mouth of the canyon. The second should come right behind, then the third. He balances himself. He's close enough to make a good shot now, and far enough to flatten himself before it hits. He lays one stick beside him on the ground and takes a firm hold on the other. The second charge from Sacramento Hill goes off.

The stick of hell-fire spirals away from him like a throwing knife. Straight for the corner of the building. Jim drops and covers his head. The stuff explodes differently than dynamite. There's less of a shock wave and, as he sees when he lifts his head, more fire. Globs of fire that catch and hold on the ground and porch. But the building stands.

The blessed thing stands. Jim pushes to his feet and steps a few yards closer. He'll go higher this time, catch the gable if he can. He draws back with the second stick. The charges from Sacramento Hill still rumble and echo. And over them he hears a new sound. He hesitates, his arm still cocked. He could swear there was a yell from inside the damn building. The fire licks up the wooden columns of the porch, and he strains to see through it. Did he hear a scream? His damn hearing is so bad there's no telling. Nobody could be in there now. And what if there is? It's a scab or a boss, like the ones last night. The thought releases the invisible catch on his arm.

The hell-fire hits the gable. Jim doesn't drop all the way, so he can watch. The gable shudders, the flagpole topples, and the whole thing sinks. Sinks like a cake falling in an oven.

Jim guesses the Cousin Jack supervisor lady rolled out onto the porch just about exactly the time the gable collapsed. No more than a second or two ahead of it. He doesn't know what it is on the porch at first. It's just something on fire that tumbles from the building. Only when he sees Shotgun Johnson leap out behind her and roll her off the porch into the dirt and throw himself on top of her does he make sense out of it. Johnson flung an open whiskey bottle as he leapt from the porch. Even Jim Brew is smart enough to figure what's been happening since the place closed.

Jim still crouches. Lord God amighty. What's happened? He didn't mean for there to be anybody in the place. His anger flashes again. It wasn't fair for somebody to be in there. Especially a woman. He pushes to his feet. Johnson is still sprawled on the woman, throwing dirt on her. She writhes and yells, but her clothes don't seem to be on fire anymore. Oh, Lord. Burning hurts worse than anything. He wouldn't mind if it was Johnson hurting, but not that woman that never did anything to him. It's not fair, goddamn it. He wants to tell the woman he's sorry.

Then, all at once, the porch roof catches. Fire leaps out over the heads of Johnson and the woman. Johnson rolls off her and commences to pull her away from the building. For the first time now, Jim realizes he ought to do something. He half runs, half limps through the scrub brush toward Johnson. "Wait!" he yells. "I'm a-coming!"

The rumbling from Sacramento Hill stops abruptly, and the spitting of the flames from the country club is loud in the quiet air. Johnson catches sight of Jim. He is no more than a dozen yards away. Johnson looks surprised, then picks up a rock and flings it. It bounces off Jim's shoulder. He stops. He's coming to help and the son of a bitch wants to fight again. Johnson backs away from the woman and reaches for his holster. Jim ducks down into the scrub brush. His leg gives him hell, but he weaves in a crouch toward the golf course behind the building. He hears Johnson's first shot sing past him over the desert. He ignores the pain in his leg and throws himself forward, behind the building out of sight.

By the time he's diving over a dip toward one of those little flags on the golf course, Johnson has reached the rear of the building. Jim hears him shoot again. Something burns his side. He can't stop for that either. He knows Johnson won't leave the woman to come after him. Once he's out of range he's okay. He stands straight now to run. He can lope pretty well if he keeps his hurt leg stiff. The burning in his side makes his breath come shorter. He's done something terrible to a poor working woman who never hurt him at all. What in Jesus' name is he doing mixed up in something like this anyway? Bo will pitch a fit.

He spots the burro trail ahead of him. What the hell will he do now? Oh, Jesus, what will he do? They'll hunt him like a renegade Indian. There's no place but Bisbee or the desert to hide in. He hurts all over. Why couldn't they have left him alone? People got to live, ain't they? Even Jim Brew.

Bo Whitley: July 4, 7:30 A.M.

The explosions from Sacramento Hill echo and stop. Bo, like the others at the long oilcloth-covered tables of Mother Moriotti's French Kitchen, looks up. Forks and coffee cups pause, as if waiting for a signal that it's over. Only Mother Jones keeps jabbing at her pancakes. "Noise," she says in the silence, "is good for the appetite."

Haywood laughs and slices off a slab of ham. He has circles under his eyes and eats more slowly than Bo thinks a man his size ought to. He sounded like he was making speeches to the walls when they brought Bo into the hotel room last night. He was still making them when Bo passed out. Haywood's boom and Mother Jones's sharp answers muffled through the wall: That's the last thing Bo remembers. But Haywood insists they all go to the parade. Can't let the plutes think they're hiding from them. The boys will have a place staked out in front of the porch of the company store, where the reviewing stand is. Right at the feet of the plutes. No matter how bad Bo hurts, he won't miss that.

They insisted on bringing Bo to the hotel last night even though he wanted to go find Brew. He slept in a room with Art Matthews. Art's moved out of his old man's house. Says he won't go to France when his leave is up. He's got some Jap or Chink houseboy named Johnny Fourth of July with him, too, sneaking things out of the house. Right now the Chink is slipping a list of names back before old man Matthews misses it. Bo was too groggy to make much sense out of what Elizabeth and Hamer and the local leaders were saying about it when he woke up this morning. But they sounded excited. Damn near a quarter of their people were potential informers, they said. And the companies knew where to find every real striker in Bisbee.

Bo can't worry about it. If the companies thought they were strong enough to do anything, they would have done it. So what if there are informers? There always are, especially in this damn town. No, it's not the informers, but this general strike thing that has everybody so wound up. Haywood and the others have been yapping about it all through breakfast. Congratulating one another on the reports every time another copper camp goes out. Bo doesn't like it. Even if they win in Bisbee, where are they if they lose everywhere else?

But Bo means to see that they don't lose here, because things are happening that he never let himself think about before this week. Things between him and Bisbee—and between him and Elizabeth. Christ, what will it be like when they take over the whole works? Bo's thirty today. Elizabeth is getting older, too. She's got to start thinking about that, just like everybody else. Bo will be somebody in the new setup here . . . in a way the damn scissorbills and plutes never guessed he would when he was a kid. Would Elizabeth want to stay here with him? Why not? He'd have something to offer her then. And hell, she's even better at running things than he is. Then there's the kid—she must be worried about leaving the kid behind with her mother all the time. His kid, too. This would be a perfect setup for them all to settle into. He's wondered what it would be like to watch a kid grow up. Why shouldn't he have a shot at being like every other stiff with a front porch to sit on and a wife and kid to give a rat's ass what happened to him?

Christ, he is thirty. Elizabeth called him naïve once. When he found out what the word meant, he agreed with her. It meant damn fool. He shakes his head to clear out the last of the laudanum that hangs in it like dust after a blast underground.

Down the table, Elizabeth sits beside Haywood. Damn but she was fine last night! Bo doesn't remember much about what happened after the country club. He knows he ran his mouth too much, though he has no idea about what. But Elizabeth was there with him the whole time—that, he's sure of. Today she's wearing her bright red public occasion dress. She leans over the table into the conversation and seems to become the center of it just by being there. Bo watches the solid but delicate way she holds her coffee cup, the poise with which she casually rests her hand on Haywood's arm. She's a woman who could be at home anywhere, with anybody—from Captain Greenway to Bo Whitley. Bo feels an almost painful pride as he watches her; yet, a kind of unexplainable resentment, too.

Haywood breaks in on Bo's thoughts by calling down the table to the local secretary, Embree, who's sitting across from Bo. "Anybody get a count on that church rally last night?"

"Near fifteen hundred, we reckon, Bill."

"How'd it go?"

Embree smiles. "Patriotism was rampant, as the *Review* puts it. Harry Wheeler was in hog's heaven."

Haywood doesn't smile back. All morning Bo has been waiting for him to mention the country club. Stiffs have been stopping and patting Bo on the back for it—telling him it's the goddamnedest spirit booster the boys have had yet.

That it put the fear of God into just the right people. But not a word from Haywood. "You boys get a chance to see that army observer?"

"He ain't talking to us."

The Yaqui kid, a hatchet-faced stiff who runs Mother Moriotti's cash box, hands Haywood a copy of the *Review*. It's about the only kind of thing he has to do now: Mother Moriotti is feeding on credit till the strike is over. The Yaqui kid claims he's never gone to bed without at least one fight during the day. He was the first to congratulate Bo. Why can't Haywood be man enough to do the same?

Haywood scans the paper. "Forty more deputies from that Merchants' Protective outfit put on, it says. Fifty more city marshals. That must give them . . . what? . . . four hundred, five hundred, all told?

"Something like it."

"Our boys staying in line pretty well?"

"Well as can be expected." Embree glances at Bo. "We start trying to hard-line 'em and we ain't no different from any other union."

Haywood looks up sharply. "I know," he says. "Do what you can. Just try not to let them start anything unless they have to. The more we provoke Wheeler, the more excuse he'll have to put on deputies. Grandstanding like busting up society dances don't help either." His look travels down the table to Bo. "Whitley, I believe it is, son?"

"Whitley," Bo says. He tries to pick up his coffee cup. His hands tremble so that he can't. He hurts everywhere, now that the laudanum is wearing off. He's managed to get some mush down, no more. He's got a tooth missing and another busted. He doesn't need any shit from Haywood now.

"You pretty bad?"

"Bad enough."

"You know you got every boss from El Paso to Butte mad, don't you?"

"Intended to."

"Sometimes that don't hurt. Now it does. You read the papers?"

Bo tries a smile. "Not if I can help it."

Haywood holds up the *Review*. "Says here Villa's

marching on Juarez. That's right across from El Paso, ain't it?"

Whitley nods.

"The Guggenheims got a big smelter there, right? We've let them be so far. Now you got their people mad, when they're scared to begin with. Give them the excuse and they'll be on us like wasps on a baby." He points at a blur of headlines on the front page of his paper. "Editorial they got reprinted here from El Paso is already claiming they ought to resurrect the Ku Klux Klan and come machine-gun us. You not satisfied with what you got here in Bisbee, son? You want the Klan and Texas gunmen and God knows what else in here, too? They stop our boys from getting through El Paso and we're cut off for damn sure."

"Bisbee's my lookout, Mr. Haywood. I know what I'm doing."

Haywood's one eye narrows, focuses on Bo like a weapon. "Do you know, Whitley, do you know what's at stake outside these godforsaken mountains?"

"I'm organizing Bisbee, Mr. Haywood, that's all I know."

Haywood's huge fist slams down on the table. He winces at the noise it makes. "Then what you don't know makes a man sick!"

Mother Jones touches Haywood's sleeve. "Bill . . ."

Bo meets Haywood's eye. "You go to hell."

"Watch your language!" Haywood roars. He pushes to his feet. Bo laughs out loud, then doubles over with the pain in his ribs. When he can see clearly again, Haywood is leaning toward him over the table. He is calm now. "I'm sorry, Whitley," he says. "Hurts a right smart, I suppose."

Bo nods, then looks for Elizabeth. She's avoided his eyes all morning. Now she's out of her seat, frozen. Art Matthews is beside her. His face is so smooth, so untouched by anything at all, that Bo blames the pain in his ribs on him. "Elizabeth," Bo says, "let's get the hell out of here."

Elizabeth looks to Haywood, then to Mother Jones. Neither meets her look. She seems lost for a moment, then moves quickly to Bo's side. Bo staggers to his feet, leaning on the back of his chair. This strike means more to him than to any of them. They don't have it in their belly the way he does, and they're telling him what to do with his strike, his town, his devils. Hamer, from the next table, rises to help. But Bo lurches toward the door, and Hamer and Elizabeth can only follow.

The outside air seems to tighten the pain into a ball he can handle. He leans against a hitching rail and breathes in quick shallow breaths until he's easier. Elizabeth takes his hands and rubs them, her eyes fixed on them. Who the hell is Haywood to talk to him that way in front of Elizabeth? He looks to Hamer. "And when Haywood's general strike goes bust, who are they going to have to come asking to hold Bisbee for 'em?" He wants to add: And who is the only one that John Greenway will talk to? Bo Whitley holds the ace, no matter what Haywood thinks. He'll use it too, damn it, if the time comes. And then it will be his decision, with nobody, not even Elizabeth, interfering. Only Hamer knows for now, and he'll keep his mouth shut.

"I don't know, pilgrim. If I didn't believe this strike could be won their way, I'd get out of town and let 'em lose it their way. Might be right rough on you, especially, being a local boy and all."

"We ain't going to lose. Anybody's way."

Hamer doesn't answer.

"Don't be too hard on Bill," Elizabeth says. "He got some bad news this morning."

"Yeah?"

"The AF of L has disowned the whole strike. Straight from Charlie Moyer at Western Federation headquarters. Absolved all the scabs, like the pope. They've been after Bill for a long time. He's on his own now, everywhere."

"That's his problem."

She looks up at him and lets his hands go. "No, it's not, Bo. It's ours, too."

"The AF of L ain't got nothing to do with us."

"Oh, Bo! It's got everything to do with us. They've got discipline, which the IWW doesn't. They've got a fat treasury, and defense funds, and politicians in their pocket. You want to just ignore them and hope they go away?"

"You're talking like a scissorbill, Lizzie."

"Am I? Or am I being realistic? Did we really do any good last night? Just how do we go about 'building the new society in the shell of the old'? We talk about it, but what do we have to show so far?"

"So you're siding with Haywood, right?"

"No I'm not. It may mean just the opposite—or something else entirely. I don't know yet . . . I don't think I know anything right now."

"You got to choose. Me or Haywood, Lizzie. You know that."

"Haven't I done enough choosing these past couple of days? Can't you give me some time just to . . . to get used to things? Why does everybody want me to choose all of a sudden?" She turns away from him sharply.

The pain in Bo's ribs grabs him again. His breath catches and he squeezes the hitching post until the blood in his fingers stops. "Lizzie?" he says. His voice breaks.

She turns, sees him doubling over, catches him up in her arms, and buries his head in her breasts. "Whitley, you son of a bitch," she whispers. "You really let them bust you up, didn't you?"

"Reckon I better hurry folks up," Hamer says. "He ain't going to last long."

"I'll last."

"Will you be all right a minute, Bo?" Elizabeth says. "Mother Jones . . ."

"Go help her. I'll be fine, I said." He pushes himself upright as the pain fades. Elizabeth looks in his eyes a moment, then brushes his hair back, and kisses him lightly.

When they're gone, Bo clamps his jaw and shoves away from the hitching post. He left this town once, whipped. He'll not do it again, not as long as he's breathing. He focuses down the Gulch to the warehouse of the company store. Like everything else, it's draped with bunting. The've gone whole hog this year. Blowing the top of a mountain off. Dragging in everything that can walk or roll for their parade. He watches a couple of Mexes painting a stripe across the Gulch for the burro race finishing line. In front of Cockeyed Jimmy's place, a gang of scissorbills sets up a block of granite for the hand-drilling contest. Whole hog. Haywood wants things to stay calm today. Bull.

A squad of Wobs rattles down the steel stairs behind the Lyric Theater. They carry large notebooks. Roll-takers, just like the company will have. Today's the day you choose up sides: Who's in the parade, who's busting up the parade. My side, your side.

Oh yeah, Bo thinks. My side, your side.

By the time the screen door slams behind him, and Haywood and the others come out, Bo is already on his way to the parade.

The parade is to be a Great Display of Loyalty, says the program. It will be led by the Legion of Honor, composed of all patriotic men of draft age. Behind them will come the floats. The local French citizens will feature the Goddess of Liberty holding aloft her huge torch, which will actually blaze. The Russians sent to Los Angeles for a double-eagled Russian flag, but it hasn't arrived, so the local Russian women have handmade one. The Mexicans plan a joyous street fiesta and have invited the state band from Sonora to play. The Serbs and Italians will jointly sponsor a float carrying Domingo Scotti's band. The Greeks, Finns, Cornishmen, and even the Turks plan patriotic floats. The Germans have not been invited to participate. Children rumor that they have green blood. There will be no Chinese. Chinese are forbidden to live in Bisbee.

Behind the national floats come those of the Elks, Moose, Masons, Phelps-Dodge, C&A, the Fair Store, and local trades. The electricians have built a float that will be attractive by daylight and majestic by night, says the program, a twinkling representation of a submarine complete with wireless and periscope. The women's club will nestle local ladies, trimmed in red, white, and blue, among yellow paper chrysanthemums. The ladies will wave. A special float of Mothers has been added this year on account of the war. The float will pause in front on the reviewing stand and the Mothers will sing "America, Here's My Boy," which is advertised as the Sentiment of Every American Mother. The children's contingent will be led by two little boys in army uniforms and one in a sailor suit.

The Cochise County Cowboys have been unable to prepare a float on account of being on the range all the time, but they will ride and do rope tricks. Anna Rey Pringle has offered every cowboy in from the range a bunk, a bath, and a place to tie a horse. They will participate in the tug o' wars, foot races, sack races, burro races, and famous push-mobile races down Tombstone Canyon. With the children they will drink Ice Cream Dreams, made from great barrels of root beer, sarsaparilla, and lemonade. They will drink other things, too, and go to the dance at the Elks Hall that night. The Mex cowboys will dance at the Blue Moon cantina in Zacatecas, and at the Tierra y Libertad club in Skunktown. They are not expected at the Elks Hall. The baseball game has been canceled. The team is still on strike.

An addendum to Bo's program announces that a Workman's Loyalty League will be added to the marchers. It will come between the Red Cross and the Boy Scouts.

Just above the place the Wobs have cordoned off for Haywood and the others in front of the company store will sit Prominent Citizens and their wives: Captain Greenway, Grant Dowell, Tom Matthews, Lem Shattuck, Harry Wheeler, Mayor Erickson—Bisbee's Best Friends, the program says.

A reminder circulates among the Wobs: Everyone in the parade is to be considered a scab, and the Wobs along the parade route pickets. No different from any other workday.

Bo leans uncomfortably against the bricks of the porch. The sun warms some of the soreness from his muscles. Haywood and the others wave at Wobs on their way to line the parade route. Runners come up now and again with reports on turnout—for both sides. At last the bosses show up. Bo sees them come in a procession down from the Copper Queen Hotel across the square. They know what to expect, too, and ignore Haywood. The Wobs clustered in the square hoot at them and throw spitballs. Everyone is in a pretty good mood.

When the bosses climb up onto the platform, Haywood turns to them and solemnly tips his Stetson. Dowell and Matthews study their shoes. Harry Wheeler stares poker-faced at him. Captain Greenway rises an inch from his chair and doffs his campaign hat. He lets his odd smile rest on Bo a moment before turning to make a remark to Mrs. Dowell that she giggles at. Bo cuts his eyes away. They stop at the side-by-side marquees of the Lyric and Orpheum theaters. William S. Hart in *The Gunfighter* faces off against Charlie Chaplin in *The Immigrant.*

The voice behind Bo catches his attention. It's Lem Shattuck. He squats at the edge of the porch, calling to Haywood. The Prominent Citizens ignore him, horrified. Haywood works his way to him. Shattuck puts out his hand and Haywood takes it. "You Bill Haywood, ain't you?" Shattuck says.

"I am," Haywood says. "And whom might I have the honor?"

"Lem Shattuck. That's my mine." He points vaguely to the top of Bucky O'Neill Hill, above the Copper Queen. "Been wanting to talk to you. I think we might understand each other."

"A noble aim, Mr. Shattuck."

"Lem. Looky here. Reckon I could get together with you and some of your leaders? Have a drink up the Gulch at my place this evening."

"I normally don't refuse to drink with a man, Lem. What you got in mind?"

"Tell you, Bill. I been having a hell of a time getting to the leaders of your outfit. I ain't sure just who they are. I'd like to deal, but I want to make sure it's with the right boys."

Haywood sweeps his hand around at the Wobs next to him, and the others who cluster across the square and up the Gulch. "Right there, Lem. All around you."

"That ain't what I mean, Bill. You know that."

"Best I can do you, Lem. If you got anything to say to us, you're welcome to say it at the next rally up at the park. Any one of these boys you see around you here is as much a leader as I am."

Shattuck rocks back on his haunches. "You're serious, ain't you?" he says.

"I am."

"How in hell you expect to get anything done that way?"

"You have our terms, Lem. What more you need? We don't sign contracts. Don't vote, so we can't use political donations. You of a mind to donate to the strike fund, we got a man right here can take it from you."

Shattuck balances his paunch and gets to his feet. "I'll

tell you something, Haywood. I been thinking this bunch of tea sippers behind me was crazy, what with holy wars and such. But I'll be goddamned if you might not be worse. Never seen so many loonies around me before in my life. All I want is my damn mine."

Haywood's scowl melts into a smile. "So do we, Lem."

"You can go to hell in a wheelbarrow."

Haywood extends his hand. Shattuck bends to take it. "Think I'd like to have that drink sometime, Lem. Under other circumstances."

"Hell of a waste, Haywood. You could of been something." He hulks back to his chair. Nobody speaks to him.

Haywood's smile hangs on as he bends to look down the parade route. The clock on the Pythian Castle shows 8:35. The head of the parade should be coming into sight down the canyon now. Elizabeth, her hands clasped behind her back like a schoolgirl, flops against the warm bricks beside Bo.

"Feeling better, tough guy?" she says.

"Yep. You?"

"Me? I like parades."

"Changed your mind about anything?"

"Nope. Never made it up. Right now I'm just enjoying. Okay?" She takes his hand. "Tresca hates parades."

A cheer goes up from the platform above him, and the people in the square back away. A line of mounted company guards prances into view. Behind them the honor guard of the Bisbee High School band, at only half strength, marches in ragged time to "Yankee Doodle." The crowd that spreads across the square, up the steps of the Copper Queen offices, into the vestibules of the theaters, that hangs out the windows of the assay offices and pool halls and rooming houses, mixes hoots and cheers. Handfuls of Wobs march along beside the band, out of time and waving to the crowd. Two or three of them carry red flags, but most are empty-handed. They caw and cackle and neigh to drown out the band, which tries its best to keep eyes front. Armed deputies push the Wobs out of the line of march, but they dance back in behind them. Bo looks up at the people on the reviewing stand. They're on their feet, hats off and hands over hearts.

The onlookers are mostly Wobs, who keep their hats on

when the flags pass. Damn near everybody else must be in the parade, Bo thinks. That's a bad sign. When the scissor-bills get together in bunches, they turn brave. And the bigger the bunch, the braver they become. Too large a turnout could give that two-gun son of a bitch Harry Wheeler bigger ideas than he needs.

The parade breaks up just behind the company store so the lead marchers and floats can watch the rest of the line pass by. As the band and Legion of Honor and floats file by, the crowd around the store grows. Wobs don't make up so much of the majority by the time the Mothers' float, pulled by a team of bunting-draped mules, slows in front of the reviewing stand. Deputies are having a rougher time keeping the way clear. The day is heating up, and an undercurrent of tension seems to be slipping through the crowd. Bo edges back against the porch. He's tried to yell at the paraders along with Haywood, Mother Jones, and the others, but his hurt side won't let him.

The Mothers stand unsteadily around a red, white, and blue maypole, holding their ribbons. They all have red, white, and blue sashes across their bosoms and hold wooden rifles. Domingo Scotti's band, heavy-eyed Italians with walrus mustaches and high collars, has stopped, too, and plays a weepy introduction to a song. The Mothers, almost together, break into "America, Here's My Boy." Bo watches Elizabeth and Mother Jones turn red. Elizabeth lets go with a Bronx cheer and Mother Jones sets up a howl like a hound dog. Several of the Mothers look unhappy but try to keep the tune.

Across the parade route, behind the Mothers' float, other Wobs take up the hooting and raspberries until enough of them get together to start a counter song. Haywood joins it in a huge baritone, and Elizabeth and the others follow. They're halfway into the first verse before the shock hits Bo. It's one of his songs. Not a one of them knows it's his, but that doesn't matter. He's in Bisbee, and those are his words stopping up the canyons! He looks to Elizabeth and grins. The song grows, drowns out the Mothers:

> I love my flag, I do, I do,
> Which floats upon the breeze.

I also love my arms and legs,
And neck and nose, and knees.
One little shell might spoil them all
Or give them such a twist,
They would be of no use to me;
  I guess I won't enlist.

I love my country, yes, I do,
I hope her folks do well.
Without our arms and legs and things,
I think we'd look like hell.
Young men with faces half shot off
Are unfit to be kissed.
I've read in books it spoils their looks;
  I guess I won't enlist.

Behind the Mothers, who struggle on with their song, the Loyalty League stands at attention. They stretch from the square around the bank, up past the electric sign of the *Review* and out of sight. There seem to be at least five hundred in view, all with flags, and God knows how many others beyond the curve in the canyon. When the Wobs finish their song and the Mothers, some in tears, straggle through their last chorus, a man with a booming voice in the front ranks of the Loyalty League yells at one of the Wobs, "If you was a man, you'd come take this flag with me!"

"Wouldn't be caught dead associating with such scum," the Wob shouts back.

The man takes a step from ranks, room enough to swing. With the flag, he cuts a swatch across the front of the close-packed crowd of Wobs. The flag comes back ripped. As he draws back again, a stiff in the baggy black suit coat of a Bohunk dives for him.

Oh, goddamn. Bo knows if this one heats up, it'll be all over town, from backyard to backyard all day, and he's in no shape for it. Haywood catches his eye, shakes his head, and he and Bo yell at the Wobs within shouting distance to keep out of it. Haywood's scowl is tight, but Bo sees something else in his face, too. Excitement. Haywood's holding back with all he's got. Mother Jones leans against the brick porch and raises her crutch. Elizabeth shifts to block her.

Wheeler apparently has his best deputies stationed here; they know what to do. A half dozen quick-form a line in front of the Prominent Citizens. Others fan out into the crowd and head for the hot spots. The whole thing hasn't exploded into a free-for-all yet, and the deputies try to shove and club the knots of fighting men apart. For the most part, the Loyalty League stands together at attention. IWWs pick off a few at the edges, but can't make them break ranks.

Harry's ready, Bo thinks grudgingly. He'll have to give him that. He's got some discipline in his boys. So far there's more heat than fire. The stiffs and frails hanging out the windows have set up a hell of a whoop and holler, but keep their places. Most of the Wobs, too, look toward Haywood and his bunch to see if they're joining in the fight. They'll stay calm until Big Bill breaks.

And then somebody gets to the mules. A swat, a kick, a hatpin in the flank—Bo can't tell. But the lead mule for the Mothers' float brays and rears and plunges forward in the traces. The Mothers' wagon jerks and one of the Mothers, a fat woman near the edge of the float, loses her balance and plops down into the sea of red, white, and blue crepe that the Mothers swim in. The rest of the mules bray in answer to the lead. The float skids, then tilts. The Mothers seem as confused as the mules. One of them leaps from the float into the heavy arms of Domingo Scotti. The maypole sways like a mast in a storm as the mules zag to the side. Most of the Mothers leap for rescuers, screaming.

All the Mothers save one have escaped by the time the float tips over. The last one, a frail woman who has gotten tangled in her red, white, and blue sash, holds on to the edge of the wagon, like the pictures of the people on the *Titanic.* It comes to rest on its side and the frail Mother slides slowly through the thick crepe paper into the arms of half a dozen waiting men.

The crowd cheers. Even the brawlers have stopped to watch the slow capsizing of the float. Wheeler's deputies take advantage of the lull to hustle the nearby fighters to the edge of the crowd. But through the taller heads around him, Bo sees that the fights have spread like splashes of water the whole length of the parade route. Brawlers roll from the line of march out onto the railroad tracks, into Subway Alley, up the cobbled hills. Flags dip as Loyalty Leaguers are pulled out of line or swing on the strikers.

Bo's spirits rise. It's turned out to be a pretty damn good Fourth after all. He looks to Elizabeth. She's beside Haywood, frowning, while Mother Jones pokes at a deputy with her crutch. Elizabeth shoves the the deputy out of range, and Bo catches her eye. He smiles. Her frown holds a moment, then melts. Bo winks. She winks back. Oh yeah, Bo thinks, might be turning out to be a good Fourth.

Bo sees Red Cross ladies from the line of march hustling Boy Scouts away from the confusion up the steps onto School and Laundry hills. The Loyalty League still more or less holds, though raggedly. There's no riot, but the parade's done for.

Something hard brushes the back of Bo's head. He ducks and turns, ready. It's nothing: One of the deputies on the porch above him has brushed him with a boot. But he doesn't like what he sees behind the deputy. It's Harry Wheeler. Bo has never seen his face other than blank, calm. But now, now it's hard, set with a kind of molded violence. His eyes stare at a point beyond the melee in front of him, as if he were somehow elevated above it. Beside him stands Shotgun Johnson, agitated, talking rapidly into his ear and waving every now and again toward Warren. His vest is torn loose on one side and his shirt and Levi's look scorched. He's hatless and his usually greased hair lies lank and blown. A sharp flash of hate tightens Bo's chest at the memory of Johnson standing above him in the floodlights last night.

Johnson pauses and Wheeler motions for him to be calm. Johnson takes a step back. Wheeler's face retains its violence, but his eyes focus on Haywood's back. He steps forward across the porch. "Haywood!" Wheeler doesn't shout, but his voice cuts clearly through the noise of the crowd. Above them on the porch, he seems taller than he is.

Haywood turns, looks up, meets Wheeler's eyes. Wheeler shifts position slightly so that his legs are spread and he's facing Haywood full on. Something in the movement telegraphs itself to Haywood. He, too, squares off.

"Sheriff," Haywood says.

"I told you I'd hold you responsible. I'm doing that now. What do you intend to do about this . . . *this*?"

"What this is that, Sheriff?"

Wheeler's jaw tightens, works. "Today is the Fourth of July, Haywood."

Haywood studies Wheeler's face before he speaks. "As I calculate it, that's correct, sir."

"Property destruction, the flag dishonored, and now a woman lying in the hospital with burns all over her body. You attract filth, Haywood. *Filth.*"

Haywood draws himself up. Wheeler throws his suit coat back out of the way of his pistol. Bo sees what maybe nobody else does: If Haywood had a pistol, they could be drawing on each other. He's sure Wheeler and Haywood both understand that perfectly. "Is there a woman I should know about, Sheriff? Somebody my 'filth' has had to do with?"

"Arson and attempted murder, Haywood. This time we have witnesses."

Greenway moves quietly up beside Wheeler. "What arson, Harry?"

Wheeler keeps his eyes on Haywood. "Ask Shotgun. Your country club was firebombed and two people damn near murdered. Shotgun was one of them."

Son of a bitch! Bo imagines the bunting, the chandelier, the bandstand all burning and collapsing, the place where Johnson leaned last night only a hole in the sky. Oh, Jesus, that's worth a tooth or two. The god-amighty country club! If he knew which of the boys did it, he'd kiss him.

The Prominent Citizens crowd around Wheeler as the news spreads among them. They're outraged. Bo can't help himself; his grin grows as Haywood's scowl deepens. Greenway throws him a look, then hurries away, his smile gone. Haywood's eye picks out Bo.

"He was with us all night and day," Elizabeth says. Haywood nods.

Hoooo, is Harry Wheeler provoked! Bo never thought he'd see the time they'd get to him. Harry's the only thing the bosses have going for them, really, the only man the scissorbills will fall in behind. Break Harry down, and they've got the strike. That's what he understands, and Haywood and the others don't. Push Harry into getting mad enough to make a mistake. Troops then, maybe, and publicity, like the time the Wobs sent the workers' kids out of

Lawrence and the bulls were dumb enough to charge a bunch of them. Get the plutes to loose faith in Harry, then the scissorbills will, too, and Harry's dead. And with no Harry, who have the scabs got to hide behind?

Wheeler glances a last time over the ruins of the parade. Then his eyes catch Haywood's again. "It's gone too far, Haywood. Too damn far," he says, does a sharp, military about-face, and leaves the reviewing stand with the other Prominent Citizens.

Oh, Harry's riled. But not as riled as he can be. Bo knows that. And he knows how to finish the job. It's his strike again, his song they're singing. It's him and Harry Wheeler and Bisbee and Elizabeth, and to hell with the rest.

Art Matthews: July 4, 8:00 P.M.

Art's pretty lonely, but relieved. Johnny Fourth of July got the list back all right and managed to slip a couple of quarts of Scotch out in the bargain. Plus some civvies and the two twenties Art had hidden away in his kit bag. He supposes the first day must be the hardest. He had really expected it to be more of a giggle than it's been so far. To tell the truth, he feels a bit like a fugitive. Not at all the way he'd pictured being bohemian. He missed the fight, he even missed what they had of the parade. All he could really see from his window was the end of the burro race—or what was left of it, after the hullabaloo.

He pours a shot of whiskey into a water tumbler and dips some water from his washbasin to chase it with. Drinking alone's a ruddy rotten thing, too. He's been pretty generally ignored all day. And after the risks he's taken!

It was a regular madhouse around this place last night. Doors slamming at all hours. That Haywood making speeches at everything. The Flynn woman has been pretty decent to him—seems appreciative—but he hasn't been able to get to first base with her. After the parade he heard Bo and her banging the springs in Mother Jones's room while the old lady and Haywood were making the rounds of the strike kitchens and union halls. That was hard to take. He's horny as a billy goat.

Bo seems to resent him and he can't figure why. After all, two fellows can like the same girl and not get all bothered about it, can't they? It's not as if Art wanted to marry the Flynn woman. Bo's been asleep all afternoon. Art supposes he has the right to a nap after the licking they gave him last night. It was damned unfair. Art doesn't regret a bit standing up for Bo. He just wishes Bo would be a little more sporting about things.

But Bo was friendlier just before he went to sleep. Asked Art if he had plans for the evening. Art thought he was joking, so the knock on the door startles him into spilling some of his drink onto his trousers. Trust an Oriental not to know any better than to bring him a pair of white ducks to wear in this weather. Bo comes into the room without waiting for Art to open the door. He is still hobbling, but looks more rested. He waves away the drink Art offers him and plops into what passes for the room's easy chair.

"Have a nice Fourth?" he asks.

"Well . . ."

"No, I reckon that ain't a sensible question," Bo says. He looks around the room, checking the iron beadstead, commode, oak dresser. "Nice enough flop here, all things considered."

Art really doesn't know what to say. He wants Bo to advise him, tell him what he ought to be doing. He's afraid now he'll have to spend the rest of this strike cooped up here like a patient in an asylum or something. He'd like to get out and make some speeches or something. He's even considered asking if they'd like him to go back East and drum up some support on campus. But with his leave status, he's afraid that's not such a good idea either.

But Bo keeps the conversation light. Talks about old times for a while, which Art appreciates. Then they swap a few stories about their lives. Bo seems genuinely interested now that the Flynn woman and the others aren't around. Not nearly so defensive. He asks Art to describe in detail some of the things he tells him about—restaurants and women and clubs and such—as if he's trying to get a clear picture of them, and can't quite. He talks about his own life, too, but makes light of it. He seems a little ashamed of it, even when Art assures him he thinks it's fascinating. Art has always wondered why fellows of Bo's class get nervous when he asks them to talk about themselves seriously. As if they're afraid he'll make fun of them, which Art knows he's too much a gentleman ever to do.

Bo seems to get more and more nervous as the conversation goes on, then suddenly surprises Art. He suggests they go up to the Line. Art thinks he's joking again. But Bo looks offended when Art tries a laugh, so Art mentions that it's raining pretty hard. Bo clicks his tongue and Art confesses his real reason for being hesitant. He'd love to get out, of course, but is afraid he might run into his father or one of his father's friends.

Bo tells him not to worry, that they'll go to one of the private cribs. Art considers sending a boy up to tell Johnny Fourth of July to bring his rain slicker, but doesn't believe Bo would think so much of the idea. What the hell, what if his clothes do get mussed, at least *one* of the laundries in town has to be open. Think of what the hoboes must put up with on nights like this. He's never seen one of them in a slicker.

Bo leads him out through the café and along the edge of the Gulch. The water stays in the center, mostly, so they can generally keep their feet dry. It's just where the Gulch twists and curves that the water boils up and they have to wade through it. Street lamps become fewer as they climb, and those that there are wave erratically in the wind. It's perfectly eerie, Art thinks. In spite of the holiday, they seem to be nearly the only people out.

They cut away from the Gulch just before the curve where the Mint and Monte Carlo clubs sit. It's even darker here, and the water laps down the stone steps like a waterfall. Water squishes in Art's shoes, something he hates violently. He's not sure this is a good idea at all.

Bo seems to know where they're going, though. He leads Art to one of the long green wooden buildings that always seemed so forbidden and exciting to Art as a kid. There's no porch light on, and only a faint red glow from inside. Art's nervous again and stands to the side while Bo knocks.

There's no answer. Bo knocks harder. Still no answer, though Art is sure he saw a shadow move inside. Bo pounds.

The curtains part a little and the face of a pretty enough Mexican woman pokes through them. She shakes her finger at them to go away. Bo pounds harder. The curtains flap back together and the door opens a crack, though the woman makes sure the screen is locked. "Closed," the woman says with a heavy accent.

"The hell you say," Bo tells her.

"Closed."

"Looky here," Bo says. "See who this is." He pulls Art into the sliver of light from the open door. "Know this boy?"

"No."

"Ever hear of the name Matthews?"

"Sí."

"Ever have anybody go down and buy you anything from the company store?"

"Sí."

"This boy's name is Matthews. His old man is a good friend of the *hombre* who runs the company store. You don't want to make him mad, do you? You'd like to keep getting things from the store, wouldn't you? Maybe even some 'special' things? This boy's daddy is even bigger than, say, Harry Wheeler. You know that."

"Sí, yo sé."

"Can he come in?"

The woman hesitates, peers out to get a better look at Art.

"Word of honor," Bo says. "I'll stay right here on the porch and set up a row if anybody comes this way. You got a back door, ain't you."

Art wonders why Bo's having such a hard time with the woman. Doesn't she want business? Most of these women fight for it. Why is Bo so interested in getting Art diddled, anyway? Does he feel bad that the Flynn woman is only giving it to one of them? Or is Bo truly trying to make him feel at home?

The woman reaches to unlatch the screen. Bo steps back to let Art in. Art hesitates. Bo takes his arm, rather insistently, Art thinks, and guides him inside.

Art feels even more uncomfortable. This room has an

odd feel to it, with a huge painted cloth on the ceiling and a cracked charcoal brazier lit in the corner to keep the chill off. Not at all like the big place he was at before. But the woman seems willing enough, and he has to admit she's a great lot better-looking than the ones he had last time. He's never had a Mexican before, but he hears they're tigers. He starts getting excited in spite of himself as she strokes his arm and helps him out of his wet shirt. Really, he is bloody horny. She smiles at him. She has a gold tooth. Imagine! What would the fellows at school say? Sleeping with a gold-toothed woman!

Art must have been asleep. He guesses he had more Scotch than he thought. The woman seemed to be nervous at first and tried to rush him. But she calmed down quick enough. Art supposes he must be a different sort of a man than she's used to. Most of the ones she gets can't be very refined lovers. She did get up once just before Art dropped off to make sure Bo was still on duty. Bo's first rate, Art has decided. True blue.

The woman is holding him damn tight now. That must be what woke him. He starts to say something and she clamps her hand over his mouth. He wonders briefly if he's really awake after all. There are voices outside, though he can't make out whose. He pushes the woman's hand away and looks at her. She's absolutely petrified. That's a hell of a note. She shoves at him and points to his clothes and the back door. She's out of her mind! He's paid his money. Let the next fellow out there wait his turn like everybody else. He'll be damned if he's going to fling himself out into the rain butt-naked.

She knows enough English. Why doesn't she speak up and explain what's going on? Bo's out there. He'll take care of things; she should know that. Silly damn woman.

But then the screen rattles. Maybe something *is* up. Maybe she's got a Mex boyfriend with a curved knife. Maybe Bo's already been done in. Art's stomach feels cold. Oh, God, there's no help around here, that's for sure. Even his family can't do any good now. He slides out of bed as quietly as he can, and reaches for his pants, which are flung over the back of a cane-bottom. The chair is light, and the pants heavy with water; as he pulls at them, the chair crashes down onto the floor. His pants flop with it, and the change in his pocket makes an awful racket. He freezes, naked in the middle of the floor.

The screen rattles again, more violently, then flings open, the latch popped. Next the door handle rattles. But only once. The silly bitch didn't lock it. It opens slowly, cautiously, and a pistol leads a hand through it. Oh, Saints and Seraphim! Art never thought it would come this way, naked in a whore's room.

Then the door kicks wide and there, in the stark red light, stands Harry Wheeler! Oh, God in heaven, is he glad to see Harry Wheeler. But no, Harry's face tells him another story. Harry is as near to being surprised as Art has ever seen him. The wind that rushes in behind him has a chill to it. Art remembers he's naked.

"Evening," Art says.

"Get some clothes on," Harry says.

The woman breaks down in tears. She flings herself onto Harry. He shoves her away. "You're naked," he says to her. Oh, boy, Art figures, this woman and Harry . . .

He reaches for his pants and slips into them. He's in such a hurry that he rips one of the legs. He throws his socks away and puts his shoes on without them. He only drapes his shirt over his shoulder. Harry stands still as a statue in a garden, gun drawn. Why in hell didn't Bo warn him? Did Wheeler threaten him, too?

Wheeler steps aside for Art. Art's a good foot taller than Harry. "Sorry," Art says as he brushes by him. Wheeler doesn't answer. The woman stays hunched on the bed, weeping. Harry leaves her there and follows Art onto the porch. Bo doesn't look at all disturbed—just sits on the porch rail like he was watching kids fish a nickel out of a grate. He's polishing his harmonica on his pant leg. What is going on?

Wheeler closes the door behind himself. "I don't hold you responsible, boy," he says to Art. His voice is tight, choked, like he had to spit. Art doesn't meet his eyes. He concentrates on buttoning his shirt.

"Whitley," Wheeler says, his voice still that funny kind of tight. And quiet, too quiet. "I think you've got what you wanted. I don't reckon I've ever hated anything in my life like I hate you and your people and how you operate. I can't stand to breathe the same air you do. You got no right to be called human beings. As God is my witness."

Art looks up at Wheeler. Harry's pistol hangs limp in his hand. "As God is your witness, Sheriff," Bo says.

Harry stares at him a long moment. Then, in a motion like a trap springing, he slams his pistol butt into the porch rail beside Whitley. Bo doesn't move. Wheeler backs down the porch steps. His eyes never leave Bo. The rain clatters on the roof. Wheeler slips away.

"Evening, Sheriff," Bo says into the dark.

Art can't put it in words yet, can't even puzzle it out, but he feels he's been betrayed in a way beyond any he ever thought possible.

Orson McCrae: July 4, Midnight

Will he never get any sleep? Don't they know what it took to get the word around to all those boys who showed up at the meeting last night? And to get the captains organized to turn out over a thousand men for the parade? When is enough? They've rousted him out of bed on this wet night and he hadn't been asleep an hour. How do they expect a man to be clear-headed when they treat him like this? Sending Captain Greenway's nigger chauffeur to pound on his door and plop him in that big Jordan touring car and drag him out to Captain Greenway's house with hardly time to take his nightcap off. If he's as important as they say he is, he has some rights, he supposes. Leaders need rest.

And then not letting him take his bodyguards either. What good are they if not to look out after him? The town is crackling, sparking all over with fights and threats like somebody had plugged a big generator into it. That scummy Whitley is lying in wait for him somewhere. His wife and kids don't need more than two bodyguards. They could at least have let him take the other two. What good is a nigger chauffeur in a pinch? For all he knows, he could be a Wobbly. The other three niggers he knows of in town have joined.

Getting through to the captain's house is like crossing a battle line. They're checked at two points on the road in front of Walter Douglas's house and again at the gate into the captain's. Sheriff Wheeler's deputies, all huddled up in rain slickers. Good boys. Harry wouldn't trust any but the best here.

He's one of the last to arrive. Grant Dowell's car is here already, and Tom Matthews's, and Sheriff Wheeler's Locomobile. Most of the lights are turned off in the big wooden house. The Mex houseboy takes Orson's slicker just the same as Orson saw him taking the others' slickers last time he was here. The crowd is more or less the same bunch as before, minus Lem Shattuck. The big guys and their security chiefs. But now in the middle of the room is a long oak table with Harry Wheeler sitting right at the center of it and Dowell at his side. There are plat maps spread all over the table, and loose sheets of paper with names and figures. Tom Matthews and Captain Greenway stand talking by the fireplace. The captain breaks off when Orson comes in and crosses the thick Oriental rug to shake his hand. Orson is embarrassed. Captain Greenway shaking Orson McCrea's hand! Who would ever!

The others take Orson's hand, too, and Captain Greenway motions the nigger chauffeur, who's waiting in his wet slicker in the vestibule, to step into the room. The nigger looks even more embarrassed than Orson feels. That relaxes Orson some. At least nobody shakes the nigger's hand.

"Where's Mr. Ellinwood?" Captain Greenway asks the nigger.

"Say he won't come."

"You gave him my note?"

"Yessir. He give me one for you." The nigger digs a sealed envelope out of his slicker pocket. Orson sees the initials E.E. on it. Everett Ellinwood. Chief lawyer for the Copper Queen Company. Mr. Ellinwood's a big deal. Planning to run for governor, they say. He doesn't blame him for not getting out of bed at this hour.

Captain Greenway rips the letter open and reads it silently. When he's done, he laughs his good, hearty laugh, and tosses the letter into the fireplace. "Everett doesn't want to know us, boys. Says the last thing we need now is legal advice, and the less he knows about what goes on, the better."

Harry Wheeler looks up sharply. Tom Matthews spits into the fireplace. "What did you expect?" he says. "Lawyers study rules, not principles. Am I right, Harry?" He looks to Wheeler and waits.

"I've known that at times to be the case."

"Some laws go beyond the books. Wars make things different. Where were the lawyers when we ran the Indians and trash out to make this damn town to begin with?" Matthews says. "Let's get on."

Even when he's speaking, Tom Matthews seems to manage to keep in the background of things, Orson thinks.

"Still . . ." Dowell says.

"Still what?" Matthews says.

Dowell looks around him. Everybody waits for him to speak. Their faces are blank. "Nothing," he says and falls back into his carved chair.

The Mex houseboy brings coffee and whiskey in. Orson takes a whiskey. Last time he tried the stuff he choked, so he makes up his mind just to hold it and sniff it this time. Captain Greenway takes a chair just behind Harry Wheeler. "Harry asked for this meeting, boys," he says. "So I'm going to let him have the floor. I just wanted to let you know how I appreciate your coming, personally."

"Thank you, Captain," Wheeler says. He clears his throat and looks down at the papers spread out before him. He pulls a folder from beneath the heap and opens it. "I've done a right smart of studying today," he says. "And I want to thank Captain Greenway and Mr. Dowell for the time they've given me, and the files they've shown me."

He looks up, directly at Orson. For a brief, hot moment, he thinks he knows how the men Harry's drawn against must have felt right at the last. There's no indecision in those eyes, no quibbling.

"I have become convinced," Wheeler goes on, "that what we've got here in Bisbee is a German plot, financed by

German money, against the government of the United States of America. There's no question in my mind now but what we're at war just as much right here as our troops in France are." His eyes never leave Orson's. He knows Harry's waiting for him to say something, but he can't. This is probably the most historic thing that's ever happened to him or ever will. The best he can manage is a nod. Apparently satisfied with that nod, Wheeler leafs through the file on the desk. "I believe," Wheeler says, "that if nothing else, the events of today would have convinced me. There is not the tiniest spark of patriotism or Americanism in these men who are trying to deliver us to our enemies. But there's a deal of hard evidence beyond that." He holds up a sheaf of clippings and papers. "Statements by people like Senator Clark of Colorado to the effect that he has secret information that proves the IWW has German links. Confidential reports from the Bureau of Investigation that link the IWW with German-Jewish socialists, Russian anarchists, and God knows who else. A letter from Governor Campbell of this very state that he intends to produce firm evidence of German and Austrian infiltration. Coded messages found in the pouch of the dead Villista aviator last week. And so on and so on. I am not inclined to disbelieve men and reports of this caliber."

"Here, here," Grant Dowell says.

Wheeler clears his throat again. "I don't believe there's a man in this room who would oppose the right of legitimate trade unions to exist, even if they disagree with their principles. Or at least I can speak for myself on that. That's not the issue. I have here two statements from Captain Greenway's files that sum it up pretty well. One of them is from the American Federation of Labor, printed in their own newspaper." He squints a little at a clipping in the light from the chandelier above him. "It starts out, 'We, the officers of the national and international trades unions of America in national conference assembled, in the capital of our nation, hereby pledge ourselves in peace or in war, in stress or in storm, to stand unreservedly by the standards of liberty and the safety and preservation of the institutions and ideals of our republic.' Etcetera."

He looks up again to make sure that McCrea is following him. McCrea nods again. Wheeler puts the clipping aside and spreads out a newspaper. McCrea recognizes the IWW emblem on it. "This statement, in their own paper, is by the IWW: 'With the European war for conquest and exploitation raging and destroying the lives, class consciousness, and unity of the workers, and the ever-growing agitation for military preparedness clouding the main issues, and delaying the realization of our ultimate aim with patriotic and, therefore, capitalistic aspirations, we openly declare ourselves determined opponents of all nationalistic sectionalism or patriotism, and the militarism preached and supported by our one enemy, the Capitalist Class. We condemn all wars. . . .' " He looks around him again. Matthews stares into the fireplace. Dowell shakes his head and purses his mouth.

"That, gentlemen, is treason," Wheeler says. "Pure and simple. It's putrid and, by God, has nothing to do with labor unions. It deserves no quarter."

"Damn long-winded, too," Greenway says, and rises. "Care to tell the boys what you told me this evening, Harry?"

Wheeler leans back in his heavy carved oak chair, so small he's lost in it. Like a little boy in a judge's chair, Orson thinks. But he slowly lets his eyes move from man to man in the room, as if he's measuring them all. There is a look in them that Orson decides is that of a man touching destiny, a man of History. "As chief law officer of Cochise County, I've decided to take personal charge of the Loyalty League. I reckon by the time I'm through, it will be the largest posse in the history of the West. I've had enough."

Part Three

Big Bill Haywood: July 10, 3:30 P.M.

You step through the double screen doors of the French Kitchen to watch the newsboys scrambling for their papers at the stand just behind the stage entrance to the Lyric. Your trunk is packed in your room above, ready for the 4:30 Argonaut to Chicago. In Chicago you will hit the speaking circuit, in spite of the pain in your stomach that tells you your ulcer is working at killing you again. Chicago, Milwaukee, Philly, New York. It's the best you can do now, since the money dried up. You knew you had to go yesterday when you watched a Mexican woman stand before the relief committee with her five kids and get a dollar bill to feed them with. She threw the bill on the committee's desk and said she was going back to work in the laundry. What good can you do her now with speeches in the park? You owe her more.

You owe them all more. You called the general strike and now that it's alive it has to be fed. Globe, Jerome, Ajo, Leadville, Butte—from Montana to the Mexican border, the boys and their families are counting on you, are still believing that *scab* is a dirtier word than *hunger.* They're stopping the wheels of the whole damnable machine in the middle of a war, and they've got to have money to do it with. If they can't find it themselves, then you'll do it for them.

You walk toward the newsstand. The *Review* should be jubilant: The damned scissorbills have begun to move. You got the news from Jerome at strike headquarters about midday. Vigilantes rounded up the entire strike committee there, plus some, and shipped them out of town on a freight. Seventy, eighty boys. Now they'll need a raft of lawyers. And that means money . . . always money.

Up and down the Gulch deputies loiter with sidearms and cartridge belts. Your boys can't get together in groups of more than three or four without a deputy busting it up. Day and night, the pressure is on. In vacant lots from Warren to the Divide, Wheeler's boys are drilling. With broomsticks or Springfields, they wheel and prance and strut in pieces of old uniforms or in overalls. For every Wob on a street corner now, there's some jackleg counting cadence down the block. And it's working. Close to 60 percent of the underground men are back at the job, escorted by squads of armed Loyalty Leaguers. The deputies come at your pickets in shifts, *keep moving, keep moving, keep moving!* until the boys are too exhausted to show up next day. And where is the army? Where is the government? They don't answer when you ask them to come. The only law in Cochise County, a territory vaster than most any state in New England, is Harry Wheeler.

But the boys have stayed in line. You've accomplished that, at least. No more hell-fire, no more brawls. Harry Wheeler has had no excuse. His scissorbill homeguards can whirl and prance all they want, but they can't move on the Wobs. The world is watching Bisbee now. Even Wheeler has to have an excuse; even this upside-down world demands that.

The money went away so damn quick; that's what bothers you. The boys here have already given all their stash, you understand that. But the outside money: You expected that would be coming in. Where is it? Spread too thin over the other camps in the general strike? Hamer says the money is being intercepted at the post office, says the assistant postmaster is siphoning it off to the Loyalty League. Maybe. But should it have dried up so quick? Hamer's trying, no doubt. He just showed you the biggest single contribution of the day, brought in by a bindlestiff on the morning ore train. Ten dollars, and a wrinkled note that reads:

> Fellow Workers:
>
> A Demonstration was just held in Sheep Camp No. 1, there being three present, a herder and two dogs. The following resolution was adopted:
>
> Resolved: That we send $10.00 for the strike in Bisbee.

You can't, you won't let that get buried. Even if you have to go to Berlin to speak and ask for handouts.

The newsboys spot you. They drop their bundles of papers and crowd around you. You know many of them by name now. These are the kids you owe most of all: It was the newsboys who first listened to you back in Goldfield a decade ago, who started the strike that turned the IWW from a theory into a union. The kids understand. They believe.

A gawky kid named Ewing, from the family the Flynn stays with, takes your hand and drags you to the flight of metal steps at the rear of the Lyric. They seat you halfway up the steps and range themselves above and below you in their too short overalls and homemade cotton shirts. You can see the newsstand owner wants to yell at them, but doesn't dare. The loitering deputies stare, and spit.

"Kids' Town again, Bill," the Ewing boy says.

"Again?" You've told them the story half a dozen times. You first told it to workers' kids in Paterson, when the children got together to make their own union and strike against their besotted schools. But you've dreamed it since Salt Lake, when they jerked you out of school and put you to work on your uncle's farm. You ran away when he beat you; your first strike, you called it.

"Again," the boy says.

You take off your Stetson and unbutton your vest. You speak loud enough so that the deputies across the alley hear you. "There might be a city somewhere," you tell them, "where the only people are kids, like you. There are no grown-ups to always say, 'Don't, don't, don't,' and nobody has more than he needs while other kids don't have enough. Everything belongs to everybody, and there's always enough to go around. How does that sound to you?"

A thin Bohunk kid, the one from the train your first day here, says, "No homework, Bill. You said that last time. Don't forget to put that in."

"And no homework." You lean back, your elbows on the step above you, and fix your eyes on the rain clouds that descend to touch the cross on the top of the Presbyterian steeple beside the Copper Queen Hotel. The world is young, you tell them, like kids, and always changing. Glaciers are always moving, making valleys. Earthquakes and volcanoes are always making mountains. All these things, and tiny creatures called microbes, are forever creating new out of the old. It's the one law of the earth. But you tell them that the hardest thing to change is the minds of old people, and that some people get old while they're still young. They're the ones who make the new world seem old. They're the ones who fasten governments, religions, and diseases on the people. They're the ones who, generation after generation, make wars. And it's all these terrible things, you tell them, that the old leave to the children of the world. The kids boo and hiss. It's a ritual by now.

Then you ask them about their own Kids' Town. What would they keep? What would they not have?

"Cops," the Ewing boy says. "No damn bulls."

"Jails," another boy says.

"Banks"

"Churches."

"Armies," the little Bohunk says.

"That's stupid," another one answers. "You got to have armies."

"What the hell you going to fight about if everybody's got everything?"

"I want lots of trees. But fruit trees and nut trees and stuff, so you can sit in the shade and eat."

"And lots of grass to sit on."

"And instead of hedges, I want blackberry bushes. With lots of birds."

"Birds eat berries up, stupid."

"Birds got to live, too."

"I want lots of tools and things. But mine, not some damn boss's."

You've heard the answers before, almost always the same ones, in every mining camp, every mill town the Wobblies have organized. No bulls, no armies, the beautiful and the useful always combined. You won't let that be dead either, no matter what it takes.

You drop your eyes from the rain clouds when the kids around you grow suddenly quiet. Just below you, at the foot of the stairs by the newsstand, Lem Shattuck leans and listens. The kids and deputies all watch him. He regards you sadly from above his walrus mustache.

"You believe it, don't you, Haywood?" he says.

"I do, sir," you tell him.

"You boys like fairy stories?" he asks the kids. Almost all of them nod, or say yes. "Be careful, Haywood. Most of them grow out of that." He takes his derby off and slicks back his graying hair. "Once I reckon I would have been with your outfit, you know that?"

"I think you might have."

"Now, hell. I reckon I even admire you. But I got my mine. I can't go back on that. It's got nothing to do with fairy stories nor ideas, nor such stuff. I just don't take to going back to mucking and eating beans. Don't imagine you take a fancy to that either, do you?"

He turns away without waiting for an answer. He walks a few paces toward the front of the Lyric and stops. "Come join me for the matinee," he says and points toward the poster of Vera the Medium. "Her fairy tales don't cost near as much as yours or Jack Greenway's." He touches his hat to you and lumbers off down the alley.

A gust of wind swirls leaves down from O.K. Street ahead of the storm. The kids' newspapers fly up; a few flap across the alley and paste themselves to the wall of the brewery. The kids clatter past you on the steel steps to retrieve them. Alone now, you watch Lem Shattuck's back until he vanishes around the corner of the theater, coattails fluttering in the wind. The rain will come soon. You're tired, every cell in your body is tired. Fairy tales! Damn Lem Shattuck to hell. Yet there's nothing you'd rather do than go to a stage show with him, then to a saloon for a bottle of Tennessee whiskey and a few rounds of low ball.

You ask yourself if you're running. If there's something in these sharp canyons that Lem Shattuck understands and you don't, maybe never have. The air is not as you remembered it, the exhilaration not as high. There is something sinister here, something you thought you had left behind, but that has tracked you all the way from those other rainy canyons in Manhattan. The clock on the castle above you strikes four. Time for your train. You heave up off the cold metal steps. Whatever, it'll have to move fast to keep up with you now.

You've asked only a few to come to the train with you. The less commotion attached to your going, the better. Gurley Flynn will be there, and Mother Jones, and a couple of the boys from the strike committee. Not even Whitley will come. Ever since word slipped out the day after the Fourth that Wheeler was looking for Brew, Whitley has been a demon. Thrown himself into a fit of organizing like this whole strike depended on him alone.

When you round the corner of the depot, you see there's somebody else come to see you off. Harry Wheeler lounges by the ticket window, Shotgun Johnson beside him. They watch as you buy your tickets. Gurley Flynn stands between them and you to block their view. But as the agent slides your tickets across the counter, Wheeler circles her and drops his hand on them. The rain slices in under the wide eaves of the depot.

"I won't ask how you knew I was leaving," you say.

He flips the corner of the string of tickets up and looks for your destination. "Chicago, Haywood? Thought you'd be heading back to New York."

"Is there a reason for your being here, Sheriff? Do you reckon to stop me from going?" You turn to face him. Shotgun Johnson slides into view behind him. The long whistle of the Argonaut cuts up the canyon from beyond Sacramento Hill.

Wheeler slips his hand off your tickets. "No, sir. I promised you something back. I wanted to see you got it." He reaches into his inside coat pocket and hands you your revolver. He offers it to you butt first. As you take it, you check and see the dull noses of bullets still in the drum. That startles you at first, then it strikes you why. You drop the revolver into your coat pocket, and leave your hand resting lightly on the butt.

The train whistles again. You pick up your tickets, put them into your other coat pocket, and bend to take your valise. Wheeler takes a step forward so that the tip of his boot touches the valise. You look up at him. "I wanted you to know something else, Haywood," he says. "I told you I was holding you responsible. I still do. If I have to track you to New York or Chicago—or Berlin—to do it. I want you to understand that."

Shotgun Johnson moves a half step closer. His sawed-off shotgun dangles loosely in his hand, his finger on the trigger guard. A scatter-shot from the thing couldn't miss. You keep your voice calm, conversational. "I reckon we've always understood one another, Sheriff."

Wheeler's mouth becomes a tight line, then consciously relaxes. "I'd never have pegged you for a man to run out like this. But I imagine it's true after all what they say about rats and sinking ships."

Behind him the black engine of the Argonaut puffs into view. You back off a step. The door to the waiting room flings open and passengers spill out onto the platform. Wheeler's eyes don't leave you. Your loathing for the man rises in your throat like the taste of bad meat. Loathing and understanding. He would draw on you, you're certain. He's here for that, to draw on you or to back you down. And in a sense you know that's just what you came to Arizona to find. But it's no good. You're Big Bill Haywood, and there are two people you don't owe: yourself and this tin-starred strike baiter. You haven't got time to stop for Harry Wheeler now. Your showdown is with something much vaster than him—or Bisbee. And you realize that he's not really after you; he would draw on this whole blessed century if he could.

You take your hand out of your pocket, off your pistol. Wheeler sees the motion. If his eyes showed you anything, you know it would be disappointment. You turn your back on him. You're in a hurry.

Mother Jones and Gurley Flynn helped you get settled on the train. Fussed over you, brought you a pillow, stuffed your pockets with messages for people back East, made small talk to keep from having to say anything. You promised you'd be back—with money. They promised they'd hold until you did. They have no choice, nor do you.

The Argonaut creeps past vacant lots with Loyalty Leaguers drilling, past crossings with deputies on guard, mine gates with your boys marching in their slow circles in front of them. You've been here . . . how long? Just eight days? You watch the sparse, silent pickets. You remember the way the boys whooped it up for you when you came in. Jesus, that was good.

You open your copy of the *Review* to the editorial page. "We need a hundred thousand well-manned airships to bomb every potato hill, chicken coop, fodder stack, granary, submarine base, and everything else in Germany," the lead editorial says. "*That* would end the war, not IWW cowardice." You slap the vile thing down onto the seat. A hundred thousand air machines, the sky black with them, leveling the earth. There's no time left, no time at all. You check to see that the conductor isn't in the car, slip a flask from your pocket, and take a deep slug.

The train slows toward Warren, where a donkey engine maneuvers a long dun private car under one of a half dozen metal awnings. Then, at last, you reach a tank stop called Osborne, where the train backs onto a siding, turns, and drops down from the mountains.

The clouds are much higher here, much less smothering. The whiskey is warm in your belly, and the rain streaks the windows. You watch the smoke from the engine flash by; on a curve, you can see it behind and in front of you the whole length of the train. Your mind slips back over all your other strikes; strikes you've won, strikes you've lost, all move by you like the smoke from the engine. Which have created things that have lasted? Even some of the towns, like Goldfield, are vanishing now. One hundred thousand air machines. Whose fairy tales created those, Lem Shattuck? Ah, but the only law of the earth is change that makes things new, you told the children. You will believe that; you must believe that. The world waits to be made new. You won't give up. You look farther ahead, past the engine and smoke, toward Chicago.

Harry Wheeler: July 10, 8:00 P.M.

They've come for you in a closed car. Picked you up in back of the dispensary, by the YWCA, and drove you in circles until they were sure no one was following. It's not needed, though. There's not one foot of the Bisbee-Warren mining district you feel unsafe on. All week that's been proved again and again. The boys are rallying, everywhere you go, like nothing you can think of since maybe Bunker Hill. You've felt that somehow this has been there for you all your life, waiting for you to find it. A sense that you, Harry Wheeler, are making something historic happen. A Cincinnatus of the desert, the *Review* says.

And yet. You've felt an awful uneasiness, too. You haven't had time to think. You look at the faces of so many of the damn Wobblies and see boys who contributed to your campaign, boys you've asked a plug of tobacco from once in a while. That's the other side of the thing. There's this feeling you've had all week, too. It comes at night, usually, after one of the incredible high spells: an emptiness, a depression, like after a fever. It doesn't last long and goes away again when you're busy. But it has a way of sneaking up on you. When you had Shotgun take Remedios back across the border it came. And when you call home to talk to Alice and little Sunshine and they sound as if they're not just up the road in Tombstone but in another country. Or when you watched the Argonaut backing out of town with Haywood on it. You know you're right; you have to know that. And yet the damn depression won't go away.

The motion of the car smooths at last as it purrs onto a straightaway. You wish you knew where you were going. All you got was a handwritten note from Grant Dowell that jabbered about "need for secrecy" and then his chauffeur leading you into Dowell's Packard machine with the top up and the curtains drawn. What the hell kind of secrecy can there be that you shouldn't already be in on? And what kind of machine is a Packard touring car for Harry Wheeler?

The Packard stops at last. You peek through the curtains and see mainly blackness and the backyards of some houses. You get a glimpse of a dozen or so cowhands you don't recognize clustered around the car with carbines. The chauffeur speaks to one of them and mentions your name. The cowhand pokes his rain-wet head into the car and says "Evening" in what you peg as a Texas accent.

"Who authorized you to carry firearms?" you ask the cowhand. He smiles and waves you on. That's not right.

The machine lurches over a rutted road for a hundred yards or so and stops again. The chauffeur hops out and opens your door for you. Never jump too quick into unknown territory: The Apaches taught you that. You step out cautiously into the drizzly night. Near you more cowhands with carbines watch you from under their hat brims. In the dark, they don't have faces except when a flicker of light from a burning oil drum washes over them.

You know where you are now. The railyard. Behind the cowboys, the dim-lit sheds for private cars stretch off into the dark. You recognize Captain Greenway's car with the C&A emblem on it, and Grant Dowell's Copper Queen car. But there's a new one now. A long grayish one with no markings on it at all. A nigger porter in white stands by the stepping stool outside it, hunched under an umbrella. From inside the car, the white light of gasoline lanterns seeps around the closed curtains. Who in the name of God could have gotten into town in a private car without you're having been notified? You've left strict orders with the telegraph office and the El Paso and Southwestern dispatchers to notify you of any unusual movements. But mixed with your indignation is apprehension. Whoever could have ordered your instructions to be disobeyed is big, very big. A general? The secretary of something? The Secret Service director?

The nigger porter trots over to you with the umbrella. You stand a moment in the drizzle before you get under it. He leads you through the mud, then steps up into the blinds of the car ahead of you and knocks. Voices come from inside, and the faint odor of cigar smoke. The door opens a crack. Tom Matthews peers down at you. He nods the porter away, opens the door wide for you, and takes your hand. Behind him in the Coleman-lantern light you see Captain Greenway and Grant Dowell, both standing. A male secretary in a stiff collar sits at one end of a long carved mahogany desk, scribbling with a gold fountain pen. At an open bar, which takes up half the far end of the car, another porter is mixing something with seltzer. Everything in the car is oak and leather, with curtains of red velvet tied back with gold tassles. Next to the bar an open door leads into a dim bedroom. Your breath catches. It's the damnedest thing you've ever seen.

"Come on in, Harry," Tom Matthews says. "Damn raw out there."

You step cautiously onto the springy wine-colored carpet. Behind Grant Dowell, seated next to the male secretary at the long desk, is another figure. He's partially hidden. A small diamond stickpin in a dark striped tie catches the Coleman light. Dowell turns to you, and the figure's face slips into your vision.

It's the face of a man in his forties, a thin Scottish face with sharp features and a tight mouth. Almost gaunt, with steady eyes below hair slicked straight back, partless. You've seen the face only once before, in a newspaper, but you've never forgotten it. Before that face, the image of a general or a mere secretary of something pales. Hell-fire. It's Walter Douglas.

Walter Douglas. Member, Saint Andrews Society; DownTown Association; Century Association; New York Yacht Club; Columbia University Club; Grolier Club; Saint Andrews Golf Club of Hastings, New York; American Yacht Club of Rye, New York; board of managers for the Memorial Hospital of New York City. President, American Mining Congress. President, Phelps-Dodge Corporation. President, El Paso and Southwestern Railway. Board member, Southern Pacific Railway and seven other railroads. Board member, banks, mercantile corporations, wondrous things beyond number. Republican. Episcopalian.

Walter Douglas of the Douglases. Son of Dr. James Douglas, the founder of Bisbee, founder of Douglas. Brother of Rawhide Jimmy Douglas, whose northern headquarters in Jerome splits the state with him. Walter Douglas. Largest employer in Arizona, emperor of copper. Secret, anonymous. The man who nobody in Bisbee is quite sure exists.

Your breath returns shallowly. You can hear the hissing of the lanterns and the soft shuffle of Grant Dowell's shoes as he moves across the carpet to you.

"I'd like somebody to have the pleasure of meeting you, Harry," Dowell says. His chubby face beams beneath his balding crown. His smile is as fixed as in a photograph.

He takes your elbow and leads you across the carpet. Douglas doesn't stand. His hand, with nails such perfect half-moons you think they're false, takes yours. It's a firm grip. Walter Douglas is shaking Harry Wheeler's hand and saying, "I've heard a great deal about you, Sheriff. We get a good bit of you back East in our Sunday supplements. It's a genuine pleasure."

"Pleased." You take heart. He knows you. He's read

about you, just as you've read about him. You've worked hard for that. You grip his hand more tightly.

"Drink, Sheriff?" he says and taps the desk for the porter.

"Coffee, please," you say. Play it close for now.

"Harry never lets up, Walter," Captain Greenway says and drops his arm around your shoulder.

"So I've heard," Douglas says. He keeps his seat, but doesn't offer you one. "I could have used you last night in Globe, Sheriff."

"Pardon?" you say.

"Don't you know? The IWW up there barricaded the sheriff in the mine property. Shameful. He had to grovel to get out. I barely made it out myself."

"Never happen in Bisbee," Dowell says behind you.

"I shouldn't think so." Douglas has a funny accent. He's a Canadian, you've heard. You don't know much about Canucks. They're kind of foreigners, but not really. Not like Mexes. "I tried to slip out for a game of billiards, and some of these I Won't Works decided I ought to be ridden out of town on a rail. These boys outside here were somewhat more effective than the sheriff's deputies, though. No one in my party had to grovel, if you understand me."

"I do, yessir."

"I've been up and down the state this past week or so, Sheriff. I've seen a great deal that would anger the most patient man I know. Last night was the worst. I'm not that patient a man. I'm angry."

"Yessir."

"Bisbee is different, I'm told. Is that correct?"

"I'd hope so, Mr. Douglas."

He looks up at you steadily. His hands are clasped in front of him on the burnished desk. The scratching of the secretary's pen is the only sound other than his voice. "How different?"

"Pardon?"

"I mean the reports I've been getting."

"What reports, sir?"

"Is it true that the woman who owns the Bisbee *Ore* was approached by an IWW deputation demanding that she sell them the newspaper. On the grounds that within six months every newspaper in the country would be expropriated in any case?"

"So she says."

"Did the mayor's wife suffer from an IWW leaping on her machine's running board and spitting on her?"

"Yessir."

"Do deputations call at the homes of my workers when they are at the mines to threaten their wives?"

"There have been such reports."

"Are the person or persons responsible for the destruction of an ore car and the country club still at large?"

"As best we can figure, the country club man has crossed the border to join the Villistas. For the other, now . . ."

"Is there a tunnel being constructed underneath the post office for purposes of blowing it up?"

"I don't know, sir. I never heard that." The man is cross-examining you, like the snitty officers used to do in the army!

"You should know. I have other reports that we won't go into. Shop owners being extorted for strike funds, merchants having to subsidize lunchrooms—things I'm sure you're familiar with. In short, chaos. Is this what my father founded this town for, Sheriff? There would be no county for you to be sheriff of without my family. You realize that."

"I do." The man's voice is getting sharper. You don't like it. Only Walter Douglas could talk to you this way, and you're not sure how long even he'll get away with it, by God.

"What about the reports that there are three hundred armed Villistas among the Spanish population? Have you checked that out?"

"I have."

"Well?"

"You have to understand, Mr. Douglas, that the Mexican is an odd kind of a species. Very close. They'll lie dying and won't tell you which one of them knifed them."

"Is that all?"

"It's hard, sir, to tell one of them from the other when it comes to things like this."

He flicks his neat head impatiently. "Do you realize, Sheriff, that when my mother rode into this town the first thing she saw were two men hanged from a telegraph pole for the birds to eat? That was your Bisbee then. Who gave the town its YWCA, its first school, its library? My mother. Does that matter to you?"

Captain Greenway takes his hand from around your shoulder, with a pat. "Presumption being, Harry, that the boys had rather read than hang one another." He laughs. Walter Douglas doesn't. "Sorry, Walter," he says. "Nobody denies the woman's good intentions."

"I've asked for troops, Mr. Douglas."

He rises. "And you haven't gotten them. I know that. I saw to it that you didn't get them. Do you know why? Because I thought this was the one town in the entire West that could show the world how to handle these Imperial Wilhelm's Warriors. Because I heard that Harry Wheeler didn't need troops to keep the peace in the United States of America. What more do you want, man? Their money is gone, and why is that? Where in hell do you think it came from to begin with? Why do you think these people were *allowed* to infest my town?" He turns abruptly to Tom Matthews. "How much was in your discretionary account, Tom?"

"Twenty-five thousand, Walter."

"And how much now?"

"A thousand or so."

"Do you understand, Wheeler?"

"Well, sir . . . no."

"It means that I've gambled twenty-four thousand dollars on you. That I made a guess I'd gauged the national mood correctly. That if I gave these people enough rope they'd hang themselves. Nothing, Wheeler, nothing that has happened in this town for six months hasn't been reported directly to me by Tom Matthews. Nothing that has transpired hasn't been overseen by Tom Matthews. Did you realize that?"

"No, sir."

"I've given you every opportunity. They're at their weakest now. Even your damn Haywood is gone. What is this Loyalty League outfit doing? How much more money am I going to have to lose before you act?"

You feel small, smaller than the lowest Mex in Skunktown. All this was allowed to happen, arranged. As if history were a game of cards and you'd been dealt this hand on purpose to see how you'd play it. The whole situation dumped in your lap as a kind of test. God in heaven, what sort of stakes do men like Walter Douglas play for? And you thought you were in control. The more fool you.

Why does this happen? Again and again. You do your best. You live by the finest code you know. You think you understand courage and manly action. You model yourself after the finest men, the straightest shooters. And then your father doesn't speak to you because you were too short to go to the Point. And your commander in Oklahoma glowers at you and tells you to send the Apaches away. And at OCS, the post commander looks down that cocky nose at you and says, "Not officer material." Then Haywood turns into a pussy and walks away from you and gives you a terrible feeling that he's not a pussy. You live by the Law, you are the Law. So where did you go wrong? What more is expected of you? Why do shame and failure always wait for you around every corner, like muggers? Who caused this? Where is your fault?

"I've done everything I lawfully can, sir. I've kept the peace."

"Lawfully? In war? And how much copper does 'keeping the peace' ship to Belgium, Wheeler? Do you 'lawfully' hold off medicine from a dying man? Or do you give it to him to drive out the disease at whatever cost?" He gestures to the porter. "My mackintosh. Do you have a mackintosh, Wheeler? I'm going to show you something." He's agitated, impatient. You know he's not putting on an act for you.

"No, sir."

"Never mind, then. You won't need it. Grant, get the cars ready."

You hear the door click behind you. The porter helps Walter Douglas on with his slicker. Douglas swears at him when he can't find an armhole. "Is your man to meet us there, Tom?"

"He is," Matthews says.

"Then get your mackintosh on. We've damn well run out of time. I can see that from talking to Wheeler here. You coming with us, Jack?"

"Wouldn't miss it, Walter. Think I'll do without my slicker, if Harry's going to."

You turn to him. He smiles his odd smile at you, and you feel grateful.

"Wheeler?" Walter Douglas says. "Jack's been no doubt filling you full of holy war talk. I hope you know how to fight a real war."

"Yessir," you say. "Yessir."

The trip into town in Grant Dowell's closed machine is quiet. Walter Douglas makes small talk: business talk with Dowell. You sit in front with the chauffeur. You want Walter Douglas to talk to you again. You want to tell him how ready you are. How you and Captain Greenway and that McCrea have organized the whole Loyalty League into companies, ten of them with ten picked captains, and each captain with ten absolutely reliable lieutenants. Like the Romans. You want to explain to him how you've got telephones installed in every captain's house, code words, passwords, battle plans, everything ready for an instant's notice. All telegrams, telephone calls, and mail into or out of town screened. A troop of five hundred sheltermen drilling in Douglas alone; fifteen hundred more in Bisbee. Good men, registered for the draft, no slackers. Americans and Cousin Jacks, mostly. Then the special subcompanies: the rifle club working at sniper training, mounted company guards organized into a cavalry company. You want to hear him say: Yes, Sheriff, you've done the right thing. All that in only a week is military genius.

To do the right is not difficult; to know the right or wrong of a thing—that's the task, your sign says. You have kept the peace. That was the right of the thing. And now it's not. What is higher than that? Where is your fault?

The machine eases up to the main gate of the Junction shaft, just at the edge of town. Pickets halfheartedly chuck mudballs at the car, but back away from the wedge of deputies who lead you in. Even for them it's an ugly night for fighting. What in hell could Walter Douglas know about the Junction shaft that you don't? What did he have to drag you up here in this wet night to show you? Why can't he just tell you about it? You're no idiot.

Dowell directs the chauffeur to pull the machine right up to the base of the gallows frame of the hoist itself, at the mouth of the shaft. When the motor stops, the constant hum and throb of the steam piston fills the night. One by one, you hear the motors of the cars behind you die. You wait in the car until the chauffeur has opened the back doors for Douglas and Dowell. They stroll, still ignoring you, to the station at the foot of the gallows frame where the elevator cage stops. You follow and wait, the cables to the cage slapping and whirring on the drum above you as a sick mule, a sling under it, is hauled out of the shaft. It brays wistfully.

Dowell sends a man running for rubber suits for all of you. He starts back toward you, then veers off toward the shadows by a machine shop. There's a wagon there you hadn't noticed before—a company flat-bottomed delivery wagon with a tarp stretched over it. What's Dowell after now? The man's always after something.

He unties the tarp and pokes his head under it. Then, by God, the tarp moves! Something's under it, alive.

The whole area is clear now except for your deputies and Walter Douglas's cowhands. Dowell pulls his head back from under the tarp and unties the straps. As he does, the tarp rolls back and the figure of a man struggles out. In the shadows you can't see who it is. Only that he's big.

A mucker you deputized trots up with an armload of rubber suits and sorts them out for you. You step into yours with impatience, keeping your eyes on the man approaching with Dowell. He's halfway to you before he hits the sharp light of the arc lamps and you make out his features.

Be damned, be goddamned! It's that fat cohort of Bo Whitley's, of all god-bless people. What's his name—Hamer, that's it. One of the big shot Wobblies himself. The fund raiser. His face is serious. He brushes his pants off as Dowell leads him directly to Walter Douglas. He stops a few feet from Douglas and waits for him to speak.

"You're the man Mr. Matthews has written me about?" Douglas says.

"I reckon, Mr. Douglas," Hamer says.

"Your company speaks highly of you. Do you have a name, or do you prefer to leave it at Agent Thirty-four?"

"It's Hamer, sir. But numbers are all right with me."

"No doubt you know your business better than I," Douglas says. "It's all rather melodramatic, though, for my taste. I understand you've something to show us."

"Mr. Matthews mentioned he thought you'd like to see it, yessir."

"Good. Sheriff?" Douglas unlatches the iron-barred door of the cage for you and steps back. You flick the flint on your carbide lantern, then get a deep breath of the cold earthy smell of the shaft. You remember the speeches of the Wobblies: stories of cheap timbers that collapse, of lack of firewalls, of the men who have gotten trapped and lost for good under here. You've never really believed it, but still . . . You hesitate a moment, then get in. The cage sways and clanks against the guide rails. You grab a bar and hold tight as Dowell, Greenway, Douglas, Matthews, and the man Hamer follow into the jiggling cage. It's cramped. You try to remember how many hundred—or thousand, was it?—feet deep the Junction shaft goes.

The cables whirr and you start down. You've been on these things before and don't remember them starting with such a jerk. You thought they had clutches on them to prevent that. You start to ask Captain Greenway about it, but the thing is plummeting before you can even speak. Falling like a rock in a well. Christ! No brake, no clutch—even the safety dogs grind against the rails, spark, and slip. Christ! Someone lets go of his carbide lantern and it slams crazily, flaming at you. Dowell screams, Hamer stumbles against you—even Walter Douglas flattens himself against the bars. The thing shimmies against the rails until you're sure it's going to split. You're almost weightless against the falling steel floor. Shit, you think. Shit, I'm going to die.

And then it's over. There's a perceptible jerk, not a sharp stop, like hitting water, but a slowing like someone threw the clutch lever. The shimmying against the rails becomes a steady clanking, and when you open your eyes you see the layers of rock slipping by you at no more than the speed of a fast walk. The others slowly right themselves, puffing and coughing and cursing softly. They look around wonderingly—all except Walter Douglas. He keeps his eyes fixed on you. He's the first to speak. "Damn fine hoistman you've got there, Grant."

Dowell is the one who lost his lantern. He's shaking and still clutches the bars. Even with your own breathing labored, you find room for contempt for him. "They're everywhere, Walter. They've infiltrated everything," he says in a halting voice.

"Did you know about this, Hamer?" Douglas asks.

"No, sir," he says. "Five'll get you ten it was a spur of the moment thing. A joke."

Douglas's eyes have never left you. "What about it, Sheriff? You think that was funny?"

"I didn't." You hold on to the anger that's rising. It gives your voice its strength back. Your security has failed, and you've been humiliated in front of Walter Douglas. That's immediate, active.

At the Level Four station the cage eases to a stop. Hamer takes the lead. The timbers are old here in this drift, as if it hadn't been worked for a long time. No one speaks except for Hamer cautioning one or another of you to watch your step. He keeps flashing his lantern along the jagged, glistening wall, as if he were looking for signs. Now and again his light passes over an arrow or an X mark burned onto the wall by a carbide flame. You twist and turn for what seems a mile, until you've lost all sense of direction. Finally, in the cold and echoing drift, his light finds a crooked O next to the partially caved-in opening to a side drift or a stope. He stops.

"We're here. Want me to go first?"

"By all means," Captain Greenway says. "Be our guest." He laughs. No one else does.

Hamer clambers over the low wall of rock. Walter Douglas motions for you to follow. Your low buzz of anger sustains you still and you make it over the wall in half the time it took Hamer.

Your lamps light a stope, a big one. It's like a chamber in a cave more than anything else, or the inside of one of those old French cathedrals, a huge room blasted out of the rock until the ore was gone, then abandoned. Its distant, irregular reaches eat your light so that you can't really see how far back it goes. Even when the others climb in after you, the combined light isn't enough to reveal the whole thing. From somewhere water cascades in a ragged plashing. In front of you, roughly halfway between you and the nearest wall, a small stream cuts across the floor. You step near it, and you see little snakes of wire silver, leached from the rocks, shimmering in the clear water. The walls are a hundred colors: blue from malachite and turquoise, greenish from leached copper, black from Apache tears, sparkling from fool's gold and mica, seamed with white quartz. Tiny white and tan stalactites cover the ceiling like fine hairs. Your footsteps crunch and echo back into the darkness. Shadows from outcroppings grow into strange shapes as the men twist their lamps.

Hamer's voice comes hollowly from behind you. "It's over this way, I believe."

You turn, suddenly panicked at being left behind. Hamer leads the others along the wall nearest the entrance to the stope. You fall in with them.

The wall cuts sharply behind an outcropping of black rock. Not far beyond the outcropping the floor ends in a pit your light can't penetrate. The stream spills over into it and vanishes. But before the pit, in a kind of alcove in the wall, Hamer's lantern picks out what they've brought you here to see.

Captain Greenway gives a long low whistle when he sees it. No one else makes a sound. But they step back for you when you come nearer for a good look, as if they tacitly expected you to do something.

The most you can think of to do, though, is to touch the wooden crates very gently. There must be two dozen of them, labeled Apache Powder Company, 90% Strength Gelatin Dynamite, Use Extreme Caution. They are stacked in the alcove so that the blast pattern will spread as widely as possible—you know that much about mining, at least.

Walter Douglas's voice comes from behind you. "How long would you say these have been down here, Hamer?"

"Best I know, Mr. Douglas, the strike committee authorized them the day after the Fourth. I reckon they were set up right after."

"Where do you estimate we are now, Grant?"

"Well, best I can plot it from what Hamer told me today

is that we're quite near the surface of the hillside here, somewhere near Naco Road."

"Close to what?"

"Reasonably close to downtown."

"What do you estimate a blast of this magnitude would do?"

"Well, you're a mining engineer, too, Walter, so I . . ."

"Never mind that. Answer me."

"First off, I suppose, the road south and all rail connection would be knocked out. There would be considerable loss of life, of course, in Cowan Ridge and part of downtown. Not to mention incidentals such as the collapse of the mountainside that would set up an air blast in the other drifts and tunnels. Make gun barrels out of them. Anybody in one, of course, would . . ."

"Thank you, Grant," Douglas says. "Sheriff Wheeler, is that clear to you?"

You're trying to picture it all. No troops could get in. Total isolation. Downtown all rubble. "It is," you say. The alcove is tight, close here. Your depression won't leave you. You try to think of something else to say, to do, but you can't.

Hamer steps up beside you. "There's a detonation wire here," he says and points to a thin wire that disappears up into a crack in the rock above you.

"Know where it goes?" Greenway asks.

"That, I couldn't find out. Most I could get is that it goes to one of the houses on the ridge above us. Could be any one."

"You prepared to swear in court that the IWW did this?" you ask him.

"I am."

Douglas gives a little impatient snort. "In court, Sheriff? After the blast? When?"

Something detonates, snaps, in your gut. You reach for the detonator wire. Hamer tries to stop you, but you sluff him off and grab the wire. It's connected tightly. Only on the third jerk does it pop loose.

"Jesus, Harry," Grant Dowell says. "Jesus."

You thrust the bare wire toward Walter Douglas. "Is that enough for you, Mr. Douglas? What in the name of God else do you want me to do?" You make no attempt to hide the anger in your voice. The man squeezes, then squeezes you again until he gets the very blood out of you. What more do they want of you? You feel as if you could pull out your Colt and blast the dynamite until you're all blown to hell and better for it.

"Come here, Wheeler," Douglas says and leads the party back toward the main room of the stope. Once there, away from the tightness of the pit and the dynamite, your depression and anger ease. But only a bit. There's still something unsettling to you in the unshaped darkness around you in the stope.

Walter Douglas sits on an outcropping of rock. The shadows from your lanterns surround him like a huge robe. "No one else knows where we are now, Wheeler, or what we've seen. Or what we'll say to one another. Can you tell me, frankly, what's troubling you? Why you haven't moved before this?"

"I can, sir." You clear your throat—surer of yourself now. "One thing. Authority. I don't see what else I could have done within the law that I haven't."

Douglas lowers his head a moment in thought. His patent-leather shoes gleam in the lantern light. "Where do I come from, Sheriff?" he asks at length.

"New York, I suppose. Washington sometimes."

"Have you heard the name Cleveland Dodge?"

"I have."

"Cleveland Dodge is chairman of my board of directors. Are you aware that he is a schoolfellow of Woodrow Wilson? That he and President Wilson spend a good deal of time together on Mr. Dodge's yacht?"

"I didn't . . ."

"John Greenway here is not only a friend of yours, Mr. Wheeler, he is a confidant of Theodore Roosevelt. I take it you know that."

"I do."

"Who, ultimately, is the 'authority' in this state, Wheeler? Who elected Governor Campbell? Whose town is this? Who made it and owns it? Whose mines feed the town? Be realistic, man."

You don't answer. He watches your face in the glowing light, then continues, his voice level and low. "How do you think things get done in this world? How could I see to it that no troops came in here? Do you expect the government to come out with a public proclamation that Harry Wheeler is authorized to be the one man charged with the historic mission of destroying the Wobbly menace? Do you? Don't be a fool, Sheriff. You *have* the authority. That dynamite over there gives it to you. I give it to you. Necessity gives it to you."

You're being pulled apart. Part of you sees light for the first time in weeks, sees a way out. Another part of you sees the face of an Apache chief in Oklahoma. You can't find your voice.

Behind you Captain Greenway says, "There are more ways than one to arrange a military commission, Harry. Valor can be rewarded. Initiative can."

Douglas nods. "The time has come, Wheeler, to shake hands with history."

Greenway's arm reaches around your shoulder. "This is Arizona, Harry. The world needs an example to follow. We have the best there is. The last hope there is."

Captain Greenway's arm comforts you. To know the right, to be sure, to have authority. Who has put you in this dilemma? The face of Bo Whitley rises up, of Haywood, of that Flynn woman, of every Wobbly in town, in the world. You see the naked body of Remedios in the lamplight. Filth. Filth has put you here. Filth submerges these mountain valleys. Against it, you see the smooth face of your father, of Captain Greenway, of Walter Douglas, of a mighty army cleansing the fields of Europe, of a mighty army cleansing the canyons of Bisbee, the plains of the West, the streets of America. It is clear. It is necessary. At last.

You've never known your voice to feel so controlled. "What do you have in mind, Mr. Douglas?"

"You have the machinery, Wheeler. Use it."

"How?"

"Eliminate them, man."

"All of them?"

"All of them."

Your breathing calms, grows easy. Your depression slips away. You feel clean.

Art Matthews: July 11, 7:00 P.M.

Misery. He can't go home, and he can't fit in with the Wobblies. Not a real pal among them, no matter how hard he tries. And Bo—he's got no use at all for Bo anymore, though he thinks he understands him. They're both hopelessly in love with the Flynn woman and Bo has to humiliate him every chance he gets. That's romantic, though, so Art supposes it's all right. Bo seems to have taken it firmly into his head that the Flynn woman is going to come back to him and live in Bisbee or Pocatello or somewhere. In a pig's eye she will. But Bo insists she is and she doesn't say no. Poor Bo. He knows so little about the way the world works, after all.

Bo's been frantic about that old Brew. Art has never seen anyone driving himself so crazy with guilt. Though he doesn't know why Bo hasn't expected something like that, the way he uses people. Maybe it'll teach him a lesson. If Art hadn't been humiliated by Bo, too, maybe he'd break down and tell him where Brew is. But it's good for Bo to wonder —and probably best for old Brew, too. Art feels a kind of sacred trust since Brew singled him out to ask for help. He's still not sure why Brew did it—the man is so bloody inarticulate!—except that Bo is a friend of Art's. Or was. But Brew is afraid that if Bo knows where he is, Bo would do something to get them both in trouble.

All that aside, here he lies between these two colored whores, one of them the mother and the other the daughter. The cheap perfume and rye whiskey and mildewed mattress smells make his stomach turn but he's too degraded and in his cups to leave. This is not romantic. It has nothing to do with Free Love and free spirits. But it's all that's left to him to drown his misery in. It's one bloody hell of a lonely life.

Today he thought it was going to get better. Some of the old excitement started to come back. Something funny is up. First those notices in the newspaper this morning, almost identical from all three companies. "All men must be back on the job by 7:00 A.M. shift day after tomorrow, Friday the 13th, or they will lose their pension plans and their lockers will be cleaned out and contents given to the poor fund." That made the Wobs mad, all right, but those proclamations all over town that Mayor Erickson and Sheriff Wheeler signed really set them off. No more meetings in the park or anywhere. No more assemblies of any kind because they threatened public order. Blam! Right out of the blue, like they wanted to make the IWW angry and get them out and fighting. Well! They don't know the IWW like Art Matthews does, that's for sure. The Wobblies aren't that stupid. The last thing they want now is to give Sheriff Wheeler a chance to use that army of his. So they outsmarted old Harry again.

It was probably the biggest funeral procession a Mex ever had that the Wobs staged this afternoon. No way old Harry could call that an unlawful assembly. Twelve hundred Wobs, four abreast all the way from Hubbard's Mortuary to the new Evergreen Cemetery down in Lowell camp. Two miles if it's a foot. Marching silent as Anglican deacons through town until they got to the cemetery. Deputies all the way with carbines, but they couldn't do a thing. And fellows from the companies taking names and making counts as usual. Art knew several of them, but they turned their heads away as he passed.

Even with all he's seen these last days, at the cemetery he was a little startled. Bo preached a funeral, but he talked about how the fellow worker had been abused all his life instead of about heaven and the normal things. He quoted some fellow named Joe Hill. "Don't waste any time mourning. Organize!" he said the fellow wrote Haywood in his last letter. Everyone was pretty much moved by that and Art didn't feel as bad when they all started to sing songs like,

> Long-haired preachers come out every night,
> Try to tell you what's wrong and what's right;
> But when asked how 'bout something to eat
> They will answer with voices so sweet:

> You will eat, bye and bye,
> In that glorious land above the sky
> Work and pray, live on hay,
> You'll get pie in the sky when you die . . .

They spent all afternoon in the cemetery singing those songs, the "Internationale" and such. Old Harry must have busted a gut.

After it was over, Art came back to Mother Moriotti's, played the slot machine in the kitchen awhile, and tried to strike up a conversation with someone. But again it was no good. All that murderous Yaqui kid ever wants to talk about is breaking people's jaws. And the other Wobs . . . good chaps, still, but he has nothing in common with them outside a political science course he took sophomore year. Where's it going to end? His leave is up in a week. Surely something will break by then. He's got to know whether this Wobbly thing will be a going concern for him or whether he'll have to go back to the Princeton Rifles. There's talk of a "new initiative" from the Wobs, but he doesn't see any new strength coming from anywhere. And besides, Art doesn't know how much longer Johnny Fourth of July can keep on snitching money out of his mother's bag for him.

The colored whores are asleep, both of them. Art might have even been asleep himself, the way he was drifting away there. He has always been told Negroes have this musk to them, but he can't tell. He tries to slip quietly from between them to reach his flask on a rickety table beside the bed. He has to feel his way in the dark room. The table is no trouble to find, but his flask is missing. Bother! He gropes for his pants and finds a match.

Holy Mother of God! There's a man in the room! And it's Shotgun Johnson, holding Art's flask. He's got this sideways kind of grin on, and lets his eyes travel up the daughter whore's body before he says anything.

"You 'bout ready to come home, Matthews Junior?" he says.

"What in hell are you doing here?" Art cringes. He's never been able to stand the man. There's something about him that reminds Art of gila monsters.

"Your daddy asted me to bring you home. Took me a right smart to find you."

"This is . . . is . . . unconscionable," Art says. "How long have you been here? Why didn't you knock?" They're both nearly whispering. Nonetheless, one of the whores stirs. The older one, the mother. Bit of a hag, really.

"Number one, I ain't been here long. Number two, a feller don't knock here on the Line 'less he's sure who's door he's a-knocking on. Reckon you better git your clothes on now."

Art gets to his feet. He tries to draw himself up tall. "I intend going nowhere with you." He knows he's swaying a bit but maybe Johnson won't notice in the matchlight.

"Reckon you will. Your daddy said to bring you. One way or t'other."

Well now. If he's this serious, maybe the old boy has something up. A reconciliation or even a plan to unfreeze Art's bank account. That would surely come in handy. He reaches for his pants as the match flames out and the mother whore wakes up.

"Who you talking to?" she demands.

Shotgun Johnson flicks a match. He takes a step toward the bed and taps the woman on her chest with his sawed-off shotgun barrel. "You got two choices, sweet chops," he says to her. "You either be on the first train out tomorrow, or the both of you goin' to visit the Tombstone jail with me. And they's smallpox up there, you know."

The woman quietly lies back down, her eyes large. Johnson snuffs his match while Art dresses. Art asks him for a slug of whiskey, but Johnson says he's got orders to bring him in as sober as possible. Hmmm, Art thinks, and is suddenly alarmed that his mother might be in trouble. Don't want to upset her if she's sick.

Johnson holds the door. Just as Art goes through it, Johnson pulls the light cord. The bare bulb floods the room and Johnson lets his look roam up the younger whore's body again. She opens her eyes and blinks, but doesn't move.

"You like 'em the way I do my coffee, Matthews Junior," Johnson says. "Hot and black. Let's went. Daddy's impatient."

Art is shocked. His house is no longer his house, so far as he can tell. There must be three dozen men spread out on bedrolls and couches throughout it—parlor, dining room, kitchen, study, sewing room. Men everywhere. They laze and chew and spit and talk to one another in twangs and drawls. Rifles are strewn among them and gunbelts festoon the chair arms and lamps. Guadalupe and Concha and Johnny Fourth of July scuttle back and forth among them with coffee and food. Johnny manages to whisper to Art that the men are Texans who came into town last night hidden in boxcars. And that Mr. Matthews says Art is to bathe and change before he comes into his mother's bedroom.

When he's bathed and warm in a cardigan and favorite pair of white bucks, Art has to admit he feels better. He even manages to slip a touch of brandy. He puts some pomade in his hair—God, how you miss little things like that—and smooths the part in the middle the way his mother likes it. Maybe he'll even get a good meal out of this. The whole family waits for him in his mother's bedroom as if they're hiding from the gunmen, too.

Art didn't realize how low he'd sunk until he sees Bunny and his mother. They hold hands on the bed. Bunny looks so fragile in her khaki lawn dress, his mother so dignified but hurt in her rose empire gown. The old man, oh, Art can handle him. But these two—one is his own mother, and the other is to be, was to be, the mother of his children. How he must have slaughtered their feelings.

They keep stoically to their places when he comes in. His father stands beside the oak commode and extends his hand. "Welcome home, son," he says. "We've missed you." His voice is warm but a little trembly.

Art hadn't expected to feel this way at all. So . . . prodigal. He takes his father's hand.

"Before you say anything," his father begins, "I want to apologize for my means of bringing you home. And to assure you that I don't intend to kidnap you against your will. But I think you'll admit you owe us at least this talk."

Art loses himself in the memories that cling to the starched linen curtains of his mother's bedroom and lowers his head. His father goes on. "There's no point in my telling you that something important is about to happen here. Those men in our home should tell you that. There's danger in it, and men will most likely die for it. I won't go into detail yet, but I want you to know that the time for choosing your side—irrevocably—has come. We wanted to give you the opportunity to make that choice knowingly and manfully." Mrs. Matthews's eyes fill with tears. Bunny stares ahead at the flowered wallpaper.

"By this time tomorrow, this town will be changed for good. Perhaps a good part of the world will be, too. All of us here know the influences you've been under. We know the things you've done or have been forced to do—the list of names, for example. But all that doesn't amount to a hill of beans now. You're our son. What you are to Bunny, we'll leave you two to talk out. I'll ask you to do one thing for us, no more. Stop playing games for one day. Come with me to a meeting tonight. Then, if after the meeting you're still undecided as to your loyalties, you'll at least know what those loyalties entail." He looks to Art's mother again. "Well, Lavinia, that's my speech. You have anything to add?"

She shakes her head. "We love you, son," she says. Her tears spill over and streak the powder on her cheeks. "God bless you."

How abject Art feels. What a reptile, a selfish toad. He's been playing games like a child while these people were living serious lives. He chokes out a "Thank you, Dad," and feels hot tears well up. Fair or unfair, these are his people, his family.

His father steps to him and pats his shoulder. "I think Bunny has something to say to you, son. You take it as you will. Concha has some supper waiting for you, I believe, and a little Dubonnet." He takes the hand of Art's mother and leads her to the door. Art stops them.

"Father," he says. "Don't try to make me promise anything just now."

"I understand," his father says. "One day. That's all I ask. No more."

He feels discomfort around him like a huge piece of liver or something after his mother and father are gone. Bunny keeps her gaze pinned to the flowers on the wallpaper, but he can feel her breathing in the room. He sneaks a look at her. He still can't imagine her naked, like the colored whore on the bed. Conscience is a terrible thing. "Bunny . . . " he begins.

"I want to say one thing, Art. I've been hurt terribly, but I still care. I want you to know that."

"I've had to live by my best lights," Art says. "I never wanted to hurt you on purpose." He takes a step closer to her. She doesn't meet his eyes yet.

"Art, I must know what I'm to expect. What my future is. Can you at least give me some clue to that?"

"Well. I still think you're a bang-up girl. That goes without saying."

"Have you slept with her?"

"Who?"

"You know who."

"Oh. No, of course not."

"Swear it."

"I do."

Her eyes leap to Art's face. "God, I loathe her," she spits, with a force that surprises him.

What she must have suffered to bring such hate out! Art's never seen it in her before. He wants to atone somehow, to give her something to let her know how he feels. The way he gave the Flynn woman the information about old Agent 34. His contrition forces the need to confess out of him like the incense does at church. "Bunny . . . I'm no longer a virgin." He can't help himself. He flings himself onto his knees by the bed and buries his head in her lap. "What can I do to make it up to you?"

"Just be *you,* Art."

"That's not easy to figure out sometimes," he says into her skirt.

"Not for me. I know who you are."

God knows he's glad to find someone who does. He's done his best. None of this Wobbly business is his fault. He didn't make the mines. He didn't make all those men workers and himself . . . Art Matthews. He's not a traitor, but he's not a superman either. He didn't make the war or the world. He can't help being himself, and anybody who thinks he can change himself into somebody else is mad as a bloody march hare. The Wobblies must have known that about him all along. "I'm sorry, Bunny. Forgive me." What will he ever do now?

She puts her thin hand on his head, tentatively.

Art and his father walk down Opera Drive in a silence. Art is terrified that some of the Wobs will see him, but his father keeps telling him it doesn't matter now. His father doesn't understand the Wobblies. It does matter. What if that Yaqui kid saw him? Or Bo? Or the Flynn woman? He could never face her, that's for sure. Art knows he'll not sell out to the plutes: he's advanced beyond that now. But just being here makes him feel dashed uneasy.

Downtown is quiet tonight, quieter than he's seen it since he's been home. The IWWs are obeying the no-assembly order all right. Even the rain has held off so the air has an echoing stillness to it that captures and magnifies sounds. His father takes him into the dispensary by way of the basement entrance.

Half a dozen men with sidearms guard the door, and Art spots another guarding the ventilation grille in the sidewalk.

It's a little after eight. He and his father enter a big storage room off the main corridor. There are thirty or so other men there already; Art knows many of them. Dr. Bledsoe, Orson McCrea, city engineer Jacob Thompson, the manager of his father's bank, Kellogg from the telephone office, Clampitt from the post office, a half dozen shift bosses. And at the front of the room, spread across it in captain's chairs, Harry Wheeler, Jack Greenway, and Grant Dowell. The rest of the men seem to be businessmen from around town, a few miners and muckers, plus Miles Merrill and the other company security chiefs. Art looks around for Lem Shattuck. He doesn't find him. Tom Matthews takes the remaining chair up front. A hush comes over the room once he is seated, as if he was the last one they were waiting for. Art finds a chair near the back, apart from the others. To avoid the curious glances and whispers that come his way, he looks around the room. And Joseph and Mary, he wishes he hadn't! He can't believe what he sees. All around the walls are crates that he thought were full of medical equipment when he came in. But they're not. They're gun crates. A hospital full of guns, of all things! Crate on top of crate, all Winchester .30–.30 carbines. And over in one corner some larger crates that look for all the world like the crates new machine guns are shipped to the Rifles in. Holy Mother, they've got an arsenal in here!

The presence of the guns somehow changes the room. Art's back muscles tighten. He is sure the rest of the men feel it, too. There is something so ruddy real about those crates everywhere, as if they had been left there on purpose like stage props. If nobody else were in the room to take the floor, Art thinks the guns would say enough.

But Harry Wheeler is here.

Art tries to concentrate on what Wheeler is saying. But his mind won't stick on it. What in God's name do these people have in mind? This is a bloody hell of a lot more serious than he ever thought it would be and he's got to do something about it. He gets snatches of what's going on as he tries to make sense of why he's there at all. Wheeler goes into a long rigamarole about explosions and fires and foreigners and patriotism and hampering the war effort and outlaws and posses and the safety of everybody's wives and little children, then gets very serious and quiet and tells about some god-awful amount of dynamite he's discovered and impounded. The time has come, he says, though Art doesn't catch for what. And he's asked all these representative citizens here for advice.

Art's stomach isn't doing well, like the time he was with the Wobblies at the Finn Hall. Things around him seem to flicker a lot, the way they do at the picture show. People stand up and say things but to Art they sound like pure nonsense, coming from men he's looked up to all his life. Dr. Bledsoe rants about hanging people in front of the company store. Miles Merrill talks about driving them across the border. Bob Clampitt stammers about stockades. Everybody seems to have something to say until one of the muckers mentions machine guns. Then the room goes quiet.

Who are they talking about? Who is the "them" that they're going to round up? Dimly it comes to Art that Harry Wheeler means everybody who's been sympathetic to the strike at all. Great God, the man is talking about thousands of people! Art knows he's going to throw up. He tries to remember all those laws and constitutional things from his history courses at Princeton. Surely some of them apply here if he could only remember them.

But Harry goes on. Things about secrecy and surprise attack. About unfortunate mistakes that will no doubt be made. About all loyal Americans tying white bands around their arms to mark them and everybody else being suspect. It's out of a melodrama, Art thinks. But no, it's not. It's real. Captain Greenway says the Wobblies are all yellow, that if you meet them with guns and enough good men they'll show their true colors. Grant Dowell goes on about the company owning the railroad and cattle cars and special trains. Orson McCrea blathers about history and leadership until Art's stomach can't take it anymore.

He flings himself out of his chair. Somebody has got to go out on the streets and yell at the top of his voice about this nonsense before people take it seriously. He's aware of stumbling past a row of men and stepping on their feet without excusing himself. And then of trying to rush past the guards at the door, but being pushed back. And of his father beside him, sternly ordering him back inside the room. Telling him that if the Wobblies are warned and ready, there will be a massacre for sure. And that the blood will be on Art's hands.

On his hands? Blessed Mother, now it's all going to be his fault? It's crazy. His father is crazy as a loon. But no, he's not crazy. None of them in the room are crazy. And what if he did warn the Wobs? They would fight, Art is sure of it. All he wants to do is throw up and go to bed. He wants the world to be right side up again.

Back inside the room the men are all on their feet. Harry Wheeler is administering an oath to them that makes them duly sworn deputies who promise to uphold the laws of Arizona and the Constitution of the United States. Grant Dowell circulates among them with pieces of white cloth to tie on their arms. Art's father nudges Art and motions for him to raise his hand.

Art has no more control over his arm. It rises. Grant Dowell is in front of him, smiling. He holds out a white rag.

Art takes it.

Bo Whitley: July 11, 10:30 P.M.

The streetcar sways down out of Jiggerville, past Skunktown and Bakerville into Warren. In the dark cactusy stretches between camps, Bo lets himself drift into a mixture of elation and dread. He left word only this afternoon at the C&A hospital that he wanted to see Greenway. And the company fink was at his door in Jiggerville by sundown with instructions. That's good; it means Greenway's eager. Bo knows that time has run out on Haywood. One after another the rest of the camps in Arizona are weakening, some begging for help. They're all looking to Bisbee, all waiting to see what happens here. Haywood has had his chance. Now it's Bo's turn.

The deputy at the car stop in Warren eyes Bo, but since he's alone lets him pass. The deputies have orders to break up any gathering, but do little more. Wheeler is going after the IWW's communications. Isolating the boys. Destroying their solidarity. Few of them have phones, and sending runners to each boardinghouse, each cabin, is an impossible task. Wheeler, the son of a bitch, has hit their most vulnerable point: Bo knows that without the rallies most of the boys won't last a week.

If they give up, Elizabeth goes away. Bo is sure of that. If they attack, they lose. They don't have the strength for it; not in these damn closed canyons. And when they lose, he loses Elizabeth, too. She either goes to jail or is run out of the state. He only has one choice. Negotiate. Talk to Greenway. Give Haywood time to raise some money, get more boys into town. It has to be Greenway. Wheeler is a jackleg, a puppet. And Dowell can't do anything without somebody in New York or somewhere okaying him.

Maybe that's what Greenway wanted all along, Bo thinks as he makes his way up the slope toward the bonfires of the deputies who guard the Greenway and Douglas houses. To look like a hero and get his mines back to work without Dowell or Shattuck or any of them. Bo knows how weak the Wobs are now. He only hopes that Greenway doesn't.

There's another thing Bo is sure of: Greenway and Wheeler know where Jim Brew is. If Brew were free and in town he would have contacted Bo. And he's not in Naco—Bo has asked everyone, Mex whores to faro dealers. Nor is he dead. His clothes, old sword, and pistol were gone when Bo went back to the room in Jiggerville after the fire. So that has to be part of his bluff. If Greenway will talk about a settlement at all, he'll damn well have to talk about Brew, too.

As he approaches the bonfire, a handful of armed men stand and strain to see him in the streetlight. One of them is Miles Merrill, fat in his too tight riding pants. When he makes Bo out, he says something to the other men and they slowly sprawl beside the road again. He steps forward to meet Bo.

"You Whitley, I recollect."

"Good memory, Miles. It's been a while."

Merrill grunts and turns to walk with Bo toward Greenway's house. "Your daddy's turning over in his grave, boy. You know that, don't you?" he says.

"No, he ain't. He never made the money to buy a grave big enough to turn over in."

Merrill cuts his eyes hard toward Bo, then speeds up. Bo feels a little better.

Greenway's big wooden house is dark upstairs. Floodlights make the eastern grass lawn glow. Long rectangles of yellow light spread out to it from the high windows of what Bo takes to be the parlor. Bo has never been this close to the house before, never been this close to any house like it. He wonders what Elizabeth would think if she knew he were here. He realizes he can't afford to have this not work. Success will be the only justification he can offer.

A houseboy, visibly nervous, lets them in. He tries to take Bo's coat and looks confused when he realizes Bo isn't wearing one. He motions for Bo to follow him. But Merrill stops them.

"Whitley," he orders.

Bo turns and Merrill's hands slide from his armpits to

his hips before he can jump away from them. They pause only a moment on Bo's brass knuckles. Bo swears at Merrill and slaps his hand away.

"Sorry, boy," Merrill says. "I'll have to have them knucks."

Bo backs away, and slips his fingers into the knucks.

"You want to see the cap'n?" Merrill says, deadpan.

Bo hesitates, then takes the knucks from his pocket and drops them heavily into Merrill's hand. "I want 'em back," he says.

The houseboy leads him alone through a big empty parlor with copper chandeliers. Their footsteps get lost in thick Oriental carpets. At a door off the parlor, the houseboy taps lightly and waits. After a pause, a voice tells them to come in. Bo has left his cap on purposely. Now, without thinking, he pulls it off.

The door opens onto what seems to be a paneled study, and the houseboy steps to the side for Bo to go in. Bo throws back his shoulders and walks too fast into the room. Greenway, looking a little drawn, stands from a desk-chair to offer his hand to Bo. Bo takes it and tries to return Greenway's squeezing grip. Greenway politely leads Bo to a leather armchair and again takes his seat by the desk, only a few feet from Bo.

"Drink, Whitley?"

"No, I don't dr—no," Bo says. Hell of a way to begin, apologizing for yourself, he thinks.

Greenway motions the houseboy away. The door closes with a solid, quiet click. Bo thinks of the thin curtains between the rooms of the cabin at the top of the hundred and six steps. There is an awkward silence.

"Well. You've come alone, then," Greenway says at length.

"I'm here as me, Greenway. Not representing nobody."

"Anybody," Greenway says. "We'll have to work on that."

"Who? On what?"

"Never mind. Do I take it that you're accepting my invitation to come, or do you have something specific you want to see me about?"

"Yeah, I got something to say."

"I see. Would you at least care for coffee?"

"No."

"Well, then. I'm listening."

"I reckon you know Harry Wheeler better than I do. There ain't no point in my telling you anything about him."

"I know Harry, yes."

"So maybe what you don't know is that he's going to get your town blown up."

"Harry? I thought you boys would do the blowing up. Or at least it was easy enough for us to convince Harry you would."

"I can't make promises no more. That back-to-work notice you and the others put in the paper today has got my outfit mad enough. But if Harry tries to stop us from getting together, nobody, me nor anybody, can tell what one or another of us might do. If you understand me."

"That's not very subtle, Whitley. Even if I could control Wheeler, what would you want me to do? Take the side of your union? You're not stupid." Greenway rests his elbows on his knees and leans forward toward Bo. He smiles, that small, almost mocking smile that Bo remembers seeing on him the day of the parade. "I think you people can control your bunch. You're being overly modest."

"And if we can control them, I still don't make no promises about what's happening Friday if that order ain't withdrawn."

"That leaves us with a stalemate. And my question remains: What would you have me do?"

"Be a damn man. Call off that order. Call off Wheeler and come talk to our strike committee."

"I think, Whitley, that you're missing something, regardless of the nobility that's motivated this visit. What oversimplifiers you people are! Do you really think you understand the principles at work here?"

"Do you?"

Greenway's smile grows. "Perhaps not. Are you in love with that Flynn woman?"

"None of your damn . . . what's that got to do with anything?"

"She's not right for you, you know. Was there anything else you needed to see me about?"

"Where's Jim Brew?"

Greenway leans back in his chair. "Now that genuinely surprises me. You mean you really don't know?"

Bo shoves himself out of the heavy armchair. "You go to hell, Greenway." That's weak, and Bo knows it. But in less than five minutes, the damn man has him going in half a dozen directions at once.

Greenway stands. "I'm sorry. I don't know where this Brew is, and never have known. If I did, I'd have had him arrested long ago. Does that satisfy you?"

"He's got to be let go. Whatever the settlement, he's got to be part of it."

"If he's found, Whitley, I doubt that I or God or anyone could pry him away from Harry Wheeler, and that's the truth. I think even you will concede Wheeler that much respect. But until he's found, the point is moot. Later, who knows?"

Bo makes no further move to go. Greenway sits again, confident. "Why didn't you come to me earlier?" he asks.

"The situation was different." Bo feels even more awkward than he has so far, standing while Greenway sits. He eases down into the armchair again.

"Do you mind if I interpret that for you?"

"Do whatever you like."

"Splendid. What you really mean is that you weren't desperate enough to. And that while Bill Haywood was here, you didn't dare because you knew he'd tell you that you were a fool. Haywood would have known the rules a good bit better than you do. Your only prayer of negotiating comes when you're strong enough for us to have to come to you. Do you really think you have the strength to make it worth my time to negotiate with you? Even if I were temperamentally capable of sitting down at a table with what your outfit represents. You've lost this bloody strike, Whitley, and you know it. The fact that you're here tells me that surer than anything else you could have done."

Bo feels the blood rush to his face. Greenway has disposed of him like he would a damn Chihuahua that was yipping at his feet.

"I don't blame you, Whitley. I'd be angry, too. But we can't let it end there, can we? We've still got my reasons for wanting you here, haven't we? There may be an out for you yet."

"There's been no strike lost. And I haven't asked for any outs."

"Not in words, no. Let me ask you something, Whitley. Why are you a Wobbly?"

"It won't do no good. I won't argue it with you."

"Argue it with me? Argue the theory of surplus value, all of that? Of course not. That all makes eminent good sense in its own way. But this business about the tools belonging to the users, and so on, has nothing to do with the reason you're a Wobbly. I've watched you. You're above all that and you know it."

"There's nothing else I got to say to you." Bo moves to get to his feet again.

"Two minutes, Whitley. Give me those." Bo keeps his seat but doesn't relax into it. "Thank you," Greenway goes on. "You're a Wobbly because there's nothing else you can be. What can a young man like yourself, of your class, from a place like Bisbee, be? A shift boss in the mines? No, you're better than that. You're a born leader. You draw people to you. And that's a flair one is born with, like it or not. So given your generation, this decade, this place, your sensitivity, imagination, and obvious intelligence—crude as it may be yet—what else can you be? Look around you. How many other young men with your background are there on every freight train in the West? Their cause has nothing to do with *you,* with Bo Whitley. And that's an abomination."

Bo eases back into his chair. Something in what Greenway is saying gives him a kind of edge over the man, an edge he can't put into words. "Reckon you'd rather I be you, Cap'n."

"Don't be naïve, Whitley—and I don't suppose that's the first time you've been called that. You can't be me. You can't acquire blood and breeding any more than you can acquire red hair. Nor can you be someone like Lem Shattuck: you're too idealistic for that. What you can do is be yourself and take what help is offered you. You don't have the instincts for selfless fanaticism, you know. That Flynn woman does. And that's why you haven't a chance with her. No, you can't be me, but you can be my great-grandfather. You can be a founder, Whitley. You can be the first step to something. That's what endures in this country. Generations. That's the future a sane man builds for, not the nonsense of a world in which people go against every trace of human nature and create bleak 'earthly paradises.' Do you follow me?"

"What are you after, Greenway? What do you want out of me?"

"There! We all want something out of each other, don't we?" He slides his swivel chair back and flicks on a lamp. The lamp lights the portrait of a woman on the wall above his desk.

Bo almost shudders at the blankness in the woman's eyes. She's a woman he knows he could never talk to. A woman you'd turn to glass if you touched.

"This is one thing I want, Whitley, and you can't give it to me. No one can. It's woman, everything woman ought to be. It's not to be touched, but not to be lived without. It's the thing a man gives to his children, the kind of mother he creates. You don't see that yet, I know. But your children might, given the right surroundings to grow up in."

He turns to Whitley with the light on the portrait still drawing all the room to itself. "But I want other things, too. I need something more to make than towns and mines. I need a human being to mold, a son. Something that Isabella hasn't—may never—be able to give me. You ask me what I want from you? You are it."

Bo can't help himself. He grins. Greenway's slight smile melts and his face becomes serious, and older. "Call yourself whatever you like—call yourself my secretary, my aide. But I can make you what you can never make yourself, Whitley. There is something . . . tangible that can exist between men, a kind of transference of potency. I've watched you, all along. You have that. I want it."

In the dimness beside the bright desk lamp, Bo is aware of Greenway moving, his chair rolling silently on the carpeted floor. His hand is on Bo's shoulder, then moves gently up the side of Bo's neck to his cheek. "I'm offering much more than I'm asking, Whitley," Greenway says.

Bo sits absolutely still, seeing. Greenway has flung him around like an empty sack. He's never felt more like a fool than he does this moment. He's been jumping and turning like a trained monkey to prove something to this man, and those like him. He's let himself be flattered into believing that he was important. He's believed in Greenway's power, believed that this thing he came back to Bisbee to take for himself was worth fighting for. And yet Greenway is as twisted by this place as Bo's old man was. He's pitiful, empty, nailed down by the blankness in that woman's eyes and all it stands for.

Great God! There has to be more worth fighting for than that blankness! He thinks of Elizabeth's warmth against the cool leaves on the mountain. Then his eyes move back to the face of the woman in the portrait. Is that what Greenway can offer him? He feels violently duped, defrauded. In one motion of his right hand, he flings Greenway's palm away from his cheek. With his left, he jabs sharp and hard into Greenway's stomach. Greenway moans and doubles over. Bo clasps his hands and slams them in an uppercut against Greenway's bowed head. The head snaps up, eyes closed. Greenway slumps to his knees on the floor. Bo draws back again, then stops. He loosens his fist and pushes Greenway over against the easy chair. Greenway, fighting for breath, crumples. Bo steps back from him, watches a moment, then slips quickly to the door. He opens it to Miles Merrill leaning against the back of a leather couch in the parlor.

"Where's the Cap'n?" Merrill asks.

Bo walks slowly, steadily past him to the door. He struggles to keep his breath even and light. "In there." He jerks his thumb toward the study. "He'll be out directly."

"Let's wait for him," Merrill says.

"Got an appointment." Bo keeps walking.

"Whitley." Merrill's rumbling voice deepens. Bo pauses. "I said let's me and you wait for him." Bo hears the click of a revolver hammer.

Bo eases himself to the frame of the double doors from the parlor to the vestibule and leans. He slides around so that he can see Merrill resting his Smith and Wesson .45 in his palm, aimed. The silence in the dim room is broken only by slight shuffling noises from the study. Merrill keeps his eyes steadily on Bo.

After a time, the light from the study is broken by a

shadow. Then Greenway's silhouette erectly divides the open door. He seems at ease, composed. "Miles?" he says.

"Cap'n?"

"Is Whitley still here?"

"Yessir."

"Would you show him upstairs, please? He'll be staying the night. Put a couple of your boys in with him, too, for his protection."

"Bedrooms are full, Cap'n. Them boys that come in on the freight will be up there."

Greenway steps into the parlor. He comes halfway across it so that the light from the vestibule strikes his face. His eyes have the blankness of those of the woman. "Double them up. I'd prefer that Whitley doesn't have to go back into town tonight. For his safety."

Orson McCrea: July 12, 2:00 A.M.

"This is the Loyalty League call."

That's all it took. Kellogg and the operators in the phone company office said it—how many?—a hundred times to the captains and the lieutenants. And that was it. Afterwards the switchboard lit up like an electric sign as the captains and the lieutenants called the troops. An hour is the estimated maximum time it should take to assemble the largest posse in the history of the West. Only one hour. McCrea imagines the jingle of phones in the dark streets and up the canyons, the quiet knocks and hushed conversations on back porches where there are no telephones. All over Bisbee, Warren, Jiggerville, Johnson Addition, Lowell, Upper Lowell, South Bisbee, Cowan Ridge, Zacatecas, Skunktown, Bakerville, Saginaw, and Don Luis camps. Up School Hill, Youngblood Hill, Chihuahua Hill, Sacramento Hill, Tank Hill, Quality Hill, Bucky O'Neill Hill, Laundry Hill. Even down to the rows of smeltermen's houses in Douglas. At last. The cleansing.

They are in Wheeler's office, beside his rolltop desk.

The district is divided into sections with deputies posted to limit passage from one section to the other. The Wobblies must not be allowed to congregate or warn each other. Surprise is essential, says Captain Greenway. There is a list of men not scheduled for picket duty that somebody called Agent 34 has furnished. They'll be the ones rounded up first, one by one, house by house, just before dawn. And then comes the frontal attack. The assault on the Finn Hall (there's a one-pound cannon captured from the Villistas for that), the Pythian Castle, and the Lowell headquarters will come simultaneously with the one on the pickets. If it's done right, no one will have been able to spread the word about what's going on until it's too late. If there's a slip-up... McCrea is glad Sheriff Wheeler has taken responsibility for any blood.

Most of the boys have rifles already. For those who don't, wagons and trucks from the company store have gone out to all the designated assembly points with the crates from the dispensary. And white bands. Enough white bands and rifles for everyone.

McCrea has been supervising that. It's an important job, and everybody knows it. There will be a national Loyalty League after this, and he will head it. Captain Greenway has promised. Times make the man, he says. Harry Wheeler is busy with other things tonight. After the meeting, he vanished into his room behind the office for a good two hours to write the notice for the morning's *Review.* The *Review*'s pressmen and compositors are standing by for it.

The post office is already in the hands of the rifle club. Wheeler has ordered the telephone and telegraph offices shut down until further notice. Squads of riflemen have barricaded every road into town. Bisbee is entirely cut off. There is no earthly authority in these canyons now beyond Harry Wheeler and Orson McCrea.

McCrea hasn't stopped since the meeting was over. He passed briefly by his house for a bite of supper and a quick prayer with his wife and the kids. His wife cried a lot, the way she always does. After supper he supervised the machine guns, when it was dark enough to do it safely. One mounted on the dispensary, overlooking the square. One in the school with a view of Brewery Gulch and the Pythian

Castle. Another in Warren in the C&A offices, ready to sweep the ball park and mall. And one for Harry Wheeler.

Wheeler makes one last change in his notice for the *Review,* then asks McCrea if he wants to walk over to the newspaper office with him. McCrea agrees. Outside, the deputies have done a good job of keeping the streets clear. They're quiet, which adds to the tension that makes the very air itself seem to want to crack. The horns of a silver-white half-moon thrust vaguely from behind ribbons of clouds. At the Eagle Theater, ahead of them, *American Methods,* with William Farnum, is playing. McCrea thinks maybe somebody will make a movie about him someday.

The editor of the *Review,* Folsom, stands to greet them when they push in through the double doors on Main Street. He is solemn. Wheeler hands him the handwritten copy for the notice, and Folsom ushers him into his private office. McCrea waits in the newsroom, which falls silent when Wheeler leaves. He checks his pocket watch. It is moving on toward 3:00 A.M. One of the linotype operators catches a centipede on the floor and pins it to the copy chair.

"It's a good omen," he says when he notices McCrea watching him. McCrea nods. Mormons don't believe in that kind of thing.

The click of the AP wire sounds loud from the next room. Downstairs McCrea can hear the low hum of the linotypes. The foreman asks McCrea if they are to be furnished with guns. He seems disappointed when McCrea tells him no.

Wheeler stays with the editor longer than McCrea thought he would. The clock on the Pythian Castle has just struck three when he comes out. In spite of not having slept, he looks alert. He tells McCrea to go get some sleep, but Orson thinks he'll stick around the newspaper office. He's nervous, and it's a good place to be when something important is up. One of the reporters might want to interview him. Wheeler leaves. Everyone stands when he passes through the double screen doors.

Only occasionally an automobile speeds by. or the footsteps of a watchman echo on the cobbles. Quiet returns, waiting returns. Orson flips through some pages of tomorrow's paper, already made up. One whole page is a subscription list to the patriotic Citizens' Protective Association. To pass the time McCrea counts the names. There are 250 local companies. In a black box the names of the nonmembers are printed. People aren't to patronize them. There are only forty-five names. McCrea shudders when he imagines bearing the shame those men must. He thanks God he'll never have to. The next page has a list of the slackers who won't register for the draft. Lem Shattuck's two boys are listed. They are called sympathizers with the IWW and the "Prussian engine of war."

Outside, the street sweepers come on duty. They make plenty of noise with their carts and shovels and brooms. They seem very normal to McCrea, as if they shouldn't be there.

Just at four o'clock the telephone rings. It's a mother, worried about her boy coming in to deliver his papers that morning. Some men mysteriously came and called her husband away, and when she went out into the street a group of armed men asked her to go home. Then a neighbor called to tell her that many men with guns were gathered behind the church. The reporter who answered the phone tells her that they'll let no newsboys out unless they're assured of perfect safety, but that it's her patriotic duty to send her boy in today.

The reporter recounts the phone conversation and then asks if anybody knew that the men of Paris wore white handkerchiefs on their arms at the Saint Bartholemew's Day Massacre. McCrea doesn't know about that, but it sounds suspicious.

Day begins to break. The boys must have swept the outer reaches of town by now and be on their way into the center. McCrea imagines bunches of surprised, half-dressed Wobblies penned behind hedges, houses, stores, and churches, waiting to be driven in with the others. His own squad should be ready to move out soon. He's asked to lead one of the first into Jiggerville. He remembers his legends of the Mormon Avenging Angels. There comes a time, everywhere.

From another room floats the sound of the foreman locking up the forms. The pressman throws a knife switch, the motor flashes, and the press begins to rattle. McCrea bids good-bye to the fellows in the room. They do not stand.

Outside it is dim and sweet and cool. The morning sun slashes across the mountain peaks and spills into the canyons. McCrea thinks it looks like light from stained-glass windows. Across the street a cook from the English Kitchen comes out to the doorway in his cap and apron. He raises his hands above his head and takes a big stretch and breath of morning air all in one. It seems to McCrea that surely his stretching muscles will crack like a pistol shot when his hands meet behind his head.

His boys are waiting for him in the dispensary. There are five of them, handpicked. Wheeler is gone already. One of the boys hands Orson a rifle. He takes it, looks at it as if it were something he's never seen before, then gives it back to the man. He will go unarmed. Let the reporters hear about that.

Only Orson McCrea knows where they are going now. Only he knows the way to Bo Whitley's room in Jiggerville. Only Orson is important enough to be able to choose his own target, to pick his own fate on the most momentous day of his life.

He steps out into the cool dawn light, in the lead.

Jim Brew: July 12, 3:30 A.M.

The shuffling, thumping noises from above have long stopped. Even the cleanup man, Nigger John Brown, has put away his broom and spread fresh sawdust and gone home. In the seven other nights he's spent here underneath the Saint Elmo saloon, Jim has learned the closing-up routine by heart. They say this cave was dug back in the time when you needed a place to hide if the Apaches came. Every night he waits like this to make sure it's quiet and deserted enough to go out. If he doesn't get out into the air sometime, he knows he'll smash his head against the wall. It's no blessed way to live. As soon as this strike is over, and all those damn gunmen and deputies are out of town, he'll get a freight somewhere. Maybe get Bo to go with him. Up to Jerome or Clifton or Christmas or Silver City. Start over.

He tries the trapdoor into the cashier's cage in the card-room above him. It's undone, as usual. Nigger John Brown don't forget. John's been good to him. Took messages to that Matthews boy, borrowed money off him, got the carbolic acid for Jim's side, bought him his food. Nobody but John and the Matthews boy knows where Jim is. Even Frank Johnson that owns the Saint Elmo don't. Frank probably don't even know this cave exists. Only those who were here in the old days, like Jim and Nigger John, remember it. Jim pats his stomach a last time to make sure he has his .38, and gets a firm grip on the Mex sword he managed to get from his wall in Jiggerville before he hid out. He blows the lantern out.

The place on his side where Shotgun Johnson got him still throbs as Jim hoists himself from the wooden whiskey crate through the trapdoor. But it's no more pain than he deserves. He's glad that poor woman didn't die, though he wouldn't have minded Shotgun Johnson burning up. All he wants now is to get out from under. Harry Wheeler's known to have tracked men halfway across the country before. He's worse than your conscience about that, they say. Jim doesn't like to think about it.

Getting involved in this strike was a bad idea. It's not like the other strikes. You can't just walk away from this one. He doesn't blame Bo—hell, Jim Brew should be old enough to know better than to go being a horse's ass to make people think he's something he's not. That's maybe the worst of this strike. Everybody is something they're not.

Maybe it's for the best, though. Lord, he's tired of the mines. This might force him to go to peddling and get ahead some. Hell, there's other women in other border towns besides the whores down in Naco. He wouldn't mind being like that Johnny Appleseed. So what if he's lost his pension? Is a pension from the mines worth so much? They hold it out like a carrot on a stick for stiffs like him, and the stiffs'll put up with anything for it. In a way, he reckons, maybe he ought to be grateful to the Wobblies, even for a bad strike.

The Saint Elmo is dark. The watchman isn't scheduled to come around until four. He's got time for a decent walk.

He unlocks the cashier's cage and feels his way into the saloon. He slips a quick snort of whiskey from the barrel behind the bar. Helps keep the chill away. Then he eases the back door open and listens. The dogs are out, like every night, talking to one another from mountain to mountain. Hundreds of them, he guesses, saying something that must matter to them. Tonight, though, they seem even more busy than usual. Like a bunch of drunks arguing over a poker game. The air is cool and sweet; the path behind the Saint Elmo is ripe with the smell of fig trees and long Johnson grass.

He strikes out up School Hill, keeping to backyards so that he avoids the street lamps. He's learned the dogs up this way already, so he can avoid them, too. He cuts past the wide set of steps they call the Broadway and makes for the close-packed jumble of cabins farther up the hill. The half-moon gives a fair amount of light, and he can make out the little patches of corn and tomatoes in backyards. He takes a tomato and listens to the dogs, then sees the men.

They're backing out of a house just ahead of him. Two of them with rifles. They've got somebody between them—a man in his undershirt. The man fights them, holds on to the door frame and cusses in a low voice. One of the riflemen jabs at the man's fingers with his rifle butt.

"My shoes, let me get my goddamn shoes," the man says as he struggles. A woman, young like the man, rushes out onto the porch. She's in her nightgown and crying. She tries to get one of the men with rifles to let her give a pair of brogans to the man. Jim crouches behind a hedge. One of the gunmen takes the shoes from the woman and throws them over his shoulder. A little girl, five or six at the most, runs out onto the porch screaming. The woman, trying to check her own crying, picks the little girl up. But she keeps screaming.

Jim backs away. The sword he carries clangs and he jabs it in the dirt to quieten it. Lights go on in some of the cabins around him. Just up the hill he hears the thudding of rifle butts on a door. He looks toward the sound. More men with rifles shove into a blue cabin beyond a chinaberry tree. In the light from the door he can see they all have white rags tied around their arms. What the hell is going on? He eases closer to the blue house until he can hear shouting and scuffling coming from inside.

"Move, Bohunk," he hears a man say.

"What the hell I do?" a heavy accent answers.

"You're a goddamn Wobbly."

"I get my damn shirt maybe?"

"Move."

"Where I go?"

"None of your nevermind. Move."

He edges to the window. A man in his undershirt, a woman in her nightgown, a boy, wide-eyed, clinging to her. This woman doesn't cry. She throws herself at one of the gunmen and tries to push him out the door. The gunman slams her in the ribs with his rifle butt. Jim knows the man, an Irishman he's played cards with. He always seemed like a decent sort. What the hell is he doing slamming women around with a rifle? The woman gasps and crumples. Her husband tries to lift her up but the gunmen shove him out the door. The woman raises her head and Jim sees her staring at one of the men's white armbands.

"Cossack bastards!" she yells as they drag the man away. "Cossack bastards!"

Jim moves away from the window. Along with the barking of the dogs, he hears shouts, knocks, and thuds from cabins all up School Hill. He thinks it must be one of those pogro whatevers that the little Jew jitney driver always talks about. In the distance he hears a rifle crack. Hell piss shit, somebody's got to warn somebody. Somebody's got to warn Bo and Miss Flynn. What will they do to them, if they're doing this to just regular workingstiffs?

He knows he doesn't have a snowball's chance of making it to Jiggerville through this. He's got to send somebody. Matthews. That Matthews boy is close, just down at the French Kitchen on the Gulch. If anybody can get through, he can. Jim just has to make it to him before the gunmen. They'll bundle him back to his daddy sure as shit.

Crouching, Jim stumbles down the hill. He doesn't worry so much about the noise. There's enough stumbling and bumping around him anyway. He crashes through tomato and corn patches, surprises a goat, zigzags past dogs and streetlights. His side throbs, and the pain in his leg from the country club fight wrenches him. He slides down the last drop of the hill, alongside a rock wall behind the Saint Elmo. The French Kitchen is just across the Gulch now. He stays close to the wall and makes his way down to the Broadway. The Broadway isn't empty though; gunmen, talking low, make their way up it along the cobbles. Jim waits until they cut off onto Opera Drive, then plunges onto the Gulch.

It's quiet for the most part. Only at the little sleeping room beside the French Kitchen, where the Yaqui kid lives, is there commotion. Four men have Yaqui just outside the door. He's swinging on them all and cussing them in Indian. They have a hell of a time holding on to him until one of them gets him a good smack with a rubber hose. Yaqui falters, staggers, and goes down. A couple of the gunmen kick him until he's still.

Jim waits, shaking with impatience, as the men pick Yaqui up and awkwardly make off with him down the Gulch. He hears other men approaching and dashes into the side door that leads upstairs to the rooms over the French Kitchen.

At Matthews's door, he waits again and listens. There is no sound inside. He knocks lightly. Again, no sound. He's afraid to knock too loud. So he tries the doorknob.

It turns. Jim waits, then eases the door open. The room is dark. What the hell should he do? Flick on the light and scare the kid, or try to wake him gently? He decides the light is safest. No telling what the kid might do if somebody commences to shaking him in the dark. He makes his way carefully to the center of the room and feels for the light chain. He touches and loses it, then grasps it. When the light flashes on, one of the men crouched against the wall lunges.

Son of a bitch! Jim sidesteps and the lunging man glances off him, but manages a hold on his leg. There are three of them—Jim recognizes only Beeman, a Cousin Jack trammer he thought he knew. Beeman levels his pistol at Jim and yells for him to throw his hands up. The man on the floor tries to pull Jim from his feet. Be goddamned if he'll let himself get trapped by a bunch of whatever-they-ares and sent to prison for the rest of his life. He doesn't have time to be afraid. He brings the sword up to his waist and slaps at the man on the floor with it broadside, like he was cutting weeds. The man yelps and lets go. Jim stumbles back toward the door.

Beeman yells again for Jim to throw his hands up, but Jim can tell from the worried look in his eye that he won't shoot. He keeps moving. Beeman takes a step toward him, and Jim swings the sword in a circle around his head. Beeman steps again, and Jim hacks at him, a foot away from his face, with the sharp edge of the sword. Beeman ducks. The man with him dives for the far side of the bed.

Jim is out the door now, slamming it behind him. A bullet rips through it as Jim clumps down the stairs. Another gunman coming up to investigate the shot gets to the outside door just as Jim does. Jim hacks at his pistol arm. He doesn't cut deep, but the man drops his pistol and, with a howl, grabs his arm. Jim keeps going.

He's got to get to Jiggerville however he can now. If he tries to go by the main road, he's bound to be stopped. The only way is around Sacramento Hill, along the company road with no houses. As he passes the front of the French Kitchen, he sees that the doors stand open, and inside, by lamplight, forms move around the restaurant. He hears glass breaking and wood splintering and Mother Moriotti's shrill French. The bastards, the low-down bastards.

It's been mesquite clump to mesquite clump, shadow to shadow, all the way to Jiggerville. The sons of bitches are everywhere, like blow flies on a compost heap. Ever since he left the deserted company road, he's passed little bunches of men being shoved along the dark streets by gangs of gunmen. He even saw John Pintek, half dead of the TB and not even a mine worker, being drug out through his bedroom window. But he thinks he's made it! His street is still deserted, and the lights in Mrs. Stodgill's boarding-house are out. Nonetheless, shivering, he checks behind and to the side of himself before he starts up the porch steps to his room. Bo's got to be home. It's not even five o'clock yet.

But the bed is empty when Jim lets himself into the room. Unslept in. Jim feels a flash of relief: Bo's got word of things and skipped town. Why else wouldn't he be here? But then the other, the more likely, possibility hits him. Bo is with Miss Flynn. Of course! What a stupid shit not to go to the Ewings' first. It was on his way. He should have checked and left word. Besides, Miss Flynn would have known what to do. She only needed somebody to warn her. Now he's stuck here in Jiggerville and it's coming up broad daylight outside. He'd never make it back to town now. It's too late. Too late to save Bo, to save himself, to save anybody.

And he knows he's too tired to. He just wants to be let alone, to sleep on his own bed again. To hell with striking. To hell with everything but staying out of those damn mines and lying down to sleep. He's drained, like a butchered hog. He flings the sword at the rocker. It hits, slashes a chip from it, and clangs to the floor. The empty rocker sways back and forth, back and forth, like somebody had just gotten up out of it. Bo was crazy about rockers when he was a kid. He was a cute little shit.

Jim slips the .38 from his belt. Heavily, he falls down onto the cool cotton quilt of the still-made bed. To wait.

They try to be quiet but Jim hears them. A waiting man is like a dog, he thinks. He hears things nobody else does. He hears them spread around his little side porch, whispering. He hears the lone footsteps come up his stairs and onto the porch. He hears the silence before the man speaks.

"Whitley!"

Jim turns his head. It feels heavy as it did the night he and Bo fought Shotgun Johnson and that outfit at the country club. The man is outlined through the screen in the early gray light. Jim puts the voice and the face together. It's that shit McCrea. But that doesn't make any difference now. It could be any one of them. Nobody is who he is anymore. It could even be himself standing at the door.

"Go away, McCrea. Let me alone." He doesn't get up.

There is a silence. "You're not Whitley," McCrea says.

"No, I ain't. So let me be."

"You're Brew, ain't you? Jim Brew."

"Don't try to come in, McCrea."

McCrea steps back from the door. Jim can hear him saying in an excited voice that they've got Jim Brew in there. They've got the man everybody else, even Harry Wheeler, can't find.

"Cover me," McCrea says in a voice that Jim isn't supposed to hear. "I'm a-getting him myself."

"McCrea!" Jim says. "I'll plug you sure as hell if you come in that door."

"You don't have a prayer, Brew. They'll shoot you like a dog. I'm coming in." He reaches for the screen-door handle.

Jim doesn't sit up. The pistol lies across his stomach, pointed toward the door. All it takes is a slight shifting of his body and raising the pistol a few inches.

"Don't, McCrea."

The door moves. The spring squeeks. With the first shot, loud and stinking of gunpowder in the small room, the door slaps closed. McCrea jerks backward, then falls forward against the screen. With the second shot, he jerks again, then slumps to the side, out of Jim's vision. Jim hears an uneven sound like a feed sack thumping over onto the planks of the porch.

And then it's quiet. Jim can hear only the dogs. Wearily, as wearily as if he'd just made a long shift hand-drilling underground, Jim pushes off the bed. There's just no damn sense in it. A man's got to get by.

Two round holes about a foot apart break the screen at gut level. Mrs. Stodgill will want to fix those, Jim thinks. They'll let the flies in. He tries to remember if he has any cotton to plug them with, but can't. The screen doesn't need to be open wide—just enough for him to throw the pistol out. It thuds, skitters, and drops off the edge of the porch. He doesn't look down at the other long shape on the porch as he puts his hands on his head, kicks the door wide, and steps out onto the porch.

The morning sun creeps down into the canyons from Sacramento Hill. The men with rifles and Jim look at one another a moment in a kind of wonder. One, a solid blond with overalls on, stands apart and a little farther down the hill than the others. His bead is drawn before Jim gets to the edge of the porch. Then something slams Jim back against the horizontal boards of the wall, boards like a rub board against his back as he slides down them. He closes his eyes against the morning sunlight.

Then somehow it's like he is far down in the Copper

Queen. The wind whips cold and loud through the unseen cracks. But he's alone, and his carbide lantern gives off far too feeble a light. He reaches to turn it up. As he does, the hiss of it grows and buries even the loud wind. But it gives no more light.

He rolls over and opens his eyes. McCrea lies spraddled beside him on the battleship-gray planks of the porch. He's an ugly shit, with his mouth open like that. He looks like he's watching a boring picture show. Jim closes his eyes again.

Boots with taps clatter up the hollow steps. "Son of a bitch," a voice says.

Jim is back in the Copper Queen. Tunnels he's never seen before bank off on all sides. He sits down and waits. The hiss of the lantern grows; its light dims.

Elizabeth Gurley Flynn: July 12, 6:15 A.M.

There were men in the house. She saw them outlined against the moonlight through the open screen door. Her first thought was that Bo had come with some of the boys and was trying to slip in to see her. But then she saw the rifles and the gunbelts. What she remembers now, as she sits on the bench in Harry Wheeler's temporary office, is not the fear she felt but the sense of violation.

Two good jerks on the wooden screen ripped the hook loose and let them into the room. So it wasn't as if they had stormed the house and smashed their way in: There was no sense of violation of property rights or anything as silly as that. But as they spread around her while she lay watching, half-asleep and silent, on the couch in the Ewings' parlor, she felt something terribly obscene was happening. They were in Mrs. Ewing's clean parlor, the bare room that she had scrubbed, arranged, taken pride in as she did in her children. Her one decoration, a piece of stained glass on a string that hung in front of a window and caught the sunlight, spun when one of the men's rifles bumped it. The man jerked it down to keep it from rattling against the window. It seemed to Elizabeth as if he had ripped it from around Mrs. Ewing's neck.

She can't remember now if she thought all that then or if it's come to her as she's sat here and sorted things out. At the time, she knows she was afraid and enraged all at once. And uncertain that she was awake at all. She lay in her nightgown on the couch while one of the men held a rifle on her and another, a fat Cousin Jack, clamped a hand over her mouth. The hand smelled of gun oil, and the man made sure his arm sawed across her breasts. She supposed that in a sense she was prepared for the usual vigilante violence. But when the other two men kicked the Ewings' bedroom door open, she was taken completely by surprise. They wanted her, didn't they? They were after the leadership. What possible good could it do to terrify a five-fifty-a-day hoistman's children?

Elizabeth struggled against the fat Cornishman. He sat on her to hold her down and she could feel him squirming his heavy ass against her. The man who held the rifle on her, a younger man, tried to soothe her. "It's all right, ma'am," he said. "We're deputized." She was baffled. It was all right. They were deputized.

From the bedroom, Mrs. Ewing's voice called Elizabeth's name sleepily, then shrilly. Men's voices rose, and the sound of a scuffle. One of the children began to make a slow choking sound. Then Mr. Ewing tumbled out into the parlor in his long johns. The fat Cousin Jack got up, threw open Elizabeth's trunk and dug a dress from it. It was her red "public" dress. The Cousin Jack thought that was funny. She dressed in front of the men, staring each one in the eye until he turned away.

While she dressed, Mrs. Ewing came from the bedroom and tried to plead—could she at least send food or money with her husband? The men allowed her to throw a shirt on him and help him, gasping, to slip into his brogans and pants. She begged them to tell her where they were taking him. The younger man, who seemed to recognize her, apologized that he didn't know. The fat Cousin Jack told him to shut up.

Elizabeth did what she could to comfort the children

and put Mrs. Ewing at ease. But Mrs. Ewing would not be comforted and tried to follow the men as they herded Elizabeth and Mr. Ewing out onto the long flight of steps down to O.K. Street. The fat Cornishman held her back. He whispered something into her ear and patted her butt through her cotton nightdress. She spit at him. As he caught up with Elizabeth and the others, he shouted back to her, "Now doan y'worry. You'll not be lonesome, lady. None of y'will."

That was over an hour ago. Mr. Ewing is God knows where. Elizabeth has seen no one in authority but Shotgun Johnson. Constantly men have popped into the office with hurried reports and questions, then popped as quickly out again. They all wear white bands on their arms. They all are excited, and each speaks with a terse self-importance. She's demanded to see Bill Cleary, the IWW lawyer, to be allowed to send a telegram, to see Sheriff Wheeler. Shotgun Johnson only smiles and says, "Yes'm. Directly," to every demand.

About six they bring Mother Jones in. She's hatless, with her hair undone, and slaps at their hands when they try to help her into the room. They're gutless sons of bitches, she says. When she sits, she swings her crutch in an arc in front of herself to get some clear space and, she says, to keep the skunk shit off her shoes. The men laugh. Mother Jones doesn't.

Through the door, Elizabeth can see that the post office plaza and square are calm. The company store, the depot, the Copper Queen offices, all seem to be getting ready for business as usual. Wherever they're taking the rounded-up men, they're keeping them out of sight. The day-shift pickets, yawning and stretching, fill the plaza already. Elizabeth imagines they must mostly be stiffs bunked in the Pythian Castle or the Finn Hall or union hall down in Lowell. Pickets must be at every shaft and tunnel in Bisbee by now. Surely they suspect. This secret is too big to be kept. But the thought strikes her like a slap: That's probably just why they don't suspect.

All morning she's expected somehow to hear from Bo. He's hung at the back of her mind from the moment she saw the men in the doorway. If anybody has slipped past them, it's Bo. He's awake at the slightest noise at night. And he knows the town and the country around it. God Jesus, Flynn, she tells herself now. As if this were a picture show and the cavalry would come!

Mother Jones keeps up a steady tirade against everyone who comes in the door. Until the blond stocky man flings in with the news that Orson McCrea and Jim Brew are both dead in Jiggerville. Johnson and the half dozen other men in the room crowd him with questions as he begs to see Sheriff Wheeler. But Mother Jones grows silent. "How many more?" she says quietly to Elizabeth. "How many more of the poor blind creatures before the day is over?"

But Elizabeth doesn't hear her. If they found Brew in Jiggerville, then they must have found Bo, too. She jerks with a panic she hasn't felt through the whole nightmare morning. If he knows Brew is dead, what will he do? What won't he do? She pulls away from Mother Jones and shoves into the ring of men surrounding the blond with the message from Jiggerville. "Was he alone?" she demands. "Was Brew alone?"

The man doesn't recognize her. "Alone, yes'm. Bed hadn't even been slept in."

"Watch who the hell you talking to," Johnson tells him.

Bo didn't even come home last night? That doesn't make sense. Unless—and she chokes the thought before it has a chance to form itself fully—he knew about the thing ahead of time. No. Not Bo. Not this Agent 34. Not . . . Bo. Is she as insane as the town? There could be a hundred reasons he didn't sleep at home. Looking for Brew again. At Art Matthews's maybe. God, she thinks. Matthews. Where in hell is he? His father will go hard on him. She checks herself; that's pity misplaced. What can his father do to him that's nearly so bad as what's happening to these working people? It's them—and Bo—she has to worry about.

Johnson and the few other men still crowd the man from Jiggerville with questions. Elizabeth slips back to Mother Jones, who is alert, watching. She cuts her eyes toward the open door and winks. Elizabeth holds out her hand. Mother Jones struggles from her chair and takes Elizabeth's arm, and lets Elizabeth half lead, half carry her past the knot of men. Johnson's back is to them; the other white banders pay no attention. Elizabeth leads Mother

Jones, hobbling, out into the little grassy park by the company offices. The deputies there have their eyes fixed on the Wobs assembling in the plaza and don't notice two women alone.

Mother Jones stops short and loosens her grip on Elizabeth's arm. "Wire the President, wire Haywood, wire everybody. They can't be fool enough to close down the telegraph."

"What about you?" Elizabeth says.

"Hell, I move too slow. I'm getting out there on the picket line with the boys. Somebody's got to let them know what's going on. For what good it'll do."

Elizabeth hesitates. Mother Jones pokes her in the ribs. "Go on," she says. "Git." She turns away and hobbles toward the plaza. One of the deputies sees her and throws his rifle across her path. Mother Jones swings at him with her free hand. The deputy grabs her wrist and hollers for a couple of others nearby.

It's pointless to try to stop them. Elizabeth breaks for the steps up from the park to the telegraph office, next to the hotel. She knows she stands out like a railroad flare in her red dress, but now she's got surprise to count on. The drummers in their skimmers and derbies, up early in the chilly morning to catch their train, gawk like men watching a sideshow fan dancer. She shoves by them on the porch and into the leaded glass doors of the telegraph office.

The operator sits behind the counter. His hands are folded. He doesn't get up when she comes in, or speak. "I want to send some telegrams." She tries to keep her voice calm, normal.

"Sorry," the operator says. "Closed."

"You can't be closed! Are your lines down?"

"No ma'am. Just closed."

"By whose authority?"

From the sending room behind the clerk, two men in dark suits, with white bands around their arms, step out. She recognizes one of them: the square-built company doctor, Bledsoe. He wears crossed canvas bandoliers, has a pistol in his holster, and a huge hunting rifle in his hand. He steps to the counter, clanking and jingling like a wagonload of scrap.

"Authority of the people of Cochise County," he says. He lays the rifle across the counter with a heavy clunk. "Which you're not one of."

"Thank God for that," Elizabeth says. "This man is going to send telegrams for me. Get out of his way."

"You're under arrest," the doctor says.

That's too much. This ridiculous doctor dressed up like an armory telling her she's under arrest is more than she ought to or can stand. She shoves through the gate in the counter. "Get out of that clerk's way," she says.

Bledsoe moves quickly, in spite of the pounds of metal that dangle from him. He spins her by her shoulder so that she faces him, slaps her with the back of his hand, and flings her toward the gate. She loses her balance and stumbles through the gate, then grabs for the counter and misses. She hits the floor full face.

The wail of a siren cuts its way into the room before she can get to her feet. She rolls to her side. Bledsoe and the other man start toward her but stop when they hear the wail. It's a long, growing sound like a fire engine, but deeper and more powerful.

"There it goes," Bledsoe's buddy says. "Forget her."

Bledsoe grabs his rifle from the counter behind her. He and the other man clump past her to the heavy door. As it swings open, the wail floods the room, a horrible sound that cuts off every other. The clerk rushes to the door behind the doctor, then turns back to help her up. She pushes him away.

By the time she's out the door, Bledsoe and the other man are running full tilt down Howell Avenue toward Brewery Gulch. She can locate the sound now. It comes from the hill above the Copper Queen Mine—the huge siren Bo told her the army set up to warn against an attack from Villa. My Lord, she thinks, they've even taken over the army installations!

Things happen too fast now for her to do more than try to keep up with them. The siren stops as abruptly as it began. She tastes blood but has no time to bother with it. She follows Bledsoe toward the mouth of the Gulch, where it opens out onto the plaza.

When she reaches the plaza, the Wobblies seem as confused as she is. Most of them look toward the source of the now silent wail. She starts for them but doesn't make it. The wall of men reaches her first.

They come from behind her, down the Gulch. There must be a hundred of them, faceless in their half-military quick march, rifles leveled, someone shouting cadence. She hears them, boots heavy on cobblestones, and backs up against the railing around the company park. As she looks for a place to run, she sees them marching from every street toward the plaza, sealing it off completely. Across the way, a line of men with rifles trained rises up in ragged unison from behind the railway embankment. Even from the post office they come, bursting out of the dark doors, dropping to their knees, and sighting their rifles. She jumps away from the railing as a warning rattle of machine-gun fire comes from the dispensary.

A few of the Wobs try to run for it. But they're shoved back by the walls of men. There's no place to go. They're trapped like cattle in a box canyon.

What's happened dawns on the men. She hears fragments of shouted challenges. "Come on," a voice yells. "Shoot your brothers!" Half a dozen others, one way or another, offer to fight the white banders man-to-man if they'll put their guns down. Fists shake in the air. A half dozen stray dogs run in and out of the crowd yelping. The white banders move in closer, shoving and pushing the wobs into a tighter and tighter circle.

The Gulch is clear now. She can make it to the headquarters in the Pythian Castle. She's got to go somewhere, talk to somebody, anybody, who's not insane. If Bo's anywhere in town, maybe he's at headquarters. If she can just talk to Bo!

She gets as far as the base of O.K. Street. And it's no good, too late. Embree and the other local leaders lean out of the window of the castle, one or two shaking pistols at the crowd of white banders below. But they're trapped, too. The steep hillside closes them off from the rear. Harry Wheeler himself is directing the white banders who storm into the stairwell. The feeling of smothering she has had in Bisbee from the very beginning overwhelms her. No way out of these canyons, no way to get to the real world, nothing but desert and mountains for farther than she can even imagine.

Wheeler shouts a last order to his troops. Embree, thank God, has enough sense to tell his boys to throw their pistols down. The white banders cheer when the guns thud onto the cobblestones. But not Wheeler.

Then an *oogah*ing, topless Ford lurches down O.K. Street through the mob of white banders. She freezes, more from shock than fear. The Ford has a machine gun mounted on its hood and a priest driving it. A priest, for God's sake! It only stops a moment for Harry Wheeler to leap into it, then lurches toward her again. Wheeler grasps the machine gun and stands as straight and tall as he can in the bouncing car, as if he were in a chariot. They're only fifty feet or so away, *oogah*ing down on her. She jumps onto the sidewalk by a closed saloon. Wheeler roars past almost close enough for her to touch. His black coat is thrown back over his pistol, and a newspaper with heavy black headlines sticks out of his coat pocket. His tin star catches the morning light a moment, then he's gone.

She follows the Ford down O.K. Street until she can see the plaza again. Wheeler and the priest drive straight for the crowd. The white banders part for him, and a cheer rolls across the plaza. Wheeler seems to be trying to say something, but the Wobs and his own men drown him. At last Wheeler takes his pistol out and empties it into the air. In the moment of loud silence that follows the last shot, he shouts, "In the name of the United States of America and the people of Cochise County, I arrest you!"

He arrests them. All of them. Everybody. In the name of the people.

She tastes the blood in her mouth again. She gags, wants to throw up. And then the other car is behind her.

It honks not three feet from her. She starts, then swirls around to see the bluff face of Bill Cleary, the union's lawyer, behind the wheel. He waves for her to get in.

Even before she's seated well, the car moves. "Saw the SOBs coming up to the castle," he says. "Made it out to the car before they got there. Embree wouldn't come. Hold on."

He swerves past the ragged edge of the crowd of white banders. They're concentrating on Wheeler and don't try to stop him. The shouting has started up from the Wobblies again, but there's no heart in it. Cleary guns the throttle and heads up the slight incline of Naco Road, southward out of town.

"Damn awful weapon, a machine gun," he says. "Can you imagine what it would do to a close-packed crowd at that range? Amazing, a real wonder that Wheeler hasn't used it yet. I wouldn't have given you a nickel for the chances that this wouldn't turn into a massacre. Amazing!" He picks up a newspaper from the seat beside him and hands it to Elizabeth. "Seen this yet?"

Dumbly, Elizabeth takes it from him. She doesn't know if he's babbling at her this way to help calm her down or to keep his own fear under control. She knows she should say something, even ask where they're going, but she can't. She can't make enough sense out of any single thought to form words.

ALL WOMEN AND CHILDREN STAY OFF STREETS TODAY, the headlines in the *Review* say. Below them, three columns wide in heavy type, spreads a statement signed by Harry C. Wheeler, Sheriff, Cochise County. She lets her eyes wander down it in the rocking car. "I have formed a Sheriff's Posse of 1,200 men in Bisbee and 1,000 in Douglas, all loyal Americans, for the purpose of arresting on charges of vagrancy, treason, and being disturbers of the peace all those strange men who have congregated here from other parts and sections for the purpose of harassing and intimidating all men who desire to pursue their daily toil."

She skims the rest of the page. "Appeals to patriotism do not move them, nor do appeals to reason. . . ." Again and again, the words "strangers" and "foreigners" leap out at her, like the titles in a moving picture. "This is no labor trouble—we are sure of that—but a direct attempt to embarrass and injure the government of the United States. . . . I therefore call upon all loyal Americans to aid me in peaceably arresting those disturbers of our local and national peace. Let no shot be fired throughout this day unless in necessary self-defense, and I hereby give warning that each and every leader of the so-called strikers will be held personally responsible for any injury inflicted upon any of my deputies while in performance of their duties, for whose acts I, in turn, assume full responsibility as sheriff of this county."

Oh, yes, Harry, she thinks. Take full responsibility. Take it for that poor hulking man, Brew, dead in Jiggerville. Take it for the whole damn exploding world. She reads the last paragraph hastily: "All arrested persons will be treated humanely and their cases examined with justice and care. I hope no resistance will be made, for I desire no bloodshed. However, I am determined, if resistance is made, it shall be quickly and effectively overcome."

She looks to Cleary's ruddy, whiskey-blossomed face. She doesn't know him, really. He's been someone on the edges of things, a man running in and out of the Pythian Castle with reports, quick advice, warnings. He could be taking her to hell for all she knows. Or, now, for all she cares. He wears a campaign hat, riding boots, khaki shirt, and bow tie—like a man who could easily be at home hunting with Teddy Roosevelt. But she has to trust him. There's no one else.

"See that last line?" he asks. " 'Quickly and effectively overcome,' or some such. Machine guns do that right well. Do you have any idea how many laws those sons of bitches have already violated? Breaking and entering, kidnapping, assault . . . hell, the list would read like a lawbook. Look there." They are speeding along Main Street in Lowell camp. In front of a grocery with a long Slavic name three white banders load boxes of canned goods into a wagon. A woman in a black shawl shakes her fist at them beside the door. Cleary snorts. "Harry Wheeler's going to be responsible for *that*?" They rock around the corner at the end of Main Street, past the Junction shaft onto the highway to Naco. "And treated humanely, eh? You know, I really think the poor bastard believes that. But does he have any idea what he's let loose? Or where it could end?"

Elizabeth leans closer to Cleary and squints her eyes against the dust that swirls up as they bounce onto the dirt road after the pavement ends. "Where are we going?" she asks. It sounds so silly to her to ask that now, after she's already gone halfway to nowhere with him.

"Naco, lady. Mexico. *La Patria.* They got telegraph

offices there, don't they? Betcha even Harry can't shut the Mexicans down. Though Christ knows he's tried. Duck, quick."

She opens her eyes wider as Cleary cranks the windshield shut. Ahead of them she sees a barricade and a good two dozen men around it. A couple of them wave their arms for Cleary to pull over. He guns the car, hunches low over the wheel, and throws out a huge red hand to push her head down.

The car lurches, swerves, and she feels a heavy thud that jerks her forward into the glove box. Then she hears cracking sounds and feels splinters of glass as bullets smash through the windshield. She stays down, even after the cracking stops. She doesn't want to see any more, doesn't want to think about what Bill Cleary has been saying. They're going to Mexico, yet she feels already she must be in another country since they passed Wheeler's barricades. And where is Bo? Somewhere in this other country, too? She needs to feel his physical presence now, to touch something warm and sane. But another thought cuts at her like the slivers of glass from the windshield. What has happened today, what might still happen, may shut something off between her and Bo that she won't be able to open again. Nothing is very clear to her yet. But she knows that Bo—perhaps all the Wobblies—may never get out from behind those barricades. And that if this automobile were the only means to stop what's going on in the canyons of Bisbee, she would stay in it even if it were driven by the devil himself. She has given herself up long ago to a kind of passion that transcends all other loves or hates or needs. She aches for Bo, but he is somewhere back there, behind her.

She raises her head. Her black hair whips in her eyes. In front of her, Naco sweeps toward the golden lonely cone of San Jacinto peak. She's any man's dog, and no man's dog.

Bo Whitley: July 12, 10:00 A.M.

Bo hasn't slept. All night boots clumped along the carpeted hall outside the bedroom, and shouts, cussing, jokes, rolled from room to room. His door was locked and he was conscious always of someone outside it. He thinks he's got it figured. They're going to round up the strike committee and organizers like himself—put some trumped-up charges against them, or just ride them out of town, like they did up in Jerome. Maybe that'll get them the publicity the union needs to keep this strike going. That's not what's kept him awake, circling the room for hours, tight as a winch cable.

It's been quiet since dawn, but now he hears voices in the hall again. One of them sounds like the deep rumble of Miles Merrill. Come for him, he imagines. He quickens. Come for him for what?

Bo's had all night to think, to try to juggle what's happened until it makes some sense. It's like Greenway is a jigsaw puzzle with some pieces missing, holes he has to fill up with things from outside: money, power, and even something he thinks he can get from Bo. Now he knows that that gives him power over Greenway. And if Greenway knows it, too, then Bo is in trouble. He was angry with Greenway at first, face-busting angry. But during the night, the anger turned inward, toward himself where it belongs. He wondered if Greenway knew something about him that he'd never admitted even to himself. All that talk about generations—for a moment while Greenway was talking it seemed so damn reasonable. He saw himself in a wool suit and patent-leather shoes and celluloid collar, imagined his portrait on some future grandkid's wall in a gold frame. Like that was, after all, what he figured Bisbee owed him.

And then he felt guilty. About that part of himself Greenway somehow dug out, and about so many other things that Bisbee has brought back. The whole awful time with his old man, and the way he walked away from his mamma because of it. The mess he's got Jim Brew into—and even about Art Matthews. And the guilt for his and Elizabeth's kid in New York, whom he's never written to. He's sure he's fouled all of them up in one way or another, like maybe he's fouled himself up with the Wobs by being here at Greenway's at all.

But most of all, there's Elizabeth. What would she do if she knew what a naïve ass he's made out of himself? He hasn't figured out how yet, but somehow he's got to get to her, explain himself. If she loves him the way she says she does, she won't let this general strike thing get in the way. Hell, she and he matter more than politics. He's always known that.

He hears a key in the lock. The door handle jiggles, turns, then Miles Merrill and a scissorbill with a rifle and a white handkerchief tied around his arm appear in the door. Merrill's hair is plastered to his forehead with sweat.

"Time to move it, son," he says.

"Move it where?" Bo doesn't get up from the bed.

"None of my nevermind, nor yours either. Cap'n wants to see you." The stiff with the rifle, a huge old Krag-Jorgensen he must have dug out of an attic, steps into the room and motions for Bo to get to his feet. Bo considers rushing the door. But now's not the time. He needs open space, room to run. He can wait. He swings his legs over the edge of the bed and stands.

They lead Bo downstairs. The house is hot already—no rain means it's going to be an oven outside. Just at the edge of the parlor, by the vestibule, Merrill tells them to hold up. He pounds up a flight of stairs that leads from the vestibule to an open door out onto a balcony. Through the door, Bo can just see three or four men seated in camp chairs, watching something down the mall toward the ball park. When Merrill steps onto the balcony, they turn. Greenway first, then Grant Dowell, Tom Matthews, and a man Bo doesn't recognize. A man in a perfectly tailored suit, with a sharp hard face. Telephone lines have been jerry-rigged up the stairs, and all the men have binoculars around their necks.

Merrill whispers to Greenway. Greenway's eyes find Bo while Merrill talks. He nods, leaves Merrill, and trots down the stairs. He's wearing an officer's automatic, tight riding pants, a military-style khaki shirt, and tall soft boots.

"I'll take him now," he tells the scissorbill with the Krag-Jorgensen. The scissorbill flips a sloppy salute and vanishes.

Bo stares up into Greenway's blue eyes and waits. Greenway speaks first. "I'm disappointed in your reaction to our talk last night, Whitley."

Bo can find nothing to say. Whatever Greenway wants, he has nothing Bo wants in return.

"I like to be fair, you know. My offer still stands—and it's your last chance for it."

"I'll tell you something, Greenway. I pitied you last night. And not for the reasons I reckon you imagine."

"Don't be so damn sanctimonious. I suppose I was wrong about you—you are acting just like that priggy bunch you associate with."

"Lots of things you might be wrong about."

"Oh, my God. Maybe I am wrong about everything—even everything I believe. Does that matter so much? Right and wrong are so bloody imprecise, Whitley. That's what drives me mad about you people. Not a one of you will ever be anything but a petty Puritan." He locks his eyes onto Bo's a moment, as if he's making a final decision about something. "Miles!" he calls, at length. Merrill pounds down the stairs from the balcony. "Meet me at the stables, will you? Bring Whitley."

"Right," Merrill says. Greenway regards Bo a little sadly, then does a loosely military about-face toward the rear of the house. Merrill rests his hand on his pistol butt and asks Bo, "You leave anything in the room, son?"

Bo shakes his head.

"Then the cap'n says go." There's something blandly good-natured about Merrill, even now, that keeps Bo from hating him. He takes a step in the direction Merrill indicates, then hears the startled "Oh!" behind him. He turns. Art Matthews stands with a tray of sandwiches in his hand. His face is in terrible confusion.

"Why, Bo!" he says. "I certainly . . . well! Just fancy."

Bo checks him over—white bucks, worsteds, striped shirt, and bow tie. Art bears the once over, then, still in awful confusion, holds out the tray.

"Sandwich?" he says.

Bo can't stand it. He breaks into a grin, scoops up a handful of the little sandwiches, and lets Merrill lead him away.

Greenway waits for them at the stables. A Mex stableboy leads his white mare from a stall. Greenway checks her over, then mounts. His houseboy hands him a hunting rifle.

"Sorry there's only room for one, Whitley," Greenway says when he's mounted. "You don't mind walking, do you? It won't be for long." He lowers the muzzle of the rifle level with Bo's chest.

They go at a leisurely pace down the graveled drive, then out into the street in front of Greenway's house. There seem to be half a hundred men in loose groups spread up and down the street, past the company doctor's wooden bungalow, and across the property of the sprawling pink-granite Douglas mansion. The whole damn world seems to have white rags tied around their arms. Greenway's mood is good: he hums and gently nudges Bo ahead of him with the rifle barrel. Bo walks in slow humiliation, but tries to meet the eyes of each scissorbill they pass.

Just in front of the Douglas driveway, the hill crests. The view there is the best in Warren. You can see all the way down the mall to the baseball park in one direction, and over the low trees to the Bisbee road in the other. But it's not the view that he sees. It's the men. Before he makes them out, he hears the singing. Ragged and uneven from a distance, it seems to come from the entire length of the horizon. And even when he realizes what it is, he can't make out the words, spread over so great a number of men.

God almighty damn. The men. There have to be thousands of them, stretched in a column from the ball park along the railroad tracks toward Bisbee the whole length of the mile's view he has. And who knows how much farther beyond that. Bo stops, and Greenway with him. Bo has nothing to compare it with; he's never seen anything like it.

It's impossible. No one could manage to scoop up so many men in so short a time. Christ, there aren't that many Wobs in town. What could you possibly do with that many men? He turns to Greenway, half wondering if Greenway really sees it, too.

"Impressive, isn't it, Whitley? A miracle of efficiency. Harry Wheeler missed his calling. He should have been an engineer."

"What in God's . . . ? Where are they going?"

"I'm not really sure. You'll have to send me a wire when you wind up wherever it is." He pats his whinnying horse. "I kept you last night. I reckoned you'd learn something. It's not really this shoulder-to-shoulder, united masses, solidarity nonsense that gets things done, is it? It's civilized authority and efficiency that creates power, Whitley. Look down there again. There's your 'power in a band of workingmen.' So don't count my people out quite yet—in case you'd planned to."

"What have you done with the women?" Bo says.

"She'll not be harmed, if that's what you mean. Harry Wheeler is old school, you know. He doesn't hurt women."

Bo should run for it now, he knows, if ever. But there's too much open country for a horse to maneuver in here. Greenway could ride him to ground like a fox. He'll not give him that goddamn satisfaction. And what good would it do? He was wrong. If they'll do something like this, they're stupid enough to run Elizabeth out of town.

Greenway lightly spurs his horse. "You wouldn't want to be the only man in Bisbee not involved in this, would you? History waits, my friend. Let's go look." He taps Bo with the rifle again.

As they make their slow way toward the ball park, the column of men does not dwindle. Once they drop down from the crest of the hill, Bo can only see parts of the line, but ahead of him he can see that the movement past the gauntlet of men with white bands into the ball park doesn't slow.

Cars and wagons are parked haphazardly on all sides. Horses and mules bray and whinny; wives and girlfriends of the strikers try to reach them, or cuss the white banders, or beg to know where their men are going. Ladies with parasols gawk from front yards. It's half circus, half tent meeting. Only when he and Greenway reach the park does the number of voices decrease until he can make out the words they're singing, a song that fades as the men enter the ball park. . . .

When our cause is all triumphant
And we claim our Mother Earth,
And the nightmare of the present fades away,
We shall live with Love and Laughter,
We, who now are little worth,
And we'll not regret the price we have to pay. . . .

Greenway hums on. They pass through the packed lines of men in white bands. Greenway's horse thrusts gently forward to make a path for them. Bo looks at faces as the men part for them. What grabs his attention most is the faces of the old men, who are everywhere in the crowd. Plainsmen, cowhands, with Colts in their belts. Men they must have dug up from Queen Creek to San Antonio, like a reunion of Civil War veterans. They look excited, as if they're remembering things.

At the gate, Greenway stops. The ball park is surrounded on all sides by a high board fence. He leans down to Bo. "I built this for my men, Whitley. Baseball is a fine game. Why in hell couldn't you people stick to it and leave my damn mines to me? You've never been a bigger fool than now." The men inside the gate spot Greenway, and a long hoot swells across the crowd. Bo catches a glimpse of Hamer shaking his fist near the front rank. Greenway straightens up, tips his campaign hat to them, and reins away. Before Bo can see where he's gone, a hand shoves him from the rear into the ball park.

Harry Wheeler: July 12, 1:00 P.M.

The damn train should have been here by now. Dowell promised twenty-five boxcars and cattle cars. That's precious few; you'll have to do a right smart of packing in. You pace through your officers and make sure they know the plans. If that fool McCrea hadn't got himself shot, you'd be free of a lot of this petty detail. Still, what's happened so far has been a triumph and a wonder. Only two men dead, and that only because one pea-brain disobeyed orders and rushed a house unarmed. You only hope now that Greenway knows what he's talking about. If you get these men into the boxcars and the rest of the plan doesn't work, you're going to look a bigger fool than McCrea.

So far the Wobblies have been smart enough not to try anything—the machine gun up on the C&A offices and the snipers on the hillsides have done the trick. Everything has done the trick so far. It's almost too smooth.

Your officers seem to have their companies pretty well in hand. So you make a last reconnaisance of the ball park before you give the Wobblies their chance to get right with their neighbors.

Through cracks in the fence, underneath the ads for the Fair Store and Coca-Cola, you scan the bunch. Two thousand of them, your best count says. Two thousand! Their speakers echo through the grandstands, as they've done all morning. Some try to signal through the fence to their women. Every kind: old hags in black shawls; foreigners in striped dresses; Mexes with babies strapped on their back; the whores from the Line. Yelling and cussing like sailors. Some of the men bleed or limp. You told the boys not to get rough, but you knew they'd have to in some cases. They were dealing with a rough outfit.

You walk along the fence, from crack to crack and knothole to knothole. Near the closed refreshment stand, a miner in long johns squats in some kind of consumptive fit while a couple of others in overalls hold him up. One of them yells for a doctor. You hate to see that, too. But the consumptives have to take responsibility for their actions just like the rest. Every man is responsible.

"Great lot of good a doctor'll do," you hear a tubby, shoeless miner with a pipe say. "Damn doctor's dressed up like a Mexican bandit, clubbing stiffs." You keep walking. You never have liked Bledsoe. He's not a man to control himself.

Other men, many half-dressed, spread on the outfield grass to try to sleep. A couple cry. That lawyer Cleary, who you picked up sneaking back across the border from Naco, wanders from group to group with Whitley and some others. He's been yakking all morning about suing the companies for ten thousand dollars for every man rounded up. Fat chance. At least when you got him, you got that Flynn woman back, too.

You pick up snatches of conversation as you walk, and refuse to believe most of it. Were it true, you'd have heard about it. You gave orders for full reports.

". . . so she thrown herself up against the door to keep the bastards from a-coming in till I had time to dress and git. They shot it in, right beside her. She's lost the baby on account of it, I got no doubt. She was cramping when they drug me out."

". . . *este, como se llama? Ramirez, sí.* He run out through the back, you know? Up over the hill. He's a dead man, *hombre,* I promise. Nothing but *puro* desert out there. He's a *muerto.*"

". . . he's laying over yonder in the grass, sweltering with the flu. Won't make it through the day lessen they git him in bed, fellow workers."

". . . *Bog znaet, malchik!* Come in store, ask do I give credit to Wobblies. Sure, I say. Damn foreigner, they say. Next I know—bang, out the door with me. What I know about strikes?"

". . . hell yes, I carry a union card, I said. But it ain't no Wobbly card. I'm AF of L and put every extra cent I got into Liberty Bonds. Give to the Red Cross and registered for the draft. But hell yes, I carry a union card."

". . . so what the hell if my name is Eisner? I was born here, at least. And him not even a goddamn citizen! Goddamn Cousin Jack!"

". . . went through my wife's bag while I was standing there watching. Took her ring and ever cent she had."

". . . gonna machine-gun us in the desert, he told me."

". . . it'll hit a hundred and six in the desert today, swear to God. Even the damn grass is hot."

". . . victims of the class war, fellow worker . . ."

". . . drug the Episcopal priest himself out till that Catholic one told them to leave him be . . ."

". . . one side or the other. You got to be on one side or the other today. Everybody."

". . . my damn feet hurt, and I ain't eat since last night's supper . . ."

You hear them but don't hear them. You've felt peculiar

all day, as if you're outside yourself watching yourself. Harry Wheeler feels sorry for some of the bastards in the ball park. But you only see him do it from a long way off. Ever since Walter Douglas talked to you, you've felt like a character in a play. You're not even sure there was a Walter Douglas. Or that it matters now. You've done what no other sheriff in history has done. You *are* history, and you don't belong to yourself any longer.

You wind up your reconnaisance by the gate. Your officers have got their best men ready, as per orders. Father Mandin sits in the idling Ford. This is the final thing you have to do. The final proof of Harry Wheeler's fairness. You climb in the Ford and take a good hold on the machine-gun handle. You raise your hand, then drop it in a "Forward!" signal. A couple of boys fling the gates open. Your picked men rush in ahead of you and fan out. Father Mandin guns the Ford.

You head for second base. The Wobblies hoot and throw bits of sod at you. But they don't try anything rougher. They're whipped and know it. You fire a quick burst from the machine gun over their heads and they shut up. All except Cleary. He runs out ahead of the others, disheveled, his campaign hat in his hand. You feel ashamed for him, being with this outfit. He's a college man.

"Wheeler," he yells at you. "On behalf of the Industrial Workers of the World and of humanity, I accuse you of the biggest mass kidnapping in the history of this country. The Constitution of the United States . . ."

Your boys are on him before he can finish. "The Constitution of the United States by God forbids treason, Cleary. Don't be a jackass," you say to him. "Now, we're here to give any of you boys a chance to prove your patriotism. I want two groups of you in good military formation spread out along the foul lines. Any of you that's been wronged will have his chance now." You signal to your men. "Line 'em up, double time!"

Bitching, the Wobblies shuffle into ragtail bunches along the foul lines. They make filthy gestures at you. "I don't aim for any man here to claim he didn't have a fair chance," you say when they're in decent order. "These citizens here"—you point to the members of the merchants' committee who came in with you—"will vouch for any loyal American they know that's been picked up by mistake. Anybody else of you who wants to renounce this outfit and put a white band on his arm with his neighbors is welcome to do so, and return to your home. Provided you're not a known troublemaker and offer to come back to work at the prevailing wage and conditions." You didn't especially want to put that last part in. But you have to keep peace with the companies. After all, they're picking up the tab for all this.

"Don't do it, boys!" Cleary yells from somewhere. The other Wobblies take it up down the line, till it turns into a chant. You stand firm. At last one of the men in the line breaks into the clear and holds out his hand. A foreman slaps a white band into it. The man runs for the gate. The Wobblies spit at him as he passes them. But another man breaks loose, and another, until all down the line they're popping into the open space like fleas off a hound. Then the merchants' committee members start pointing to one or another of the men they know and shouting to them to come out. Most do. The Wobblies try to get hold of some of them, but your men crack a few skulls and things go in good order.

When the trickle of men dries up and the chanting dies, you've made a dent. The IWW has lost maybe 30, 40 percent. Down to, say, twelve, thirteen hundred. You scan the ranks a last time. They're silent now, watching. They've had their chance. They've convicted themselves. Justice, done best, is swift, sure, unequivocal. It's always been so out here. You'd have it no other way.

You ask Father Mandin to move out. He backs the Ford in an arc, rocks it straight, and nearly kills the engine, then bounces toward the gate. Your men fall in behind you. They walk backward with their rifles trained. At the gate, Father Mandin pauses to let the men catch up with you. The Wobblies still make no sound. The sun is violent overhead now. Suddenly, from the back of one of the groups, a voice breaks the silence. "Fuck the plutes!" The yell echoes in the empty grandstand. No one answers it. Father Mandin jerks the Ford into gear. The gates close behind you. They've had their chance.

Late, but at last. Twenty-five cattle cars and boxcars, as promised. You've mounted your horse now and sit beside

Captain Greenway on his white mare. He's come for the show, he says. The train, with only a single engine, whistles into the tiny wooden Warren depot. All around you, the boys break into cheers. It's the first train today. The El Paso and Southwestern has canceled all the others. As you gallop to meet the engine, you catch the odor of dung from the cattle cars. Damnation. You'd think they could have cleaned the things.

But at the engine cab, the engineer explains that they had a hard time getting a crew. Unions again, refusing to take part. They got so far behind that there was no time to do any cleaning, and the bread and water Mr. Dowell ordered didn't really make it either. Only a couple of barrels of water in the first car. But Mr. Dowell, the engineer says, telegraphed that the train was to come ahead anyway.

Nothing to be done. You'll be damned if you'll let night fall on them in the baseball park. So you give the go-ahead sign and your officers quick time their men into position. A long double snake of a line has already half formed by the time you trot your Appaloosa back to Captain Greenway. The line will be an unbreachable channel of men from the ball park to the train.

The IWW women have a fit. Scratch and pound on your men till you have to order some of them taken off. When the gates open for the Wobblies to come marching out, a couple of strapping boys in overalls try to put on white bands. But their mamma flails at them, screaming for them to get back in line and be men. Some of the other women come pushing around you to ask where their men are going. Half a dozen try to get in line with the men. Some throw food to them. But all in all the loading goes efficiently. A few Wobblies have to be persuaded more than others to get on board, and the ones in the front car throw the water out. There's more than a little swearing about the dung in the cars, but Captain Greenway says the stuff's appropriate. The women squawk when the doors to the cars are shut and try to climb aboard. But you've posted two hundred guards—crack shots all—on top of the cars. There'll be no trouble.

As the last car fills, Captain Greenway trots up beside you. He's in good spirits.

"Harry," he says. "I've never seen a finer operation in

my life. I'd be proud to have you serve under me in any man's army." He leans over in his saddle and slaps your back. "By the way, I hear you caught that Flynn woman."

"She's in custody, yessir."

"Do me a favor?"

"I'll try."

"I don't really know what you've got in mind for her—and don't particularly want to. But if you ship her out, hold her here a couple of days first."

"Got a reason for that, Captain?"

"Oh, say she's less trouble here than somewhere out there on a soapbox. Agreed?"

You'd be just as happy to get rid of her today, but there's sense in what Greenway says. "I don't reckon they'll start yelling for us to let her go for a couple of days at least."

"Capital!" He slaps you on the back again and gallops to the train. He reins his horse in at the engine, rears it, then gallops the full length of the train. The Wobblies in the slotted cattle cars poke their arms out to slap at him.

The last door slams. The train gives a long warning whistle. Steam hisses. The cars clank together and shudder. The pistons thrust, drive wheels spin. The train moves. Over the chug of the engine, you hear a noise from the string of cars, a mixture of voices that sounds like a long sigh.

Greenway sits on his mare at the end of the train, a little apart from everyone else. As the last car moves away from him, he takes off his campaign hat, waves it, and throws back his head. He whoops, a long yippie-aye-yea whoop that draws every head in the thousands of watchers. Almost to a man, from voice to voice the whoop rolls back to him. It's a sound you've known from Oklahoma to Arizona, a sound you've never heard anywhere outside the West. In spite of yourself, you find your voice taking it up, throwing it back into the crowd. It stays and rolls and echoes up the canyons of Bisbee behind you. Loud, hot, cleansing.

Bo Whitley: July 13, Noon

Bo stays low and sprints. The road has got to be just ahead of him, over the cactusy rise. He saw rooster tails of dust from automobiles at least a mile back. More than a few of them. And there are houses here, too, set under the few eucalyptus trees that stand out above the desert mesquite. The Mex tank tender's directions back in Hermanas were sound. And it's good that Hamer didn't come along after all. He'd never have made it this far in the desert.

At the top of the rise, Bo drops to the ground just behind a clump of prickly-pear cactus. He was right. It's a main road, running east and west. The town isn't much—a saloon and general store and more of the adobe houses he's already seen. It's only a crossroads town, but that's enough. He can get news and a ride. The place should be safe, but he'll take no chances. If Harry Wheeler can track a man to Texas, there's a chance he can send his gunmen into New Mexico to pick up runaway strikers. He darts from stumpy cactus patch to stumpy cactus patch until he reaches the wall of the clapboard, false-fronted saloon. There's only one car out front, an open touring Studebaker, not new.

He hears a laugh, and a soldier bursts through the swinging doors with a case of whiskey in his arms. He nestles it in the back seat of the Studebaker and covers it with an army blanket. It's all right. They're on a whiskey run from Arizona, sick of Bisbee's rotgut bootleg. The last thing they're after is trouble. Bo brushes his overalls off and kicks a dried piece of sheep dung from his brogans, then steps up onto the wide boards of the saloon porch. He hasn't had anything to eat since he took the sandwiches from Art Matthews yesterday morning. Thank God Hamer had a couple of bucks to lend him before he left the train.

The train. The memory of it, of the smell of the ankle-deep sheep and cow shit, won't leave him even here in the open dusty desert. He knows he should have stayed with the boys back in Hermanas and listened to Cleary. Cleary is all right. But the idea of settling his claim with Bisbee through years of lawsuits and lawyers' double-talk is no good for Bo. It was his town, his strike, and it's blown. Period. Elizabeth, he's certain, is on a train heading east. Once she's settled there, back with people like Tresca, his chance to square with her is gone for good. He's got to forget Bisbee and get to her before they do. What use would there be in staying with the boys at the train? Hell, Bisbee's whipped him. He'll hitch a ride to the nearest freight yard, then head east, toward the only thing that really matters now.

He walks into the saloon as nonchalantly as he can. He must look enough like hell as it is—two days' beard, smelling like a stockyard, clothes filthy, no cap. The saloon's only light spills from the door onto the raw plank floor. The soldiers look up as he takes a place at the end of the bar, then go back to their poker. One of them flips through a newspaper, an *El Paso Herald.* From time to time he reads a passage aloud to this buddies. They don't seem interested. But Bo is.

The news should be out by now. A trainload of men sent a hundred and seventy-five miles across the desert and left on a railroad siding in the middle of no-goddamn-where can't stay quiet too long. The boys were in bad shape when he left them. The hottest day of the year, fifty stiffs to a closed boxcar or shit-littered cattle car. No room to sit or lie down, no food, nothing but brackish water from a railroad water tank to drink—and that only after a full day in the heat. And in one of the cars, riding for hours with a man dead from the flu.

It was a pretty smart move. Ship the Wobs over to Columbus, in New Mexico, where Villa raided last year. The army had stockades already built for all the refugees Pershing was supposed to bring back with him when he caught Villa—which he didn't. Evidently the plan was to surprise the army with the strikers, and they'd have no choice. They'd have to take them over.

Except they didn't. The sheriff in Columbus tried to arrest the damned white-bander guards riding the cars instead. And the army told them to get the hell back to Arizona. So the guards backed the train out of Columbus just ahead of the sheriff, dumped it on a siding at a tank stop called Hermanas, and lit out for Bisbee on the Drummer's Special just before daylight. Cleary loves the idea. Says the government will have to send them back to Bisbee now with army protection. Bo doubts it. The day the army escorts a bunch of Wobblies back onto the picket lines—especially in the middle of a war—is the day he'll become a Republican. He told the stiffs with families to give him any messages they wanted him to mail before he left. They'll likely not be seeing them for a while.

Just before Bo left at daylight, the army did show up. Or at least some shavetail on horseback did. Said he'd been authorized to see if the men needed food or medical supplies, but nothing else. Cleary told him hell yes, and that he was holding Woodrow Wilson personally responsible if it all wasn't there by noon, plus somebody from the Associated Press to take a statement. The shavetail got upset and promised. The boys had already bought out everything in the little store in Hermanas and were in no mood to wait another forty-eight hours for chuck and a smoke. That's good. They can settle with the government now, like Haywood can settle his general strike with the copper trust. Bo wishes them all the goddamn luck in the world. For his part, he's already been settled with.

He orders a glass of tonic and cheese and crackers and tries to figure the soldiers. Are they here for the day, or heading back soon? Should he wait for somebody heading east and hitch a ride, or try to steal the car?

"Listen to this shit, troops," the one with the newspaper says. "Bisbee's done seceded from the union." He holds the paper to catch the light from the door and reads, " 'Beginning today every stranger entering the Bisbee mining district must bear a passport signed by the Los Angeles chief of police, or secretary of the El Paso chamber of commerce, or the mayor of Tucson. Foreigners are being prevented from entering the district by armed guards posted along the roads in this region by Sheriff Harry Wheeler.' "

"Somebody ought to horsewhip the son of a bitch," a square-faced corporal says over his cards. "I was a union man before I enlisted myself."

"Oh, hell," the man with the newspaper says. "Wobblies ain't unions."

"Ought to horsewhip the son of a bitch," the corporal says again. "And nobody's doing nothing about it?"

"Says President Wilson has asked them to please stop. Everybody back in Washington and New York is issuing statements and raising hell. Big Bill Haywood's threatening to invade."

"Anybody *doing* anything, I asked," the corporal says.

"Don't seem to be."

"Well, there you are. They ain't going to neither. Mark me."

Bo moves to the table beside them. "Mind if I take a peek at that paper, soldier?" he says.

The private looks Bo over, shrugs, and hands him the paper. Bo scans it. The news is mostly what he knows, except that it looks like Sheriff Harry must have his name on the front page of every paper in the country today. From the way the paper talks, it's the biggest thing since war was declared. He looks for details, and his eye stops on a name. Elizabeth's.

". . . only two women were apprehended," the article says. "Mary Harris 'Mother' Jones and Elizabeth Gurley Flynn. Flynn lists her address as New York, Jones as 'everywhere.' Both are being held in Bisbee until further notice. Meanwhile, the establishment of 'citizens' tribunals' was announced by Sheriff Wheeler. With members appointed from the Bisbee Loyalty League and Citizens' Protective Association, these tribunals will assume all judicial functions of state and federal courts until the district is stabilized . . ."

She's still there then! Harry Wheeler's got himself declared the Law West of the Pecos, and Elizabeth is there. If Bo could have one day, one day to talk to her alone . . .

And then his eye picks out the other name. Brew. Orson McCrea and James Brew. Something about a statue to McCrea and a funeral with full military honors. And that he was murdered by Brew, who was "killed in the ensuing fray." Jim Brew? Jim's dead? He reads the short article again. Oh, God Jesus. All the guilt he felt at Greenway's house that he thought the anger of the train ride had squeezed out of him surges back. He let his old man die alone, and now the next thing he ever had to an old man is dead. And because of him.

He slaps the paper down on the table. The private looks up at him, mildly startled.

Bo walks swiftly out onto the dusty, fly-busy porch. Clouds move west overhead. They're coming from Chihuahua. Monsoon clouds that should reach Bisbee by evening. He pushes his mind ahead. Bisbee is sealed off tighter than an Apache war camp. A man would have to be a bigger damn fool than even Bo Whitley to try to get back into it. But if there's anybody who knows the country around it as well as Harry Wheeler, it's him.

He turns back to the dark room. The corporal has thrown his hand down and calls the bartender for their bill. The private picks up the newspaper. It's as if Bo has been sent a message, through the paper and this place. You're not done with Bisbee yet, Whitley, it says. Come home. Settle with me.

"Corporal!" Bo calls. The man turns to him. "You against giving a union man a ride home?"

Elizabeth Gurley Flynn: July 14, 4:30 P.M.

Elizabeth watches a drop of water fight its way down the windowpane of the Argonaut. Outside, bands of deputies question the few arriving passengers. Rain drips from the deputies' hat brims and ponchos. Above them, a machine gun's black barrel still pokes from the roof of the dispensary. And above that, the tops of the mountains are hidden in dark swirls of clouds. The deputy Harry Wheeler assigned to ride as far as El Paso with Mother Jones and herself looks uncomfortable; he sits across from them and keeps his eyes on the carpet. His rifle lies on his lap. Mother Jones claims they're lucky. They could have been dragged before that damn kangaroo court they call a citizens' tribunal and had their heads shaved. She's seen it done before.

Elizabeth supposes they'll never know why they weren't—or why they were kept here at all after Thursday. And now they've been given special treatment: tickets to El Paso, where they can wire for money to go north. It will be the first wire they've been allowed to send. Her mother will be frantic.

Beside her, Mother Jones is quieter than usual. She twists and untwists a ribbon of her black dress.

"Well, Lizzie," she says. "How do you feel about it?"

Elizabeth thinks a moment. "Angry, I suppose. And a little afraid."

"Me, too. But do you know what? I'm more afraid this time for what we might find when we do get out of here."

"That's not like you, Mother."

"No. But then I ain't seen nothing like this since I worked the abolition movement. I was your age then. It was easier to take."

"Where do you head now?"

"Speaking, I reckon. Fund raising—and hell raising. This general strike thing's dead as day before yesterday. We'll be lucky if we can keep the goddamn union alive. The sons of bitches."

The conductor's "All aboard" sounds along the platform outside. Elizabeth continues to search the faces there. She knows none of them. But feels she recognizes all of them.

"And yourself?" Mother Jones asks. "Back to Tresca?"

"I haven't thought about that yet."

"Well, it's none of my nevermind, I reckon."

Elizabeth's eyes travel back to the sharp bare mountains outside the rain-streaked window. They reminded her of Bo when she first got here. Everything did. Now . . . Bo, Tresca—how little room there's been to think of either of them these past two days. She feels as if she's coming off a kind of drunk. Has been trying to get something back that was gone, over with, before she even got there. Gone from herself, maybe from the world.

And now it's the future that has, that must have, all her mind—and all her emotion. There's been a terrible and new kind of violence let loose here. It doesn't have to do with just bosses and strikebreakers anymore, but with new words, and with the workingpeople themselves. The old words, the old dream, failed here. Harry Wheeler's guns didn't.

How slowly it will have to go now! The *Review* said today that the mining companies were organizing all over the state for the expulsion of foreign and unpatriotic labor. Is the rest of the country next? They'll need legal funds, publicity, solid inch-by-inch organizing, arguing, convincing. A hundred thousand details she'll have to think out. Things that will take root, build, hold, until they're stronger than Harry Wheeler's guns. Before her stretches middle age, years of sewing a world together, single stitch by single stitch. Years with no time for busting up country club dances, for parades, for red dresses, for stupid mountains and stars and . . .

The familiar male voice startles her. "Well . . . Miss Flynn! Here we are again." Art Matthews, in uniform and cape and riding boots, stands beside her in the aisle with his military cap in his hand. He looks nervously at the deputy, who seems to know him. "I thought you had already gone —I mean that you would have . . ."

Elizabeth's anger flashes. Of all the damn people to see. And in that uniform! But she forces herself to speak calmly. What would be the use now? "No, Art. We were . . . guests a few days."

"Oh! How—nice." He drops his eyes to his cap brim and wipes imaginary rain from it. "I hope you're well. You, too, Mrs. Jones."

"It does look like a bellhop's uniform, don't it?" Mother Jones says to Elizabeth. She doesn't look up at Art.

Art tries a smile but it doesn't stick. "I'm, ah, in the next car. I'd sit here, but, ah, well, you know how railroads are."

"No, how are railroads, Art?"

His eyes meet hers at last. "I'm sorry."

"For what?"

"That the things I did—the list of names and all that—didn't help. I'd have liked them to."

She wants to keep her anger but can't. She might as well be angry with a child for dressing up in a soldier suit. She relaxes into the seat. "I know you would have. It's all right."

He keeps his eyes locked on hers. They're sadder than

she has seen them before. "You're going back East?" he asks.

"Yes."

"Will you see Bo?"

"I don't think so. I'm not sure."

"Oh." He drops his eyes and wipes his cap brim again. "I'm off for France, I suppose."

"I imagined you would be."

"I'll not be coming back to Bisbee, though."

"Never?"

"Not to live." He glances at Mother Jones, who is pretending not to listen. "Miss Flynn, I want you to know something. I'm glad I met you. You're a swell woman. And . . ." He looks to Mother Jones again. She's smiling now.

"Yes?" Elizabeth says.

"And it wasn't really all wasted. I'm not one of you—I suppose you knew that all along, didn't you?"

Mother Jones chuckles.

"But I'm not really one of *them* anymore, either. Will you believe that?"

"I'd like to."

"Well. Fine." He stands awkwardly a moment more, then pokes out his hand. Elizabeth takes it. Art holds on to her too tightly. She makes a slight motion to take her hand back. Art, with his face fixed somewhere between tears and embarrassment, drops suddenly to one knee. He kisses her hand. Then, his face averted, he rises as quickly as he dropped to his knee and strides away down the aisle.

Elizabeth looks at her hand. "No one's ever done that before." She slowly wipes her hand on her skirt.

Mother Jones is still smiling. "Nor is it likely to ever happen again. Thank God."

The car jerks. She hears the couplings clank tight one after the other the length of the train. The station platform slowly moves past. The train picks up speed until Lowell, where it creeps past the small, empty depot. In front of the union hall there, which is now the Citizens Tribunal hall, a line of miners in dark suit coats and overalls and brogans waits to be taken inside for judgment. She scans their faces quickly for Bo's. She knows she doesn't really expect to see it. Except, for the rest of her life, whenever she looks at the face of their son. She feels old, even older than Mother Jones.

"I wonder," she says to Mother Jones. "I wonder if Bo would ever understand. I've got to try and make him do that one day, I suppose."

"Save your breath, honey," Mother Jones says. "Never in a million years. The best thing you can do for the boy is never see him again."

Elizabeth's eyes remain on the line of miners huddled against the rain. I do love you, Bo, she thinks. Every one of you. Understand, please understand.

The train picks up speed again. They'll be in El Paso by morning.

Bo Whitley: July 14, 8:00 P.M.

With the soldiers to Douglas; by clanking ore train next morning to High, Lonesome Road, deserted since Geronimo's time. A stop at Walnut Springs to rub the juice from green, bitter walnut husks onto his face until it is dark as the darkest Mex's. Then with the Mex woodcutters' burro train, slanting down the mountainside into Zacatecas as Bisbee's streetlights flick on in the gray half-light of evening. The monsoon blows into the darkness, flailing the Mexes' adobe huts. Elizabeth is here, and the body of Jim Brew. He's home again.

Elizabeth's at the French Kitchen, the Mexes tell him. There's no secret to it. *La Gringa Famosa* and the other one, the old woman, have been there since Thursday. It's dangerous to go down onto the Gulch, though, they say. None of them have been down since they heard about the Drive. Only those who have jobs. And the *policia* don't come to Zacatecas. They know better.

Bo knows he has to go now. If he waits he'll break Wheeler's curfew and run the risk of being picked up automatically. How the hell he'll get past the guards Wheeler is sure to have posted around Elizabeth he doesn't know. He can't figure that until he sees the setup. One of the Mexes gave him a white band for his arm and a sharpened kitchen knife. It's not much, but it'll have to do. If he's recognized, he's out of luck anyway, no matter what he's carrying. His best hope is Wheeler's conscience. The son of a bitch hasn't had anybody killed so far. If Bo has him pegged, he's going to want to stay as clean as he can.

Bo doesn't know what he's going to do when he does find Elizabeth. Sneak her out of the French Kitchen like some maiden in a tower? To where? No. All he can try for is time to talk to her, arrange something. Then get the hell back out of town. After he collects for Jim Brew.

He knows who's got to pay Jim's debt. Not Wheeler—Wheeler was set up for this thing like the Wobblies. Only one man really knew all along what was happening. It doesn't matter now whether he pities Greenway or not. The debt's too large for pity to matter anymore.

He remembers the night he brought Art Matthews up to the Line as he makes his way down the rushing Gulch. He thought he could get Wheeler riled enough to make a false step. Naïve, Whitley. Naïve.

He feels good. Light. Ever since he stopped thinking and began only to do. This is what he's wanted all along, he realizes. No One Big Union now, nothing but Bo Whitley and Bisbee. He stays close to things as he heads into the lower Gulch. The rain drips down his face. He doesn't feel it.

Past the whiskey warehouse, past Lem Shattuck's lumberyard, past City Park with all the cardrooms under it shut tight. No one stops him. He passes sparse groups of white banders huddled in doorways. They ignore him: He's a Mex white bander, so far as anybody can tell.

He stops just above the French Kitchen, in front of the dark Saint Elmo. He's grateful for the rain. Even Harry Wheeler's finest won't stand outside in rain like this. The Gulch is clear. He can make it. Once he's inside, he'll be okay. A knife in a quick enough hand stands a better chance against a rifle at close quarters.

At the French Kitchen, he flattens himself against the wet bricks. Down the way, a patrol of white banders darts from doorway to doorway. He rolls along the wall to beat them to the stairwell door. If he can get inside before he's spotted—and if there are no guards just inside the door . . .

He opens the door to the stairwell as quietly as he can. A single bulb burns at the top of the wooden stairs. The stairwell is empty. He lets the door slip closed and ducks behind the staircase in the shadows. And waits. The patrol stops at the door. One of the white banders jerks it open, looks quickly around, and slams it. Thank God for the rain; they're in too big a hurry for a cup of coffee to stop here.

He steps out of the shadows, toward the stairwell. And the voice stops him.

"Don't you reckon you'd best wait to make sure they're gone, pilgrim?"

Bo whirls. A chair creaks behind him in the shadows underneath the staircase.

"You didn't check under here as good as I would have thought you might. I'd nearly 'bout gone to sleep waiting for you." Hamer's bulk moves out of the dark into the pale light from the top of the stairs.

"Oscar? How in hell did you get here? Jesus, brother, you scared the piss . . ." Hamer stops a yard away. He raises the pistol so that the light catches it.

"I'm sorry, pilgrim. Swear to God, I am. I done my best to let you know you ought to git while the gitting was good."

Bo takes a step back and sinks down onto the steps. "Christ all mighty, Oscar." He feels sick.

"I got to buy my beans just like everybody, Bo. Don't mean nothing by it."

"Elizabeth . . .?"

"Gone. Left on the Argonaut this afternoon. No harm come to her."

Pieces begin to slip together, like gears in a huge machine. Elizabeth's gone. Hamer's here. They never meant for Elizabeth to stay. "Why this way, Oscar? Why didn't it happen Thursday?"

"Harry Wheeler would have knowed about it then. Old Harry'd of had a fit if you'd just disappeared during the roundup. Harry's a fair man."

"I reckon I ought to laugh or something, Oscar. But I ain't got the heart for it."

"Me neither, pilgrim. I hate this, if you want to know the God's truth."

"You're a low fucker."

"Some thinks so. Others don't. But I got to turn you over, Bo. I ain't got no more choice in this than you do."

"You know what's coming?"

"No. I hand you over. That's all for me."

"God damn, Oscar. Just . . . God damn."

"I'm a-going to have to ast you to stand up, Bo. They're waiting for us upstairs."

Bo breathes deeply and gets up. He's afraid. It's a feeling he's not used to, not like this. Not as sharp as this is; this is more like being in a room in a dream and knowing you can't get out of it. But his hand doesn't go for the knife in his belt. Somehow—again like a dream—he knows he's supposed to be here. That this is supposed to be happening. And that it will be all right soon. He takes hold of the banister and pulls himself up the stairs. He feels as heavy now as he felt light a while ago.

At the top of the stairs, Hamer unlocks the door to a room. Inside, he motions Bo to the wall and has him turn his back. He slips the knife from Bo's belt and flings it behind the bed. Bo hears a telephone being unhooked, then a pause, and Oscar says, "Eight fifty-one, please, ma'am."

There's another pause. "He's here," Oscar says into the telephone. Then, "Yessir, they're waiting in a room down the hall. I ain't going." Bo strains to hear the voice on the other end of the line. He can only make out that it's a man's. "I'm sorry, no sir, I just ain't going with them. It ain't part of the job."

Bo hears the other man's voice give a sharp answer, then the sound of the receiver being dropped back into the hook. "Out the door ahead of me, Bo."

Bo opens the door. With a pang, he remembers that this was Mother Jones's room. He spent afternoons with Elizabeth here. He looks around for some trace of her. There is none.

Hamer raps three sharp times on a door at the far end of the dim wainscotted hall. A voice from inside says, "Who is it?"

"Hamer. It's time."

"Just a minute," the voice says.

Bo hears bedsprings squeak and chairs scrape and mumbled conversation. Rain washes heavily across the roof. The door opens a crack first, then wide. There are four men in the room. They wear white bands, but have no faces. Each of them has a mask, a cloth with eye holes, draped beneath his hat. In the dim light, nothing is visible behind the holes.

The railroad tracks cross the Naco Road at Skunktown, or Tintown, as the Mexes who live there call it. Skunktown sprawls roadless over the hills between Lowell and Warren. It is dirt-floored adobe huts and lean-tos made of the flattened tin from five-gallon kerosene cans. It is bleak in any weather; in the rain, at night, it is the bleakest part of a bleak city.

The delivery van bounces off the Naco Road onto the railroad right-of-way. None of the men have spoken except to give a direction or ask for a plug of tobacco. The delivery van smells of wet hay. Bo's hands and feet are tied, but he's not blindfolded. In the headlights, he watches three of the men get out into the rain and drag a handcar from a clump of creosote bushes. They struggle with it up to the gravel of the railroad embankment and right it on the tracks. This is no mainline. The tracks go to only one place: the new ore crusher on the hillside between Skunktown and Warren. The yellow glow of lanterns and candles falls from glassless windows in Skunktown. Bo sees shadows move by the windows; no one will come to investigate the van. *No es mi negocio,* he knows they're saying. It's none of my business.

The terror that Bo felt above the French Kitchen has gradually grown during the ride. It tastes like brass, and something in his stomach pushes against his throat. But beneath the terror lingers the odd sense that this is supposed to be happening, and that it will be all right soon.

When the men settle the handcar on the tracks, they come for Bo. They pull him from the rear of the van, and he loses his balance in the slick, clayey mud. He strangles in the sheet of water that rushes from the hillside, and fights for breath. One of the men turns him onto his back with a rifle, as if he were a beetle. The man holds an American flag the size of a biscuit pan.

"Git him on his knees," one of the others says. He is a big avocado-shaped man who seems to be the leader.

Two of the men grab him under his armpits and pull him up to a kneeling position. Bo recoils when they touch him and wrenches himself loose. The leader holds the flag out in front of Bo.

"Kiss it," he says. "Be a man for once in your life, you son of a bitch, and kiss it."

Bo doesn't move. The leader slaps his hand over Bo's head and draws his face toward the flag. Bo turns his face away. He feels a boot slam into his ribs and doubles over. The pain jerks his breath away. But it is almost welcome as it spreads up his side. The leader grabs Bo's hair and pulls him upright again.

"Hold the fucker's head straight," the leader orders. Bo twists, struggles, but two pairs of hands hold his head tight. The leader brings the flag up to Bo's lips. Bo can smell whiskey and tobacco on the leader's hands, even through the clean new odor of the cloth. When the man pulls the flag away, Bo spits on it. The man backhands him. Bo tastes blood.

"You the worst of all, friend," the leader says. "I can forgive them foreigners better than I can you. You know what you doing." He grabs Bo's head again and flings him back down in the mud. For a moment, Bo wants to tell him to kiss his ass. But what's the use?

"Let's git on it, boys," the man says. Again Bo is flipped over on his back, and one of the men ties a lasso around his feet. He and another take hold of the rope and drag Bo toward the railroad tracks. Bo's shirt rides up out of his pants, and the sharp caliche rakes his back. In spite of himself, a moan slips out.

At the tracks, the men flop Bo onto the wet floor of the handcar. It's cold, with leaves stuck to it. They arrange themselves two on each end of the handle. As they pump, the car moves silently up the tracks, toward the crusher. Who are these sons of bitches? Who was Hamer? Does it matter? Does it matter who *he* is? He could be the Mex or Bohunk or nigger that he looks like and the bastards would still have to do this. Through the pain, the sense that something will be all right remains. He's glad Elizabeth isn't here. He's glad she doesn't know he fucked up again.

He watches the silhouettes of wet low shrubs and ocotillo and mesquite slide by. The heavy hiss of the rain muffles the clack of the handcar's wheels and the four men's puffing. Somewhere a chorus of coyotes yips after a kill. He's never felt more alert. He knows he could even hear the carpenter ants at work on the mesquite leaves.

One of the men leaps off to throw the switch that will put them onto the siding beside the crusher, then catches up with the car. They sway onto the smooth curve of the siding. The car rolls to an easy stop.

"Stand his ass up," the leader says.

"This don't make shit for sense to me," one of the men says.

"Don't to me neither," the leader answers. "But I got the sense to do things the way I'm told to. Stand him over yonder." He points to a spot beneath the security lights, just at the edge of the dumping platform.

Bo feels hands under him. He stiffens. Then, as the men lift him to his feet and drag him upright toward the crusher, the clutching in his stomach relaxes. There's nothing to fight anymore. The men's hands feel almost as if they're caressing him. And with the lightness is something like elation. He thinks of the hundred and six steps, of Elizabeth, of Jim Brew, of the twelve hundred men in the desert. He's doing what he's supposed to do. What he came home to do. There's nothing to fight, to settle, anymore.

At the platform where the ore cars dump their tons of rock into the crusher, the men let him go. Behind him the mouth of the ore chute falls away into the dark like a huge well. He manages to keep his balance and stand facing them, his back to the crusher. In the distance, the lights of Bisbee reflect off the low clouds and send a gray glow down onto the barren muck dumps and the town. Nearer, the gallows frames of the Campbell shaft stand stark against the floodlit air. Wind skitters the cold rain across the dumping platform. The mines are at work again now. There will be full ore cars here in the morning.

The ore cars will dump their ore into the crusher. The company claims it is the largest piece of machinery in the world. The cars turn upside down on huge gears and let their ore fall far down a steel funnel to a gigantic set of jaws. Then the ore drops three stories down the mountainside, in chutes, along conveyor belts, through cone crushers and then ball crushers. Each kind of crusher makes it smaller and smaller. When at last it reaches the cyanide of the precipitation ponds, it is no more than powder. Engineers come from all over the world to look at the crusher. It is a marvel. It is the sum of Bisbee.

The leader orders Bo blindfolded. The man who does it is nervous. He ties the cloth too loosely. In the security lights from the crusher, Bo can still see to the edge of the scrub woods. The men's voices seem very far away from him, as if they were at the end of a long flight of steps.

"We gonna do it all together?"

"Hell, one of us is enough."

"You want to be the one?"

"No goddamn more then you do."

"Shit. I want a drink."

"You take a drink and you'd throw it up."

"I'm a-going to anyway."

"You chicken shit?"

"No, I ain't chicken shit. I just don't want to be the only one to do it."

"Goddamn, man, let's just do it."

"All of us then?"

"All of us."

"Good."

They're not talking about Bo. In a month, two months, Bo will be part of a roll of copper wire, a shell casing, a penny. It's not so terrible. In a little while it will be all right. Through the loose blindfold, he sees a movement at the edge of the light, as if something were watching from the scrub woods.

"Everybody ready," the leader of the men says. "When I say 'fire,' everybody go at once. And aim, goddamn it."

It's all right. It's as it's supposed to be.

Big Bill Haywood: September, 1917, 8:00 P.M.

You know there is an auditorium, and a dark dry street stretching out behind it with puddles of light from street lamps. It is in Philadelphia or Indianapolis or Los Angeles, you're not sure. You're scheduled for one of them this week. There is an ugly glare in the small dressing room, which is bare brick made stark by the naked light bulb from the ceiling. Your huge hand covers the open mouth of a half-empty bottle of rye. The taste of the whiskey lingers. From time to time someone rattles the handle on the locked door and tells you that it's time, you have an audience. Of sorts.

The chanting from outside the high small window keeps up. Not many will have made it through that to hear you tonight; you'll barely cover the rent on the auditorium. It has been the same in every city. The mobs that prowl outside the auditorium, men and women, with flags and slogans and brickbats. The bulls who keep them from smashing property but not bones. The thing with no shape, no name, that you've tried to drink away, to drive away by will, and have failed at both. And behind the faces of the workingstiffs in every city, the blankness, the spent quality, the tiredness. Something you can't get to anymore. The earliest memory you have is of your father's funeral. When they covered him, you dug down as far as your three-year-old's arm could reach to try to bring him back. You kept trying until they dragged you away, your sleeve dark with mud. If you lose the workingstiffs, you lose yourself. You know now that is the thing you fear, have feared all along, most of all. That has followed you from New York to . . . here, whereever it is.

Bisbee is lost. Butte, Globe, Jerome, Leadville, the general strike . . . all lost. You're tired, bone tired. There is an audience waiting that you don't have the strength to rouse.

Your one eye fixes itself on the whiskey bottle. You try to focus, but it is a blur—everything in the room you try to focus on is a blur. Nowhere can you clear your vision now. A little while ago a telegram came from Chicago. It was confused, hurried: unclear, too. The government has raided IWW headquarters. Everywhere. Files all seized, membership lists, treasury, correspondence. And there are arrest warrants out. Not just for you but for everyone, the whole leadership, hundreds of you. There is a face behind that, too, a face you couldn't stop for before. It has tracked you from Bisbee, has multiplied a hundred thousand times, waits for you in every city.

The door handle rattles again. There will be a marshal here before you finish your speech. But you take a last shot of rye and stand. They're waiting for you, for Big Bill Haywood, who can't walk away from them.

Harry Wheeler: July 12, 1923, 7:00 P.M.

Outside your hotel room, traffic circles and honks. You pull the curtains back each time a honk is particularly close-by. It could be your taxi. You'd be up shit creek without your taxi. The most you've been able to figure out about London in the month you've been here is that you're on one of those damn little squares. But they all look alike to you. You'd never find your way back here. And you're Harry Wheeler, the man who tracked a robber ten days in the snow once, back in Cochise County.

But you're not Sheriff Harry Wheeler anymore. You stopped being Sheriff Wheeler back in the spring of '18, when you became Captain Harry Wheeler, United States Army. And then you stopped being even that by the fall, when the war was over. You may not have gotten yourself blown up in the trenches and brought back home to a hero's funeral like that Matthews boy did, but you made it for a little while, by God, let that be clear. Even though the pussies tried to take that away from you. You think about that a great deal. Especially today, six years to the day after what they wound up calling the Deportation. No matter what happened in that awful time afterward, you made it for a little while. You were able to write home to the *Review* that line every paper in the West picked up. "The Eagles in France have nothing but contempt for the vultures at home." You did your part.

Even when they shipped you home from France early for the trials, and took you away from your machine-gun company, you didn't flinch. You had faith. You knew they'd never dare bring you to trial. They indicted you and Jack Greenway and Walter Douglas and Grant Dowell—all of you. But they knew you were too hot to risk on a witness stand. So they tried that Loyalty Leaguer instead—Wooten, it was. Owned a hardware store. And they couldn't even get a conviction against him. Justified by "the law of necessity," the jury ruled. Besides, the lawyers were right. How could any of you be convicted of kidnapping? You gave every Wobbly in the bunch the chance to step out of line and come back to work. Those who got deported went voluntarily. The jury was smart enough to see that. Those lawsuits have been a nuisance all right. But since the IWW has been busted up so well, the company has been able to settle them out of court right simply. So that way, at least, it's worked out for the best. They've got you to thank for that. With a lesser man in command, they'd have had a massacre on their hands.

Oh, that commission Woodrow Wilson sent down to investigate gave you a hard enough time for a while. But since kidnapping isn't a federal crime, they were as useless as tits on a nun. Deplored things a lot, but what could you expect? Sending down that Felix Frankfurter as their counsel! He's a foreigner himself. A Jew. But Wilson kept him in line. Wilson had a war to get on with, too.

You like to think that Wilson himself learned from you. In spite of all that newspaper cant about the Deportation being "the exclamation point at the end of the Frontier era," "the last great vigilante raid," and so on, you showed the way. Would the government have dared to raid all those IWW headquarters just two months later if you hadn't shown the way? Have dared to pass the laws that have sent every man jack of the damn Wobbly leadership to Leavenworth since the war?—all except for that Haywood, who ran away again, just like he did from you. Harry Wheeler is the man who showed how weak the IWW really was. Who broke their backs. They pushed too hard, too far, and against the wrong man. This new bunch they call Bolsheviks, or whatever, some say, is worse than the Wobblies. Maybe. You'd like to try 'em. You're going back to the States before the year is out. It's time to run for sheriff again.

Of all the hell that's come of the Deportation, the sheriff business has been the hardest to bear. Nobody wants to know you now. When you walk down the street in Bisbee, they turn their eyes away or mumble a few pleasant things and don't invite you for a coffee. And there's no more campaign money from the companies. Greenway has left town, Dowell is transferred, Tom Matthews says he's sorry but the company doesn't want to be partisan these days. When you ran in '20, you got swamped. It's treachery. Like the whole town was ashamed to know you. The companies have even hired back some of the scum you deported.

Your only comfort is that the rest of the boys are in the same boat. Not a man in Bisbee connected with the Deportation has been elected to office again. People are pussies. They don't have the courage to take responsibility. You did. You came home from France to announce that you took personal responsibility for the whole thing.

But you're not whipped yet. You lived by the best code you knew. You proved that the West was alive. And you stood by it. You'll keep on doing it, by God, till they slip you six feet under in Boot Hill cemetery back in Tombstone. You beat the meanest, roughest, most feared union in history. You commanded the largest posse in the West. And you did it honorably.

The honking outside your window doesn't go away this time. You pull yourself together and look through the window. It's your cab. You can't afford to be late tonight. You're performing before the king, the king of England himself, at the Court of Saint James. There are those who have made fun of you for joining a Wild West show. But it was the only honorable course to take. You were the fastest draw in Arizona, the most accurate shot with any kind of weapon. And you still are, even in those furry chaps and ten-gallon hat they make you wear, like William S. Hart. How many other sheriffs have performed before the king of England? You're a legend. You'll be one king in the presence of another.

You buckle on your silver spurs.

About the Author

Robert Houston has published nine novels in addition to *Bisbee '17,* including *The Nation Thief* and *The Fourth Codex,* and a book of translations of the poems of León Felipe. One of his novels became a feature film, while another toured as a play. *Cholo* won the *West Coast Review of Books'* Golden Palm Award. His nonfiction has appeared in *The Nation, The New York Times* (for which he reviews regularly), *Mother Jones,* and elsewhere. He has been a Fulbright professor to Peru and has frequently been on the staff of the Bread Loaf Writers' Conference and the Bread Loaf School of English. He is the director of the Creative Writing Program at the University of Arizona.